D0733499

Other Titles by Susie Bright

Full Exposure
The Sexual State of the Union
The Best American Erotica 1993, 1994, 1995, 1996, 1997, 1999 (editor)
Nothing But the Girl: The Blatant Lesbian Image (with Jill Posener)
Herotica, Herotica 2, Herotica 3 (editor)
Sexwise
Susie Bright's Sexual Reality: A Virtual Sex World Reader
Susie Sexpert's Lesbian Sex World

edited by

Susie
Bright

A Touchstone Book
Published by Simon & Schuster
New York London

the

Best

American

Erotica

2000

Sydney Singapore

TOUCHSTONE

Rockefeller Center
1230 Avenue of the Americas
New York, NY 10020

TOUCHSTONE and colophon are registered trademarks of Simon & Schuster, Inc.

Designed by Gabriel Levine

Manufactured in the United States of America

10 9 8 7 6 5 4 3 2 1

ISBN 0-684-84396-X

Acknowledgments

Thank you to my father and constant *Best American Erotica* series collaborator, Bill Bright; to my agents, Joanie Shoemaker and Jo-Lynne Worley; and to my editor at Simon & Schuster, Airié Dekidjiev, for all of their devotion and care to this volume. I'd also like to thank my assistant, Jennifer Taillac, who helped immeasurably, and every one of the magazine, book, and Web editors who supported and published these outstanding writers. My appreciation to all of the editors and publishers who supported this work, and to the many fans who wrote to me to introduce me to new work and artists.

This twenty-first-century edition is for my twenty-first-century daughter, Aretha, whose best feature is her vision.

Contents

Introduction

Here I am, holding the year 2000 edition of *The Best American Erotica* in my hands, and it feels like an extraordinary climax is called for.

"Why don't you announce that there will be no sex in the new millennium?" one of my friends wisecracked as I approached my deadline. "That would be new, that would set a tone."

Of course, my catastrophe-minded pal made this suggestion in 1999, months before the clock had actually hit 21st-century proportions. To his dismay, I had already rejected most of the Y2K dooms-day predictions about the end of life as we know it. If the power fails, the banking stops, and the material world grinds to a halt—the fact of the matter is that *more* people than ever will be having sex in the year 2000. I remember that phenomenon during the last "earth-quake baby boom" we had in California in 1989, the year my daughter was conceived. People just love to huddle together under the covers when calamity strikes.

But what about our erotic lives? What is the next century holding in store for us, for our sexual·imaginations? I have already seen many new trends come and go in erotic literature since I started editing this series in the early nineties.

One of the events that's emerged over the last year is what I call the beautiful-people backlash. In so many stories I've read, the plot turns on a character who—for either supernatural or quite pedestrian reasons—is physically grotesque. Ugly people seem to be calling the shots, ranging from the disabled to the strange to the terribly plain.

In contrast with the sentimental message of a Beauty and the Beast fable, these anti-cutie characters do not change as a result of a magic kiss; they don't transform in any way in the end. They offer neither apologies nor pleas for understanding. It's the people and lovers around them who change as a result of meeting them, without necessarily getting a pat on the head for it. Some of the conventional-looking characters even end up yearning to be distorted in some way themselves: Their sexual hunger has gone beyond a pretty face and latched on to a new kind of passion.

This sort of literature is the dead opposite of everything that one would think is attractive from looking at the mainstream media. The skin of our magazine-cover models is still dewy, their chest-to-waist proportions are ever Barbie-like. Like glowworms, the beautiful people shine on and on and on, as epitomized by airbrushed celebrity myths. They are the icons of the consumer culture. Some observers point out correctly that advertising is not quite so blond anymore, that the glossy media have even glamorized the plump and the aging. But I suspect that this craving for "diversity" is motivated by market-niche scouring rather than genuine appreciation of what's different.

Meanwhile, back in eroticaland, not everyone is taking a daily bath, not everyone's teeth are straight, not everyone's nipples line up in perfect symmetry. It is this very dirtiness and waywardness in their physical features that often makes these characters so irresistible.

I think erotica authors who explore the imperfect side of the human body are reflecting a sexual truth: We may know what perfect beauty is, we may stand in awe of it—but what arouses us comprehends every shadow, every image. We get wet dreaming of the unknown; we get hard contemplating risk. Yes, we wouldn't kick Supermodel Baby out of bed, but we might want to invite her Evil Twisted Twin for an even more intriguing ménage.

No one ever said our intentions and actions aren't contradictory. I often wonder: with the popularity of plastic surgery, will the critical mass of pert noses, Hostess Snow Ball titties, and curveless thighs finally fold in on itself? Will we end up creating an appetite where everything that is desirable is dark or crooked or pendulous? I remember when blond hair coloring became available to every woman, and the advertised message was that now, at last, anyone could be platinum, anyone could score. Of course, the specialness of the fair elite was diluted. Now, if we have one life to live, as the slogan goes, many will choose to live it as a raven-, plum-, or even a magenta-colored hair diva.

There is also a dramatic quality at work here. Erotic writers are often drawn to the spectacle of the awkward and deformed, simply because that element adds a twist to the genre "Person A meets Person B and they must get it on." An outstanding erotic story is one that makes you forget that you know that formula backward and forward. By adding a physically unsympathetic character to the mix, writers test the boundaries of a reader's expectations.

Interestingly, what is coveted and rhapsodized today, more than any other quality of beauty, is youth—pure, childish sensuality and teenage bloom. Certainly young people *are* beautiful in their new skin and wild vitality, but as the twentieth century closes, it seems that we have fetishized their "innocence" beyond all reasonable recognition.

My friend David Steinberg is an author who has spent a lot of time thinking about the various sex panics of our age. He notes that in our American culture we treat sex as something chaotic that must be constantly guarded and suppressed. Over time we've developed the concept of an "idealized class of innocent, supposedly nonsexual individuals onto which society can project its yearning to escape the conflicts generated by overly repressed sexual desire." This virginal category used to include both women and children, but in modern times, since liberated women have thoroughly ruined the feminine ideal of unblemished virtue, we have come to mythologize our children, as David puts it, as the "designated innocents."

Of course, the problem with being a designated *anything* is that the targeted individuals may feel their true selves do not coincide with their designated label. Our young people naturally go through puberty, begin their adult lives, and feel all of the powerful sexual feelings that come with such maturity. Unfortunately, American politics has reacted by giving young people a big abstinence program to stuff all those nasty feelings back in their pants. How about a nice cold shower to go along with that, my little darlings?

Meanwhile, the people who reject the Just Say No propaganda—who give in to chaotic feelings instead of stifling them—these are the folks who get called perverts, who arouse the public's suspicions. It's clear that many, if not all, erotic writers have been targeted as perverts simply because they have crossed the very first line of sexual repression: They have written down something that turns them on. They have articulated an erotic feeling that can't be denied. They have taunted the Thought Police.

Nowadays, the irrational hysteria surrounding youthful sexuality has spurred many erotic writers to reminisce about their sexual awakenings. Many publishers won't print those stories anymore, but that hasn't stopped the stories from coming. In them, we hear about the experiences of young people feeling the first spin of lust, of wanting to connect with someone else intimately—not knowing the rules, but wanting to touch. Time was, this would not be considered an unusual topic for erotic reverie—in fact, for any aficionado of erotic literature, it's a classic coming-of-age tale. Yet in the era of designated innocents, this topic is a sin.

We face the year 2000 with a national education and health-care establishment that warns the public that sex will have an apocalyptic effect on their lives. Shame and fear are their operative tools. The mystery of AIDS has linked sexual risk with death in most people's minds. Parents have focused their efforts on making their children more and more infantile in an effort to protect them from what will inevitably be their experiences of real life. For all these reasons, we have now produced a millennial generation of neopuritans. The kids think of the older generation as "sluts," and they swear that they won't let it happen to them.

Erotic artists have realized that, in this climate, speaking of their early sexuality produces the most shocking story of all. If we say that the teenyboppers can't feel that way, then why did we feel that way once upon a time? Why could we entertain risk and imagination, but they can't? Why are the stakes now so high that we have to lie about the most natural facts of life? When *do* today's young people get to learn about sex and death—in grad school?

Erotic storytellers are frequently truth tellers as much as they are fantasy writers. They perform the function of pointing out what is real under surreal conditions. There will always be fashionable notions in the body politic of what *ought* to be—but the truth about sex will belie every institutional myth, every consumer-crazed folly, every bright shining bit of nonsense. I don't think that I'll understand the spirit of erotica in the year 2000 until I'm at its tail end; but I do know that, throughout, I will hear voices from the sexual underground, and they will carry the weight of a new century's most blatant fears and desires.

Susie Bright
February 2000

Innocence in Extremis

Debra Boxer

I am 28 years old and I am a virgin. People assume a series of decisions led to this. They guess that I'm a closet lesbian, or too picky, or clinging to a religious ideal. "You don't look, talk, or act like a virgin," they say. For lack of a better explanation, I am pigeonholed as a prude or an unfortunate. If it's so hard to believe, I want to say, then imagine how hard it is for me to live with.

I feel freakish and alien, an anomaly that belongs in a zoo. I walk around feeling like an impostor, not a woman at all. I bleed like other women, yet I feel nothing like them, because I am missing this formative experience.

I won't deny that I have become attached to my innocence. If it defines me, who am I without it? Where will my drive come from and what will protect me from becoming as jaded as everyone else? I try to tell myself that innocence is more a state of mind than body. That giving myself to a man doesn't mean losing myself to a cynical world. That my innocence doesn't hang by a scrap of skin between my legs.

In college, girls I knew lost it out of impatience. At 21, virginity became unhealthy, embarrassing—a female humiliation they could no longer be burdened by. Some didn't tell the boy. If there was blood, they said it was their period. I cannot imagine. Some of those same boys thought it was appalling, years ago, that I was still a virgin. "I'll fuck you," they said. It sounded to me like, "I'll fix you," and I did not feel broken.

I don't believe I've consciously avoided sex. I am always on the verge of wholly giving myself away. I think emotionally, act intuitively. When I'm attracted to someone, I don't hold back. But there have been only a handful of times when I would have gladly had sex. Each, for its own reason, did not happen. I am grateful to have learned so much in the waiting—patience, strength, and ease with solitude.

Do you know what conclusion I've come to? That there is no concrete explanation, and, more important, there doesn't need to be one. How I got here seems less important to me than where I am.

This is what is important. Desire. The circle of my desire widens each day, so that it's no longer contained inside me, but rather, it surrounds me in concentric circles.

Desire overrides everything and should be exploited to its fullest potential. It is the white-hot space between the words. I am desire unfulfilled. I hover over that fiery space feeling the heat without knowing the flames. I am a still life dreaming of animation. I am a bell not allowed to chime. There is a deep stillness inside me. There is a void. A huge part of me is dead to the world, no matter how hard I try to revive it with consoling words or my own brave hand.

I am sick of being sealed up like a grave. I want to be unearthed.

I pray for sex like the pious pray for salvation. I am dying to be physically opened up and exposed. I want to be the source of a man's pleasure. I want to give him that one perfect feeling. I have been my only pleasure for too long.

Do I have dreams about sex? Often. There is one recurring dream in which I can't see whole bodies at once. But I know which parts belong to my body. I know they're mine. I know, better than anyone, my curves, my markings, my sensitive places. If I close my eyes now, I can see the man's body. Thin, smooth, light-haired, limbs spreading and shifting over me like the sea. A small, brick-colored mouth opens and closes around the sphere of a nipple. Moist eyes, the color of darkest honey, roam up and down my spine. A sensation of breath across my belly induces the first wave of moisture between my legs. This reaction crosses the line into wakefulness, and I know when I awaken, the blanket will be twisted aside as if in pain. My skin itself will feel like a fiery blanket, and I will almost feel smothered by it.

In some versions of the dream, I am on top and I can feel my pelvis rubbing against the man's body. Every part of my body is focused on the singular task of getting him inside me. I try and try and am so close, but my fate is that of Tantalus, who was surrounded by water he could not drink. Thank God for masturbation.

My fingers know exactly how to act upon my skin—they have for over half my life now. There is no fear or hesitation. When I masturbate, I am aware of varying degrees of heat throughout my body. It is hottest between my legs. Cool air seems to heat the moment it hits my skin, the moment I suck it in between my lips. After, my hands shake as if I'd had an infusion of caffeine. I press my hand, palm down, in the vale between my breasts, and it feels as if my heart will burst through my hand. I love that feeling—knowing that I'm illimitably alive.

Though I've never had a man inside me, I have had many orgasms. I have talked with girls who not only can't have one with their lover but can't bring themselves to have one. I was shocked at first, until I saw how common it was. And then I felt lucky. My first one scared me. At 12, I did not expect such a reaction to my own touch; I thought I'd hurt myself. But it was such a curious feeling, such a lovely feeling, that I had to explore it further. I felt almost greedy. And, well, I got better at it until it was ridiculously easy. Still, it is always easy.

I don't expect it to be so easy with a man. I've come to believe that sex is defined by affection, not orgasm. There is that need to be held that doesn't disappear when we learn to walk on our own. If anything, it intensifies.

I love being a girl. I think of my body as all scent and soft muscle. It is an imperfect body, but beautiful still, in its energy and in its potential. I love looking at my curves in the mirror. I love feeling them and admiring their craftsmanship. I love my hipbones—small, protruding mountains. Or maybe they are like sacred stones marking the entrance to a secret city. I trace the slope of my calf as if it is a slender tree trunk and I am amazed at how strong, yet vulnerable, the human body is. I am as in awe of my body as I am of the earth. My joints are prominent, as if asserting themselves. I know my terrain well, perhaps better than any man ever could—the warm, white softness of my inner arms; the hard, smooth muscle of my bicep like the rounded swelling in a snake that just swallowed the tiniest mouse; the sensitive skin between my thighs; the mole on my pelvis nestled by a vein like a dot on a map marking a city beside a river. I have stared at my naked body in the mirror wondering what the first touch from a lover will feel like and where it will be.

Masturbation is pleasurable, but it cannot sustain a whole sexual life. It lacks that vital affection. I am left with the rituals, the mechanics of masturbation. I crash up against the same wall each time. It becomes boring and sad and does little to quell the need to be touched. I long to let go of my body's silent monologue and enter into a dialogue of skin, muscle, and bone.

There are sudden passions that form in my mind when I look at a man. Thoughts of things I want to do to him. I want to follow the veins of his wrists—blue like the heart of a candle flame. I want to lick the depression of his neck as if it were the bottom of a bowl. I want to see the death of my modesty in his eyes. Although I am swollen with romantic ideas, I am not naïve. I know it will not be ideal. Rather, it will be bloody, painful, awkward, damp, and dreadful—but that is always the way of birth. It is an act of violence. The threat of pain in pleasure, after all, makes seduction stimulating. I want the pain, to know that I am alive and real—to leave no doubt there has been a transformation.

The fear is undeniable. It's a phobic yearning I have for a man's body, but I have to believe that everything, including fear, is vital when expressing desire. If sexual thoughts are either memories or desires, then I am all desires.

I am powerfully attracted to the male body. I want to watch him undress. See him touch himself. I want his wildness in me—I want to touch his naked body and feel the strength of him. His sweat sliding down the slick surface of my skin until it pools in the crooks of my limbs. I imagine the rhythm of our sex like the slick, undulating motion of swimmers. I imagine my own body's movements suddenly made new, so that we would appear to me like two new bodies. I imagine the sound of our sex—a magnificent, moist clamor of limbs.

I want to hold him inside me like a deep breath. I want to leave kisses as markers on the sharp slices of his shoulder blades, then surrounding the oasis of his belly button. I want to slide him in my mouth like a first taste of wine, letting the bittersweet liquid sweep every part of my mouth before allowing it to slide down my throat.

I will hold my mouth to his ear, as if I were a polished seashell, so he can hear the sea inside me—welcoming him. I will pause and look at him—up into his face. I will steady myself in his gaze, catch the low sun of his cock between my smooth, white thighs, and explode into shine. I will look at him and think, I have spent this man's body and I have spent it well.

Space Girls Are Easy

from Rock 'n' Roll Babes from Outer Space

Linda Jaivin

Back in the saucer . . .

Baby looked down at Jake's prone form. She prodded him with her foot. Though sound asleep, his mouth pursed slightly, as though anticipating a kiss. Underneath heavy lids and a thick fringe of curly brown lashes, his eyes darted, chasing a dream. The bold arcs of his eyebrows, pierced on the left by a silver ring, lay motionless on his high, clear forehead. Baby bent down and touched his cheeks, then brushed her lips lightly over his neck. A potent Earth-boy smell, part bourbon and Coke, part sweat, wafted up into her nostrils and set off delicious vibrations in her antennae. She closed her eyes and breathed in deeply.

"When you're finished . . ." Lati yawned.

"Oh, sit on my faculae," Baby retorted, snapping out of her reverie. "And don't just stand there. Give us a hand." Together, Baby, Doll, and Lati picked Jake up and carried him into the sexual experimentation chamber, where they dumped him unceremoniously on the gleaming laboratory table.

Doll watched with studied indifference as the other two pulled off Jake's boots and socks and tossed them onto the floor. Next, they hoisted him up to a sitting position and yanked his T-shirt up over his head. As his long arms slid out of the sleeves, they slapped heavily down on his sides. There was a sharp intake of breath, but he didn't wake up. Around his neck hung a leather thong, upon which were threaded a couple of pieces of flattened metal. Pulling this off, Lati experimentally bit into what was in fact Jake's house key. "Yum."

Baby traced with her finger the tattoo of a scorpion that decorated Jake's right shoulder blade. "Looks a bit like one of those guys from Zeta Reticuli," she observed. "I hope this doesn't mean he's had contact before," she added, a trace of apprehension in her voice. "I was hoping we'd get an alien virgin."

As they laid him back down, Baby's eyes roamed over the breadth of his shoulders, the gentle curves of his long freckled arms, the soft, light down carpeting his forearms and chest, the lean lines of his torso, and the neat pink mounds of his nipples, one of which strained erect over a small silver barbell. A wee tuft of brown hair poked up out of the top of his trousers and curled around the strange little hole in his stomach. Now where would that line of fur lead to?

Baby tugged impatiently at his jeans, but couldn't pull them down past his slender hips. "Damn," she cursed.

Lati, who was wearing 501s herself, shouldered Baby aside and unbuttoned the fly. Together, they shucked the jeans off Jake's long legs.

Baby was rapt. Jake's smell clung to her nostrils, the touch of his skin set hers aflame, and the very sight of his handsome face was causing a liquid longing to mist her ears. (Nufonians had *very* sensitive ears.) This Earth boy, she was thinking, was truly a thing divine. Lati, if asked, would have said she was having fun. Then again, she always had fun. As far as she was concerned, Jake wasn't a bad biological sample, but that was about it. Doll, for her part, was utterly unmoved. She was thinking about drum kits for their band—Pearl or Brady?

It all boils down to chemistry, really.

Baby slipped trembling fingers into the waistband of Jake's red jocks and eased them off. She gasped. What was this? The other parts of the Earth boy's body had not contained so much surprise, for they were but variations on the forms the babes themselves had taken. But this fat pink plaything resting on its plump pillow and crowned with a coarse burst of hair, this was something else. She put a tentative finger upon its head. It twitched under her curious touch.

Lati began to spool out Bind-a-Bean tape. According to the manual that came with the Abduct-o-matic, Bind-a-Bean was the best method for securing a live abductee. Bind-a-Bean felt like silk and held like steel. Baby reluctantly stepped aside so that Lati could tape Jake's hands and feet to the table.

"Well, girls, this is it!" Baby exclaimed breathlessly when he lay spread-eagled and naked before them. She rubbed her hands together. "The moment we've been waiting for."

"*One* of the moments we've been waiting for," Doll corrected. Earth girls were *her* weakness. Still sitting on the bench, she picked up a speculum and began tapping out a beat on a row of carefully labeled beakers and jars. "Personally, I'm hanging out for the day we become rock stars."

"Yeah, yeah, yeah," said Baby, leaning over and sniffing at Jake's armpit. "Sweet," she remarked. Lati walked around to the other end of the table. Scrutinizing Jake's crusty toes, she recoiled at the smell. "Eeyuurgh!" She waved a hand in front of her face. "What d'ya reckon we should do now?"

"According to the manual," Doll replied, "you wake them up. Then you get some long hollow steel needles, point them at the abductee's head, and scare the shit out of them."

"It doesn't really say that, does it?" Baby protested, shocked—and a little excited, too.

"Nah, it doesn't," Doll admitted. "I got that from the film *Communion*." She was kicking her ankles together. Doc on Doc. A good sound. Solid. "Did you know that movie was based on a true story?"

"No way!" cried Lati. "You don't believe in *aliens,* do you?"

They all fell about laughing hysterically. Jake slept on, oblivious.

"You know," said Baby, wiping a blue tear of mirth from her eyes, "this is making it really hard to get into the mood. Oh no! Now look at *this.*" With one hand resting possessively on Jake's thigh, she pointed under the table with the other. "*Someone's* in the mood," she chuckled.

Revor, their pet oioi, had insinuated his long narrow snout deep into one of Jake's woolly socks and, clutching it to his furry red face with eager claws, was rolling and tumbling and wriggling ecstatically around the floor, burbling and sniggling and cooing. The sock may have been old, unwashed, threadbare at the toe and down at the heel, the kind of footwear that was an embarrassment to mothers, a disgrace to sheep, an aesthetic and olfactory repellent to normal affection, but to Revor, it was sex incarnate.

"Now *that's* a sick puppy," commented Doll.

Lati was getting antsy. "Pass the strigil." She indicated a small instrument near where Doll had resettled herself on the bench. "Something has to be done about these toes."

Baby, meanwhile, turned her attention to Jake's testicles. "These look like fun." She stroked and pulled the dark, cool scrotal skin curiously. "Ohhhh," groaned Jake, now semiconscious. She cupped the balls in one palm. She bounced them up and down. She rocked them back and forth and pinched them between her fingertips. "I wonder if maybe this sexual experimentation thing isn't a bit over-rated," she posited, a trace of disappointment in her voice.

Then something occurred to her. "Maybe," Baby wondered, her antennae trembling at the thought, "it would be more fun if he were awake?" Performing sexual experiments on an Earthling who was actually conscious—too *transgressive* for words. She leaned over and, not too hard but not too gently either, bit Jake's balls. His eyes flew open.

"It's awake now," Doll noted dryly.

"Hey!" yelled Jake, trying to raise his head. What the hell was happening to him? Who the fuck were these, um, girls, and what were they doing to his *balls*?

"Mind telling me what's going on?" Jake asked in as normal a tone as he could muster.

Baby shrugged. "Sex," she replied, gripping his balls in her hand. He was *very* cute, she thought.

"Sex," Jake echoed flatly, attempting to pull an ankle free of its Bind-a-Bean. No go. Jake was not into bondage. Sure, he'd tied up a few girls with scarves when they'd asked for it, and had even used handcuffs on one kinky older woman, but he had never let anyone tie him up. Ever. He did not like feeling vulnerable and powerless. Not one bit. And finding yourself utterly starkers, bound hand and foot to an examining table under mysterious circs at the mercy of three very attractive, sexually predatory chicks, did tend to inspire feelings of vulnerability and powerlessness. Not to mention intellectual confusion and spiritual crisis. Christ. It was almost as bad as being in a relationship. He tried to jerk a hand free. "Ow," he grumbled.

"What's a relationship?" asked Baby curiously, reading his mind. She wasn't kidding. Relationships were, if you'll pardon the expression, an alien concept in the Outer. Alien civilizations had evolved way, way beyond relationships. Earthling society, which in universal terms was still dragging its knuckles on the ground, was only just beginning to shed the concept that a moment's fuckability did not automatically lead to a lifetime's compatibility. Aliens had long ago figured out that it was usually best just to give the night's mateling breakfast and a kiss and send it on its way.

Jake's jaw dropped. He stared at Baby. He stopped struggling. His eyes widened and his whole body visibly relaxed. A bright white light filled his vision and formed a shining halo around her head. It suddenly occurred to him that here standing before him—looming over him, whatever—was a beautiful, clever, full-on babe who *didn't know the meaning of the word relationship*. This was the girl of his dreams. Granted, his dreams had never accounted for antennae or green skin, and he'd have to have a serious word to her about this B/D scenario, but . . . *kyooool.*

"Oh, you know," he explained, gazing at her with eyes gone soft with longing, "relationships are when you hang out a lot, you know, for more time than it takes just to get each other into bed, and pretend to like the same films and music and each other's friends, and have really dumb arguments over things like, you know"—the pressure of her hand on his balls was starting seriously to distract him—"you stealing the covers at night and stuff, which really is dumb because, if you're bigger, you need more covers, right?"

Baby was nodding her head in agreement, but what she was

thinking was: Why would anyone steal the covers at night? Weren't they just old songs sung by new people? How did you steal a cover anyway? She was also studying his legs with their soft matting, his lean torso with its coat hanger shoulders, and the curious geometric manner in which the fur covered his chin. (Goatees hadn't yet caught on in the Outer.)

"The worst thing about relationships," he continued in a voice choked with confusion and lust, "is that they inevitably lead to a situation where one person starts talking *love* when the other person was still just thinking *like,* and that turns the *like* into *fear,* and then things get fucked up." Jake paused. Jesus. He sounded like a cynical bastard. If the truth be told, Jake had been in one or two relationships where he'd been the one who started talking *love.* Not that he was prepared to admit that. Not even to himself. "Yeah," he concluded, breathing heavily, "relationships are the pits."

God, her hand felt good. He had to call on all his willpower to resist the temptation to thrust his pelvis into those warm green hands of hers.

"Relationships sound *awful,"* Baby commiserated, absent-mindedly tugging and tickling and squeezing Jake's cock. She wondered what it would be like to fall in love. It could be fun. On the other hand, she had the impression that love was, oh, she didn't know, suspiciously *pop* or something. She wasn't totally ruling it out or anything, but she needed to know more about it first. Now sex, on the other hand, *that* was definitely rock 'n' roll.

Holy Hyades! Now what was happening? This Earthling was *full* of surprises.

"Check this out," she called to the others excitedly. Before their eyes and under Baby's fingers, Jake's penis was dramatically lengthening, the flesh hardening, the skin stretching taut and smooth. Jake was breathing fast now, his head twisting from side to side, his hands and feet struggling against their bonds.

"This bit . . ." Lati grabbed the *Whole Earthling Catalogue* off the shelf and turned the pages frantically until she located the reference. "The, uh, inseminator," she read, "is not of static proportions." She yanked open a drawer marked MEASURING IMPLEMENTS and began rifling impatiently through its contents. "Where the hell . . . this'll have to do," she said, holding up something that an Earthling scientist might have recognized as a micrometer screw gauge but to Jake looked frighteningly like a miniature vise. Fresh fear churned the rapids of weird emotion that were surging through him but, instead of counteracting his desire, it only served to harden it.

Baby reluctantly relinquished her hold on Jake's penis so that Lati could insert it between the micrometer's anvil and spindle. Lati took a reading. "It's already thirteen illion nufokips. And it's still growing," she said, impressed.

Doll had turned her back on them and continued to leaf through the catalogue until she found the section on females.

"Twenty-four illion," Lati announced.

"You can make a clitoris grow too, you know," Doll said. "If anyone's interested."

Baby nodded vaguely. She was interested, sure, but *later*. She wasn't sure whether it was the novel sight of an expanding Earthling inseminator or the appealingly demented lust in Jake's eyes, or just her own general excitement at having finally abducted an Earthling after dreaming about it for abso-fuckin-lutely *ages,* but she was feeling *very* turned on.

"Thirty-five illion . . . Fifty-one illion!" Lati whooped. "But hey, look at this," she cried, doing a double take. "There appears to be a spot of seepage."

Indeed. A small pearly drop had oozed up through the glans of Jake's cock. All systems were go. The balls were in position, the shuttle was set for launch. Countdown commenced. Ten. Nine . . .

On a whim, Lati opened her mouth and bent over.

Eight.

"Don't touch it!" cried Doll, waving the *Whole Earthling Catalogue.* "It says here that it's necessary to build up a tolerance to Earthling bodily fluids over a period of time. It says here—"

Seven.

Baby dived at Lati to shove her aside before she could touch her lips to Jake's cock. If anyone was going to do that sort of thing to Earth boy here, *she* was. He was *her* Earth boy, she fumed. Who was the leader here anyway?

Too late. They were both too late.

CHICK-A-BOOM!

It wasn't entirely clear what had happened, but Lati now lay panting and disheveled on the floor, and Jake's countdown was temporarily suspended. Her T-shirt was twisted around her torso as though she'd dressed in a tornado. A lemon-yellow aura pulsed over the surface of her skin, heat poured off it in visible waves, and her form oscillated for a few seconds between Nufonian gray and Earth girl. A smell like that of jonquils filled the room. Her antennae vibrated and hummed. "Wowie zowie," she slurred.

Jake wasn't feeling quite so robust as a moment ago. In fact, he was feeling rather disoriented. "Mum," he whispered. "Mum. I wanna go home." But Baby grasped Jake's flagging cock possessively and under her warm green fingers, Jake's shuttle was soon ready for launch once more.

Lati was still lying motionless on the floor. Doll crouched at her side. She shook her shoulders and stroked her cheeks. "I bet this wouldn't have happened if we'd started with an Earth girl," Doll grumbled. "Baby, leave it alone for a second and come over here, will you? I'm not sure that Lati's all right."

Baby reluctantly turned her attention to her misdemeaning mate. "You okay, Lati?" she asked, secretly hoping she was suffering for her sins. She was *out of fuckin order,* that girl.

They were both attending to Lati when a bevy of anxious squeals and groans drew their attention back to Jake.

"Ow! Oh! Aaaaaaargh!" hollered Jake.

"For love of Saturn . . ." Doll exploded with laughter.

Revor, unnoticed by any of them, had abandoned the sock, shimmied up the legs of the table, and was now sitting between Jake's spread legs. He sucked Jake's erect cock up his tubular snout. It was a snug fit. As Jake struggled in vain to shake him off, Revor drew on Jake's cock with a manic intensity that made his little pop-eyes protrude even further. His shag-pile fur stood on end and small arcs of electricity rainbowed the spaces between his tensely splayed toes and fingers. His little tail was wagging so fast that it was a cherry-colored blur.

Jake was practically weeping by now. With one final shriek, he came in Revor's mouth. A huge crackling sound traveled the length of Revor's little body. Revor flew backwards into the air with jet propulsion, a small furry meteor that cratered the wall and then slid down to the floor, a tangle of damp fur and wild eyes.

Lati picked up her dizzy head. "Rev," she cried weakly, her shoulders sinking back to the floor again.

Revor threw her an unfocused glance. Then the lids snapped shut over his eyes.

Baby picked him up and held her hand up to his snout. "Still oxygenating," she noted. How was it that Revor and Lati had managed to have *all* the fun?

"So that was sex, eh?" remarked Doll, not quite as unimpressed as she liked to make out. She snuck another glance, this one lingering, at Lati's prone and peaceful figure.

"I think there must be more to it than that," Baby said wistfully. "Still. Yeah, I reckon that was sex."

"But was it rock 'n' roll?" said Doll.

Jake, feeling like he'd just returned from a very long journey, picked his head up and looked at them, blinking. Did someone say rock 'n' roll?

The Maltese Dildo

Adam McCabe

My latest client still hadn't told me his name. He sat upright in the Chippendale, facing me, his legs spread against the chair arms so I had a front-row seat for the action. Wearing nothing but a long silk robe, he played with his asshole during our interview, watching me for a reaction. His hole, puckered and red, looked resigned to this treatment. He slid two fingers back and forth inside of himself as he waited for my reply.

"Well, Mr. McCabe?" he said, not stopping his rhythm.

"I'm not sure I can help. I usually look for things of value. You can buy a dildo at any sex shop."

He stopped and sat up. His dick parted the folds of the robe, throbbing in the surrounds of silk. "It's not any dildo. It's invaluable."

"Why? Lose your virginity on it?"

He smiled languidly. "No, that might make it an antique, but hardly worth the effort. This dildo has a jewel-encrusted handle. Rubies and sapphires along the outside and emeralds near the base. My family brought it from Malta—generations ago."

I barked out a laugh which disappeared in the heavy drapes of the darkened drawing room. "You mean to tell me that you shove precious gems up your ass?" I was a top-man all the way. How could anyone want to have another man up his ass?

He pulled the robe around him so that his hard-on disappeared from view. Maybe I'd overstepped my boundaries. "If you want to phrase it like that, yes. Will you take the case?"

I nodded. "Four hundred a day plus expenses."

He leaned back again in the chair and ran a finger down between his balls to explore his hole again. The poor thing never got any rest. "Very well, let me tell you the story."

"The facts will do. Stories are for children."

Three fingers went up his hole to the second knuckle. He seemed to be missing his dildo quite a bit these days. I could see that a butt plug wouldn't be enough for this guy.

He sighed, whether from exasperation or lust, I couldn't tell. "As you wish, the facts. Three days ago, I hosted an orgy here at my home. One of the guests stole the dildo at that function."

"So someone you know did it? Why don't you just ask for it back?" Some people had more money than sense.

"Not that easy. My friend, Albert Gutman, set up the event. My house, his party, his friends."

"Does Gutman keep a guest list?"

His fingers started a rhythm that barely left him energy to speak. "If I had a name or a better description, I would appeal to him directly. You see, all I know is that this particular thief is well-endowed: eleven inches at least. I heard people refer to him as the Fat Man, but that's the only name I know for him. Albert might know him, but it's a rather embarrassing situation."

"So how do you know he's the thief? Could have been anyone at the party."

His cock pulsed like a metronome in time to the movement of his fingers. Pre-come flowed off the head of his dick and into the folds of his robe. "We were—becoming acquainted, this big man and I. When I came, I closed my eyes to savor the moment. I opened my eyes to find that he and the dildo were gone. Simple as that."

"You got Gutman's number? Sounds like the place to start." I watched him, feeling my own cock press against the leg of my pants. His act was reminding me how long I'd been celibate.

He pointed to a small marble table. "Better than that. On the table is an invitation to Albert's next party. It's tonight. Albert has assured me that the guest list is the same, except you'll be going in my stead." As he finished his words, he came. Milky-white liquid shot out of him and ran down his shaft in torrents, disappearing into the robe.

I took a deep breath. Most cases didn't get me this horny. I'd be ready for tonight if I could wait that long. "Fine. I'll be there. But what makes you think this mystery man will be interested in me?"

"Mr. McCabe, trust me. He will. Just bring me back the dildo."

■

As promised, I left with an invitation to a small soiree that evening: its engraved lettering and thick vellum envelope revealed no sign of illicit sex. The whole scene stank of money, though. The rent on the office was due next week. I didn't have a lot of choice in how the bills got paid at this point.

Never having been to a fuckfest, I wasn't sure how to dress. Intimate scenes with a single partner were my forte. I couldn't get that interview out of my mind as I threw on a sports coat with my jeans and white Tommy shirt. No use getting too spiffed up since the clothes would be doffed inside the door.

I arrived at eight per the invitation. I'd hoped for a chance to scout the place before most of the others got there, but the house was packed. House, hell, it was a mansion. First time I'd ever seen a crowd of punctual gay men.

A valet led me into a drawing room where five men stood, stripping. I followed along, trying to look like I knew the score. No one looked familiar and none of their dicks matched my client's description. I undressed in a hurry. The valet placed my clothes into a private locker and gave me the key attached to a wrist-strap. The hallway was packed with men looking to score. I had work to do.

The first floor was a series of showrooms, each space filled with antiques and mahogany furniture. I wasn't sure how the old masters would have felt about this place. I walked around, trying to ignore the variety of dicks in my path. None came close to the description of the Fat Man's. A winding marble staircase led to the second level and I began a search of the upstairs bedrooms. Plenty of action, but no eleven-inch dicks.

I decided to take a piss. Even with the mass nudity, I wanted a little privacy and shut the bathroom door behind me. Someone entered while I was going and watched from the doorway. When I looked up, I knew I'd found my prey. Even at half-mast, his cock was the biggest I'd ever seen. Thick, with the ropy veins that meant plenty of blood to the organ.

He held up a dildo and smiled. "Interested in some fun?" The toy was nearly as big as he was: probably ten inches, thick, and the color of night.

I couldn't make out the handle so I wasn't positive that this was my client's dildo. I shook the last drops and stepped toward him. "I'm always up for some fun."

He smiled and pulled the door shut. His dick grew, almost bridging the gap between us. I didn't know what we could do with a cock that size. He held up the dildo and the light sparkled off the handle. I'd found what I'd come here for.

"Bend over." The Fat Man pulled a rubber and some lube out of the medicine cabinet. With one hand, he protected the end of the toy and made the device slick to the touch.

I smiled. "I'm not really into that." My own dick didn't look up to his standards.

He matched my smile and tapped the dildo in his hand. "Everyone says that the first time. Trust me." He moved closer to me, blocking my exit. The tile wall cooled my back as I looked for a way to escape, but I didn't see any. Not if I wanted to do my job. I didn't have what I came here for yet. I felt a finger slide up inside me as his monster dick rubbed against my stomach. He lubed my abs with his juices.

The sensation and heat of our cocks thrusting in time made me want to come now. A second finger entered me and the moment was lost. The pain was bearable, but made me twinge, imagining what he could do to me. The dildo slid down into his palm and I felt the head of the toy penetrate me. I lost my erection as the sex toy filled my ass. I'd never been fucked before and a mingling of excitement and fear swept over me—wanting the sensation and dreading the pain.

He turned me to face the wall and slid an arm around my waist to pull my ass out. I was almost bent at the waist by this point as the dildo traveled inside me. I could feel it push against my pucker. He rested a second and moved it inside me. My sphincter protested and then gave in. The dildo gained entrance and filled me.

I moaned so loud that the Fat Man laughed. "You're getting into this fast, aren't you? Maybe it's time for the real thing."

My knees nearly buckled as I thought of his huge dick penetrating me. I didn't know if I could handle all of it and remain conscious. Four hundred a day didn't begin to cover this. He gave the dildo a few more thrusts in me. I imagined the jewels scratching my ass.

The dildo clattered to the floor and I pushed it with my foot under a towel near the wall. He didn't seem to notice as he made preparations with lube and another rubber. Even facing the wall, I could smell his sweat as he approached me again. "Ready for ecstasy?"

I grunted, trying to prepare. Nothing could have helped. The first push made my eyes roll up in my head. The pain filled every cell and yet felt delicate in a way I'd never known. His arms slid around me to keep me standing as he started to thrust. The oversized biceps held me in place and I began to lick one. When he was sure I wasn't going to fall to a pile on the ground, his hand slipped down to my crotch and began to massage my limp dick. All my attention was on the feelings in my sphincter.

I could feel the ripping in my ass as he explored. I leaned back against him and felt the rough pressure of hair against my back. He nibbled on my neck while he squeezed my dick slowly in one hand. I wanted him to come so this moment could be over, but he had just gotten started. His balls slapped against my ass and he pushed me up against the wall again. I couldn't move as the heat of his dick filled me. I expected my stomach to explode like the scene from *Aliens* at any moment. He began to bite my back and shoulders as he massaged my dick. I started to feel the familiar stirrings as he clamped down on my cock and stretched it to full length.

"You'd be good as a top-man, too. Wouldn't you?" He whispered the words in my ear as he pulled on my lobe with his teeth.

Through clenched teeth, I said, "I've done that before."

A savage thrust made me whimper. "I'll bet you have." The words released him, and his balls contracted as he shot his load inside me. The sensation was unlike any I'd had. He continued to work me and I shot my wad against the bathroom wallpaper. I noticed a young guy lying on the floor by the towel and dildo, letting my come splash his upper body. I hadn't realized that anyone else had entered the room, but three guys were jacking off to the scene we provided. The Fat Man pulled out and threw the rubber into the toilet. I staggered out of the room, still feeling his dick inside me, gripping the towel and dildo to ensure that the experience was worth it.

■

The next day I returned to my client's home carting his prized possession. A butler led me into the study where my client sat in a robe with the hood pulled over his face. I laid the dildo on the table between us and chose to stand. "Here's what you wanted. And here's my bill."

The hood nodded.

"Have you heard any complaints from Gutman? Any noise from the Fat Man?" I leaned up against the back of the chair and watched him.

He shook the silk cloth covering. A whisper said, "The Fat Man had nothing but compliments for your performance. Said you were a natural."

I straightened up and stared at the cloaked figure. If he knew these people, why had he hired me? What was going on here? I limped across to his chair and pulled back the hood. My ex-lover's face came into view.

"What the hell?" I stepped back and bumped my ass against the table. Pain shot through me.

"Hello, J.J. Have a nice time last night? Thought you needed a little loosening up, so to speak." He smiled at me.

"This was all just a revenge plot?"

He nodded. "Not bad, huh? Now I think we're even." He stood up and walked out of the room.

I was left to limp back to my car and gingerly make my way home.

Triple X

Shay Youngblood

The summer I was sixteen years old, me and my aunt Sofine took the number thirteen bus downtown to the Triple X theater on North Main Street every Thursday afternoon. This idea came to Sofine one morning early in June. We both sat on the floor in my grandmother's kitchen in our bras and panties, sweating in front of a loud table fan set on high and a chipped white enamel bowl of melting ice. We dipped our hands in the bowl, flicking our cool, dripping-wet fingers at each other from time to time. Sofine laughed low down in her throat; her big breasts decorated with black lace trembled when she came across the small black-bordered ad in the movie section:

> First–run features. High–Quality Adult
> Movies. Air–conditioned. Thursday Ladies
> Free. Must be 18 years.

"Ladies free," she said.
"Air-conditioned," I repeated. I dipped my hands up to the wrists

in the bowl of ice and water, then leaned forward, pressing my wet palms to Sofine's face like she'd taught me to do when I was a little girl and we'd spent hot summer days in my grandmother's house. She closed her eyes and smiled in my hands.

"This could be educational." Her long, thick fingers selected a small piece of ice and began sliding it back and forth across her bare, buttery shoulders.

My mother, when she left me at my grandmother's for the summer, insisted that I do something educational, that I think about what I wanted to do with my life. She and my father were not happy when I announced that I was thinking about dropping out of high school at the end of my junior year, just thinking about it. I was considering pursuing a career in acting, after knocking out the audience at Malcolm X High School with my original interpretation of Ophelia as a homegirl in a contemporary staging of *Hamlet*. Mama said I was just acting myself, she didn't seem to think the reviews I got in the Afro-American weekly newspaper meant that I was Broadway stage material. Parker Henderson, the cultural critic, said I had promise, that my Ophelia was the most original he'd ever seen. My father, although he said he was proud of my performance, said he hoped I'd go to college before making my final decision to be a stage actress. I worked my behind off for that part. In Mr. Brandon's English class, the others were always laughing because I was a slow reader, but I fixed them. Mr. Brandon chose me to be Ophelia, and he helped me to create my role. He stayed after school with me for three weeks straight, helping me read Shakespeare. It might've been Greek, for all I understood in the beginning, but he took his time with me, and we cracked open the door to understanding.

"So you want to be an actress?" Sofine didn't act surprised or even laugh at me like my mama had when I told her.

"I *am* an actress. I was Ophelia . . ." Then I stood up in my grandmother's kitchen in front of the table fan in my underwear and gave Sofine and the kitchen cabinets all the drama of a mad Ophelia, heartbroken and abandoned. Sofine clapped politely.

"Mona Lisa, honey, get real; you can't afford to be playing Ophelia for the rest of your life. You a black woman living in America."

"Maybe I'll make movies," I said. "As a backup career."

"Well, there's an original idea." She took down my grandmother's coffee can filled with change from on top of the refrigerator and counted out bus fare for the both of us.

"Let's go do some research," she said, filling my hand with dimes.

The first time we went to the Triple X, the clerk, a bulky black man with a wild Afro and the mean gaze of a prison guard, asked us for ID. Sofine started to flirt with him, talking about how hot it was. He smiled, showing a gold tooth left of center, and winked at her.

"We get a lot of ladies come in, just want to be cool," he said, looking at her driver's license through the thick, dirty glass. She told him I'd lost my license at a baseball game two weeks ago. Her story was beginning to get long and I was losing my nerve, shifting my feet nervously, but the clerk wasn't interested and waved us in. The second time we came, he didn't bother to ask at all.

We lived in Atlanta then. My daddy delivered trailer homes cross-country. This particular summer he and my mama decided to use one of his long-distance deliveries to go on a second honeymoon. On their way out west they dropped me off in the small town in south Georgia where my mama grew up. I'll admit I was jealous of their adventure, I'd already begged on my knees at the dinner table to stay home alone so I could rehearse for my audition for Juliet in the Atlanta Festival of Stars Dinner Theatre production of *Romeo and Juliet* in the fall, but they just kept piling meat and potatoes on their forks and shoveling it into their mouths. Unlike most of my friends' parents, my mother and father were in love, and what I wanted didn't matter at all. The only saving grace to a hot summer in south Georgia was that my aunt Sofine was staying with my grandmother, and I knew she knew how to have a good time.

My grandmother was hard of hearing and spent her days piecing together quilts on the front porch when she wasn't watching afternoon soap operas and talking to the TV as if the villains inside could hear her harsh judgments of their sinful behavior.

Every Thursday all summer long, me and Sofine slept till ten o'clock, took a cool shower, and dressed in brightly colored tank tops and shorts and lace-up Roman sandals. We lotioned our bodies with cocoa butter, talcum-powdered between our legs and breasts, took three swipes of Mum deodorant under our arms, and picked our hair into big curly Afros that framed our faces.

I wasn't allowed to wear makeup at home, but Aunt Sofine put a thin line of black eyeliner on me, a little bit of blue eye shadow, and pink lip gloss that made my lips shine like glass. I began to feel glamorous. I had to look eighteen to get in the movies. Sofine let me wear her gold hoop earrings. I tried to give attitude like Lena Horne in *Stormy Weather.* I had to keep my glasses in Sofine's pocketbook until we got inside the theater. She said my glasses made me look like a square. It took Sofine longer to put on her face. The first layer was a liquid foundation that made her face look like a flat, dry pancake, then she painted on a thick line of black eyeliner, making points at the corner of her eyes to emphasize their slanted shape. My daddy said she looked Chinese, which she took as a compliment. Her lips she outlined in dark rose and filled in with Hawaiian Orchid, a kind of fuchsia color that matched her stretchy tube top. Me and Sofine walked slowly to the bus stop, so as not to encourage perspiration, and stood waiting for the Number Thirteen to take us downtown. We could have walked the eight or ten blocks, but it was hot, hotter than I imagined hell could be on a summer day.

A hand rests on a swollen breast, thighs spread open like a Bible. A man bows his head in prayer before them, holy. Her head thrashes from side to side, eyes squeezed shut. Small whimpers. Pleasure out of sight.

"You want some more popcorn?" Aunt Sofine whispers.

"No, I don't want no more." I cross my legs, shift in my seat, and let out the air I've been holding in my lungs, but I don't take my eyes off the screen. My mouth is dry, and although the air conditioner is on full blast, my hands and crotch are sweaty. I try to memorize the expression for desire.

A wide, red satin skirt lifted delicately above the knees. Thighs spread, lowered to the floor, hips dipping, picking up twenty-dollar bills. Smoke rings emanate from deep in her private parts. Perfect circles float in the air.

At home I take off my panties, squat down, and try to pick up a dollar bill, but my legs get a cramp and I lose my balance and fall and scrape my elbow against the bathroom door. I'm not allowed to smoke, so I can't try the smoke rings. Miss Kitty makes it look so easy to be a movie star.

A pool stick aimed at the eight ball aimed at the center of a womanly body spread open on a field of green felt.

My uncle High Five won't let me in the pool hall. He says I can't play pool and besides, "This ain't no place for skirts." He and his friends laugh and keep playing for quarters stacked on the edge of the pool-cue rack.

"I ain't no skirt," I say. "And anyway, blind Miss Lily could beat you shooting pool." I knew I could beat him, too. All I had to do was use my imagination. When I see High Five leave the pool hall, I sneak in and rub my hands across the green felt, hold the smooth, cool white cue ball in my hand, feeling the weight of it, wondering if my aim would be sure. Practice . . . rehearse . . . make believe . . . make it look easy . . . make it look real. . . . Eight ball in the corner pocket.

The frame is filled with moist flesh, steam heat; a white washcloth makes a trail in the water of her bath. The sound track is bland, nothing you could dance to, but my body is rocking on the beat.

At home I turn the volume on the radio up loud and sit in my grandmother's room in the dark, rocking in her rocking chair with my legs pressed together, a cool washcloth wadded into a ball stuffed in my panties. I rock through the top ten soul hits before my aunt Sofine bursts into the room and throws a comic book at me and tells me it's time for bed. My bed is a narrow single cot next to the bed she sleeps in with her one-year-old baby boy we call Honey because that's the color of his skin.

A man and a woman, both naked, gallop through a meadow on a white horse. Cut to interior bedroom. Day. The man lies still on his back. The woman sits on his lap and rides as if he is the white horse.

My aunt is munching loudly on the tub of popcorn balanced on her knees. She slurps her orange soda and watches the screen as if it is a documentary on the secret life of a tree. She watches as if she has seen it all before and is reduced to looking at the background. Sometimes we see the movies twice if the temperature is over ninety outside. We like it cool. Sofine comments on almost every new scene: "I hope that horse don't have fleas." Or "I would never sleep with a man had a butt bigger than mine."

A hand on my shoulder, a whisper in my ear.

"You don't want to go for a ride with me, do you?" A voice inviting, whispers in the darkness behind me. His breath smells like licorice, his voice sounds like a little boy's, a boy who is afraid the answer will be no.

"What you whispering in her ear?" Aunt Sofine turns around to look him in the eye.

"I'll whisper in yours, too, if that's what you into." He seems eager to please.

"We trying to watch the movie. Keep your comments to yourself, soldier," she says without missing a beat. He gets up and moves two rows behind us.

Sofine can tell a soldier from two hundred feet in the dark. She should know. She's only nineteen years old, but she's been married twice, both times to army men. Her first husband married her when she was just one year older than me. The problem with him was that he was already married to a girl in New Mexico. Her second husband was a short, chunky brick-colored sergeant from Pittsburgh, who was twice her age and expected her to cook dinner and make up the beds every day. She left him after two weeks. She says she didn't have to work that hard at home. Honey's daddy was in the marines. Men liked Sofine and she loved men. She was sexy in a way that made them whistle, stop their cars in traffic, and made them want to give her things.

I want men to give me things—flowers on opening night and diamond rings for each of my fingers and toes. I want applause for a job well done.

The fourth Thursday in July, Sofine says she has a date with Honey's daddy. She gives me money to buy a loaf of bread, some sliced meat, and a carton of Coke at the grocery store. My grandmother is on a trip to the mall with a group of senior citizens. By eleven o'clock, heat rolls through the open windows of the house in thick waves. The fan just stirs up dust and blows dead flies onto the bed. I keep wondering what the movie this week will be. If I'll learn some new acting technique. I am itching to learn something new.

I am nervous and sweaty at the thought of going to the Triple X by myself. I take another cold shower and decide to put on my aunt Sofine's face and catch the bus downtown. One block from the theater, I put my glasses in the pocket of my shorts and the world becomes a blur. I manage to wave in the direction of the clerk behind the window who barely looks up from the comic book he is reading. I am a regular. I open the door and a blast of cool air freeze-dries the sweat rolling down the back of my neck. With the money Aunt Sofine gave me, I buy a tub of buttered popcorn and an Orange Crush. I sit in our usual spot three rows from the screen on the aisle. There are less than a dozen other people in the theater, scattered mostly in the back rows. The movie has already started, so I can't see their faces.

Underwater. Bodies in slow motion. Graceful as dancers. Slow-motion sex. Wet sex. Sunlight dances on their bodies. Two women kiss on the mouth. A man watches from a distance.

I wonder if they could drown underwater, staying so long. Sofine would certainly comment on the man's hairy back or the woman's big feet. I squeeze my legs together, take a sip of Orange Crush, and hardly blink at the images on the screen. I want to be kissed underwater like that. I want the man to lift me onto his lap. There is a sudden movement next to me. I don't look directly, but out of the corner of my eye a body, a large male body, eases into the seat beside me. I sneak a look sideways. Muhammad Ali handsome. My guess, Air Force. His elbow takes over the armrest between us. His breathing is labored as if he is out of breath. He leans in my direction, close but not quite touching me. He smells freshly showered and shaved. His breath is minty.

"I could do that to you," the mouth next to me whispers, cool in my ear.

A girl and a boy are sitting on a sofa, watching TV. The boy tries to kiss the girl. The girl says no, but she is smiling. The boy tries to touch the girl underneath her dress. The girl says no, but she is smiling. The boy is frustrated. He pushes the girl against the sofa and pins her down with his body. The boy rips open the girl's blouse. The girl says no, she is breathing hard, putting up a fight, but she is still smiling. The boy is so overcome with passion at the sight of the girl's naked breasts that he tears off the girl's skirt and panties. The girl resists, but the boy is stronger. The girl struggles for a while, but eventually she gives in.

My head thrashes from side to side, eyes squeezed shut. I am the girl in the movies who takes pleasure out of life. I am the girl who rehearses to become the woman who will win Academy Awards for her performances, the one who loves the sound of applause. I am the girl who takes the hand offered in the darkness. Small whimpers. Pleasure out of sight.

Sophie's Smoke

Mark Stuertz

t was my father who brought me to it. Sophie took it to another place, a deep place.

When I was young I could take the strength of the clouds and hold them, feel how they pricked and burned. "Where do they come from?" I asked him.

"They're grown. They're made of leaves." My father had little patience for questions. But for this he made an exception. "You see the leaf?" He held it in front of my eyes and ran his finger along the veins hidden in the leathery tan wrapper.

"What about the inside?"

"The same," he said. "It's rolled tight, squeezed together, then cut." He sat in his leather chair with a book next to the all-in-one lamp and end table. I was next to him on the floor, sitting Indian-style. My mother was in a chair to his left. She thumbed through magazines. She didn't mind it. Seeing him there, putting it quietly between his lips, taking in the smoke, letting it out. It brought her some peace. It gave his breath form and was there for all of us to see.

It was loud when he struck the match; a screaming hiss. He used large kitchen matches, never the books they gave him at the tobacco shop. "More sulphur on the head. A bigger, hotter flame. The tip has to have an even light," he said. The first cloud was the most aromatic. The tobacco was fresh, more vaporized than burned, and it mixed with the sulphur and wood from the match. It opened the senses like the first cold wind in the fall.

I was fourteen when my father gave me my first cigar. He taught me how to hold it, how to clip the butt, how to strike the match, always a large wooden match, and how to pull in the flame. He taught me how to smoke it: how to puff, then wait, then puff again.

"Don't puff too hard," he said. "Hold it away from your face after you take it in. Let it breathe and cool. You never want it to overheat. And it never hurts to look at it after you take it out of your mouth."

■

Sophie is tall. Her hair falls straight to her shoulder and folds under like a dried-out leaf, a rich-brown one. Tiny freckles speckle her skin like bits of ash fallen from the sky signaling some distant inferno.

"Do you mind?" I ask.

"I love the box," she says. "Cedar is a smell I wish I could drink."

I open it and pull one from the bottom row. I slip off the red and gold ring. She holds her thumb in front of my lips. The ring goes over her thumb easy. She kisses it. "You'll need some help with the match. I can see the tip better than you." Her smile is like the stretch of elastic.

I bite the butt and flick a wet brown wrapper speck to the floor with a spit of air. She likes this crassness. I put it in my mouth, taking in the cool freshness before the burn.

She picks up the box matches. I hear the cardboard scratch as she slides it open. She pulls one from the box. "These are gold," she says. "You can get them with colored heads?"

"Strike it," I say. "My mouth is watering. I'm soaking it."

"Someday, I'm going to poison you." She says this slowly while she strikes the match. The sulfur bursts into a fizz as "poison" leaves her lips. She brings the flame to the end and holds it. "Make the clouds big, big enough for me to hide myself naked."

I suck in her flame with my eyes closed, drawing it gently, firmly. My puffing thickens the air with gray. She pulls the match away from the tip of the cigar and douses it in a sizzle on the flat of her tongue.

"You're crazy enough to poison me," I say. She holds her hands in the clouds and pulls the gray smoke to her face where she sucks some of it in. I take her head from behind and press it hard into my chest, puffing above the top of her head.

She twists her head so that her mouth is close to my ear. "Play with it," she says. "Get it going. Then pull it from your mouth and show me the wet part, the part you soaked."

■

I do pretty well for myself. I know how to make deals, size up situations, maximize opportunities. I'm making enough money for a cushion on my cushion. "It's like a museum," my father said. "Why do you want a museum in your house?"

My humidor is small, a bit larger than a phone booth. I had it built out of a useless coat closet. I had a carpenter do it. Work was slow for him so I made him an offer we could both live with. He installed the compressor, the fans, the lights, and the glass door. He wired the whole thing together, but probably not to code. The shelves are oak.

I stocked it carefully, and I have some prizes in it. There are the Cubans: the Romeo y Julieta and Hoyo de Monterrey Churchills, the Davidoff Château Margaux and the 4000's. I have the Partagas #2's and the #10's from the Dominican Republic, and the Honduran Aliados Valentinos.

"Pick one," I said.

"Sure, it smells good, but why in your house?"

"It keeps them fresh. I can age them."

"Age them?"

I brought my father to see it when it was finished, completely stocked. I wanted him to have the first one, to christen it in a sense. But he didn't understand the purpose, what it was I wanted.

"Listen," he said. "This is what it's about. You find one you like. You shop for it like a car. You go to the tobacco shop and go into the room and smell them all together. Then you look, pick them up, feel the weight, how they hold. Get a half a dozen this way. You might have one with the clerk before you bring the rest home.

"Try each one, live with the damn thing in your own living room. Then you go back and get a box or two of the best of the six. When you're getting low, you go back and do the whole thing all over again. But this, this is hoarding. You expecting a war?"

We had our smoke. The room had its christening. But it wasn't how I had imagined it. We talked a little. I didn't ask too many questions. He enjoyed the smoke, I could see that without asking. Through the smoke, through the talk and the non-talk, I could see some of his way.

Eight months after that he died of an aneurism in the aorta. I went through his things with my mother and found a box and a half in his sock drawer. They weren't expensive, but they were good. I don't remember what they were. I took them along with his watch and some cuff links. The boxes are on the top shelf in my humidor, behind the Davidoffs.

■

Sophie is dark and smooth, like a fresh sable brush. I whisk the back of my hand over her face, draw her to my chest, close my eyes, and hum low enough so that she can't hear, only feel. She turns her head up and drives her lips into my throat. "I want you to smoke for me," she says.

"For you?"

"You don't know what it does to me." She doesn't say this in a teasing way. She wants me to know of the mystery of the smoke and how it works her.

"We should go to the humidor. I'll let you choose," I say.

Sophie is like a stab wound for the good, one that draws off dangerous fluids. She moves at me brutally from all sides, looking for the fundamentals. She cuts to those dark, unexpected spaces that bring the pain you would never bring upon yourself, even if you knew it was good for you. But once it's there, you revel in it.

Sophie opens the boxes, touching each cigar, lifting them from their rows. She holds them under her nose and takes deep breaths, rolling them in her fingers, rubbing them on her cheeks. She kisses one, imprinting the leaf with lipstick.

One stops her cold, drawing off her attention from the others. "This one," she says, "is remarkable." It's a Cuban. The band is gone, so I'm not sure exactly what it is. But I see it's a chocolate-brown Colorado. This much I know. She holds it in both hands: the tip in her right, the butt in her left, each end pinched between her fingers.

"Look at the shape," she says. She lifts it to her eyes and stares it down like it's a string of diamonds. "The end looks like a nipple," she says. "And the butt is tapered, like a cock with the foreskin still attached." Her eyes widen when she says this. She closes them and passes it under her nose.

■

My father never smoked Cubans. He thought the embargo was a worthy thing, more worthy than enjoying the best smoke in the world. He never said much about my Cubans or how I got them. He would refuse my offers to try one with a quick wave.

"I don't want to put any change in Fidel's pocket," he would say. "Let him and his revolutionaries drive their '50s Chevies and smoke their cigars until they drop. But they won't get any working change from me."

I would light one of mine and he would smile, peeling the cellophane from a cheap Jamaican. "You think I don't know," he said. "You think your old man doesn't know as much as you. Well, let me tell you, before you were born, before the Bay of Pigs, I got them by the box. I still remember, too, the thick flavors and the spice; going down to shop for them like you would a pound of pork chops. Now you have to take a vacation and smuggle them back, or find a way to smuggle them in without having to trouble with a 'vacation.'" He said "vacation" with a sneer. "Does getting them this way make it smoke better?"

"You know Kennedy picked up thousands of them before he put the embargo in place," I said.

"That's just like a politician. Make rules for everybody else and exempt yourself. But I still think it was the right thing to do, you know."

■

Sophie asks me to kiss her hair. I fill my hands with it and bring it to my face. I smell the soap and the sweat through the strands. I kiss her scalp while she fills herself with the smell of the Cuban. "The wrap, look at the wrap," she says. "The veins are thick and they're sprawled over the length of it in branch after branch after branch. It's like the purple veins that weave through a cock."

She asks me to kiss her ears, then her neck. Her smell is crisp and sharp. I drill my tongue into her ear holes and move down her neck. A chill rolls through her. I seal my mouth over a patch of her skin at the base of her neck and let a flow of fresh saliva warm her there. The Cuban is under her nose the whole time.

I pull her sweater back and kiss her shoulders, long hard kisses so that I can feel her bones in my mouth. I stretch the sweater collar, pulling the shape out of it. She licks the tapered butt of the Cuban. My mouth floods, like it does at the first bite of a lemon. I slip my tongue under the straps of her bra.

She asks me to lift her arms and lick the sweat from her pits. "I don't use anything. I'm all that you'll taste," she says.

She is rich and strong, like dried apricots. I lick and take in all I can from the delicate, prickly pit skin. She shivers and from this I know I've reached her. I lick until the taste fades, and then move to her other arm. She growls. The sound comes from her chest. I move back to her throat and suck on her larynx as she hums. She rubs the Cuban against her cheek.

"Please."

"Sophie."

"Smoke." Everything she says will be all breath now.

I'm hard. I feel myself grow, turn sticky with sweat, the drops of liquid pushing from me. Sophie pulls away and leaves the humidor.

She has the Cuban in her fingers, pinching it at the part she said was like foreskin. I follow her. She drops to the floor and stretches her legs out straight in front of her, pulling her skirt up along her thighs, rolling it to her hips. Her green panties darken with a spreading patch of moisture. She pinches the elastic edge and slides them down her legs, pulling one leg out of them, leaving them dangling from her other ankle. She folds her legs into her body, spreading them out from her hips, poking the carpet with the sharp, thin heels of her shoes. The space between her thighs bristles in its fullness, glittering with sex salve.

"Please, sit down," she says. "Hold me. Let me help you with this."

She holds her hands out to me and I clutch them, dropping to my knees. My prick drains heavily. The head of it sticks to the fabric of my briefs. I squeeze her calves and draw her legs further apart, exposing more of her thickness to air. The salty seaweed smell mingles with the spice of the Cuban tobaccos. Her soaked pubic hair shimmers like a fruit glaze. She brings the Cuban between her legs and parts the lips, swollen and full, with the tapered butt, the uncircumcised tobacco cock. She twists it there slowly, working it like a drill bit, pushing the folds away from their center, pressing it into her body. Her lips encase it, soaking the leaf wrapper.

She moans and raises her ass from the floor, working the Cuban deeper. With her eyes closed, she rolls her head from side to side. Her pussy drools generously, dribbling down the scrunched inner cheeks of her ass in thick, yellowish trails, spotting the carpet. The chocolate wrap of the Cuban blackens, drinking her in.

I can see how she works her pussy muscles, squeezing the cigar into her body. I feel the muscles in her calves tighten and relax erratically, like jolts of car-battery juice shooting through her.

She moves like this until she has the Cuban completely hidden in her body. The narrow nipple cigar tip pokes past her lips like a second clit. With her head snapped back, she rattles in her throat. I watch how her wet turns to tobacco spit and I hear locomotive roar in my ears.

Then she stops. She raises her head and opens her eyes. "Let's smoke this." She pinches it by the nipple and slowly withdraws the

Cuban, twisting it a little, moving it from side to side. It shines like chocolate frosting. I wonder how she could have gotten so wet. She raises her ass off the floor when she passes the butt from her pussy. She offers it to me, pinching it in her fingers at the nipple. I grip it in the center and put the butt between my lips. I taste the sweat, thick spice, and sea spray.

It sizzles when she puts the match to the tip. I draw on it gently, her juices coating my lips. The nipple burns quickly. Sophie moves her face close to mine as I puff. She licks the length of it as I smoke.

She asks me for a puff. I take it from my mouth and touch the butt to her lips. She licks it as I run it over them. She pulls in some smoke.

I kiss her in a cloud of thick, musky smog. Then I give her the Cuban and undress. She smokes it through the unbuttoning of my shirt and through the unbuckling of my trousers. Naked, I take it from her and smoke. Driving between her tobacconized pussy lips, I puff hard. Then I let her taste it, blowing her face with smoke. She screams, leaving a hard ring in my ears.

Her screams plow a silence in my head, like a bulldozer clearing deep-rooted trees. Through the ring I open to her warmth and everything stops. Through the silence I hear my father's footsteps on the sidewalk. I hear the crunch of gravel and ground glass on the soles of his leather shoes as he walks to the tobacco shop to get a box or two of the best of the six.

Calcutta

Bob Vickery

At five in the morning, I usually don't expect to run into anybody on the streets. Which is fine with me. This is the time of day that I like the best, when most people are still in bed and the city is quiet. The streets take on a whole new feeling: peaceful, empty, the stores and cafes shut down, the yellow blinking traffic lights providing the only distraction. It's also my favorite time to work out. I belong to one of those 24-hour fitness centers, and at this time of day the place is almost empty: no lines for the weights, no guys waiting impatiently for you to wrap up your set.

So, I'm just walking down the street toward the gym, enjoying the quiet, not thinking of anything in particular, when I notice this guy in a wheelchair on the corner ahead. I size him up in an eye blink: the torn Grateful Dead T-shirt, the long, ratty hair, the powerful arms, and . . . no legs, just jeans pinned against the stumps of his thighs. When I pass him, I avoid eye contact, hoping to escape getting caught up in some little street encounter. Dream on. He reaches out and lightly touches my arm. "Hey, buddy," he says, "can you give me a minute to help me out?"

Shit, I think. I turn to him. "Sure. What's up?"

The guy points up the block, which rises before us in a long, sloping hill. "I got to catch a bus at the next street over," he says. "Can you give me a push up this hill?"

Well, what am I going to do, leave him stranded there? "All right," I say. I get behind his wheelchair and start pushing. The guy twists around so that he's half facing me. "My name's Mike," he says. He holds out a hand to me that is large and none too clean.

I shake it reluctantly, wedging my knee against the chair to keep it from rolling back. "I'm Paul," I say. Mike's grip is powerful, and I can feel a ridge of calluses rub against my palm. Looking at him more closely now, I can see how broad his shoulders are, how much his muscles bunch up beneath his T-shirt. I resume pushing Mike's chair, bending down and leaning forward, my face right above him. I get a whiff of something that isn't exactly roses, and I start breathing through my mouth. Pushing Mike is turning out to be a harder job than I expected: there's something wrong with the chair; it keeps swerving over to the right, and the wheels keep getting stuck. Now I see where Mike got his biceps.

"This chair's a piece of shit, isn't it?" Mike says, as if reading my mind.

"It's pretty beat up," I agree.

"I got it from the VA hospital. I get to go there because I'm a Vietnam veteran. That's how I lost my legs: stepping on a fuckin' land mine two weeks before my tour of duty was over." Mike's tone of voice is conversational, almost cheerful.

"That's a tough break," I say, because I can't think of anything else to say.

Mike gives a laugh without any bitterness. "No shit!" He jerks his thumb in the direction we're coming from. "You know that Highway 80 overpass, a few blocks away?"

"Yeah. What about it?"

"I slept under there last night. I'll probably sleep under there tonight too."

Why is he telling me all this stuff? I wonder. But it's pretty fucking obvious. I can smell a touch coming on a mile away. "Why don't you just sleep in one of the shelters?" I ask.

Mike snorts. "Those fleabags. I never go to those places. Only bums hang out there."

I maintain a diplomatic silence. After a little while we finally make it to the top. I wheel Mike next to the bus stop. "Here you go," I say.

"Thanks, man," Mike says. He holds out his hand again, and, again, reluctantly, I shake it. Only he doesn't let go when I try to pull away. "Listen, Paul," he says, his voice suddenly low and urgent, his words coming out fast, "I wonder if you could help me out with a little contribution. I'm trying to make it to the Y so that I can get a room and clean up. I smell like shit, I know that, do you think I like being this dirty? Only they charge twenty-five bucks for a room and I'm kind of low on cash. My disability check isn't due for another week. Do you think you could spare a few bucks?"

I pull my hand out of Mike's grasp and clear my throat. "Look," I say. "I have a standing policy not to give money to panhandlers." Mike doesn't say anything, he just looks at me, his gray eyes narrowed. "I mean, I give to charities," I say, talking faster. "I belong to the United Way, I'm a member of the Sierra Club, it's just that I get hit up for money all the time so I decided that I just wouldn't give any more money in the streets . . ." *Jesus, will you stop babbling!* I think. I take a breath and look Mike in the face. "I'm sorry."

Mike shrugs. "Don't be." He spins his chair around and wheels down the street. "Thanks for the push," he says, over his shoulder. I watch his retreating back for a few moments, and then turn and go to the gym.

The place is almost deserted, just me and a couple of other guys in the weight room. I go through my routine quickly and efficiently, keeping my mind blank. There's some guy there I haven't seen before, a kid in his early twenties: blond, milk-fed, downy-skinned, his body smooth and beautifully defined. I think of Mike and the contrast between the two is grotesque. The guy asks me to spot him when he does his presses, and I lean over him, ready to catch the weight if I have to. His T-shirt is hiked up to his chest, and I check out the hard torso, the cut of the abs. A little later, he returns the favor as I do my bench presses, and I catch a glimpse of the bulge in his jock strap under his gym shorts. We talk briefly; he tells me that his name is Jeff and that he's a student at U.C. San Francisco.

When I'm done with my workout, I go back to the locker room, strip, and enter the steam room. Except for me, the place is empty. I lean against the tile wall and close my eyes, listening to the hiss of the steam, feeling the rush of heat pour over my body. I hear the click of the steam-room door open and close. After a couple of beats, I open my eyes again. Jeff is sitting on the bench across from me, naked, knees spread apart. He watches me intently as his dick slowly gets hard. After a pause, I reach over and slide my hand over his torso, feeling the hard muscles beneath my fingertips. Jeff hooks his hand around my neck and pulls my mouth against his; we play dueling tongues for a few seconds. I drop to my knees and slide my lips down his dick, until my nose is mashed against his dark-blond pubes.

Jeff lays his hands on either side of my head and starts pumping his dick in and out of my mouth. I suck on it greedily, my hands still exploring his torso. I find his nipples and twist them, not gently. Jeff groans.

He pushes me back. "Stand up," he says, his voice urgent. I climb to my feet, and stand before him, my arms at my side. My dick is as hard as dicks get. Jeff wraps his hand around it and starts stroking, his fist sliding rapidly up and down the shaft. He replaces his hand with his mouth, and I close my eyes, letting the sensations sweep over me. The steam hisses out of the vents and pours over my body, and I feel my sweat trickle down my face, my torso, my back. Jeff tugs gently on my balls as he deep-throats me; his hand wanders to my ass, squeezing the cheeks, burrowing into the crack, massaging my asshole. I feel my load get pulled up by his mouth, and one sharp thrust of my hips sends me over the edge. My body spasms and I groan loudly. Jeff pulls my dick out of his mouth and jacks me off as I shoot, my load raining down onto his upturned face. And right at that moment, while the orgasm sweeps over me, the image of Mike's face floods my brain. *What the fuck . . . ?* I think. All I see is Mike, his narrowed eyes, his weatherbeaten face, the stumps of his legs. I try to shake the image out of my head. Jeff is jerking off, and then he cries out as the sperm pulses out of his dick. I reach down and twist his nipple until he's done.

We're silent for a few beats. "That was hot!" Jeff finally says, grinning.

"Yeah," I say absently. "Real hot."

When I'm out on the street again, I walk back to the bus stop. If by some chance Mike is still there, I'll give him a couple of bucks. But the place is deserted.

For the whole morning at work, I can't get Mike's face out of my mind. After a while this gets annoying. *What the fuck is this?* I wonder. *Some spasm of liberal guilt?* At lunch I leave the office to run a few errands; for some reason I notice the street beggars more than I usually do. They're on every corner, squatting down in doorways or against newspaper racks or street lamps, their Styrofoam cups in front of them, along with their cardboard signs, hand-printed with their hard-luck stories. Nobody gives these guys a dime. I don't either.

I still think of Mike that evening, while I wait in a line to see a movie, with my friend Tony. Tony's going on about some guy he's been dating, how this might turn into something. I listen patiently. Finally, when Tony winds down for a second, I clear my throat. "I had this weird encounter this morning," I say. "I can't get it out of my head."

Tony looks at me expectantly. "Somebody hot?" he asks, grinning.

The absurdity of Tony's comment makes me laugh. I shake my head. "It's nothing. Skip it." Tony continues talking about his new boyfriend.

It doesn't take long before I'm sick of him, of the idea of spending the next few hours sitting next to him in a movie theater. I clear my throat. "Look, Tony," I say. "I'm sorry. I'm just not in the mood for a movie. Do you mind if I take a rain check?"

The blood rushes up to Tony's face. "Hell, yeah, I mind. We made plans. I drove to the city to do this."

"I'm sorry," I say. And I am. But all I want to do is get away.

Tony leaves, none too graciously. I put my hands in my pockets and start walking. I'm in an upscale commercial district, the streets flanked by department, jewelry, and clothing stores: Macy's, Gump's, Saks, I. Magnin. And yet, in every doorway, figures are huddled under blankets and beat-up sleeping bags. I pass by a woman panhandling in front of Tiffany's, a small girl in her arms. The girl watches me with shrewd, bright eyes. *Where the fuck am I?* I think. *Calcutta?*

When I reach my car, I climb into the driver's seat. I sit there for a long time, my hands grasping and ungrasping the steering wheel. "Shit!" I mutter. I stick my key in the ignition and start up the car.

My headlights make a tunnel of light under the highway overpass. Everything on either side of me is pure darkness; the only other light source is from a street lamp over a block away. I cruise down the street slowly, peering out the window, trying to make out the details of the forms I see lying on the pavement. My nerves are raw. I half expect some crack addict to pull out a Saturday-night special and blow my head off. I finally spot Mike sitting in his wheelchair, wedged into a concrete corner. He squints into the headlights.

I get out of my car. "Hi, Mike," I say. "Remember me?"

Mike looks at me for a long time. "Sure," he finally says. "How ya doin', Paul?" If he's surprised to see me, he doesn't show it.

I talk fast, before I have a chance to change my mind. "Look, if you want a place to spend the night, I can take you back to my apartment. I have a fold-out couch you can sleep on."

Mike gives me a hard, shrewd look. A full thirty seconds of silence passes. "Okay," he finally says.

I wheel him to the passenger side of the car and open it. He slides into the front seat with surprising agility. I open my trunk, and after a hard struggle, I get his rusty, beat-up, piece-of-shit wheelchair folded up. By the time I close the trunk, sweat is dripping down my forehead.

We ride back in silence. I keep my mind blank. Every time a thought tries to rise to the surface, I push it down savagely. I don't speak to Mike until I've pulled into the garage of my apartment house. "There's no elevator," I say. "I'm going to have to carry you up the stairs."

Mike regards me calmly, like we do this every day. "Okay," he says.

Mike is not a small man, and I stagger up the stairs with him in my arms, praying to God that I don't drop him. Up close, the smell of stale sweat from his body is almost enough to make me gag. His torso under my arms is powerfully built; I think with grim amusement that he ought to rent out his wheelchair as a workout machine. I deposit him on the sofa and then go back down for his wheelchair. When I'm back in the apartment, Mike is the first to speak. "Mind if I take a bath?" he asks.

"No problem," I say.

I help him into the bathroom and turn on the faucets for the tub. Steam rises into the air. Mike peels off his clothes and drops them on the floor. His torso is packed with muscles. There's a tattoo on his left arm of a growling bulldog, with U.S.M.C. written underneath. The ink under his skin has started to run, blurring the image. A scar runs from his left pectoral down his side. Mike sees me staring at it. "I got that in a knife fight with some coked-up street crazy," he says. He lowers himself slowly into the tub. "Sweet Jesus, that feels good!" he groans.

I pick up his clothes. "I'm going down to the laundry room and throw these in a washing machine," I say. Mike is too busy soaping down to answer.

When I come back, Mike is sitting naked in his chair, toweling himself dry. The water in the tub is several shades darker. I reach in and pull the plug, and then throw Mike a terry cloth robe. "You want something to eat?" I ask.

Mike looks at me with half-lidded eyes as he slips on the robe. *What does it take to get a rise out of this guy?* I wonder. "Okay," Mike says.

Over dinner, Mike starts loosening up a little. He tells me about life on the streets, about the crazies he runs into, how he got his arm broken four years ago in a fight over his cashed disability check, and how it never really healed right. It surprises me to realize that he's a handsome man: the skin around his eyes is puffy, and his face is lined, but his features are regular, his mouth well formed, his chin strong, his gray eyes fierce and intelligent. There's a no-bullshit, direct way about him, stripped of self-pity. He laughs once over some story he's telling me about life on the streets, and in that instant he looks years younger.

Shortly after dinner, I open up the sofa bed and make it up for

Mike. "I'm going to go to bed," I say. "Let me know if you need anything."

Mike shrugs off the robe and slips naked under the blankets. He folds his hands under his head, his biceps bunched up like meaty grapefruits. "Why don't you hang around for a minute?" he says. "Keep me company." He grins. "These new surroundings have got me all wired."

His grin is so boyish and good natured that I'm immediately suspicious. He doesn't look wired at all. If anything, he looks completely in control. Uneasiness floods over me. *I don't know anything about this guy!* I think. *What the fuck was I thinking of, bringing him into my apartment?*

Mike waits patiently, his eyes trained on me. I sit down next to him, my body rigid. He reaches up and squeezes my shoulder. I flinch. "What's the matter?" he says. "Do I make you nervous?"

"Yeah," I say. "As a matter of fact, you do."

We sit silently for a few beats, Mike's hand still kneading my shoulder. He pulls me down, and we kiss, first gently, and then with growing fierceness. Mike's tongue pushes deep into my mouth. I slide my hand across his furry chest, feeling the hard pectorals, the nipples. I pinch one and feel it swell. Mike sighs. "Yeah," he says, "that's good. Play with my tittie."

I lean forward and flick his nipple with my tongue, then nip it gently. Mike's body stirs. He reaches down and cups my crotch with his hand, giving it a squeeze. He pulls back and looks at me, his eyes hard and shrewd. "Why don't you get naked?" he says.

I stand up and pull my clothes off as Mike watches. *This is fucking insane!* I think. But my dick is fully stiff and my heart is hammering hard enough to crack a rib. I can't remember when I've felt this excited.

When I'm naked, I slip into the bed, next to Mike. He reaches over and pulls me against him, wrapping his huge arms around my torso. We kiss again as Mike presses our bodies together. I can feel his hard dick rub up against my belly. He increases the pressure of his hug, and I find myself struggling for breath. Mike's eyes gleam with a wolfish light, and suddenly I'm scared shitless. I'm a strong guy myself, but I can't break free. If Mike wanted to, he could snap my spine in two right now. But he just releases his grip, laughing.

"What was that all about?" I ask.

"Nothing," Mike says. "I'm just fuckin' with you."

"Oh, yeah?" I say. I grab his wrists and pin his arms above his head. Mike doesn't resist, and his eyes gleam with amusement. But I don't kid myself that if this were a real brawl, I'd probably be fighting for my life right now. "Why don't you just suck my dick for a while, tough guy?" I growl.

"Okay," Mike says, laughing. All of a sudden he's as mild as a spring day. I release his wrists and sit up, pressing my thighs against Mike's torso. My dick sticks straight out, inches above his face. He opens his mouth, lifts his head, and I slide my dick in. His lips nibble down the shaft and his tongue wraps around it. I don't stop until my balls are pressing against his chin. Mike takes it all like a trouper. I start pumping my hips, fucking his mouth in long, slow strokes. Mike twists his head from side to side, sucking on my dick with noisy gusto. He wraps his hands around my balls and tugs on them as his head bobs up and down. I reach back and start jacking him off. His dick feels meaty and thick in the palm of my hand, and the pre-come that oozes out helps me slick it up nicely.

I whip off the blankets so that it's just our naked bodies on the bed, with no covers to hide under. I want to see Mike's body. I pull back from him and sit at the foot of the bed. Mike shows no sign of self-consciousness; he lays there, his hands once again behind his head, watching me calmly as my eyes drink him in. I lean forward and run my hands over his arms, tracing the bulge of his biceps. I knead the muscles of his torso, feeling their hardness: the powerful pecs, the hard, furry abs; then run my finger along the length of his scar, noting the texture of the rubbery red skin. I place my hands on his hips and slide them down over the stumps of his thighs, massaging the flesh. Mike's dick lies hard against his belly, twitching slightly, a drop of pre-come oozing out of the head. Mike has a beautiful dick: red and meaty, thick, veined, the head flaring out. His balls hang low, covered with a light fuzz. I lean forward and press my face against them, breathing in their faint musky smell, feeling the hairs tickle my face. I open my mouth and suck them in, rolling the loose scrotal flesh around with my tongue. I look up, my mouth full of ballmeat; Mike is watching me intently, his eyes narrowed, his eyebrows pulled down.

I drag my tongue up the length of his dick and around the flared, red head. I open my lips, and slowly, inch by inch, I take Mike's dick full in my mouth, sucking on it, wrapping my tongue around it as my lips nibble down the shaft. Mike exhales deeply, the rasp of his breath a hairbreadth shy of a sigh. I start bobbing my head up and down, and Mike pumps his hips in sync with my mouth, thrusting his dick hard into my mouth with each downward swoop of my head. I run my fingers through the forest of hair on his chest and twist his nipples hard. This time, Mike does groan, and when I glance at his face, I see the composure beginning to break, the eyes widening, the mouth opening as he breathes harder. Mike firmly grips my head with both hands and starts plowing my mouth in earnest, his thrusts hard and deep. With a sudden, quick movement, he pivots us around, so that I'm on my back now, with Mike straddling my chest. His huge hands grip my temples with greater pressure now, and the head of his cock is banging against the back of my throat like it's knocking on Heaven's door. This suits me fine, I can't get enough of his dick in my mouth, I'm feeding on it like a shark on chum. I reach behind and grab his ass cheeks, feeling their muscularity, how they relax and harden with each thrust of his dick.

Mike's face looms over me. His lips spread wide in a savage grin. "I would really love to fuck that pretty ass of yours, baby," he growls.

I pull his dick out of my mouth and return his grin. "Just hold that thought," I say. I slip out of bed, make a run to the bathroom, and return with a condom and a jar of lube.

Mike leans back, propped up on his arms, as I roll the condom down his dick. I give my hand a liberal squirt of lube and grease his dick up good. Mike pushes me back onto the bed and hoists my legs over his powerful shoulders. He works his dick into my asshole with killing patience, inch by slow inch. I push my head against the pillow and close my eyes. When he's full in, Mike just lays motionless on top of me for a few beats. He looks down at me and grins. "I just want my dick and your asshole to get acquainted first," he says, "before they start dancing." I laugh. Mike begins to grind his hips, slowly at first, almost imperceptibly, and then with increasing thrust.

It doesn't take long before he's giving my ass a savage pounding, his balls slapping against me.

I throw my head against the pillow. "Oh, yeah!" I groan.

Mike bends down and plants his mouth over mine, his tongue thrusting back in as his dick works its way deep into my ass. I match him stroke for stroke, squeezing my ass tight against his dick, matching his rhythm. My heels dig in between his shoulder blades, and my hands hold on to his hips for purchase. We're both working up a sweat now; drops trickle down Mike's face and splatter on me, mingling with my own sweat. Mike's chest is heaving, and his breath comes out in ragged gasps. He pauses long enough to squirt a dollop of lube on his hand and starts jacking me off; it doesn't take long before my groans are mingling with his. Mike's teeth are bared, and, with each thrust of his hips, his grunts become louder and more drawn out. Finally, he shoves his dick in hard and cries out. I feel his body shudder, and he leans down and kisses me hard as the orgasm sweeps over him. Mike's greased strokes on my dick never slow down, and it's just a matter of seconds before I'm groaning and squirting my load out as well, the thick drops splattering against my chest and belly. Mike collapses on top of me, smearing his body with my come. I feel his chest rise and fall, and we kiss again. He pulls his softening dick out of my ass and nestles against me, his face nuzzling my neck. After a couple of minutes, he starts snoring. I drift off to sleep soon afterwards.

I wake up early the next morning and get dressed for work. Mike is still asleep. My mind is full of ideas: contacting social agencies, finding Mike some kind of permanent place to stay, getting him off the streets. After a while, Mike wakes up. His eyes follow me around the room.

"I'll be leaving for work in a few minutes," I say. "You're welcome to stay here a while longer."

Mike shakes his head. "Once you leave, I won't be able to get out. You'll have to carry me down those stairs."

I stop and look at him. "Why don't you just stay here for the day? When I get back, we can talk about figuring some way of finding you a place to stay."

Mike smiles. "Thanks, but I got things to do."

I carry him down to the sidewalk outside, set him on the stoop, and get his wheelchair. "I'll be back from work around 5:30," I say. "You going to be here?"

Mike shrugs. "Yeah, sure."

He's not there when I return that evening. Somehow, I'm not surprised, though I stay indoors in case he shows up. Later, I drive by the overpass, but he's not there, either.

Every evening, for a couple of weeks, I make a ritual of cruising under the overpass, searching out in the dim light for a figure in a wheelchair. I never find him. Maybe the thought of some do-gooder trying to get him off the streets is so abhorrent to Mike that he's moved on to another place where he can't be found. Eventually, I give it up.

But I can't get the son of a bitch out of my head. It's not lust or pity; it certainly isn't love. I don't know what the fuck it is. But Mike, wherever you are, hustling passersby with your "will you push my wheelchair for me?" routine, I hope you're doing what you want to do. And I wish you luck, man. I wish you luck.

S & M

Gabrielle Glancy

All my girlfriends' names, without exception, have begun with S or M. It was not until Sasha, however, that I had my first official S/M relationship. When I tell you the circumstances, the frustration, the attraction, the particular curve of her particular elusiveness, you will perhaps want to hit her too.

We were in Brooklyn, sleeping in the living room of her friends Linda and Lani's brownstone. Linda and Lani were a warm, wealthy lesbian-activist couple who were trying to have a baby. She had not picked me up from the airport. True, she was waiting for me, but she had made me suffer.

Stiff at first—it had been three months since we had seen each other—Sasha got up from the couch and put on music. Of course, she played the tape she had sent me from Moscow. I began to cry. Then when she got into bed, I fucked her in the ass. I had two fingers of one hand up her ass and two fingers of the other in her cunt. I could feel the thin wall that separated one from the other, slick, hot between my fingers. I fucked her good and hard. She was on her stomach. I stood over her. When she came, I thought she would cry.

I myself was exhausted. I rolled over next to her.

For a long while we lay without talking. Then I said: "That was really good for me. I like fucking you in the ass. Was it good for you?"

"It was great," she said. "But you know what I really wanted?"

"What?"

"When you were back there?"

"Yeah?"

"I wanted you to spank me."

I felt dizzy with desire.

"To spank you?"

"Yeah," she said.

"With my hand?"

"Yeah."

We were both breathing heavily.

"To fuck you and spank you?"

"Yeah."

"Jesus."

You can imagine what happened the next night.

"Turn over," I said.

Sasha obeyed.

"Spread your legs."

She was wet to the touch, her lips silky.

I found her asshole. I ran my index finger around the edge of it.

"Does that feel good?" I asked.

"Mmm," she moaned.

"Do you want me to fuck you in the ass?"

"Mmm."

"Do you want me to spank you?"

She gasped.

"You do, don't you?"

I ran the palm of my right hand over the smooth curve of her checks, the middle finger of my left hand still up her ass. Sasha had a beautiful round butt, small, but beautifully shaped, solid, supple, inviting.

I touched her with delight and calculation. I was about to do something I had only dreamed of and I was plotting my course.

If she had turned her head at that moment, she would have seen my left hand halfway up her ass and my right hand poised in the air, ready to strike.

The preparation lasted a good ten minutes. What I was about to do was momentous. It was a boundary I wasn't so sure I wanted to cross, not because it disgusted me or because I felt it was morally wrong, but because I had the feeling if I crossed it I could never go back. All my life this act had existed only in fantasy. To make it real, to embody this fantasy, terrified me. It was as if in allowing my imagination to find physical form, it would spring loose entirely. I might completely lose control, say everything on my mind, or worse, do everything I had ever fantasized about.

I took my fingers out of her and held the small of her back firmly down, steadying it. Sasha squirmed in marvelous anticipation.

"I'm going to spank you," I said, breaking the silence.

"Do it," she ordered.

She was breathing heavily, could barely speak.

"You want it?"

"I want it."

"Say what you want."

"I want you to spank me really hard."

I couldn't hold back a sigh.

"Go ahead," she said. "Punish me."

The rest is like a dream. When the boundary between fantasy and reality is broken, the world collapses into a moment the size of a dime.

I spanked Sasha red. My hand stung with the blows.

And all the while I was saying something. Without words, I was trying to get her to understand: all the while in the breath of my heart, screaming its awful whisper, back behind the light-spill, I called her. As if to spell it out, with each stroke I gave her, over and over, I was saying: Now! Now do you understand me?

Somewhere I Have Never Traveled

Claire Tristram

t is 1981. I live in Japan, under the shadow of Mt. Fuji. I'm twenty-one, and I've been hired by a Japanese teacher's college to recite books on tape for the English department. Every day I spend eight hours reading *Sister Carrie* into a studio microphone. That's all they want from me. No one speaks to me unless I stumble in my delivery. Then a voice from the recording booth will ask me to begin again.

Each night I go home to my one-room apartment, where I listen to the train run past my window every fifteen minutes until midnight. I live alone. I don't know the language. I am the only non-Japanese person in town. Since I am blonde and nearly six feet tall, I attract a good deal of attention. Adults whisper and stare. Children point at me, and will scream if I come too close. On one particularly bad day, the boldest of them runs up and plucks some strands of hair from my head, before running away again squealing with laughter and terror. That night I write a long letter to a former lover in California about the peculiar and deep xenophobia of the Japanese people.

In the evening as I walk home from the train station to my apartment, I pass a rustic building about the size of a basketball court, where a group of twenty men are practicing a martial art on a shiny wooden floor. The men are tonsured, like monks, and wear cotton uniforms of blinding whiteness. Sometimes they are punching and kicking the air in precise unison when I walk by. Sometimes they sit in meditation, backs perfectly straight. One of the men will march slowly and silently among the others, carrying a bamboo pole before him, his elbows out. If any of the others begins to slouch, he is struck across the shoulders with the pole, viciously and without warning. Every night I watch for a few minutes, from the darkness, before going home to my rice cooker and futon. I have a television, too, but rarely turn it on, since I understand nothing at all.

One night a latecomer rushes by me as I stand there, watching in the dark. He graces me with a close-palmed gesture of greeting before slipping off his shoes and stepping inside, into the light. I feel a rush of gratefulness towards this man, that he has acknowledged in any way that I am human, in a country where I have begun to feel like a freak of nature. It bolsters me when, one evening many weeks later, I find the courage to slip off my own shoes and step inside, myself.

I sense a reaction to my presence, immediate, organic, entire, as if a body has swallowed something it doesn't know how to expel. I feel an awareness, without acknowledgment, even as the men sit in meditation, eyes closed. I wait for something to happen.

When the meditation is over, the men get up and begin to spar with one another. Still I wait. Finally, a small man who seems to be the teacher approaches me, bold and jovial, as if he has just noticed me for the first time. He knows no English. I know no Japanese. Much later I learn that I was asking to join the martial-arts team of a men's technical college. The teacher doesn't try to explain this to me. Perhaps the challenge of explaining it is too much for him. Instead, he barks out a command, and another man runs to his side.

"Yoshimoto," the teacher says.

Yoshimoto. Now I see you again in my mind, as if for the first time. Your head is shaven like the others. But a moustache follows the line of your upper lip, thin and provocative, the only facial hair

I've seen in Japan. You are an inch shorter than I am, and stocky and solid, like a brick. You gesture for me to follow you to a corner of the practice area.

This is how it begins, then: Our first meeting, our first touch, still seared in memory. You bend your knees a little, and gesture for me to do the same. You extend your arm, a right cross of glacial slowness, so I can observe the slight turn of the wrist at the end, the final snap. When I try to follow, you shake your head in disgust and grab my hands roughly, molding my fingers impatiently into a proper fist. It is the first time in months that anyone has touched me, except for the random and soulless pressings of the too-crowded train at rush hour. I want to cry out with the relief of it. I want to break, like an egg, and flow into you. I will do anything for you. You don't notice.

The next evening you are annoyed to see me show up again: your irritation pulses towards me with each clench of your jaw. The other men call out to you, laughing, as they spar. You frown more deeply. I begin to understand that I am your special trial; that the teacher has chosen me, this odd, large, white, awkward woman, to test his finest student. We retire to our corner once more to begin our slow drills. But tonight you don't touch me, as if you know already that I am aching for your touch.

The next night you force my body into strange and painful positions. You make me stand on one leg, the other stretched out to one side at right angles to the floor until I think it will break and fall off. Then you walk away and leave me there. You seem to forget about me, never looking in my direction, even as I follow you with my eyes from one side of the floor to the other. When you come back at last, it is not to relieve me, but to apply more torture. Now you force my body into a submissive crouch, knees bent, until my thighs burn with pain and rage. When you come back again, you gesture for me to kneel in meditation, sitting on my feet until I can feel them no longer. You walk away.

And still, each night I come.

You change tactics. You stand with your arms flung wide apart, taunting me, daring me to strike at you. Your uniform opens in front to reveal your hairless golden chest, and the small, perfect, delicate roundness of one nipple. You dance in front of me, and when I try to hit you, or to kick you, or in my fury and frustration to reach you in any way, you grab me easily and throw me to the floor, your knee applying pressure between my breasts, pinning me there. Over and over again.

I come back. Night after night you force me to submit. You never say a word to me, in any language, and yet I learn to understand your commands. My life has become an endless progression of tense and sweaty couplings without any hope of consummation. Your approval becomes the most important thing in my life. You must touch me often, to put my body into the correct position. You have touched my body everywhere now. But you won't look at me. Your eyes are dark, like a Noh mask, but a golden light breathes out from your skin. You are very beautiful.

One night, a hot fury rising up in me, I manage to grab one of your wrists as you taunt me. I force it into a particularly agonizing lock, one that you have demonstrated on me many times. You drop to your knees before me in surprise and pain. You look up, and your golden neck arches forward, like a woman's. For the first time you look at me. I see in your eyes such longing and intense fragility that I hesitate, and my hold on your wrist grows less secure. Then I am on the floor again, and you are over me, breathing hard, your knee applying the familiar pressure to my chest.

Yoshimoto. I come to understand that you desire me, too. You tell me so by the way you begin to say my name with a soft, fuzzy-edged intimacy, even as I'm crying out from the torture of your teachings. You tell me so every time you defeat me. You tell me so every time you press your knee into my chest, or between my thighs, or into my ass. Sometimes as I lie beneath you one bead of sweat will drop, like a tear, from your temple to my cheek.

Now you are over me again, your body rocking, your breathing hard and fast, your lips parted with exertion and elation. You have pinned me by the wrists this time, behind my back. My face is pressed against the cool floor. Your knee is shoved between my thighs, making my vulva sing and ache for you. You make a sound low in your throat, like a big cat purring, as you exert the final pressure on my wrists to master me completely. Only when I cry out will you release me. I know I need only make a sound, and the pain will be over, and so will be this unbearably sweet throbbing between my legs. I clench my jaw and taste the floor and writhe beneath you for as long as I can stand it, before I must cry out, both from the pain and from the disappointment of feeling you let go of me once more.

We never make plans to be alone together. It is unthinkable. Neither of us knows how to break the rules of this strange and secret game. The tension between us is too precious, too forbidden, like an addiction. It is here, each night, in the company of twenty sweaty and grunting men, that we make love to one another, over and over and over again. When it is done, I go home alone to my bed and rub my little hooded knob and imagine that my finger is your tongue, that your face is buried in my cunt, until I ride one glorious spasm and find liquid release. When we do one day find a way to be together at last, I know that you will continue to taunt me and to tease me, and when you finally take me it will be in the ass, hard, swift, mercilessly deep, until I split apart, until you break me utterly.

Now each night there is a small crowd of spectators by the door, amazed at the large white woman who has learned the ways of Japan so quickly. Their presence adds to the voyeuristic pleasure of our fierce duet. I earn my brown belt in record time. At this pace, I'll earn my black belt in a year. Only you, Yoshimoto, understand that my devotion to the art isn't about earning a black belt at all.

Then, disaster. The teacher gives me over to another sparring partner. Now I feel your eyes on me now from across the floor, watching as I and this other man, this nothing, perform the same intimate couplings that you and I performed together. I want to tell you it is not the same thing, that it means nothing to me. But I don't know the words.

Your lust makes you clever. The next night you strike me with the bamboo pole for the first time, as I sit in meditation with the others. The blow is sharp, clear, and relentlessly hard. It sings out your desire even as it cuts through the air.

I wait each night for your blows. It is all we have. I try to anticipate them, to hear your cat steps behind me before the stick lands. Always you take me by surprise when the blow finally falls, sending such a vicious flame of want through me that I feel my wet dripping lips open with their need for you, so much so that I want to bend over and let you enter me right there, while the others meditate, unseeing and unknowing. Each night your blows grow harder. Each night when I go home, I touch the bruises that mark my shoulders, and you are with me. But it is not enough. I feel your frustration building with each blow, and I know that your yearning matches my own.

One night my regular partner does not appear, and you and I are together again. We fight fiercely, the relief of touching you at last! My reach surprises you and I strike a sharp jab to your kidney, just barely checking my thrust as I hear you grunt with surprise and approval. We clash again. Our sweat mingles. You enfold me in your arms, a neck hold that forces me to my knees, pressing me forward, forward, until I must bend over in a tight ball and crawl away from you to escape the pain, and still you do not release me, and I feel myself spasm, the joy of it! When you finally let me go I feel my soft sweet juice between my thighs, and I can see from your eyes that you know my secret, that I have come.

I stand up again. I think of planting a swift kick to your ass, a love tap, but something goes very wrong, somehow your knee gets in the way and I collapse in a heap. Pain comes, the wrong kind of pain. The men all huddle around me, whispering. I have broken my foot. The teacher shouts out the news in slow Japanese and asks me over and over if I understand, even as my pulse sends a jagged torment from my foot up my spine and makes me dread each heartbeat.

Somehow, in my haze, sitting there on the floor at the center of this throng of sympathizers, I know that this is our chance.

A taxi is called. You conspire to be the one who rides with me to the clinic. Just as I knew you would. When the taxi comes, you and another man carry me outside, stretching both of my legs across the back seat. Then you get in and close the door, holding my bare feet in your lap.

We drive away into the darkness. We are alone, alone at last, save for the anonymous white-gloved driver in front. He won't tell, Yoshimoto. Surely you understand that this is to be our only chance. Surely you understand that I will do anything for you, anything at all, be your rough concubine and let you hit me across the shoulders every night with your bamboo pole. Even as my mind explodes with pain from my broken foot, I hold my breath and wait for you to unlace the drawstring of my uniform trousers and to unfold me, petal by petal, until you find the small and secret place that is singing for your touch.

You sigh. It is a sound that strikes me, then and now, as unbearably sad. You raise my good foot to your lips. I feel your breath. Then you kiss my instep. The kiss is long and full, a caress so focused, and so sweet, that I understand at once that I haven't understood you at all. Tears come.

That is all.

After a month with my foot in a cast, I earn my black belt. My name goes up on a plaque on the wall, never to be removed. I go home to America. We never learn to speak to one another. We never find a way to be alone.

But now, seventeen years later, walking along the tide line on a beach near my Northern California home, I find myself thinking of you. The tide is coming in. One foot feels the cool shock where a wave has just left the sand. The other feels the warmth where the tide has not yet reached. One foot I broke. The other, you kissed. Even as we travel away from each other, with each step you are with me. Whenever I think of you, Yoshimoto, it is with this exquisite tension between the pain and the light, never to be resolved, like a hot wind rising just before a storm that never breaks.

3 Shades of
Longing

Jack Murnighan

he party is like any other, but it's my last night in town and we all know what that means. The chalky promise of the last chance, the final desperate stab at what might happen now and only now 'cause I'll be gone in the morning. But the one I really want has her rhinestone husband in tow, and my chances are looking pretty slim.

Come here a minute.

What?

Just come here.

I take her out the apartment's kitchen door into the back staircase. We're drunk as hell, and I can feel the pulse in my temples. Her skirt is a couple of inches too short to be tasteful, her legs a couple of inches too wide to be perfect, but the combination has my sodden head reeling. There's nothing I can do to stop myself:

We've known each other a long time, right?

Yeah.

You know there's only one thing I regret . . .

What's that?

That I never got to taste your pussy.

For a second she's surprised, perhaps even shy, but it's only a second. Then she turns, takes a long look at the kitchen door, and slowly turns back. We're both still, and she keeps looking at me out of her right eye, even as a long smile unfurls from the side of her mouth.

Is that right.

My hands are trembling. She looks at me hard—she's all hair spray and eyeliner, worry lines and a molespeck beside her eye. It's the face of a predator, the face of a widow. Without saying another word, she slides her ringless hand between her knees. I watch breathless as her fingers drag the edge of her China-print skirt up her thigh; I see a flash of pale panties, watch as her fingers disappear. She pauses a bit before she takes her hand back out, stares me down as she deftly wets two fingers on the flat of her tongue and slips them back under.

I try to stand still, but I'm breathing in heavy spurts. A few eternal seconds tick before she turns her eyes away; tilts her head a little and sways, her face growing more serious. Then, raising her head in a relaxed parabola, she looks up, this barroom valkyrie, smiles full, lifts her hand from beneath her skirt, and with the serene majesty of an aging pope, drags her two redolent fingers down my lips in a slow, wet benediction.

■

Halfway through Ohio I start to smell my clutch burning. The gears aren't taking—I shift, but the car just revs like it's in neutral.

I've got to wait a day for the part.

The motel is a standard no-frills affair. Plaids, brown carpet, HBO. I go out into heavy rain and walk to the A&P for supplies.

Thanks for wipin' your feet.

'Scuse me?

You're the first person who's walked in here tonight who wiped his feet.

I'm not from around here.

I know.

She starts to scan my meager groceries: a bag of carrots, a six-pack of Milwaukee's Best, a loaf of generic wheat bread and a jar of peanut butter. Her nails are better cared for than the rest of her: air-brushed glue-ons, starry nights, blue fading to black. She's shortened slightly by her polyester work smock, but her green-gray eyes, her cavernous dimples and her small-mouthed cocky half-smile all bespeak barely legal mischief. I stroke my lower lip with an index finger.

I had some car trouble and gotta wait till tomorrow for a part, so I, uh, got a room at the motel up the road and was just buyin' some dinner.

Hmm. You gonna drink all that beer?

I was thinkin' about it. Why, you wanna give me a hand?

I just might.

Why don't I just buy some more then?

I can bring somethin'.

All right then. Room nineteen.

Okay.

When the door finally knocks, there are only two beers left in the melted ice in the bathroom sink. I had started to nod off, boots and TV still on. She comes in dripping, smelling of peppermint schnapps.

I thought you weren't comin'.

You didn't ask me when I get off.

No, I guess I didn't.

And I'm here ain't I.

Yeah.

So . . .

Here, lemme take that coat.

Life can be lived both from the in- and the outside. You can be caught up in every moment, consumed, in the throes, the minutes of the spectator and pariah, naked and abject and jilted out of time. In the exquisite fracture of this latter world, things lose the form of their familiar meanings, nature stops being natural, and words disassociate from the sounds that compose them. Each event stands alone, separate from and unparticipating in all others. The fragility of being is exposed; all existence wavers on the razor's edge of its own possibility, miraculously not different from what it is, miraculous to be at all.

What is it?
What d'you mean?
You got a kinda faraway look.
Hmm.
It's weird sometimes, isn't it, I mean, when you don't know the person.
Yeah. Totally.

■

She didn't know I was coming, didn't know I would ever come, but I knew I'd find her. Knew she'd be out behind her place, sitting in cutoffs on the back of her car smoking Salems and drinking from a can. I'd park around the side and she wouldn't ask too many questions but smile a big knowing sexy half-drunk jaded woman's smile and take my hand and drag me to the bedroom where she'd start with the T-shirt that would go in one pull, then the top button of the Levi's, then she'd press herself to me with that rotgut ashtray breath and an older woman's insistence. Her knowing hands would get my zip down and inside the crease and I'd be shocked again at her imminence, surprised by the speed of her assault, the power of her breath, feel again her desire descend upon me like the locusts. It would be the same now despite my bidding, despite my confidence; she would come with the same authority she had in my youth, in my trembling, the first time she dragged me uncertain and fearful around the car, up the back stairs, to the dimly lit bedroom above the garage.

She tries not to wake me because of the hour, but I feel it anyway as her body moves away. I roll on my side, but I don't go back to sleep. I hear her in the kitchen opening the cans, I hear the pawed feet come running, then I see her come back naked through the doorway and go into the bathroom with the door half open and when I see her with the toothpaste I get up and as the brush starts going back and forth I get on my knees behind her tight curved belly, down the insides of her thighs and back up, pressing tighter on her waist and circling wet kisses on the small of her back. She tries to push me away with her free hand and mumbles something through the toothbrush, but then she finds herself, leaning further over the sink, forgetting the toothbrush, lifting and pressing harder to me as my tongue slow snakes along her tiny crevice. I take her ass in my hands and spread her wider as she presses against the sink with her waist, clutching with her free hand, pushing and lifting for me as my tongue dips into her, tasting her sharp jungle mulch, her tin vibrato, her burnt-rubber trace. Then I press a hand firmly between her thighs, cupping her heat, my fingers rubbing her lengthwise with gentle pressure at the tip. When I feel her wet in my hand I wrap my other arm tightly around her and, in a single movement, stand and lift her further up on the sink. She starts with her catnip moans as I lower her down onto me, my arm still around her waist, she still clutching the edge of the sink, pressed hard against her stomach. With a firm slow rhythm I urgently raise and lower her with both hands wrapped all the way around, my shoulders tight on her back, until finally I tremble, face pressed against her sideways, arms clenched, and gasp like a boated mullet for breath.

■

Years before, she had said that if I ever learned to love my cock, I might make a halfway decent lover. I had wanted to come back to her, to show her, to say yeah baby here I am with my well-loved cock and my wry smile and my traveling man's flannel and ain't I just the cat's meow. But now she just says that if I ever learn to love somebody I might make a halfway decent lover. And I say what do you think I'm doing and she says leaving.

From Glamorama

Bret Easton Ellis

In the shower in the bathroom Jamie and Bobby share Bobby's admiring the tans we acquired on the yacht today, at the shocking whiteness where our boxer-briefs blocked out the sun, at the white imprints Jamie's bikini left behind, the paleness almost glowing in the semi-darkness of the bathroom, the water from the massive chrome head smashing down on us and both our cocks are sticking up at sharp angles and Bobby's pulling on his prick, stiff and thick, his balls hanging tightly beneath it, the muscles in his shoulders flexing as he strokes himself off and he's looking at me, our eyes meeting, and in a thick voice he grunts, "Look at your dick, man," and I look down at the cock I'm jerking off and past that, at my thickly muscled legs. . . .

In the shower Bobby lets me make out with Jamie and Bobby's head is between her legs and Jamie's knees buckle a couple of times and Bobby keeps propping her up with an arm and his face is pushed up into her cunt and she's arching her back, pushing herself onto his tongue, and one of his hands is gripping my cock, soaping it up, and then Bobby starts sucking it and it gets so hard I can feel the pulse in it and then it gets even harder, the shaft keeps thickening and Bobby pulls it out of his mouth and studies it, squeezing it, and then he flicks his tongue over the head and then he lifts it up by the tip and starts flicking his tongue in brief, precise movements over the place where the head meets the shaft as Jamie hungrily moans "do it do it" while fingering herself in the semi-darkness and then Bobby places the entire shaft into his mouth, taking as much of my cock as he comfortably can, sucking eagerly, wetly, while crouching down on his haunches, still stroking his own prick, and below it the curves of his thighs keep swelling as he repositions himself. I'm bending my neck back, letting the water stream down my chest, and when I look back down Bobby's looking up at me and grinning, his hair wet and pressed down on his forehead, his tongue extended, pink against his face. Then Bobby motions for me to turn around so that he can spread the cheeks of my ass and I can feel him extending his tongue up in it and then he removes his tongue and sticks his index finger halfway up my asshole and keeps fingerfucking me until he's pushed the entire finger as far as it can go, causing my cock to keep twitching uncontrollably. . . .

I drop to my knees and start licking Jamie's pussy, my fingers spreading her lips, and as her hands massage my hair I lean her against the shower wall—Bobby still behind me on his knees, his finger moving in and out of my asshole, another hand running over my hard, cubed abs—and I keep running my tongue from her clit to her asshole and placing one of her legs over my shoulder I suck her clit into my mouth as I fuck her with two then three fingers and then I move my tongue into her asshole, fucking it with my tongue while my fingers tug on her clit, and when I stand up Bobby's finger slips out of my hole and I turn Jamie around and squatting down behind her I spread her small, firm ass cheeks open and start pumping my tongue in and out of her asshole and then I slide my tongue deep inside her anus and keep it there while rubbing her clit until she comes. . . .

After we dry off we move into Jamie and Bobby's bedroom, next to the giant bed which has been stripped of its sheets, and all the lights in the room are on so we can see everything and Jamie's squeezing my cock, sucking on its head, and I'm watching Bobby walk over to a drawer and when he bends down his ass cheeks spread wide, briefly exposing his asshole as he picks up a bottle of lotion, and when he turns around his cock is sticking up in a full erection and he strides back to us as I'm watching Jamie put one finger inside her pussy and then pull it out and then she starts stroking her clit and then she brings that finger up to my mouth and I start sucking on it. She sticks her finger back into her vagina and when she pulls it out she offers it to me again and I take her hand, licking the saltiness from her finger, sucking on it, and then I pull her face to mine and while I kiss her my hands slide down to her ass, then up to her waist and then up to the heavy firmness of her tits, my palms passing lightly over her tiny nipples, causing them to harden, while she keeps trembling, moaning. Then I lay her on the bed and kneeling at the side of it I smell her cunt lips, inhaling deeply, beads of water still clinging to her pubic hair, and I'm breathing gently on her and with one finger I trace the outline of her labia, not parting them yet, just teasing, and then I slide one finger deep into her pussy, playing with her clit as I watch it deepen in color, and she's lying back on the bed, her eyes closed, and then I'm strumming my tongue along her clit and then I lift her hips up and I'm spreading her ass open until I can see the pink inside it. . . .

I move my mouth back up to her tits, sucking hard on the nipples while squeezing the breasts beneath them, and then I slide down again, my tongue traveling down the line bisecting her body, and Jamie raises then spreads her legs, her clit totally engorged now, but I barely touch it at first, deliberately avoiding it, causing Jamie to shift around continuously, trying to place herself against my tongue, whimpering, and when my tongue lightly laps at it her clit gets firmer, bigger, and my hands are squeezing the backs of her legs and then the insides of her thighs and I'm still fucking her with my tongue and when I lift her hips up again I start sucking on her asshole. Bobby's leaning in, staring intently as my tongue goes in and out of her anus while he strokes his prick off. "God, you're so wet," I'm whispering. "You're so fucking wet." I start pumping a finger into her vagina and Jamie's bucking her hips as I move my mouth up and suck the whole labia into my mouth and then I lick her clit again, causing Jamie to thrash out another orgasm. . . .

In front of me Jamie steps into Bobby's arms and he places a huge hand under her chin and tilts her face upward and he kisses her deeply, their pink tongues entwined, and Jamie's hand falls onto Bobby's cock and she squeezes it and then she eases Bobby down onto the bed next to where I'm lying, his head at my feet, his dick at my face, and Jamie drops to her knees beside the bed and starts licking the sides of Bobby's prick while she's staring at me and Bobby's moaning and he's tonguing my feet and Jamie raises then lowers her mouth, taking in as much of his cock as she can while Bobby's hips keep thrusting upward. She climbs onto the bed and raises herself over Bobby's dick then slowly lowers herself, her eyes riveted on mine as his cock slides into her pussy, and then she pulls it out until she's rubbing her slit over the head and then she falls onto it again and it slides into her effortlessly and then she stops, stays still, letting her cunt accustom itself, and then she starts riding Bobby's cock, rising up to its tip then lowering herself down hard onto his pelvis, Bobby groaning as he pumps into her, and suddenly all her muscles contract at once and she's trying not to come but she loses control and starts yelling "fuck me fuck me fuck" and somewhere across the room a beeper goes off, is ignored. . . .

I'm on my knees in front of Bobby and he's urging me to lift his penis up so I can smell his balls and then he pushes my head back and slides his cock all the way into my mouth and I'm gagging, choking for air, but Bobby keeps it there until my throat relaxes, his hands on either side of my head guiding me up and down on his penis, then pulling it way out but keeping the head in my mouth and then pushing his cock back into my throat until my upper lip is buried in his pubic hair and my nose is pressing against his hard, taut abdomen, his balls tight against my chin. When I look up, his head is thrown back, only the point of his chin visible above the thickly corded column of his neck. Bobby's abdominal muscles taper down from under his chest to the narrower ones at the base of his stomach and one of my hands is rubbing over them, my other hand on the place where his back fleshes out into the curves of his ass, and I'm swallowing hard, my lips slicked over with my own spit and Bobby's pre-come, and I run my tongue around the head, sucking up and down, going all the way to the base of it in a slow, steady motion, my nose buried in Bobby's sweaty pubic hair, and then he starts fucking my face harder. . . .

Bobby falls back on the bed and hoists me up, positioning me so he can start sucking my dick while I'm sucking his, and he's deep-throating me, his head going all the way down and all the way up each time, sucking hard on my cock as it emerges from his mouth coated with saliva and then swallowing it as he goes back down, our hips rotating slightly, in rhythm. Then Bobby rolls over and lies flat on his stomach, one knee cocked, his balls resting on the bed beneath the crack of his ass, and Jamie's spreading the cheeks of Bobby's ass apart and, panting, I lean down and kiss his asshole, immediately sticking my tongue in it, and Bobby's responding by raising his hips until he's on his knees and elbows and I start drilling his asshole with my tongue, feeling it expand slighty then contract and then expand again and then Jamie moves to the top of the bed and spreads her legs in front of his face, holding his head, and he tries to get at her pussy but she's sitting on it and he moves backward taking Jamie with him until she's lying on her back, raising and spreading her legs in front of Bobby's face, and he starts eating her pussy until he turns her over onto her hands and knees and starts eating her pussy from behind and he's emitting loud groaning noises that are muffled from between her legs and I start lubing Bobby's asshole with the lotion he brought to the bed. . . .

I'm sitting back on my heels and Jamie leans over and starts suck-ing my cock, spitting on it until it's slathered with saliva, and then I stand on my knees and push Jamie away, keeping Bobby's ass spread with the fingers of one hand and lubing my cock up with the other, and then I guide the head of my penis up against his asshole, grasp-ing his hips, holding them steady, shoving gently forward until I can't help myself—I start fucking him really hard, my stomach slap-ping up against his ass while Jamie holds on to me, bringing me back each time I lunge forward. I let go of one hip and reach down and around to find Bobby's hand stroking his stiff dick, jerking it off, matching each stroke with my thrusts, and I close my hand around Bobby's and the rocking motion we're making causes my hand to automatically go back and forth and I start riding him harder, breathing so fast I think my heart's going to stop, totally flushed.

"Easy, easy," I hear him moan. "Don't come yet. . . ."

Bobby grabs my cock and helps me guide it into Jamie's pussy and I slide my penis up into her while holding her thighs from beneath, reaching my arms around them, doubling her up, and then I grab both her tits and start sucking on them while I'm fucking her, her cunt sucking on my cock as she rocks from side to side, her pussy totally responding and sucking me in when I pull back, and then I'm slamming into her, grunting with each thrust, and her face is bright red and she's crying out, heaving against me, and then I pull out and turn her over, spreading her ass cheeks with the thumb and finger of one hand and while I'm sliding a finger in and out Bobby slathers my cock with more lube and, grasping Jamie's hips while rotating my own, I push my rock-hard cock slowly into Jamie's rectum, feeling it stretch out, not even waiting until she's loosened up to start fucking her ass really hard. Bobby leans down, watching my dick disappear then reappear, Jamie's asshole clinging to it, and then positions himself at the head of the bed and grasping the headboard for leverage he slides his hips forward, raising and spreading his legs so Jamie can eat out his asshole while he jerks off. Releasing a hip, I reach down and squeeze Jamie's breasts again, running my hand down her stomach until I find her clit, and with two fingers I start rubbing it, then fingerfucking her while she continues eating Bobby's ass out, sometimes sucking his dick. . . .

Jamie stands up on the bed and straddles Bobby at hip level. She lowers herself over his cock and grasps it with one hand and then feeds it up into her cunt until she's sitting down on it, leaning forward, flattening out on Bobby, her breasts pushed into his face, and Bobby holds them with both hands while sucking on her nipples. I'm crouching between Bobby's legs inside Jamie's and I spread her checks and start fingering her asshole, which is pushed out and distended from the pressure of having Bobby's large cock filling her. I sit back on my heels, my erection twitching, and when I spread Jamie's cheeks even wider she raises her hips, causing Bobby to slide out of her until only the head of his cock remains inserted between the lips of her cunt and then my cock slides effortlessly back up into Jamie's ass. Carefully Jamie settles back down on Bobby's cock while I bounce gently up and down, Bobby's cock going all the way in while my dick slides halfway out, and we can both feel Jamie's vaginal muscles contracting powerfully during her orgasm as she convulses between us. . . .

"Here, lift up," Bobby's saying as I raise my hips, and he quickly slides a towel under my ass and I'm touching the contours of his chest, tracing the line bisecting his body, and he's spreading my legs while leaning over and kissing me hard on the mouth, his lips thick and wet, and one finger, then two fingers, start moving in and out of my asshole and both of us are glistening with sweat and my head's in Jamie's lap and she's holding me, whispering things in my ear, leaning over and stroking my erection. "Yeah, show me that dick, Victor," Bobby says. "Keep stroking it, that's it. Spread your legs. Wider. Lift them up. Let me see your asshole." He lifts my legs up and pushes my knees back and I can feel him spreading my legs open, inspecting that area. "Yeah, you've got a nice pink butthole, man. I'm looking at it right now. You want me to fuck it, huh?" I'm bracing myself, gazing intently up at Bobby, who is expressionless, and I'm not sure how many fingers are in my ass right now and his hand starts moving in a circular motion, fingers moving deeper until I have to grab his wrist, whispering "Easy, man, easy" and with his other hand he keeps twisting my nipples until they're sore and burning and my head's lodged in Jamie's armpit and I have to strain my muscles to keep from coming too soon. . . .

"Wait," I groan, lifting my head up. "Do you have a condom?"

"What?" he asks. "Oh man, do you care?"

"It's okay." I lean back.

"You want me to fuck you?" he's asking.

"Yeah, it's okay."

"You want me to fuck you with this cock?" he's asking, hoisting my legs up over his shoulders.

"Yeah, fuck me."

Jamie watches carefully as Bobby slides his long, thick cock in and out of my asshole and then starts increasing the length and depth of his thrusts, pulling his prick almost all the way out and then slamming it in again, his cock pumping my prostate, and I'm looking up at him and shouting out and his abs are straining with each thrust and he tries to steady himself by holding on to my shoulders, the muscles in his arms bulging with the effort, and his eyebrows are furrowed and his face—usually impassive—now scowls briefly with pleasure. "Yeah, fuck him, fuck him harder," Jamie's chanting. Bobby keeps slipping his cock in and out of me, both of us groaning with relief, intensity rising, and then I'm yelling out, convulsing uncontrollably, both of us bucking wildly as I start ejaculating, shooting up onto my shoulders and then my chest as Bobby keeps fucking me, my anus contracting around his thrusting cock. "Yeah, that's it, that's it, man," Bobby groans, coming, collapsing on top of me. . . .

ReBecca

Vicki Hendricks

As her Siamese twin joined at the skull, I know Becca wants to fuck Remus as soon as she says she's going to dye our hair. I don't say anything—yet. I'm not sure she's even admitting it to herself. The idea doesn't sit well with me, but I decide to wait and see just how she plans to go about it.

It's a warm, clear night, and not a bad walk to Payless Drugs. Becca picks out a light-magenta hair color that to me suggests heavy drug addiction. "No, siree," I tell her. "I know my complexion colors. I'm a fall, and that's definitely a spring." No spring that ever existed in nature, I might add.

"Oh, stop it, Rebby. We'll do a middle part and you can keep your flat brown and I'll just liven up my side. I want to get it shaped too—something that falls around my face."

"It better not fall anywhere near *my* face."

When we get home from the drugstore, she reads the instructions aloud and there are about fifty steps to this process by the time you do the lightening and the toning. Then she starts telling me which hairs are hers and which are mine. We've gone around on this before. It's a tough problem because our faces aren't set exactly even: I look left and down while she faces straight ahead and up. For walking we've managed a workable system where I watch for curbs and ground objects and she spots branches and low-flying aircraft. She claims to have saved our life numerous times.

"Oh, yeah? And for what?" I always ask her. And she always laughs. But now I know—so she can fuck Remus, the pale, scrawny clerk with the goatee who works at A Different Fish down the corner. Now it's clear why Becca didn't laugh when I pointed out his resemblance to the suckermouth catfish. Also her sudden decision to raise crayfish. Those bastards are mean, ugly sons of bitches, but they suit Becca just fine. They're always climbing out of the tank to dehydrate under the couch, so we have to go back to the store for new ones. Fuck—I'd rather die a virgin. We entertain ourself just fine.

It's two A.M. when she finishes drying that magenta haystack and we finally get into bed. Then she stays awake mooning about Remus while I put a beanbag lizard over my eyes and try to turn off her side of the brain. I know where she's got her fingers. There's a tingle and that certain haziness in our head.

We barely make it to work on time in the morning. Then Becca talks one of our coworkers into giving her a haircut during lunch. The woman is a beautician, but she developed allergies to the chemicals, so now she works at the hospital lab with us.

They're snipping and flipping hair in the break room to beat shit while I'm trying to eat my tuna fish. "Yes!" Becca says, when she looks in the mirror. Her side is blunt-cut into a sort of swinging pageboy. She tweaks the wave over her eye, making sure we'll be clobbered by a branch in the near future.

We get home from work that evening and—surprise—she counts the crayfish and reports another missing. I try to scramble down to look under the couch in case the thing hasn't dried out yet, but she braces her legs and I can't get the leverage.

"You know how much trouble it is for us to get back up," she says. "Anyway, it'd be covered with dust bunnies and hair."

At that moment I get a flash of guilt from her section of the brain—she's lying. There is no fucking anthropod under the couch. She wants badly to get back to that aquarium store.

I catch Becca smiling sweetly at me in the hall mirror. I forgive her.

She insists on changing into "sleisure wear"—that's what I call it—to walk down the street. The frock's a short fresh pink number with cut-in shoulders. I'm wearing my "Dead Babies" tour T-shirt and the cutoffs I wore all last weekend. Becca has long given up trying to get me to dress in tandem.

We see Remus through the glass door when we get there. He has his back to us, dipping out feeders for a customer. His shaved white neck almost glows. The little bell rings as we step in. Becca tugs me toward the tank where the crayfish are, and I can tell she's nervous.

Remus turns. Straining my peripheral vision, I catch the smile he throws her. I can feel this mutual energy between them that I missed before. He's not too bad looking with a smile. I start to imagine what it's going to be like. What kind of posture they'll get me into. Maybe I should buy earplugs and a blindfold.

Becca heads toward the crayfish, but I halt in front of a salt-water tank of neon-bright fish and corals. A goby pops its round pearly head out of a mounded hole in the sandy bottom and stares at us. "Look," I say, "he's like a little bald-headed man," but she just keeps trudging on to the crayfish tank where she pretends to look for a healthy specimen. Remus comes back with his dipper and a plastic bag.

"What can I do for you two lovely ladies tonight?"

Becca blushes and giggles. Remus reddens. I know he's thinking about his use of the number *two*. He's got it right, but he's self-conscious . . . like everybody.

She points to the largest, meanest-looking crawdad in sight. "This guy," she says. I figure she's after the upper-body strength, the easier he can knock the plastic lid off our tank and boost himself out over the edge. "Think you can snag him?" she asks Remus.

He takes it as a test. "You bet. Anything for my best customer—s." He stands on tiptoe so the metal edge of the tank is in his armpit and some dark hair curls from his scrunched short sleeve. He dunks the sleeve completely as he swoops and chases that devil around the corners of the tank.

Remus is no fool. He's noticed Becca's new haircut and color. I'm thinking, Get your mind outta the gutter, buster—but I'm softening, I'm tuned to Becca's feelings, and I'm curious about this thing—although, it's frightening. Not so much the sex, but the idea of three. I'm used to an evenly divided opinion, positive and negative, side by side, give and take. We might be strange to the world, but we've developed an effective system. Even his skinny bones on her side of the balance could throw it all off.

Remus catches the renegade and flips him into the plastic bag, filling it halfway with water. He pulls a twist-tie from his pocket and secures the bag. "You have plenty of food and everything?" Remus asks.

Becca nods slowly and pokes at the bag. I know she's trying to think of a way to start something without seeming too forward. Remus looks like he's fishing for a thought.

My portion of the gray matter takes the lead. "Hey," I say, "Becca and I were thinking we'd try a new brownie recipe and rent a video. Wanna stop by on your way home?"

Becca twitches. I feel a thrill run through her, then apprehension. She turns our head further to Remus. "Want to?" she says.

"Sure. I don't get out of here till nine. Is that too late?"

"That's fine," I say. I feel her excitement as she gives him the directions to the house and we head out.

When we get outside she shoots into instant panic. "What brownie recipe? We don't even have flour!"

"Calm down," I tell her. "All he's thinking about is that brownie between your legs."

"Geez, Reb, you're so crude."

"Chances are he won't even remember what we invited him for." Suddenly, it hits me that he could be thinking about what's between my legs too—a natural ménage à trois. I rethink—no way, Remus wouldn't know what to do with it.

Becca insists that we make brownies. She pulls me double-time the four blocks to the Quickie Mart to pick up a box mix. I grab a pack of M&M's and a bag of nuts. "Look, we'll throw these in and it'll be a new recipe."

She brightens and nods our head; I can feel her warmth rush into me because she knows I'm on her side—in more ways than one for a change.

We circle the block to hit the video store and Becca agrees to rent *What Ever Happened to Baby Jane?* She hates it, but it's my favorite, and she's not in the mood to care. I pick it off the shelf and do my best Southern Bette Davis: "But Blanche, you *are* in that wheelchair."

It's eight o'clock when we get home, and the first thing Becca wants to do is hop in the shower. I'd rather start the brownies. We both make a move in opposite directions, like when we were little girls. She fastens on to the love seat and I get a grip on the closet doorknob. Neither of us is going anywhere. "Reb, please, let go!" she hollers.

After a few seconds of growling, I realize we're having a case of nerves. I let go and race Becca into the bathroom. "Thanks, Rebelle," she says.

At 9:10 we slide the brownies into the oven and hear a knock. Remus made good time. I notice Becca's quick intake of breath and a zinging in our brain.

Remus has a smile that covers his whole face. I feel Becca's cheek pushing my scalp and can figure a big grin on her too. I hold back my wiseass grumbling. So this is love.

Becca asks Remus in and we get him a Bud. He's perched on the love-seat. Our only choice is the couch, which puts me between them, so I slump into my "invisible" posture, chin on chest, and suck my beer. I know that that way, Becca is looking at him straight on.

"The brownies will be ready in a little while. Want to see the movie?" she asks.

"Sure."

Becca starts to get up, but I'm slow to respond.

Remus jumps up and heads for the VCR. "Let me," he says.

"Relax," I whisper to Becca. I'm thinking, Thank God I've got *Baby Jane* for amusement.

The movie comes on and neither of them speaks. Maybe the video wasn't such a good idea. I start spouting dialogue just ahead of Bette whenever there's a pause. Becca shushes me.

The oven timer goes off. "The brownies," I say. "We'll be right back." We hustle into the kitchen and I get them out. Becca tests them with the knife in the middle. "Okay," I tell her. "I'm going to get you laid."

"Shh, Reb!" I feel her consternation, but she doesn't object.

The brownies are too hot to cut, so Becca picks up the pan with the hot pad and I grab dessert plates, napkins and the knife. "Just keep his balls out of my face," I say.

That takes the wind out of her, but I charge for the living room.

Remus has moved to the right end of the couch. Hmm. My respect for him is growing.

We watch and eat. Remus comments on how good the brownies are. Becca giggles and fidgets. Remus offers to get us another beer from the fridge. Becca says "No, thanks." He brings me one.

"Ever had a beer milkshake?" I ask him.

"Nope."

"How 'bout a Siamese twin?"

His mouth falls open and I'm thinking suckermouth catfish all the way, but his eyes have taken on focus.

I tilt my face up. "Becca would shoot me for saying this—if she could do it and survive—but I know why you're here, and I know she finds you attractive, so I don't see a reason to waste any more time."

The silence is heavy and all of a sudden the TV blares—"You wouldn't talk to me like that if I wasn't in this chair—" "But Blanche, you are in that chair, you *are* in that chair."

"Shut that off," I tell Remus.

He breaks from his paralysis and does it.

I feel Becca's face tightening into a knot, but there are sparks behind it.

I suggest moving into the bedroom. Remus gawks.

I'm named Rebelle so Mom could call both of us at once—she got a kick out of her cleverness—and I take pride in being rebellious. I drag Becca up.

She's got the posture of a hound dog on a leash, but her secret thrill runs down my backbone. I think our bodies work like the phantom-limb sensation of amputees. We get impulses from the brain, even when our own physical parts aren't directly stimulated. I'm determined to do what her body wants and not give her mind a chance to stop it. She follows along. We get into the bedroom and I set us down. Remus sits next to Becca. Without a word, he bends forward and kisses her, puts his arms around her and between our bodies. I watch.

It's an intense feeling, waves of heat rushing over me, heading down to my crotch. We've been kissed before, but not like this. He works at her mouth and his tongue goes inside.

The kissing stops. Remus looks at me, then turns back to Becca. He takes her face in his hands and puts his lips on her neck. I can smell him and hear soft kisses. My breathing speeds up. Becca starts to gasp.

He stops and I hear the zipper on the back of her dress. She stiffens, but he takes her face to his again and we slide back into warm fuzzies. This Remus has some style. He pulls the dress down to her waist and unhooks her bra. She shrugs it off.

"You're beautiful," he tells her.

"Thanks," I say. I get a jolt of Becca's annoyance.

My eyes are about a foot from her nipples, which are up like gobies, and he gets his face right down in them, takes the shining pink nubs into his mouth and suckles. I feel myself edging toward the warm moist touch of his lips, but the movement is mostly in my mind.

Remus pushes Becca onto the pillow and I fall along and lie there, my arms to my side. He lifts her hips and slides the dress down and off, exposing a pair of white lace panties that I never knew Becca had, never even saw her put on.

He nuzzles the perfect V between her legs and licks those thighs, pale as cave fish. Becca reaches up and starts unbuttoning his shirt. He helps her, then speedily slips his jeans down to the floor, taking his underwear with them. I stare. This is first time we've seen one live. I feel a tinge of fear and I don't know if it's from Becca or me.

"Got a condom?" I ask him.

"Oh, yeah," he says. He reaches for his pants and pulls a round gold package out of the pocket. Becca puts her hand on my arm while he's opening it, and I turn my chin to her side and kiss her shoulder. We both watch while he places the condom flat on the tip of his penis and slowly smoothes it down.

He gets to his knees, strips down the lace panties and puts his mouth straight on her. His tongue works in and I can feel the juices seeping out of me in response. Becca starts cooing like those cock-atiels we used to have, and I bite my lip not to make a noise. Remus moves up and guides himself in, and I swear I can feet the stretching and burning. I'm clutching my vaginal muscles rigid against noth-ing, but it's the fullest, most intense feeling I've ever had.

Becca starts with sound effects from *The Exorcist,* and I join right in because I know she can't hear me over her own voice, and Remus is puffing and grunting enough not to give a fuck about anything but the fucking. His hip bumps mine in fast rhythm, as the two of them locked together pound the bed. I clench and rock my pelvis skyward and groan with the need, stretching tighter and harder, until I feel a letting-down as if an eternal dam has broken. I'm flooded with a current that lays me into the mattress and brings out a long, thready weep. It's like the eerie love song of a sperm whale. I sink into the blue and listen to my breathing and theirs settle down.

I wake up later and look to my side. Remus has curled up next to Becca with one arm over her chest and a lock of the magenta hair spread across his forehead. His fingers are touching my ribs through my shirt, but I know he doesn't realize it. I have tears in my eyes. I want to be closer, held tight in the little world of his arms, protected, loved—but I know he is hers now, and she is his. I'm an invisible attachment of nerves, muscles, organs, and bones.

It's after one when we walk Remus to the door, and he tells Becca he'll call her at work the next day. He gives her a long, gentle kiss, and I feel her melting into sweet cream inside.

"Good night—I mean good morning," Remus says to me. He gives me a salute. Comrades, it means. It's not a feeling I can return, but I salute back. I know he sees the worry in my eyes. I try to take my mind out of the funk, before Becca gets a twinge.

Remus calls her twice that afternoon, and a pattern takes shape over the next three days: whispered calls at work, a walk down the street after dinner, a 9:10 Remus visitation. I act gruff and uninter-ested.

When we go to bed I try not to get involved. You'd think once I'd seen it, I could block it out, catch up on some sleep. But the caresses are turning more sure and more tender, the sounds more varied—delicate but strong with passion, unearthly. My heart is cut in two—

like Becca and I should be. I'm happy for her, but I'm miserably lonely.

On the third day, I can't hold back my feelings anymore. Of course, Becca knows already. It's time to compromise.

"I think we should limit Remus's visits to twice a week. I'm tired every day at work and I can't take this routine every night. Besides," I tell her, "you shouldn't get too serious. This can't last."

Becca sighs with relief. "I thought you were going to ask me to share."

I don't say anything. It had crossed my mind.

"Just give us a few more nights," she says. "He's bound to need sleep sometime too." I notice her use of the pronoun *us*, that it doesn't refer to Becca and me anymore.

She puts her arm around my shoulder and squeezes. "I know it's hard, but—"

"Seems to me that's your only interest—how hard it is."

I feel the heat of her anger spread across into my scalp. I've hit a nerve. She's like a stranger.

"You can't undermine this, Reb. It's my dream."

"We've been taking care of each other all our lives. Now you're treating me like a tumor. What am I supposed to do?"

"What can *I* do? It's not fair!" she screams. Her body is shaking.

"It's not my fault, for Christ sakes!" I turn toward her, which makes her head turn away. She starts to sob.

I take my hand to her far cheek. I wipe the tears. I can't cause her more pain.

"I'm sorry. I know I'm cynical and obnoxious. But if I don't have a right to be, who does?" I stop for a second. "Well I guess you do . . . So how come you're not?"

"Nobody could stand us," she sniffs.

I smooth her hair till she stops crying. "I love you, Becca . . . Fuck—I'll get earplugs and a blindfold."

That night we take our walk down the street. There's nobody in the store but Remus. He walks up and I feel Becca radiating pleasure just on sight. He gives her a peck on the cheek.

I smell his scent. I'm accustomed to it. I try to act cheerful. I've pledged to let this thing happen, but I can almost feel him inside of her already, and the overwhelming gloom that follows. I put a finger in my ear and start humming "You Can't Always Get What You Want" to block them out. Then it hits me.

"Headphones—that's what I need. I can immerse myself in music."

"What?" asks Remus.

"Oh, nothing," I say, and then whisper to Becca, "I've found a solution." I give her a hug. I can do this.

The little bell on the door rings. Remus turns to see behind us. "Hey there, Rom," he calls, "how was the cichlid convention?" He looks back at us. "Did I mention my brother? He's just home from L.A."

Becca and I turn and do a double take. In the last dusky rays of sunset stands a mirror image of Remus—identical, but a tad more attractive. A zing runs through my brain. I know Becca feels it too.

Fish Curry Rice

Ginu Kamani

I can hear my aunt's voice through the wall again, matchmaking. In Bombay, conversations on the telephone are always louder than in person.

"See, this girl is very stubborn. She will never come to your house to meet your boy. But we're going to the club for lunch tomorrow, so why don't you just drop by? That way all of you can take a good look at her. I tell you, she's quite silly. Insists she has a boyfriend in America and is not interested in anyone else. Well, we'll soon take care of all that."

Matchmaking. The favorite hobby of idle adults in India. Sentencing each other's children to a fate worse than . . .

"How many times have I said to myself, It is an absolute curse having good-looking girls in the family. Better if my niece were an ugly duckling. Then we could take care of her right away without fuss. But once they become aware of their looks, these girls just lose all their sense. Then *we* have to run around trying to fix them up with someone decent! Thankless job, I tell you."

I couldn't move. I was fascinated by the way my aunt was ignoring all my unique qualities and treating me like a commodity. I knew I would go to the club for lunch with her the following day and I could almost predict the fortyish couple who would drop by the table: the man with tired eyes, whitening hair, restless to move on to his tennis game; the woman plump, with perfectly sprayed tresses, chiffon sari and diamonds, unwilling to acknowledge my presence until my aunt introduced us. Then her eyes would turn on me and her lips would part and she would say with perfectly rehearsed surprise, "Oh! So *you're* the daughter of Jamini! We've all heard so much about you. But don't worry, only good things."

She would giggle on cue, pull up a chair, and commence an endless session of gossip with my aunt, from which I was pointedly excluded. The man would look around, spot one of his men friends, and excuse himself in a hurry. I would watch my aunt's friend glancing at me from the corner of her eye. The bearer would arrive with our lunch and I would grab my usual plate of mutton samosas and finish them off before my aunt had even started on her soup and toast. The two older women would watch me eat with fascination.

"Eating fried food is bad for your figure," my aunt's friend would admonish sharply. "You should give all this up now, while you still can."

"Oh, don't worry," I would retort with one of my stock replies. "I'll go to the ladies' room in a minute and vomit it back out."

"What a sense of humor this one has!" the friend would gasp, suitably shocked.

"Just wait." My aunt's voice would rise as she adjusted her sari over her bulk. "After you get married, you'll never be thin again."

"Actually," I would yawn, "I was a lot heavier before I started having sex. Steady sex in a marriage should do wonders for me."

By this time the friend would be quite insulted and draw my aunt into another long cycle of gossip. I would close my eyes and lean back in the rattan armchair, drifting to the hoarse chugging of a dozen ceiling fans, the clink of glasses and silverware. I'd hear excited shouts from the cricket field and the sharp crack of the bat. These were some of the oldest, most familiar sounds embedded in my consciousness. The effect of hearing them once again was hypnotic.

"If only your parents would come to their senses, they would realize how important it is to fix you up with a nice boy. But even they had their heads turned after living in the States all these years. Believe you me, one word of encouragement from your mother and I would be dragging you all across this city to meet boys. At this very moment, I have at least thirty boys who would agree to you, sight unseen. What's the harm in at least meeting a few of them? Other girls aren't fortunate to have me for their auntie. You're an attractive girl from a good family with a university degree and a green card. Who knows, you might even decide to move back to Bombay if you meet the right man."

■

I make a list of questions for my aunt: Will you let us use your house to have sex? Will you introduce me to your gynecologist so she can put me on the Pill? Will you rent us your other apartment so we can live together for a couple of years? Can we borrow your vibrators?

■

My aunt's cook, Ramesh, was an utter sensualist. His food was so delicious that each mouthful entered my body like some ethereal nectar. I could barely stand to chew it. One night when I was alone in the house, I asked Ramesh if he had ever cooked fish. He said, Of course, many times, but not in this house. He said he had a special fish curry that he used to make for his previous employer, a Swiss engineer who lived in Bombay for three years. I asked if he could make it for me and he nodded. I was surprised.

"What, here?" I asked, laughing. "In this pure vegetarian household?"

He nodded again, said, "No problem" in English, and left the house. It was dark outside. Where would he find fish at this time of the night?

Ramesh returned in ten minutes with a thick filet of *surmai* in his hand. He had begged it from the Muslim cook on the seventh floor. I stood there with my mouth open, as excited as a little girl. Ramesh was shy, and after a few minutes of pretending that he was alone in the kitchen, he turned to me blushing and asked if I wouldn't prefer to sit in the living room until the curry rice was ready. I said, No, I had to watch him. And, I said to his burning red neck, he had to join me in eating the meal. At that he giggled and stammered: "No, no, *memsahib,* how can I, you are not yet married, it will be a shame on us."

The fish curry was astonishing, its flavors as distinct, yet as blended, as a rainbow. I took two bites of the curry rice and, without realizing, started to cry. Ramesh stood at the far end of the kitchen, watching me eat my first few bites, to be sure I approved. When he saw my tears, he approached me nervously. "It is too much chili, *memsahib?*" he asked anxiously. "Shall I give you a little yogurt?" I took control of myself and wiped away the tears of joy.

The gift of his curry was profound. After years of eating fish fingers in America, my body was overwhelmed by the real taste of fish.

I resumed eating. I inquired whether Ramesh was from Goa. He smiled broadly and said yes. "Don't you drink *feni* with your dinner?" I asked. "Let's have some."

He shook his head sorrowfully. "*Memsahib,* very sorry, but this is not possible. If I drink in this house, I will lose my job."

"I understand," I said. "Where can I get some for myself?"

"No problem," he said in English. He walked into the adjoining servant's room where he unrolled his bed every night, came back with a bottle of clear liquid, plucked a teacup off the drying rack, and poured out a small amount. He handed it to me, still grinning. "Very strong, *memsahib!*" he warned. "Only for sipping."

I took the cup from him and drank the liquid in one gulp. The burn down my throat was smooth, and it filled my face with heat. Ramesh watched me with open mouth and rapidly shifting eyes.

"It's very good," I acknowledged, and held out my cup. "One for me and one for you," I said, motioning Ramesh to get himself a cup.

Ramesh shook his head. "Sorry, *memsahib.* I am happy for you, but it is not possible for me."

"Call me Renu." I smiled at him. "When you call me *memsahib* it feels like you're talking about someone else."

■

"Want to come with me and get your hair done? You have very little imagination, I think, always leaving your hair open like that. Just collects dust all day. My Chinese hairdresser is very good. She'll show you some tricks. And while we're there, I'll tell her to fix your blackheads. You really should get them removed before it's too late. And also that hair on your chin looks like a nanny goat. There are only two or three of them, but my god, how vulgar! What will people think?"

"Do Indian men really care about my blackheads?" I teased my aunt. "I think it's just an obsession for Indian women. None of my American boyfriends ever notices such things."

"That's exactly why I'm telling you not to waste yourself on an American boy. Leave them for those girls who aren't so eligible. Americans will marry anyone, you know. Comes from not having a sense of their own history. Mongrels, all of them."

To do or not to do Indians, that was the question. I had more than a month to go in Bombay. Could my aunt really rustle up an interesting man for me? To be or not to be sexual around my relatives, that was the real issue.

"Okay. Find me someone. But no virgins. And no anatomical illiterates. And no chaperones, meddlers, or parents, please."

My aunt looked at me in shock—she couldn't believe I'd said yes. She smirked with ill-concealed victory, then broke into a triumphant, generous laugh.

"You naughty girl, there's nothing wrong with virgins! In fact, it's a blessing because you can teach them exactly how you want it. Just don't brag about where you got all your experience."

■

Ramesh and I began a series of nightly trysts. He cooked me fish—one piece was enough to satiate my craving—and then watched me eat. It took me close to an hour to eat the single piece of fish and the bowlful of rice. The flavors were so intense, so overpowering, that I had to stop after each mouthful and let my quivering taste buds settle into some semblance of calm. If I took two bites in a row, my stomach felt unbearably full, as though I had eaten well beyond my limit and would burst.

After that first night, Ramesh saw that conversation was not the right accompaniment for my meal. Instead, he settled down on his haunches and stared at me with intense fascination as I ate. I might as well have been a child or an animal, given the ease with which this normally deferential, barely literate employee entered into my space. If my aunt had seen the two of us together in the kitchen, sitting so intimately on the bare floor, she would have suspected the worst— that I had lost my mind and become the cook's lover.

Never in my life in Bombay had I been able to look a male servant in the eye without overtones of power, dominance, cruelty, indifference. But every mouthful of Ramesh's fish became a whirlpool flooding my entire being with ecstasy. I was too dazed to be bothered with the codes of domestic hierarchy. With great difficulty I softened my moans of pleasure into mewing sounds, which Ramesh took as a signal to bring out the *feni,* surreptitiously presented in a teacup.

■

"Haven't you found someone yet?" I asked my aunt impatiently.

She looked at me with tired eyes. She'd been on the phone nonstop for the past few days. Quite a few of the thirty "sight unseen" prospects had moved to the United States for postgraduate studies. Several others were engaged to be married, or close to it. Two families with Gandhian roots were morally and ethically opposed to green card marriages. And word had gotten around that my sister had divorced her Bombay–born-and-bred husband. His unhappy family had put out the word that the girls in our family were fickle and bossy.

■

Ramesh's fish was having an explosive impact on me. The curry rice seemed to wander off the normal digestive route and lodge instead in my groin, creating a slow burn. I hungered for contact. Bombay was unexplored sexual territory for me, still connected in my mind to the trusting dependencies of childhood.

I asked Ramesh about the men in the apartment building. He was incredulous that I wanted information on servants, drivers, watchmen, and janitors, as those were the only men he knew. But he answered my questions with great gusto. Who were the most handsome? Who bragged about being the most virile? Which of them were married, which had girlfriends, who visited prostitutes? Ramesh had an astonishing range of information about most of the domestics—apparently these men let their guard down around the sweet-natured cook. Ramesh related these stories to me with the childlike trust I associated with a prepubescent boy. I was surprised to discover that he was married and had three children in his village, whom he saw perhaps once or twice in a year.

One night after an exquisite meal of several kinds of spiced roe, I told Ramesh that Big Memsahib was searching out a husband for me. The cook's eyes lit up and he broke into a grin. In a rush of sentences he congratulated me, blessed me with good luck and fertility and shared his conviction that I would be matched to a very good man. Seeing my skepticism, he stopped smiling. "Bad thoughts will hinder the process," he gently scolded.

I looked hard at Ramesh, wondering whether I could trust him with my deepest desires. His youthful face stared back at me, still glowing with the news of my impending matrimony.

I put his hand on my forehead and told him to feel the heat. He admitted that my skin felt feverish. I nodded slowly and added that I felt the same fever burning in my groin and placed my hand meaningfully over my pubis. Ramesh did not understand at first, but then his mouth fell open. He lost his balance and fell forward, almost landing in the remains of the food. He sprang up and brushed himself off.

"You think only men feel a burning between their legs?" I asked sharply.

Ramesh coughed nervously, then began laughing with his hand

clamped over his mouth. *"Memsahib,"* he said, smiling, "the truth is that if you take a lover from among us poor servants, we will definitely lose our jobs. But if you don't care whether we work or starve, then surely someone among the servants is senseless enough to say yes. Do you want me to ask around?"

Ramesh's words were like a slap in the face; I felt the sour taste of shame in my mouth. Is that what I had seriously been contemplating? Did I expect reciprocation of my sexual urge from men who were in constant fear of being sacked, humiliated, abandoned?

"I didn't make myself clear," I said. "I don't want anyone losing their job, least of all you. So just think very carefully before you do anything. But if there is a *sahib* in the building—unmarried, good-humored, a decent person—who might be alone, just the way I am, then perhaps you could mention to one of his servants that Big Memsahib's foreign-returned niece is in town for a while and likes to have company in the evenings."

Ramesh nodded and cleared the plates. He disappeared into the back room and returned with two teacups of *feni*. Without a word, he placed one cup in front of me and took the other in his own hand.

"Chin-chin," I murmured, and tapped my cup against his in salute.

"You can use my bed," Ramesh offered before draining his cup in one gulp.

■

"I just don't know why I'm having such bad luck finding someone for you. When you need them, these dashing Romeos disappear into the woodwork like cockroaches."

In a week of hunting, my aunt had found no one. She was beginning to despair. She had lost her appetite. In the past, there had been nothing easier than finding partners for her stable of youngsters.

"I wish your mother had told me openly about your sister's divorce. Honestly, I could have saved face and at least come up with *some* bloody excuse, even if it was a complete lie, who cares, in this city it's all about appearances. It's one thing for you children to have forgotten our Indian customs, but I can't understand what happens to women like your mother when they move abroad. Do they get amnesia or what?"

"My parents supported her divorce. They're quite wonderful that way. If any of us kids are in trouble, they rally around without judgment."

"What a waste, I tell you. Those two were good for each other, really good. The problem was that they waited too long to have children. You have to know how to work a marriage!"

Divorce was a sore topic for matchmakers like my aunt. They took personal offense at the inability of couples to muddle along through life.

"Anyway, Renu darling, there's still hope for you, I've sent your horoscope to be matched through a computer service. Only thing is, the boy may be of a family I don't know. If someone turns up, naturally we will do a full investigation on him. These days you can hire a detective at very decent prices—it's almost become routine, you know, with these caste-no-bar marriages happening all over the place. Personally, I can't imagine being married to anyone besides a Gujarati, but youngsters these days seem to have quite the imagination that way, probably comes from reading too many novels. Oh, look, there's someone at the door."

My aunt's bulk blocked the doorway and I couldn't see over her shoulder. There was a brief tussle at the entrance and then she dragged in a protesting young man carrying a ribboned box of sweets. His name was Nemesh Shah, said my aunt, and he was a distant cousin. He looked no older than nineteen or twenty. He shook my hand firmly and introduced himself as Nemo. He said he was just passing through and his mother had sent him with the sweets, and no he really didn't want any tea and he had to get going to the club. I asked Nemo for a ride to the club and he assented.

We drove in silence, Nemo in front with the driver, me in the back. Once at the club, Nemo visibly relaxed. As we signed in, a group of Nemo's friends greeted him with resounding backslaps and cheery hellos. They looked older than Nemo. I studied his face more carefully and saw lines at the corners of his eyes. He was older than I'd thought.

"This is Renu. She lives in my building. She's visiting from the States."

All smiles, the friends began walking toward the tennis courts. I placed my hand on Nemo's arm, signaling him to hang back for a minute.

"I didn't realize we're in the same building! Auntie just said you were a distant relative."

"Oh, that's an old joke, you know, how we're all supposed to be 'related.' Your parents and mine are old friends. We must have met when we were kids."

"So did my aunt call and tell your mother that I was in town?"

"No, no, not at all. The servants were talking, and I overheard them discussing you. Your chap Ramesh is always up there chatting with our cook, Hassan."

"You're the ones with the Muslim cook? But . . . but you're Gujaratis!" I sputtered.

Nemesh laughed. "My mother is a Bohra Muslim. Hassan is from her father's village. He's a fantastic cook. Even if the religious fanatics descended on us, the family wouldn't part with Hassan."

Nemesh's laughter brought a mischievous sparkle to his eyes. His smile was brilliant, open, lingering. I looked at him in astonishment, and he stared back. Fast work on the part of Ramesh—here was the *sahib* of his choice. I felt the thrill of the chase engulfing me.

"You . . . you must be circumcised!" I blurted out before I could stop myself. Nemo, who had just turned away to follow his friends, stopped dead in his tracks.

"I've heard about you foreign girls being bold, but honestly, this takes the cake! How would you know?"

"Servants these days know everything." I chuckled. "Isn't Hassan a barber as well as a cook?"

Nemo slapped his forehead in mock distress. His lingering smile proclaimed a sweet challenge.

That night Ramesh and I had an urgent *tête-à-tête*. I congratulated him on his quick work, then interrogated him about Nemo. How old? Not sure, somewhere between twenty-three and twenty-six. Work? Family business, garment manufacturing. Marital status? Single. Series of girlfriends the family had trouble with, and

Nemo *sahib* was too obedient to go against his parents' wishes—but too passionate to miss any sexual opportunity. Hassan had often turned over his bed to the *sahib*. Very good lover, according to Hassan, very satisfying to his women. Girls begging not to be sent home in the morning. Some mornings sleepy *sahib* even came to breakfast with the girl's juices on his unwashed face, and mother holding her nose tightly, saying not to eat fish so early in the day. Mother prefers nice Jain Gujarati girl for her son, even though she herself is Muslim. Boy has brought home all kinds—Hindu, Muslim, Parsee, Christian, foreign. All leave Hassan's bed with big-big red bug bites. For the first time I noticed that Ramesh himself had red marks on his arms and neck.

"Who else has been sleeping in Hassan's bed?" I asked, pointing at the bumps. He blushed and turned away but seemed pleased to have been caught. "Hassan is my best friend," he whispered confidentially.

■

"Darling, I have the most exciting news! Two very nice boys are coming from the suburbs, one for lunch, the other for tea. The lunch-*wallah* is just back from an assignment in Delhi. He's quite shy, so you'll have to do your best to draw him out. Normally, of course, these boys would come with their mother or someone, and are not used to having to speak for themselves, if you know what I mean. But these two are willing to try. The tea-*wallah* actually lives in the U.S. and, surprise-surprise! is in town looking for a wife. He lives in Detroit or Denver or Delaware or something."

My aunt looked quite relaxed as she chatted about the boys from the suburbs. I knew she felt tremendously relieved at having drummed up some hopefuls. Ramesh was preparing another one of his master meals in the kitchen, and the wonderful smells had us feeling slightly tipsy.

"I'd like to invite Nemo over for the day as well, if you don't mind," I said. "He's easygoing and comfortable with everyone, and that way the two guys won't feel like it's us against them, okay?"

"Hmmm. That's not a bad idea, Renu. Why didn't I think of it? That Nemo, isn't he darling? He's going to be quite a catch one of these days when he grows up. They're all so sweet until a certain age, and then, I don't know exactly what, but something happens."

■

Lunch-*wallah* turned out to be a fashion photographer, just as shy as my aunt had warned. The ubiquitous Indian mustache sat dark and thick over his lips, and his round face was made even rounder by comically oversized glasses. Mohan photographed mostly teenage boys from the suburbs who were hoping to make it big in modeling. He had brought along his portfolio and passed it to my aunt, who quickly immersed herself in the semi-nude shots of airbrushed hopefuls. She murmured and clucked over each provocatively posed boy, and even took down the names of a few of them.

Mohan asked me a series of questions about life in the States, but before I could answer he interrupted me.

"You have such a straight nose!" he stated emphatically. "You should consider modeling."

The doorbell rang and I excused myself to answer. Nemo stood at the door, his wet hair hanging in a curled bunch across his forehead. I tried to read his face, but like every good Indian, he had on his social mask. He sensed the impatience in my eyes and produced a bouquet of flowers from behind his back. He held my gaze warmly, effortlessly, like an old friend. Ramesh's cot and mattress swam into my mind's eye. Just that morning the cook and I had fumigated the cotton bedding and set it out in the sun. It would be baked dry and clean, ready for a post-lunch respite.

Nemo's arrival caught Mohan by surprise. He did not like surprises. He thawed a little when I introduced Nemo as my distant cousin, and further relaxed when he saw the flowers were meant for my aunt. Finally he smiled and commented on the family resemblance. Ramesh brought out the food, and my aunt and I attacked it in silence.

As expected, Nemo put Mohan at ease, and the two men chatted up a storm through Ramesh's glorious lunch. As happened after every meal by Ramesh, I sat in stunned silence. Mohan grew more animated, his voice rising higher and higher, making him seem like a twelve-year-old. At one point my aunt looked at me inquiringly, and I shook my head in a definite No. She nodded agreement and winked at me.

Mohan had an appointment right after lunch, so he left in a hurry. As the door shut behind him, my aunt sighed with a mixture of frustration and relief. She declared that she needed a recharge before the next one arrived, and retired to her bedroom for a nap. Ramesh cleared the table and brought out cups of *feni* for Nemo and myself. He announced that he would be gone for many, *many* hours, buying food for the evening. Ramesh was nothing less than a genius.

■

There is no greater aphrodisiac for me than having a man open himself up to my probing, revealing himself with subtlety, honesty, and wit. The *feni* proved to be just the right lubricant to bring out Nemo's eloquence. He was surprised more than once at my questions, but he spoke with ease about his family, his girlfriends, his work, his dreams. I asked questions that I knew would provoke laughter. His response brought the heat to my face, and I knew he could see the flush. We reached for each other's hands at the same moment, our fingers greedily entwined on top of the table, our bare feet hotly entangled beneath. I leaned over and fed him *feni* from my mouth. We melted together at the lips, rolling the strong liquor around, allowing it to blister our palates and tongues. Like divine Indra exploding under his mythical burden, I felt a thousand vagina-eyes swelling and surging along the length and breadth of my skin.

■

Ramesh had left his bed tidy and turned on the fan to keep out flies. There was still much left to be said between Nemo and myself, but the dialogue now would be wordless. He sat on the mattress with his back against the wall and I sat on his lap with his hands under my clothes. With shirts unbuttoned, our erect nipples prodded each other's skin, sizzling like hot coals on ice. Like the slowpoke game of childhood, where each contestant "raced" to be the last one to the finish line, I set the pace for the slowest, most unhurried arousal.

I swept my tongue across his nipples, and they wrinkled and reddened. I struck them again and again until they were purple and bulging. The twin ridges of his ribs rising over his sunken stomach signaled the breath held in anticipation. I bit a nipple. He turned his dilating eyes on me, struggling to focus, pleading, laughing, challenging me to arouse him further.

Nemo's hungry gaze was thrilling. Not since childhood had I felt comfortable enough to drown in the gaze of an Indian man; not since viewing those open-shirted, sardonic actors whose posters used to line my walls. Searing eyes, fleshy pink mouths, chests thrown back with the promise of unending embrace. But this was no movie star in bed with me. I felt more and more like I was making love to a beloved companion. We must have met as children and perhaps even snuck an embrace or two in a dark corridor.

Nemo curled his legs around my back and rolled me over. Finding my armpits unshaven, he rubbed his nose in the soft tangles. The thousand vagina-eyes coalesced into the throbbing recesses under my arms and between my legs, and soon we were wrestling on the bed. The drops of his musk scent spread slickly over me as we stroked together in the hot afternoon breeze. I spread apart his lips to get a look at his tongue. Out it came, dangling over me like the hood of a cobra. I grabbed at it with my teeth, but he moved down, down, winding and coiling his tongue around and between my thighs, the slow full burn of a heated rope climbing inside me, opening me wider and wider. My thighs stretched to their limits, and I tucked my feet under his chest as my legs began to tremble. His tongue braved the currents like a homing salmon climbing the steep rapids of my desire. I felt my breathing begin to stall, felt the rush of blood humming in my ears, heard my mind command, "Inhale!" but the tongue hammering out a Morse code on my aching, stretching skin signaled a different demand, and there was no breath to be had because my nose and lungs and mouth and arms had all rushed down and were pushing up from under his tongue, pushing up a molten iceberg of immense proportions through the tightening mesh of his strokes and like snow yielding to water, his pressing tongue melted into the tunneling wave of my heat, which finally erupted through the roof of his mouth. My screams shot through the ceiling and down the shuddering walls, scattering into the skyscrapers of Bombay.

■

At five o'clock Ramesh knocked and cracked open the door just enough to announce it would soon be teatime. I was dozing and oozing, too aroused to actually sleep. I sniffed the odor on Nemo's fingers and brushed against his distinctly fishy mouth. Nemo couldn't possibly settle for an arranged marriage either.

I remembered the way the lines around his mouth hardened with anger when he'd told me how he had allowed his mother once, just once, to "bring a girl home." It was maddening. The parents were pigs, disgusting, selling their daughter, like the newest gadget from Hong Kong. The girl couldn't even look him in the eye—or anyone else, for that matter. She was a Bohra girl, so beautiful . . . fifteen, maybe sixteen. Nemo was so upset, he took her father by the collar and told him to get out of his house. He was horrified at their expectation that he feel excited by this young chit of a girl. He asked his mother whether she was planning to pimp his younger sister the same way. Nemo had mimed a hard slap across the face, and I'd winced in sympathy.

It didn't end there. Nemo had become "eligible." Complete strangers found some excuse or other to parade their daughters in front of him—at weddings, movies, even right there in the building while he was waiting for the lift; he started taking the stairs because of them. He dreamed of running away to some country like the U.S., where no one would know him, where no girl would be dragged in front of him, where no parents would dare shower their filthy money on him.

■

Tea-*wallah* introduced himself as Nick. "Short for Nikhil?" I asked blandly, and he smiled sheepishly. He'd been born and raised in the

U.S., and every member of his family had a practical Anglo nickname for their traditional Indian appellations: Jay for Jayant, Vicki for Malavika, Candy for Kundanika, Sid for Siddhartha. Nick was a software programmer being actively recruited by a company in Bangalore. He hadn't been back to India since childhood, and was here to check out the scene.

Nemo sat beside me, the fingers of his left hand trailing secretly along the inside of my thighs. He seemed to know a lot about software, and soon Nick and he were heatedly debating the merits of various accounting programs. I let my head rest against the back of the chair and closed my eyes. Nemo's fingers were like tentacles of dry ice, alternately scalding and freezing the surface of my skin. He felt the trembling in my muscles and dug deeper in acknowledgment.

Ramesh brought out the fragrant ginger tea and an assortment of crisp patties and cutlets. Two he placed directly on my plate, and I knew without being told that they were fish patties. I asked Nick whether he was vegetarian, and he said he was. "Too bad," I said, popping one of the patties into Nemo's mouth. An uncertain smile hovered around my aunt's lips as she registered this sudden intimacy. Propelling food into the mouth uninvited was an accepted Indian custom, but generally reserved for relatives and intimates.

It would be just a matter of time before I told my aunt that Nemo and I were lovers. However conservative she appeared on the surface, she cherished her confidential relationships with her nieces and nephews. We all confided in her, and she maintained our trust without exception.

After a while, Nick forgot that he had come to see me, so animated was his conversation with Nemo. My aunt and I excused ourselves from the table and retired to the swing on the balcony.

"The things you don't find out about young men until you have to deal with them alone," sighed my aunt. "Usually, when the boy comes to see the girl, it's us oldies who do all the talking, you know. This rule of yours of not allowing parents to accompany their sons is turning out to be a social disaster!"

My aunt paused. "You really should let me take you to the hairdresser, Renu. I'm sick of seeing your hair flying in all directions.

How many Indian women do you see roaming around with their long hair open?"

"That's the first time you've ever referred to me as a woman. Up to this point I've always been a girl. What happened?"

My aunt looked at me as though I were daft. "Honestly, darling, you find the most unusual ways to torture your old auntie." I took her hand in mine and massaged her fingers. Her eyes took on a far-away look and she sank back against the padded silk of the swing. "Well, if all goes well you'll be married soon. It's hard to remain a girl once you're married."

"You know, Nemo isn't nearly as young as you think."

"Hmmm . . ." My aunt exhaled pleasurably as I pressed the ball of her thumb. "It's his Muslim blood. Makes him look more child-ish."

"He's just two years younger than me, you know, twenty-five."

"He's that old?" My aunt looked at me lazily. "I suppose I'm always confusing him with his younger brother."

"How come Nemo didn't make it onto your list?" I whispered. My aunt's arm tensed and she drew away.

"In the old days, we were all families of equal standing. It didn't matter whether we were Muslim or Hindu. Not anymore."

"You know," I said, choosing my words carefully, "I'm not really looking for a man to marry at this point. I love you and was curious to see who you'd pull out of your hat, but I don't think I'm destined to be married anytime soon."

"Hunh!" she snorted. "That's what they all say, until they tie the knot. Then they wonder how they managed to live so long without it!"

"But honestly, Auntie, is it the sex or the marriage that people find so thrilling?"

She rolled her eyes and swatted me on the arm. "You know you can't ask that around here. Most have never had the one without the other."

"But I have, and so have my sisters and most of my cousins. You know that."

My aunt lashed at me with the loose end of her chiffon sari. "You youngsters think you'll end up in fairy-tale marriages because you've slept with a few horny men? You're wrong. Eventually you'll come to see the error of your ways. We're from a different generation— duty first, and all that. We hardly even knew that sex was something separate from marriage. We've all been brought up in terror of it."

She sprang off the ornately decorated metal swing, which jangled with the sudden movement. Her eyes betrayed her hurt.

"You obviously don't understand that an old woman like me would be forgotten like a rusted nail in the wall if I didn't find some way to keep myself in the picture. At least I make the effort to get to know all of you. I do a decent job, all in all."

I took her hand and kissed it. "I understand all that," I said gently. "But I'm talking about me. Things have changed, and you know it." My aunt turned to go, but I held on to her hand. She sighed, and tilted my chin upward.

"I don't want to know," she whispered. "Do what you must do, but please be discreet. *I don't want to know.* All I can say is, don't ruin your chances for the future. You might just change your mind."

Inside, the two men stood up and walked toward the front door. The visit was over. At the last minute Nick remembered my aunt and me and turned to wave good-bye. Nemo graciously saw him out the front door, then staggered back to the couch and flopped down with a thud.

My aunt whispered to me under her breath. "Isn't he the cutest? You may think it's all your good luck, but it's not. I told his cook Hussan that you were in town and that you needed a little company. You owe me one." She wiggled her bulky hips at me and blew me a wet kiss.

I gasped. My own aunt setting me up for an affair? I felt the knot of anxiety tightening in my stomach. My aunt's eyes darted hungrily over Nemo, taking in his languid limbs and his fatigue-softened lips. She rubbed her abdomen and sighed.

"Ramesh, oh, Ramesh," she called. "Where are you hiding, my love? I wonder if Ramesh has learned anything useful from that boyfriend of his. Don't know what it is, but these days I feel like eating fish."

Midsummer of Love

Simon Sheppard

"A dream is all wrong, absurd, composite, and yet at the same time it is completely right . . . Why? I don't know."

—*Wittgenstein*

"For this is all a dream we dreamed one afternoon long ago."

—*The Grateful Dead*

Far out! The smoke moved down from the bowl, making its lazily intoxicating way through glass tubing, bubbling through murky water, swirling into the waterpipe's chamber, then out through another tube, the mouthpiece, his mouth, his lungs, his brain. Far fucking out.

A hit, a very palpable hit, thought Sandy Stein, leaning into the waves of music coming from the speakers in the hall. Janis Joplin, and life was good.

He heard, or thought he heard, the door to the flat open and close. He'd been alone in the place, except for Ronn and one of his boys fucking in the next room. He'd been alone with Janis and the waterpipe. No longer. He hoped it wasn't Demetrius. He took another hit, held it in until he thought his lungs would burst.

It *was* Demetrius. Oh shit.

Okay, so Demetrius, with his curly black hair, his lean and muscled body, his very bright smile, was what a lot of guys thought was "sexy." Even Sandy *could* have thought that. He might have overlooked Demetrius' self-absorption, his ego trips, even the slightly absurd name he'd chosen for himself, if only Demetrius weren't, for some unfathomable reason, after Sandy's ass. If only he hadn't tried, more than once, to fuck him. Because Sandy didn't mind fooling around with guys like Demetrius—lean, smiling boys with dazzling smiles. But Alexander Stein had never been, and most certainly did not want to get, fucked.

"Hey, Sandy," said Demetrius, kissing Stein right on the lips, a kiss Sandy wasn't sure he enjoyed. "A few of the Cockettes are downstairs, and we're all headed to the Park. A bunch of Hare Krishnas are doing some kind of parade or something. Sounds like it could be pretty groovy. I thought you might like to join us." Demetrius, shameless slut that he was, batted his long, dark eyelashes at Stein. "Can I have a toke?"

Stein passed the waterpipe to him and, with an audible sigh, pulled his sandals on and struggled to his feet. Not that it would necessarily be a bummer, but he felt duty bound to go. Since he'd moved into the Page Street commune half a year ago, Sandy had been criticized for being "insufficiently communal." He was the college boy, English Lit. The uptight one. The one who didn't get fucked. Okay, so he felt awkward about Demetrius and his insistent attempts to plow his virgin ass. And, okay, so a lot of the Cockettes were silly, effeminate glitter queens. Even so, a walk to Golden Gate Park might be cool.

Demetrius handed the pipe back to him, and he took one last hit. "Down on me," kvetched Janis, as Sandy hit the turntable's reject lever. "Down on me, looks like everybody in the whole"—and the needle lifted off the groove. In the sudden quiet, the sounds of vigorous fucking became clear. Ronn had left his door half open, and on the way out, Sandy snuck a look. A young, thin boy, just Ronn's type, was lying on his back on Ronn's waterbed, legs in the air, his long hair splayed blondly over the paisley patterns of the Indian spread. Ronn's hairy goatbody hunched over him, plowing into the boy's ass. The older man had the boy's thin wrists pinned down against the amorphous waterbed, which sloshed and shifted with every stroke.

By the time Sandy and Demetrius had gotten down to the front door, Ronn was shooting his load, his grunts and bellows echoing down the stairs.

It was a typical summer day in San Francisco, which is to say a gray, cool, foggy day. As the six of them headed through the park, Demetrius chattered on about his role in the Cockettes' upcoming show. The troupe of glitter-bedecked genderfuck drag queens was staging a musical extravaganza entitled *Greek Love,* set in ancient Athens, and based loosely—very loosely—on *A Midsummer Night's Dream.* Ever since the Cockettes had hit the big time with shows like *Pearls Over Shanghai* and *Tinsel Tarts In A Hot Coma,* they'd become the toast of gay San Francisco, their raucous, sloppy shows attended by both stoned hippies in thrift-store drag and rich A-list fags out for a night of slumming. Even Truman Capote had been to the Cockettes. Or maybe it was Gore Vidal.

"My first starring role!" Demetrius was saying. "And dress rehearsal is tonight. Girls, I am SOOO excited."

"Well, honey," Glamoretta purred, "take a Valium." Glam had come from LA, where he'd actually worked in the costume department of some studio or other, and this genuine professional experience reflected itself in a hauteur which might have been off-putting, Sandy thought, if it weren't so damn silly.

Taheetee, the self-proclaimed Star of the Cockettes, put his hand to his ear in an exaggerated flourish. "Could those be the sounds of the Mystic East? Are we there yet? And does anyone have a joint?"

Mary Moonglow, the only real, genuine, actual woman among them, grimaced comically. "Taheetee, honey, you are already stoned to the TITS!"

"You should talk," little Johnnyboy lisped.

Mary Moonglow smiled. "No hope without dope."

"Over that way," said Sandy Stein, feeling, as usual, a little put off by all the flamboyance in full sail. "I think I can see the parade."

When they turned a corner near the Japanese Tea Garden, there it was, the procession, a gaggle of Hare Krishnas in saffron-colored bedsheets, leaping, chanting, playing finger cymbals. The more muscular among them dragged along three big carts loaded up with garlands of flowers and a few weird-looking idols. *Hare Krishna, Hare Krishna, Krishna Krishna, Rama Rama!* Skinny white boys with shaved heads danced around wildly, caught up in some faux-Eastern ecstasy. And Taheetee plunged right in, his beaded gown whirling above his hairy knees. "Harry Kirshner, Rammer Rammer!" he sang.

"Psychedelic!" said Mary Moonglow. "That looks cool!" And soon all six of them had joined the procession, though rational Sandy Stein chanted halfheartedly and danced reluctantly. He was, in fact, about to slip away when he spotted the Krishna boy, the cute, tall, skinny Krishna boy, and the Krishna boy spotted him.

■

"I don't think I'm supposed to be doing this," the Krishna boy had said as Sandy led him back to Page Street. But now he was lying there naked, his gangly legs trailing off Sandy's mattress, his orangish robes heaped in a corner of the room. And though he'd said he'd never done it with a guy before, his extravagantly long cock was pointing straight at the ceiling.

Sandy looked down at the boy's pretty face, his closed eyes and blissed-out smile, his shaved head with the single long lock of hair. At the boy's thin but well-defined body and his throbbing cock. "Just lie there," Stein said, "and I'll make you feel real good." Sex with straight guys, he thought. It's what I majored in at college.

Krishna Boy still had his sneakers on. Sandy pulled them off and moved his mouth down to the boy's sweaty right foot. Starting at the toes, he moved his tongue up over the boy's ankle, up the stringy calf, swirled it behind the knee, then proceeded up the boy's thigh 'til he could feel Krishna Boy's balls against the top of his head. He buried his face in the guy's crotch, feeling the long, silky hair against his cheek, sniffing in the smell, the unmatched smell of dick. When he licked the boy's big, floppy balls, Krishna Boy said, "Mmmm."

So Sandy moved his tongue down to the ridge beneath the boy's ballsac and, wrestling those long legs into the air, licked at the tight, puckered hole. Which quickly relaxed, just as a more experienced asshole would, for Sandy's probing tongue. As Sandy slurped his way inside, he reached up and played with the boy's long boner, already damp with pre-cum. "MMMM," said Krishna Boy, louder this time. Sandy, still half-dressed, humped the mattress as he ate out the boy's musky-tasting ass. Sweet and smooth as clarified butter. Just ready to be fucked.

Sandy's still-stoned brain was tripping on images of Indian princes fucking in the Taj Mahal or somewhere when he heard Krishna Boy grunt, "Oh shit! I'm gonna . . ." And the butthole contracted around his tongue, the dick throbbed in his hand, and spurts of cum hit the back of his head. *"Hare Krishna!"* the long, skinny boy yelled. And Sandy would have giggled, except he still had a mouthful of ass, and then he was coming himself, shooting off stickily inside his bell bottoms. The smell of fresh cum joined the waft of incense in the air.

■

"Didn't know you were going in for religion," said Ronn to Sandy when Krishna Boy, orange bedsheet and all, had gone on his way. Ronn, the oldest of Sandy's flatmates, was the commune's leader. He was, for one thing, an actual published author. Sandy thought his novel, *Dogsbody,* was just pornography with pretensions, but Grove Press *had* published it. Lately, though, Ronn's writing had consisted largely of articles in the intercommunal newsletter, *KaliFlower,* where he was waging a campaign to convince people to clean their butts with water and their left hand, Indian-style, instead of using toilet paper. Ronn even knew Ginsberg. Supposedly.

"So where is everybody?" asked Sandy, ladling out a bowlful of tofu and brown rice from the big pot on the kitchen stove

"Valentine and Jeff are hitching up to the river, Peter is fucking some weekend hippie in his room, Demetrius I don't know, oh that's right, dress rehearsal, and Bear is still at the clap clinic. And I have a friend from New York who just got into town, got to the house while you were busy with the horny idolater. He's out buying a beer." Alcohol was one intoxicant rarely seen in the house.

The doorbell rang. "There he is now." Ronn struggled up from the waterbed and went to buzz in his friend. While he was in the hall, Ronn put a record on the stereo. The Airplane, *Surrealistic*

Pillow. "Don't you want somebody to love?" they taunted. "Don't you need somebody to love?"

Ronn and his friend stood in the doorway. "Sandy, this is Pug, from New York." Sandy blinked. Pug was no hippie. He was big, muscular, short-haired, bearded, and dressed in black leather from head to toe. He was also *old,* about Ronn's age, thirty, thirty-five.

"Hey, Sandy." Pug reached down to shake Sandy's hand, and damn near busted Stein's fingers in his muscular grip.

"I'm sure you and Pug will have a lot to talk about," grinned Ronn. *"He's* a total top, too."

■

"You guys are back early," Sandy said to Demetrius and his Cockette friends. He tried to remember whether it was exactly the same bunch that he'd gone to the Park with, but while Pug had been knocking back the beers, quite a few beers, Sandy and Ronn had been sampling a new shipment of Acapulco Gold that Ronn was going to sell.

"Well, the dress rehearsal ended early. Hollywood Hills threw a hissy fit and then everything kind of fell apart. And anyway, we're *perfect* as is," Johnnyboy preened. He was a cute little thing, Sandy knew, but he fucked like a wildcat, all scratching and Spanish curses once he got a dick up his ass. Sandy knew firsthand.

"Lookie what I have here," Mary Moonglow chirped. "Blue Lightning. You guys want any?" She held out her grimy palm, in which there was a baggie containing a handful of little blue pills. Blue Lightning, the best acid out there right now. Rumor was that Owlsley himself had made it.

"How much?" asked Ronn, ever the stoned businessman.

"On the house. Saraswati laid them on me." Saraswati was a sugar heiress who lived in an ashram in Pacific Heights.

Mary Moonglow opened the baggie and passed it around. Each of them took a little blue tab and popped it in his mouth. Everybody but Pug. "Nah, I'll stick with alcohol, thanks. I know that makes me old-fashioned, but fuck it," he smiled.

"Give me his," said Ronn.

■

By the time they reached Hippie Hill, Sandy had started to come on to the acid. On full-moon nights like this, Golden Gate Park was alive with activity. Conga drummers. Witches and warlocks dancing in circles. Newcomers to the Haight in the bushes, screwing or smoking or trying to get some sleep in well-used sleeping bags. But now, as he lay back on the grass of Hippie Hill, Sandy realized that the Park itself was alive, a pulsing, magical organism that rippled beneath his back. He looked up, dizzily, and began to feel sick to his stomach.

"Om," chanted Taheetee. "Om om OMMMMM!"

Om, om on the range, thought Sandy, and began to get a severe case of the giggles. And then he floated clear off the Earth and looked back on himself lying there stoned in the moonlight, and the world began to melt, thaw, and resolve itself into a dew.

I'm just stoned, he heard himself thinking. *I know what this is.* Only there was no way to define "this," just the overwhelming kaleidoscope of patterns that had begun to pinwheel behind his eyes.

He suddenly refocused on the full moon after, what, a minute? A year? What meaning did time have, anyway, when it was omnidimensional, Godhead in a Mickey Mouse watch?

"You okay?" It was Mary Moonglow's voice, though her face, staring down on him, refused to settle down, and kept shifting and shifting and shifting. First he tried to understand what her question meant, could mean. Then he tried to nod his head without it flying off into space. Then he tried to say something, maybe he *was* saying something, but . . . every . . . word . . . became . . . a . . . solid . . . object. And then Mary Moonglow laughed, became a witch, and was gone.

He was on his feet, walking, walking with these people, his friends. Friends. Friends. He began to cry. It was all so beautiful. So fragile and beautiful and eternal.

And prehistoric. They were in a prehistoric jungle now. Though some part of him realized that it was just the fern grotto near the deYoung Museum. But if it *was,* what were those dinosaurs doing there? And—oh, how beautiful!—his friends—friends!—were naked now, some of them, dancing around in the moonlight, and their glowing flesh held the secret of life. And goatish Ronn's dick was hard, a hard-on, what a funny thing to have. And cute little Johnnyboy dropped to his knees and looked so vulnerable as Ronn lumbered up, stegosauruslike, and waved his big, hairy cock in the young boy's face. "Ommm," chanted Taheetee as Johnnyboy wrapped his lips around Ronn's bulging purple dickhead and suddenly Sandy was so much closer, just inches away, so he could watch the wondrous sliding of hard cockflesh into wet mouth. And then Ronn reared back on his goat legs and pushed the young man to the ground, and Johnnyboy raised his legs so that Ronn could go inside of him. Inside and outside, it was all one, each defining the other as veiny mancock pierced boyass and Johnny began to moan and shout. Maybe in some foreign language. Though *all* words were foreign, and only flesh and desire and fucking were true. And as Johnnyboy rammed his fingernails into Ronn's furry back, Taheetee stood over them, golden naked body dappled by full-moonlight, and stroked his own long cock until he arced his body backward, every sinew tensing beneath mortal flesh, and spurted long shining ropes over their straining bodies. But Johnnyboy and the goatman were not finished yet, and Sandy realized he was stroking his own hard flesh as he knelt there in the forest, and it felt so amazingly good. Someone's hands were on his shoulders, moving down his back, and he did not look to see who it was, because he was afraid he already knew. It was one of his friends, a friend who wanted what he was not prepared to give, the hand moving down to his ass, down the crack of his ass, down to the place, the forbidden place, the dirty place . . . He looked up. It was Demetrius. As he knew it would be. "Sandy, I love you," Demetrius seemed to be saying.

He probably pushed Demetrius away, because he was suddenly on his feet, pulling his pants up, and no one was touching him. And through the moonlit woods he went, past the sound of drums, past maybe the sound of the Grateful Dead, and part of him must have been functioning well, the homing-instinct part, because he opened a door, went upstairs, and was home. Home. What a concept! He glided into his room, lit a single candle and a stick of incense, and closed his eyes, sinking deep into the flow of feelings and thoughts.

"Hey, you're back. How're you doing?"

Sandy's eyes flew open.

"Huh?"

Sandy tried to figure out who he was, the bearded stranger in his home.

"Pug, remember? Ronn's friend."

"Pug? Pugpugpug." It was all too funny.

"What's so funny?" But Pug's voice sounded like he was in on the joke.

"I'm just . . . just . . . just . . ."

"Stoned on acid, hey?" The bearded man's face kept changing, became friendly, then scary, then beautiful, very very beautiful. Those are pearls that were his eyes. "Must be good stuff," the beautiful man said, and he took another swallow of, of . . . beer, that's what it was. And he put his arm around Sandy's shoulders. It felt good. He realized he must have been cold from being naked in the park. Half naked. Half a naked's better than none.

"Gotta piss," the man in leather said. "Be right back." But Sandy followed him and stood there watching him take out his dick and then the two of them were standing side by side, both draining all this fluid from their bodies, it was something Sandy did every day, all the time, draining fluid from this tube in the middle of his body. A body, what a weird thing to have. He laid his hand on Pug's dick, felt it draining, watched the last of a yellowish stream spurt from the tip, felt the flesh becoming bigger in his grip. Pug drew him to his leather chest. Sandy looked into the bearded face. His friend's bearded face. Wise and handsome and frightening, all at once. For a second, it became his father's face, and then Demetrius's, and then it was the face of every man he'd ever wanted but had not let inside. His dick felt so good. He looked down at the water containing their mingled piss, the liquid that had flowed from both separate bodies, now indistinguishable, mixed and unable to be unmixed again. Pug moved his hand and it all swirled down into a whirlpool and disappeared like magic.

"Let's go back to your room," Pug said.

Sandy's mattress was covered with books and clothes and stuff. He swept it all onto the floor, kneeled on the bed, and waited.

Waited for whatever Pug wanted to do, for whatever Pug would make him do. Sandy was coming down a little; the acid rush had ebbed enough so that Sandy was able to figure out that he was on acid, coming down a little. But he still wanted Pug to do whatever Pug was meant to do that moonlit night.

The bearded man pulled off Sandy's shirt. When he felt the strong hands on his torso, Sandy trembled.

"Don't be afraid, boy. Ain't gonna hurt you."

Sandy looked up into his eyes. *Do thy worst,* he thought.

"Ain't gonna hurt you more than's necessary," Pug added, and laughed.

And then Sandy was on his back, looking up at the ceiling, at the Fillmore posters on the walls, and Pug was pulling at Sandy's clothes. Naked. Alexander Stein was naked with another man. A man who kissed him gently on the lips, then moved his mouth down over his chest, stopping to suck at an intense nipple, then his belly, down to his dick. The man was going to put Sandy's penis in his mouth. Sandy shut his eyes. There was a swirl of rainbow patterns, shining bright as crystal. But the mouth didn't stop at his dick. It moved between his legs, his legs which were being hoisted into the air. It moved down, the mouth, down to his ass, to his crack, his hole, his asshole. He tried to shut it tight. Only he didn't, because he didn't want to, because it felt so good, this amazing connection, this short-cut in the food chain, this wet tongue probing inside him, the place his Dad always told him was dirty. But it wasn't dirty, it was shining as full as the moon. And then the tongue, the sensation, disappeared. He jerked open his eyes. Pug's face was inches from his own.

"Never been fucked before?" the handsome old man asked, only he was ageless, and all of time had brought them both to this place.

"No." The words came out of Sandy's mouth. They must have. "No, but I want you to."

"Ronn warned me when I asked him about you. Don't worry, I won't hurt you. Just relax. You're too cute to hurt." The face smiled broadly. "Much."

A wet finger pressed in on Sandy's hole, which closed up, unfriendly. "Just push out a little and then relax. If you relax, it won't hurt."

"No."

"No what?" Pug asked.

And Sandy thought he wanted to say *No, I won't let you fuck me,* but instead he said, "No, it won't hurt."

"Wait. Be right back."

And Sandy could have gotten up, pulled on his clothes, shut his door, but he lay there, legs in the air, till Pug returned. And Pug knelt between his legs, pressed at his hole, and this time the finger just slid right in.

"See, I told you. All you have to do is want it."

And Sandy *did* want it, want that finger inside him, no not the finger, as good and startling as it felt. He wanted something else inside him. He wanted Pug inside him. He wanted Pug's cock.

"I want your cock inside me."

"I know you do."

"Ahhhh . . ."

"Just getting a second finger inside you. Loosening you up."

Make room for Daddy, Stein thought. Weird.

"Let me see it before you stick it in. Let me see your dick."

Pug shifted position and knelt over his face. A big, hard dick protruded from Pug's leather pants. A big, hard, shiny dick sticking out of a leather crotch. "It's so shiny," Sandy said.

"Vaseline. That's what I went to get. Vaseline."

And then Pug was between his legs again, his legs which rested on the man's broad shoulders, and the man's strong fingers kneaded Alexander Stein's secret hole, and made it feel so so good, so hungry, and then the swollen, shiny-slick head of the animal dick was pressed up against the hole and Sandy thought, *This is it, where I lose my cherry,* and "cherry" seemed so funny, like he was a sundae or something, that Sandy almost laughed, but before he could, the shaft of flesh slid inside him and he gasped and it might have hurt a little bit, but Sandy couldn't tell because he felt like sparks were shooting out of the top of his skull. The word *kundalini* flashed through his brain, and then his mind was blank and free of words and there was just this incredible joining, a feeling that was almost too much to bear, but Sandy wanted it never to stop. He felt like a man. He felt like a woman. He felt like a faggot. He felt like a happy little boy.

"You're crying?" Pug sounded concerned.

"Just fuck me."

And then Pug slapped him on the ass, which should have hurt, should have upset him, but just added to the intensity, as though there were even *more* than the ultimate, a mystery beyond the mystery, and then he thought of the man's big, blood-swollen sex tube ramming over and over again into his guts. Weird. And animal. And right.

"I got you, boy. You're safe with me."

Sandy threw his arms around the man and held on tight.

"That's better," said Pug. "It's nice to see a smile on your face."

The room kept on spinning for hours.

■

Stein slept till noon. He lay among his rumpled sheets for a while, feeling simultaneously drained and renewed. Ravaged. Reborn. Trying to recall just what had happened the night before. His ass still pulsed with pleasure.

When he staggered into the kitchen for tea, the first thing Bear said to him was, "Well, looks like *some*body got well and truly laid last night."

"Does it show?" Sandy smiled blearily.

"Yep." Bear's chubby face broke into a grin.

"So is Pug around?" Sandy hoped he sounded at least a little nonchalant.

"Ronn's friend? Nope, left this morning."

"Left? For where?"

"Didn't say. But it sounded like he wouldn't be back for a while. He left you something, though." Bear pointed to an envelope, addressed to Sandy, on the kitchen table.

Sandy tore it open. There was a single sheet of paper inside. He unfolded it. Two words: "Nice ass."

■

Sandy spent the afternoon in his room, listening to Dylan, trying to recapture the visions of the night before, drawing elaborate patterns with colored marking pens.

Ronn would come in every once in a while and smile enigmatically, or tousle Sandy's hair. But he never talked about the night before. And he swore that he didn't know where Pug had gone.

At sundown, Sandy took his three Chinese coins and threw a hexagram. Lots of changes. "Obstruction" changing to "Inner Truth." "Pigs and fishes," the *I Ching* read. "Good fortune. It furthers one to cross the great water. Perseverance furthers."

He went next door to Bear and Valentine's room. "Hey, Bear. Going to the show tonight?"

"Yeah, I originally figured I'd go on Saturday, but I'm afraid Miss Demetrius won't forgive me if I miss her Big Debut." When Sandy felt emotionally raw, like he did today, Bear's big smile could be a lifesaver.

■

Bear and Sandy took the 30 Stockton bus to Chinatown, went to Sam Wo, and ordered steaming bowls of jook from Edsel Ford Fong, the world's rudest Chinese waiter, whose insults achieved the status of High Comedic Art.

"Still thinking about Pug?" Bear asked, licking the porcelain spoon.

"Yeah. Does it show?"

"More where he came from. Take my word for it."

Sandy decided not to bring up Bear's ex, who'd left him for a woman. It had taken Bear months to smile again.

"You finish?" barked the waiter. "Pay the check already."

They walked up to North Beach, where a crowd had gathered at the Palace Theatre. The marquee read: TODAY: CHINESE OPERA. TONIGHT: THE COCKETTES IN *GREEK LOVE*. And beneath the marquee, queer San Francisco had turned out in force. Drag queens. Gay hippies. Fag hags. Trust-fund kids from the Art Institute. "John Apple?" a voice called out. John Apple yelled back, "Over here, Miss Pajama!"

Sandy and Bear bought tickets and walked inside. The air was drenched with a potent blend of marijuana smoke and cheap perfume.

"Yoohoo! Bear!" It was a guy from Hungadunga, the hippie house generally recognized to be home to the prettiest boys in town. Sandy had always kind of resented them.

"Come sit with me," the boy called. "Your cute friend, too."

Bear maneuvered things so that Sandy, not he, was sitting next to the boy from Hungadunga. It was getting to be show time, which meant about an hour after the announced curtain time, and the theater was filling up. Miss Teddy, in his usual Chinese-opera drag, swept up the aisle and screeched "Okay, girls, let's get your goddamn motherfucking show on the road!" And as if by magic, the house lights dimmed. A chorus of screams and squeals arose from the crowd. The Hungadunga boy's hand settled into Sandy's crotch. And the show began.

"Ladies and gentlemen," a resonant voice boomed from the loudspeaker. "The fab-u-lous world premiere of *Greek Love,* starring the all-singing, all-dancing, all-cardboard Cockettes!"

A single spot lit the stage. A pretty blond boy in a toga that stopped well short of his flopping dick struck a pose and lisped out, "What fags these mortals be!" And the curtain rose on a pasteboard scene of Athens: Corinthian columns liberally doused with glitter, and statues sporting enormous hard-ons. Center stage, Sylvester stood, dressed in a sequined black gown, his black skin dusted with gold paint. A slave of some sort, he was manacled to a very wobbly painted wall. Scrumbly struck a chord on the piano and Sylvester began to sing, in his eerily pure falsetto, "I'm just a prisoner of love."

As the last notes faded, Demetrius and Glamoretta strutted onstage, Glam radiant in a chartreuse taffeta dress, Demetrius wearing just a tiny posing strap, his oiled body gleaming in the spotlight. "Theseus, honey," Glam vamped, "Let's get married, so thou wiltest be the Duke of Athens and I shalt be thy Douche-ess."

Demetrius, chest aglow, looked out into the audience and overemoted. "Only if we can invite all the fairies."

The next hour was filled with missed cues, half-naked dancers with glitter in their beards, and a hilariously bad pastiche of Shakespeare cobbled together from *A Midsummer Night's Dream, The Comedy of Errors,* and the funnier parts of *Timon of Athens.* By the time the first act climaxed in the Astaire and Rogers–style dance-craze number "Do the Bumfuck," no bit of scenery was left unchewed.

But, despite the attentions of the Hungadunga boy's hand, which had made its way inside Sandy's fly and was clasped around his hard cock, Sandy hadn't been able to take his eyes off Demetrius. He'd never quite realized before how sexy the curly-haired boy truly was. How nice it would be to have sex with him.

"Want to go for a walk during intermission?" the Hungadunga boy smiled, flipping his long blond hair and batting his long blond eyelashes.

"Thanks," said Sandy, "but I have to go backstage."

Bear raised his eyebrows in surprise. *"I'll* go for a walk with you," he said to the Hungadunga boy.

■

"You may be the Queen of the Fairies," Taheetee screeched at Mary Moonglow, "but you're stepping on my fucking lines!"

"Oh, take a Valium," Moonglow retorted, popping a tit out of her gown and waving it in his face.

"Mary, darling," purred Glamoretta, pleased to be making trouble, "don't make an ass of yourself."

Mary Moonglow turned her back to Glam and pulled up her skirt, revealing her ample, naked butt. "Kiss my *tuchis,* Miss Thing."

It was Sandy's first time backstage at a Cockettes' show. He was gratified to discover that what went on behind the scenes was at *least* as amusing as the goings-on onstage.

"Where's Demetrius?" Stein broke in, but before he got an answer, he saw him, standing by a cardboard chariot. Then Demetrius saw him, too, and smiled. A dazzling smile. As Sandy walked toward him, he felt his dick getting hard.

"Hey," said the curly-haired boy, "what are you doing back here?"

"Demetrius . . ." Sandy began to stutter.

"Yes?"

There was nothing to do but to say it. "Demetrius, I love you, and . . ."

"That's groovy, we should talk about it later."

"I want you to fuck me." He pressed his body against Demetrius, grabbed the boy's hand and guided it to his butt. "I want you to fuck me now."

"Here?"

"How about over there, in that dark corner?"

"NOW?"

"Why not?"

"Because act two is about to start?"

"When's your entrance?"

"Not till the second scene."

"Then fuck me now."

■

The second act curtain rose on a big cardboard wall standing upstage right. Two bearded men in drag introduced themselves as Pyramette and Lesbo, "two dyke lovers separated by a vile wall."

"Ah, but there's a hole in yon wall," trilled Pyramette, "So put thine divine lips up to the hole, that I may suck upon them." And the two, joined by a dancer in a tacky lion's costume, launched into the heartfelt ballad "Kiss My Hole."

Meanwhile, backstage, Sandy was on all fours on a dusty old sofa, sprung springs biting into his knees and hands, while Demetrius stood behind him and eased his spit-lubed hard-on, inch after throbbing inch, into Sandy's hot, wide-open hole.

"Oh, Pug!" moaned Sandy, as the hot shaft of flesh plunged into him.

"*What?*" grunted Demetrius.

"I said 'Oh fuck!' Come on and fuck me good and hard!"

Meanwhile, Pyramette and Lesbo's falsetto duet rose to the flies. "Oh, stick thy head between my hips / and put thy hot mouth to my lips. / Tongue my hole / 'pon my soul / kiss my hole!"

And the queen in the lion suit whirled and spun and backed into the flimsy cardboard wall, which shuddered for a moment and then collapsed onto the stage, exposing the ratty old sofa upon which Demetrius was vigorously, if somewhat inartistically, screwing Sandy up the butt.

The audience exploded in cheers and screams and catcalls. Sandy looked out into the jam-packed theater and smiled a secret smile. And Demetrius just kept plowing away.

■

Demetrius and Sandy's wedding took place out at Land's End, on a glorious, warm October day. Each of the communes had contributed something to the celebration. The boys of Hungadunga had baked the whole-wheat wedding cake, having first collectively jacked off into the batter. The Cockettes provided extravagant white gowns for both the brides. And Ronn made sure there were enough hash brownies for all the guests.

The only guest conspicuous by his absence was Pug. Every few weeks, Ronn conveyed the latest rumors of Pug's whereabouts: He was dropping acid with Leary at Millbrook. He was living with Jesus freaks in New Mexico. He was shacked up with Mick Jagger. Like the spirit of the times, he was everywhere at once and nowhere in particular. Sandy suspected he would never see hide nor hair of him again, and as it happened, Sandy was right. Though every so often, when he was being fucked by Demetrius or the men who came after Demetrius, the sweet memory would arise, unbidden, of that first night so long ago.

And Bear, who was a minister in the Universal Life Church, concluded the wedding ceremony with a reminder of that now-legendary night at the Palace Theatre, reading a selection which came, more or less, from *A Midsummer Night's Dream:*

> *If we shadows have offended,*
> *Think but this, and all is mended:*

That you have but slumbered here,
While these visions did appear.
And if we still offend you do,
We all in chorus say, "Fuck you!"

The Manicure

Nell Carberry

Last week, when I had some time to kill, I noticed that my nails were in sad, sad shape. I felt gray and washed out, invisible in the big, loud city. But, wandering through Greenwich Village at sunset, the air was bright, like someone had opened a bottle of champagne and let it spray. So I found a little nail parlor on one of those streets that run at cross angles to everything else. The manicure shop was painted pink and red, like the inside of a womb.

Within the pulsing room, there was only a single manicurist, a small Asian woman with gorgeous brown eyes.

"I was going to close up," she said. She glanced at my hands. "But I can help you."

She wore a long, pink cotton smock, and her I.D. badge read "KAREN."

I asked her what her real name was, and she looked annoyed.

"That is my real name."

I was embarrassed. What I'd meant was that somebody so beautiful should have a beautiful name. But the damage was done. I told her my name was Nell.

She locked the door, and turned out all of the lights except the one over her manicurist's table. She practically pushed me into a chair and began to file at my ragged hands.

"Shouldn't I pay you first?" I said.

"It depends on what we're going to do," she said. She smiled, I think. "You don't take very good care of your hands," Karen said, "and they're beautiful hands. You should be punished for what you've done to your hands." At least, I thought that's what she'd said. I was tired and the fumes from the polish, the wax, and the soaking fluid were making me woozy.

She filed and soaked my nails, then went to work on my hands with pink lotion. Outside, it was getting dark, the wind was rattling, and I looked toward the door.

"Look only at me," Karen said.

My hands felt boneless. My groin felt warm, weightless.

"I really should pay you," I said, and my voice came out all soft and dark, too.

The door rattled, but it wasn't the wind. It was a woman trying to get in. She was dressed in black jeans and a shiny, red silk shirt, and even in the dark, I could see she was desperate. She yanked at the door.

"No more customers," Karen shouted.

"Customer!" the woman shrieked. "I'm not a customer, you bitch!"

Karen shook her head. "Crazy people in New York," she said, looking at me sympathetically. "You would never do such a thing, would you?"

"No," I said, more fervently than I expected. "I'd never do that to you."

Karen wore some kind of perfume, roses and spice, something off, like jazz, but right, like jazz, too. The woman outside howled some more.

"Hey, you, you in there with Karen. Get out now!"

Karen held my gaze with hers.

"If you ignore her, she'll go away," said Karen. "And you want her to go away, don't you?"

I looked only at Karen's eyes. I heard the woman walking away.

I wanted to turn around then, but Karen tightened her hands around mine. How could such a tiny woman have such powerful hands?

"You wouldn't be rude like that, would you, Nell?" she whispered. "Not after I've done so much for your hands . . ."

That's when I saw the man step out of the darkness from the back of shop.

I must have passed out.

The next thing I felt was a mouth on my mouth—smoky, male, wet.

It was now completely dark outside, and inside the shop was only lit with a couple of high-intensity lamps.

My legs were cold.

My legs were naked. My cunt exposed.

Karen worked on my cuticles as if this was the way she did all her nail jobs.

The mouth continued to explore my face: a tongue on my lip, a nip on my ear. I was dizzy, and my eyes wouldn't focus. I had been tied to the chair and stripped from the waist down. Sensations came and went. The male mouth travelled over my ears, licking, and down my neck, biting. My clit began to swell, and sweat, and trickle. The moisture hit the plastic of the seat, making it sticky. Karen gave me a glance, and stood.

"Don't you ruin my chair, you sloppy girl," she barked. Suddenly, she tilted the light down to the floor. My stubby square toenails had been painted bright red. They looked like the feet of a slut. My clit grew some more. I didn't recognize those feet as my own.

Karen noticed me looking at the color. "You like it? I call it 'Wench.' "

I turned back to the shop window. Karen hadn't pulled the metal grate down, or pulled a curtain. If anyone had looked in, they could have seen us plainly: a half-naked woman being gently mauled by a silent man in tight black jeans, a white cotton shirt, and a ponytail, while being watched over by a stern, tiny mistress. I couldn't really see the man's face, but I could smell him. I hated men who smoked. But not this one.

"Show me her breasts," Karen snapped, and without warning,

the Mouthman grabbed the front of my white Oxford shirt and yanked it open. The buttons fell on the floor with a clatter. Somehow that made me hot, too.

"What an ugly bra," Karen spat. "We'll have to do something about that."

Mouth pulled a knife out of his tight jeans and flipped it open, like a biker boy. Carefully, he placed it on the material between my breasts and slit the fabric. He was gentle, but still he drew blood. Karen sighed, and picked up a cotton ball. She dabbed it with rubbing alcohol: I could smell it rising in the air. She swabbed my wound down hard, and I gasped from the stinging.

But my nipples got hard, and my cunt was slick with juice. My shirt dangled from my arms, and my bra was ruined.

"I would never have taken you if your hands hadn't been such a mess," Karen whispered. "Now I'll have to do all of you."

Mouth flung my shirt into a corner, along with my bra. Occasionally, I could sense people stopping outside, staring into the window, wondering if they really saw what they thought they saw in the shadows.

My wrists were bound to the arms of the chair, just a little too tight. Then they gagged me with a ball gag. There was a click of metal: clips made of silver filigree grasped my nipples fiercely— again, a little too tight.

"No sound," Karen ordered as she finished. "No talk, no moan, no pant." The Mouth said nothing, only opened and closed his knife once more.

Then Karen yanked on the chain between the nipple clips, and something between a pant and a grunt escaped from my mouth, despite the gag. I waited for a whip, a slap, a blow.

Instead, Karen sat down deliberately and pulled the manicure table to the side. She grabbed a bottle of bright red polish, leaned into me, and painted the pinkie finger of my left hand. She smelled like heaven. Her jazzy perfume was breaking down, mixing with her sweat. I wanted to lick it off, even though I'd never touched another woman. She rose from her chair and perched on my left leg to finish the job, careful not to touch me anywhere else. This was my punishment—that she would sit right next to me, right on me, but draw no nearer. I tried to look on the bright side; I thought, this might not be so bad. Stripped naked by a dangerous man. Painted like a whore by a beautiful woman. I could be a silent, good little girl through that.

Then Karen nodded to Mouth, who had donned a pair of black rubber gloves when I wasn't looking. His smell had changed. He, too, was sweating, and his erection was obvious. I tried not to think ahead, tried not to wonder whether I'd get to see any more of his body. Then he walked directly behind me and tied a blindfold around my eyes. The sour-sweet odor of the polish rose in the air.

Blind and mute, I felt as if I could smell everything in the room, like my skin had doubled in size. Karen was on the "fuck you" finger, stroking my palm with one hand while decorating it with the other.

I would be her good girl. I could be quiet. Then I felt a rubbery hand stroke my mound, as Karen continued stroking my palm. Mouth went to work below, while Karen worked on my hands. What a bitch she was, I thought. That woman had been right.

I writhed in the chair, but I kept quiet. I ground my ass into the sticky, cheap plastic of the chair, trying not to come, trying to avoid his hand, ever advancing . . . I yanked at my wrist restraints. I was only trying to do what Karen demanded: to absorb the pleasure without a sound. Then someone slapped me hard on the face. It was Karen, I guess; the slap was scented with perfume and lotion.

Karen hissed, "Ruin this nail job, bitch, and you'll never leave this place."

"Let's teach her something," said Mouth. His voice was smoky and dark, too. My outer lips ballooned at the sound. Everything was making me hot. How could I possibly do what Karen wished? But I wanted to. I knew I wanted to.

Mouth's hand withdrew from my crotch, and Karen stopped her nail job. I felt ashamed. I had failed her. I couldn't even get my fucking nails done without failing.

I felt Mouth grab the back of my chair, dragging me across the shop, dragging me toward . . . the storefront window. I could tell, even with the blindfold, that there was a streetlight shining outside, and that we were close enough to the glass to give anyone a very good view of my nail job.

"Will you be a good girl, Nell?" Karen whispered in my ear. I wanted to feel her tongue there, too, but it wasn't going to happen. She yanked at my nipple clip chain. "Will you be a good, quiet girl?" I nodded, biting my cheek to keep the sounds inside my mouth.

I was a liar. I wanted to come, I wanted to scream. I wanted Mouth to plunge his hand deep into my cunt, and Karen to suck on my tortured tits. But I wanted to please her. The truth was, from the moment I'd sat down in that chair and put my hand in her hand, I was hers.

Karen kept up the pace of my nail job while Mouth worked me below, kneading my mound until he flowed onto my clit, teasing it between two fingers. Sweat poured off my neck, my breasts, down my legs. I could hear Mouth begin to pant himself, and outside, I sensed, people were gathering.

Karen switched to my other hand, and Mouth's fingers drew patterns around my labia. How big was the crowd watching me?

I didn't know. I could hear a couple of people talking outside, another tapping on the glass, tapping. The blood rose in my chest, and I could feel my pale skin turn red from desire. I wanted to move my hips against Mouth's persistent motion, press hard against his long fingers, but I knew, I just knew, this was wrong.

"It's a bigger crowd than usual," Mouth said, and I could feel him smirking. The ball gag was making my mouth dry, my jaw tired. Bigger crowd than usual? I thought. What the hell did that mean?

And then, as Karen began painting my right hand, Mouth slid two fingers into me. I bit the inside of my cheek as his fingers found my G-spot and stroked it slowly. At the same time, Karen brought her mouth close to my breasts and just . . . breathed.

Outside, the crowd was quiet, but I could feel them watching. "They usually give up by now," I thought I heard a woman say, but maybe I'd imagined it. With his other hand, Mouth began exploring the crack of my ass. Karen withdrew her breath.

"Only four more fingers to go," Karen said brightly. As if in response, Mouth slid a third finger into my cunt. My knees shook, and my shoulders quivered. The ropes cut into my legs, and my circulation slowed.

"You clean up good, Nell," Mouth said mockingly. I felt him

kneel in front of me, to one side of Karen, both hands wedged deep in my crotch. My asshole was still tender, untouched. I could feel his eyes on my clit and my cunt.

"Three more," said Karen, and for the first time, I heard some heat behind the ice. More heat against my crotch: it was Mouth, doing what Mouth did best. I twisted, as if I imagined I could still avoid him. Karen slapped my breasts.

"You almost ruined that one," she shrilled.

"Either she's melting, or her juices are dripping off the chair," said Mouth.

"And she looked like such a dull little thing when she came in. But I knew you for what you were, Nell," said Karen.

Mouth now lapped me in earnest, from cunt lips to the tip of my clit. I heard a thump, thump, thump.

"They're pressing themselves against the glass, Nell, because they want a piece of you," Karen said, as she finished with my index finger, the one I liked to use to touch my breasts. Below, Mouth shoved his tongue into my cunt and licked the deep red walls inside me.

I was desperate not to come until Karen was done, but I didn't know how I was going to hold off. I thought about taxes, Republicans, white vinyl belts. I thought about bad TV movies and Barry Manilow. But Karen was on the last digit now, my right thumb, and she was massaging my palm again. Nothing was working. I imagined a world where everyone, even John Denver, got tied up, worked over, and painted up like a slut. And we all loved it.

More thumps against the window. I thought of Hitchcock's *The Birds,* the thud of the predators.

"They all want you, Nell," said Karen. "But you're mine, aren't you?" Suddenly, my eyes were full of tears, and I nodded.

"All done," said Karen. And everything stopped. The Mouth withdrew, with a final tug at my clit. Karen dropped my hand. Outside, silence. I was on the verge of coming, and I suddenly felt completely alone. Were they going to leave me here? Was this my reward for obedience?

Karen whipped off my blindfold, untied the gag, and Mouth undid my bonds. He put his hands under my arms and forced me to stand. I shook, but I didn't fall.

And then I saw them: a crowd of twenty outside the glass—men, women, mouths, little O's of lust, their sweaty hands applauding. I was naked, my hands and feet sparkled red, the color of the whore I was, the whore I wanted to be. I was swollen, I was ashamed, and I was Karen's. I wanted to be Karen's more than I wanted to moan, more than I wanted to come.

I turned, and there she stood, in a pink smock and nothing else. Nothing else, that is, except a black leather harness and a white marble dildo. And a mean gleam in her eye. I wanted to ask her permission, but I had lost my voice.

"Bend over the chair," she said. I eagerly complied.

But then she shook her head and gave me a mean little smile.

"No. Let's wax your legs first."

Essence of Rose

Poppy Z. Brite

The city of Nashville straddles its polluted stretch of the Cumberland River like a lover, nestles into its fertile patch of Tennessee land like a cluster of rhinestones sewn on to rich cloth of earth brown and malachite green. The streets of the downtown area are brick, dating from the early days of the city. Above these cobbled paths, towers of glass and chrome soar up and up, some for thirty stories or more, elegant hotels and shopping centers and temples of commerce, catching the southern sunlight by day, reflecting the million colored fairy lights of the city by night. Many of the tallest buildings have glass elevators that can be seen from the street after dark, ascending the sheer faces of the buildings like shimmering insects climbing toward the moon.

Or spiders, thought Anthony, going up to spin their webs between the few stars that were faintly visible through the haze of city light. Yes, he could paint that: white and silver spiders, spinning gossamer threads between points of light in velvety, purple-blackness.

But he thought Rose might paint it better. The image was more suited to her style.

He stood naked at a window on the thirty-first floor of a grand hotel, pressing his body to the cool glass so that a foggy outline began to form around him—his body heat made visible—and gazing out over the city. Only the faintest shadow of his reflection was visible in the glass: sharp-featured, big eyes staring, skin very pale and hair paler still. He was backlit by the Christmas lights strung around the room, the candles burning, the tiny orange eye of an incense stick smoldering here and there. A room lit by juju.

From what Anthony had seen, the hotel staff consisted of impeccably dressed black men with gleaming bald heads and big-haired white ladies who wore their makeup like an extra face, so thickly applied that it seemed to hover a fraction of an inch above their actual features. They would certainly suspect juju or worse if they saw the room now. But they never entered, nor did the housekeepers, not during this week. Anthony met them at the door to receive towels and soap for the long, steaming baths he and Rose took. The bed could not be changed because it was in constant use, so that by the end of the week it would be a swirled, jumbled confection of sheets and pillows and small creamy stains, rich and ripe with the many scents of sex. And, this year, with the faintly sour tang of spilled champagne.

He placed his hands flat against the glass—two perfect, long fingered handprints lined in a nearly phosphorescent mist—then pushed himself away from the window and reached for the ice bucket. A half-full bottle of champagne was chilling there. *Magie Noire,* the strange brand Rose had brought with her. She said it came from a winery near New Orleans, where she spent the rest of her year.

"Cajun champagne?" he'd asked, a little nervously, the first time she had poured it for him.

"You'd really have to call it sparkling wine, I guess," she'd said. "But that sounds as if it ought to be pink and served in Dixie cups. *Magie Noire* is a *potion.*"

All the rest of the year Anthony was a sherry drinker. He had never been able to make himself like the taste of beer, and liquor mutated his personality, made him a mad thing, unable to paint. Rose always drank champagne. This year she'd begged him to drink it with her, and he had given in. There was an underlying spiciness, a slight burn like the essence of Tabasco without the garlic and vinegar, like oil of cinnamon, a subtle heat stitching across the tongue. Still, he could not detect all the flavors Rose said were in the bouquet; she knew the names and tastes of herbs he'd never heard of. It produced a strange drunkenness he'd never known before, balloon-headed, almost numb.

"You're mine," she had whispered the day before in drunken reverie, standing over him in the empty bathtub as recycled champagne flowed out of her, over Anthony's chest and stomach in a pale yellow stream. "You're mine, no one else's, not hers, only mine now."

Her words, as much as her act, had given him a jolt. Rose never referred, even so obliquely, to the uncomfortable fact of Anthony's marriage.

Now he poured some more of the potion into a tall fluted glass and sipped slowly. Bubbles exploded against the roof of his mouth as he turned to look at the woman who shared this room and this week and this city with him. The woman who slept the sleep of the sated, sprawled across the white expanse of the enormous bed. Every year the beds seemed to grow huger, softer, more enticing. Every year their bodies seemed to fit together more precisely, their hearts seemed to bleed into each other more willingly.

Rose LeBlanc. He knew so little about her, not even whether that was her given name; the symmetry of its syllables seemed too perfect. But he could imagine no name that would suit her better. And that was what it said on her Louisiana driver's license, next to a tiny snapshot, all disarrayed hair and fierce, camera-hating eyes: Rose LeBlanc of New Orleans.

They had met in Nashville, two up-and-coming young artists invited to exhibit paintings in a museum show. Anthony's wife wasn't with him; his career did not interest her. He'd been at some cocktail party sucking down the free sherry, and suddenly there was Rose wrapped in black lace and silk, hair in a wild purple cloud around her head, a glass of champagne already in her graceful, gloved hand. When he saw her work, Anthony knew he had to fuck her.

Rose's paintings seemed ready to crawl off the canvas and

entwine tendrils round your wrists, almost too beautiful and too morbid to bear. Psychedelic washes of color twisted into intricate, mandala-like patterns, seeming to swarm on the wall. Black-green swamp scenes so lush and organic that you swore the leaning tree trunks could be made of bone, the draping foliage and shadow a thin network of viscera, of stretched flesh and trailing, looping vein. Her paintings glistened and seethed. It was as if she mixed quicksilver into her tempera, LSD into her watercolors.

They made Anthony think of creation and destruction, sex and voodoo, broken skulls resting on candlelit altars, eye sockets blazing dead black light. Of the thousand ghost stories that must pervade any block of her native French Quarter, of the thousand deaths and pains inflicted there daily. And of the sodden, decadent pleasures.

Looking at Rose's work—even the Polaroids of new canvases she occasionally sent him between visits—was like being in a hotel room with her, her tongue working him over or her legs wrapped tight around his hips, burying him deep inside her. Sometimes Anthony felt stupidly, nigglingly jealous of the other people who must see her work, wondering if it seduced them in just the same way.

But they didn't get to hold the artist herself the way he did. They didn't get to bite her throat and lick her nipples, they didn't get to spread her thighs and consume the nectar of her cunt under a rainbow of Christmas lights, thirty floors above the city. They didn't get to drink *Magie Noire* with her. At least, Anthony hoped they didn't.

He approached the bed. The folds and ripples of the white sheet caught all the colors in the room; they spread like a watercolor wash over the hills and hollows of Rose's body. A corner of the sheet was draped across her face, trembling with each breath. He took hold of the sheet and gently pulled it away.

Flawless skin paler than his, pale even against the white sheet. Mouth raw from the days they had already spent together—from the kissing and the sandpaper rasp of Anthony's scruff, since he did not often leave the bed long enough to shave—too dark in the pale face, like an overripe plum. Lashes smudgy against cheeks, twin streaks of charcoal. Hair of a curious purple-black, the color of a bruise, teased and tangled around her head; there were a couple of patches at the back where it had begun to knot into dreadlocks. The soft bush of hair between her thighs was the same strange color; when wet with his saliva or sperm, it glistened nearly violet.

Rose was thin and lithe, the upper part of her body almost boyish in the hollowness of its shoulders and collarbones, its small, vivid nipples, the subtle framework of ribs visible beneath skin white as parchment. But her hips were wide and strong, and her ass was as round and heavy as fruit, delectable. With the tips of his fingers Anthony brushed her cheek, then ran his hand down the side of her neck and cupped the small swell of her breast in his palm. The nipple puckered at his touch, and Rose opened her eyes: all great black pupil and glittering purple iris, hectic even at the moment of awakening. Huge, wild eyes, feral eyes.

"How long did I sleep?" she demanded.

"A couple of hours."

He expected her to ask, "How many more days do we have?" It was the only thing that disturbed the flow of their time together each year: halfway through the week, Rose would start counting off the days until they had to part, then the hours, and finally the last, excruciating minutes before Anthony boarded a plane for the other side of the continent, back to the wealthy wife he could not bring himself to leave, and she hopped a southbound Greyhound. The diminishing time seemed to twist inside her, to cause her actual physical anguish. At the end she could not even bear to lose time to sleep. If Anthony slept, she would sit awake watching him, studying the tightly drawn, compact lines of his face and body as if memorizing them for another year.

But she didn't ask the question, not this time; just pulled him down to her.

Her voice became thick with sex, clotted, like slow southern sap, like sweet oil. Her pleading sobs and moans were curiously muted, as if her strongest emotions burned pure and hot enough to drain the air of oxygen. "Come into me," Anthony heard her say faintly. "Come to me now. *Come into me now . . .*"

He descended into the moist, fragrant world of the bed and the body of his lover. Nothing mattered but Rose's tongue in his mouth, his hand between her legs, sliding up and down the wet length of her cleft, then sinking two fingers deep inside her, where it felt like the slow rippling muscles of a snake. She groaned way down in her throat and moved hard against his hand, forcing it deeper. For a moment his fingers found her rhythm, heightened it.

When he pulled away, Rose caught at his hand. Anthony brought her fingers to his mouth, kissed their small, sharp tips. Then he pulled her legs wide. *A passage more ancient than the river, with an ocean-tide pull* . . . He lowered his face to her, ran his tongue around the swelling bud, then let it slide into her ruby depths. Her smell was like flowers crushed in seawater, her taste like fruit ripened and slightly fermented. Anthony thought he would die before he could drink enough of it.

"Inside me," she hissed. He could not disobey. He tumbled Rose onto her back and found the heart of her womb with one liquid thrust. Her scream displaced sound, her movement, time. He might have spent minutes or hours inside her before his orgasm finally brought him a sense of release, however false.

They lay tangled together, too spent to speak. Anthony's penis felt as if it were melting inside her. In fact, his whole body felt ready to melt. The slight, pleasant numbness he'd felt earlier had grown to vast proportions. It weighed down his body, his thoughts. His brain buzzed dully. He hadn't drunk enough to feel this woozy, had *never* drunk enough to feel like this.

Rose looked at him, her huge eyes shining, and smiled.

"I'm afraid you won't be going back home to your wife this year. I get so lonely, Anthony. I haven't painted anything for months and months. I spent all that time perfecting my recipe . . . my potion."

Anthony tried to react, to question her; he wanted to get up and get some distance between them, to get some air and clear his head. But he could not twitch a finger or an eyelid, could scarcely remember his own name. He was paralyzed.

She leaned over, held up a bottle of the champagne and whispered, *"Magie Noire,* darling. Black magic. *Bufo marinus* . . . itching pea . . . children's bones . . . and datura, the *concombre zombi."*

Zombie, he heard dumbly. The word ought to mean something to him, but he couldn't think what.

"I don't have much money, but that's all right. You can go out and work while I paint. You can do anything I tell you to do . . . and not a damned thing more, my love.

"Now come here and fuck me again," she ordered.

He would not move. He would simply refuse to move, would exert every ounce of his will to resist her. But even as he thought this, Anthony felt himself take her gently in his arms. He strained against his own treacherous musculature.

"Fuck me!" she commanded.

He looked on as if from a distance as his body propped itself up over Rose's. Unconsciously hard and ready again, he entered her and began moving in her favorite ways, without a second thought. Soon the buzzing filled his skull and eradicated all thought.

"Perfect," Rose sighed beneath him.

It Will Do
for Now

Molly Weatherfield

JONATHAN: My hotel was small, no elevator. I was glad of that. We'd sat quietly in the taxi, a little space between us. Hardly touching each other—I mean, not *not* touching, every so often one of our hands would creep over that little space. But hardly touching. Waiting. Which wouldn't have worked very well if we jammed ourselves into a little French ascenseur. I kept my eyes on her butt as we climbed to the third floor.

We were silent as we entered the room. She wandered to the window, opening it out wide, and looked out into the courtyard, the geraniums in pots, deep red and pale purple. You could hear birds, and you could see two young women taking in the fragrant, billowy sheets they'd hung out to dry that morning. "Nice," she said.

I stood next to her, facing her, and closed the curtains. I looked down at her neck, rising from the crisp, oversized white shirt under her leather jacket. She didn't have a bra on—the shirt was loose and opaque enough so that wouldn't immediately be apparent. But, trust me, I knew. I looked at the inverted triangle of chest at the neckline of that shirt, the shadow at the apex where I knew her breasts began.

I almost reached up to unbutton it. And then . . . I had a better idea.

I took off my own jacket instead, tossing it on a chair. Sweater and shirt, too. T-shirt. Her mouth twitched a little at the corners, and I kicked off my shoes, reached down and pulled off my socks.

She put her hand on my belly, and I knew she could feel it tremble. I leaned over to kiss her, lightly, quickly, just grazing her lower lip with my teeth.

She sighed, and then she backed up a step and folded her arms across her chest. Well, she'd certainly gotten into the spirit of this vacation thing. She was smiling now, full out, looking tough in her leather jacket. And her eyes were on my belt buckle. Hungry, amused, challenging. If she'd ever, during the time we'd been together, if she had ever dared look at me that way . . . well, it would have been unthinkable—she'd have gone off the chart, that informal and arbitrary chart of punishments and transgressions I'd maintained in my head. Arrive late at my house, five strokes with the rattan cane, forget to address me by name, ten. . . .

Well, if I'd wanted to guarantee her (hey, and *me*) a monster erection, I guess I'd succeeded. Probably it was the memory of those beatings—coming in loud and clear amid the static of little signals she was putting out now. I fumbled with my belt, remembering those beatings, using them to keep myself focused. Tossing aside my pants, pulling off my shorts. And then there was nothing for me to do but stand there and submit to her appraising gaze.

"Well," she murmured, "you're still a very beautiful man, Jonathan. And you're right—it's crazy how little I know about you in some ways. Like how old are you anyway?"

"Thirty-eight," I answered, trying to sound casual. *Still* . . . the word had a cold edge to it.

She nodded noncommittally. "Help me take off these boots, please?"

She sat on the bed and I knelt to take off the stiff, pretty new boots with their intricate, multicolor stitching. She took off her jacket but sat still. I pushed her skirt up. She had on long black stockings, a black garter belt, no panties. Slender, very white thighs. Her pubic hair was short, like the hair on her head; they'd shaved her cunt, the hair was just now growing back. The black stripes of the unadorned garter belt drew the stockings up very high, very taut. The whole effect was so ambiguously situated between whorish and conventlike—after a year, did she really remember so precisely what I liked? Or maybe it was just what Constant—the guy who'd bought her at the auction—liked.

I undid the garters. And then I put my head down and grabbed the embroidered edge of a stocking with my teeth. I could feel her thigh under my lips and I slowly pulled the stocking down, my mouth sliding over her knee, her calf, her foot. I kissed her bare instep and then I did the same thing for the other stocking, the other leg, the other foot. She had just the slightest, heartstopping trace of a purple welt on that second thigh, not quite healed—I lingered on it. It made me want to eat her alive.

I reached for the hook of the garter belt, pulled it softly, and it fell away. The little black miniskirt was made of some stretchy fabric. It was easy to pull off, and she helped me, lifting her ass slightly. I pushed her back on the bed, very gently, so that she was still sitting up, and straddled her. And, much more slowly than I wanted to, I unbuttoned her shirt, while she kissed my neck, my shoulders.

And there she finally was, and I stopped caring about what she might want. I fell on top of her, grabbing her ass, tonguing her breasts, moving her up to the pillows. Later for sensitive lover tricks like the stockings; at that moment all I wanted to do was get as much of her into my hands as possible, before I got as much of me as possible into her. She moved against me, wrapping her arms around me, arching her back, so that our fronts were pressed together, and then I was in her, her legs around my neck, her hands on my chest. I stroked in and out, long, slow strokes. I wanted to last forever, I was afraid I wasn't going to last at all, I guess I lasted long enough—to hear her cry out, anyway, loudly.

And afterward, after a space of time that I can't describe, I felt her come, once more, just a last little one—she was hardly moving at all except inside. And then I heard—maybe felt—a low laugh in her throat, bubbling up from somewhere deep inside her. I'd forgotten that laugh, but now I remembered it—her laugh that meant when it was especially good there was always something just a little ridiculous about it.

She hadn't let me hear that little laugh too often. And rightly—I would have had to punish her for it. So, as she'd gotten to know me better and had become cleverer, she'd only let me hear it when she knew that I'd fucked myself into a stupor—that I was too wiped out to whale her for such flagrant disrespect. I liked hearing that laugh again. And I'd like punishing her for it. Not right now, of course, but soon, soon enough. For now, though, it was good enough that she was here, under me. For now, anyway.

■

CARRIE: We must have fallen asleep. Because the next thing I remembered was the sun coming through the curtains. It was low, and the light was pink. Sunset.

I was lying on my side. Jonathan was behind me, one arm flung across me, his hand on my breast. Long, tapering fingers, beautifully articulated bones spreading out from his wrists. My skin looked pink in the light, pale pink against the olive of the back of his hand. I could probably bend my head down to kiss that hand if I tried, I thought.

I wanted to, a little. To show him how good I was feeling. Not that I'd exactly been keeping it to myself, but still. It was all so luxurious, so warm and indolent. During the past year I'd occasionally thought of his hands, the bones in his wrists. They'd drift, these images, unbidden, into my thoughts, late at night, perhaps when the day's challenges had overwhelmed my defenses. I'd remember the weight of them on my body, their elegant curve around my breasts. And I'd remembered correctly, too, I thought. I'll move, I'll do something soon, I kept promising myself. But right at that moment I didn't want to do anything but lie there with the slanted light of that sunset lengthening against us on the bed. Well, perhaps I could shift backward a little, a little closer to his hip . . .

His hand tightened. He was beginning to wake up. I lifted my head and licked his fingers. I inched my ass closer to him. He turned a little, and I could feel his cock—still a little moist, but not yet hard—jumping a little against me.

I turned a little more so that my ass was directly against his cock, and he moved his other hand under me, reaching for my other breast. He kissed the back of my neck. I arched my back, stroking his belly, his stiffening cock, with my ass until I felt him move into its furrow. Slowly now. I moved back and forth—teeny movements really, stomach contractions, rotate an inch forward, an inch back—while he grew against me.

"Okay," he whispered, and we moved onto our knees, him on top of me.

The bed had a headboard. I grasped it. I didn't want him to have to balance on his hands. I didn't want him ever to take his hands off my breasts. He spread his fingers a little, enough to catch my nipples between them, and then tightened. And while I gasped at the pinch, while I lost a beat in thralldom to that sensation and he felt me lose that beat, he moved his cock against my asshole.

I wasn't ready for him, quite. He knew that, he'd been looking for that moment. He wanted to feel me yielding to him. He pushed slowly and I gave way, arching my back, opening to him, forgetting everything except that yielding, that opening, that always-frightening letting loose.

It hurt a little on every thrust. (It always does. I hope it always will.) I pushed back against him, making it hurt just a little more. He moved more deeply into me, and I began to cry out guttural, unrecognizable sounds that came from deep inside. I teased myself a little. It hurts, I thought, I have to ask him to stop. Yeah, right. I felt myself opening my mouth and trying to shape some words—*please,* or *slower,* or something—and the words lost their form and became cries of pain, of pleasure, of desire and delight, and I heard and felt myself coming loudly.

He moved his hands from my breasts to the wall above the headboard, leaning heavily forward, surrendering to his own loud orgasm. Somehow we slid down together to the bed, my sweaty back plastered to him while I felt him shrink slowly in me.

I began to believe, for the first time that day, that I was actually here. With Jonathan. In a hotel with faded blue shutters at the windows and geraniums in the courtyard. There were lavender and lemon vervain in a vase on the dresser. And the sheets of our bed still smelled of sun and fresh air. Well, of sweat, too, and of cum. Wonderful, I thought. Well, but right at that moment, I was finding just about everything wonderful. No fantasies, no reciting his little letter to myself as though it were a catechism, no dreams about romantic endings. Just this lovely, wonderful, all-enveloping lust. Vacation. No rules, no plans, no idea what would come next. It would do for now. It would do quite nicely.

Two Cars in a Cornfield

William Harrison

There were eight of us, and we all worked hard in our high school classes, played on the teams and kept things normal with outsiders, including our parents, so our secret stayed intact.

The girls were Dana, Sylvie, Joanna and Tibby. The guys were Brad, Chase, Tim and me. They called me Kipper in those days, a name that came out of the baseball squad, who knows what it meant. Even my father called me that after a while.

My father also seemed concerned about who my steady girl might be. One night at supper he started again, saying, "Okay, I think Dana's your best gal, am I right?"

"We're all just good friends," I explained. "You know, for all the movies and ball games. We don't want to get serious."

"That's perfectly smart of you," my mother put in.

"True, you don't want anything complicated," my father admitted, drawing on his heavier baritone, the voice he sometimes used at town meetings.

"Real friendship is wonderful," said my mother. "You're all intelligent kids. Romantic love is probably a silly idea to you."

I nodded with relief. The roast beef that night was cooked rare, the best cut. We ate well at our house because my father owned the big market and butcher shop in our little Missouri town. He was putting on weight that year, moving toward the heart attack that took him away.

"Can I use the delivery car again this weekend?" I asked that night.

"One accident or one ticket and you don't use it anymore," he reminded me, as always. I delivered groceries for my father's store, but we went through this ritual every weekend. Most of our group had driven farm tractors or pickup trucks from the time we were thirteen years old, driving illegally, covering the whole county and beyond, and our parents gave us permission—because of our good grades, our mainstream lives, our innocence.

At school the eight of us agreed there would be no meaningful glances between us, no touching, no bragging, no confessions if caught and no falling in love with just one of the partners. Looking back, wondering how it all happened, I remember all the guys as slender and muscular. Both Dana and Joanna would become school queens although Sylvie and Tibby in their separate ways were even more stunning.

Things began the night we drove over to Nevada, a nearby town. Afterward, driving back from the movie, Chase and Tibby started undressing each other in the backseat. I gripped the wheel of the old Chevy, stunned, as Dana kept peering over at them and breaking into nervous laughter.

"You keep doing that," she warned them, "and I'm going to keep watching." She nudged me, jerking her head toward them and trying to get her giggling under control.

"They're in a trance!" Dana squealed, and she clawed at my shirt, urging me to stop the car and to become a spectator with her. After another mile I pulled in to a roadside picnic area, stopped, turned off the headlights, and turned around. By this time Tibby had shed the rest of her clothes, and I found myself addled with the sight of nakedness. Dana began to gently stroke my backside. Dumbstruck, empty of thought or language, I didn't know what more to do until

Dana moved against me, making her own signals clear, then as I started unbuttoning her denim shirt I thought, hey, this is it, we're all virgins but this is it. This is ignition. The endowment inside her bra filled up my puny imagination.

Chase made deep groaning noises.

It was a moonless April evening: the hawks silent in the new leaves of the trees, the fields alive with the smells of earth and honeysuckle.

"Go ahead, touch me there," Dana whispered, and the car became hot with movement and starglow. We opened the car doors that faced the nearby woods. As Dana and I started our awkward contortions, Chase and Tib reached a loud crescendo. Moments later they leaned forward, looking over the seat to become our grinning audience. We became exhibitionists in our first coupling, oblivious, proud of our bodies, part of the wonder of the night, mysterious and reckless.

As I emptied myself into Dana's clumsy thrusts, she arched herself, reaching up, her heavy breasts flattened, stretching out as if in a delicious yawn, and found Chase in her arms. They kissed in a long, delirious, wanton hello as I found Tibby's eyes fixed in mine. A capricious tick of the psychological clock in us all: Tibby held out her hand and I took it. The girls passed one another as they climbed over the car seat, then we all groaned and started again. Tibby's slender body became a new intoxicant and she came to me like an oiled, experienced woman.

Half an hour later we stood and sat outside the car, naked, cooling ourselves, our thoughts obliterated. Chase, our quarterback, our first baseman, the friend who worked in my father's grocery store at my side, leaned against the old Chevy with his muscular arms folded across his chest, a two-hundred-pound god, serene, as if the night belonged to him. I sat on the fender with my arms around both girls, listening: I could hear the wheeling of the stars overhead, the cosmic winds, mortal voices from other planets, and I felt both drained and wise.

Occasionally, a car passed on the highway below us. Tibby addressed us in that throaty voice of hers. She was our intellectual, the debate squad member, a writer of notebooks that no one was ever allowed to read, and she was musing on what had just happened, yet in that special way of hers. "Now I'm sixteen years and one hour old," she sighed, and I loved her voice.

Then a car cruised up beside us in the darkness and stopped. It happened with Tibby's sighing observation covering the soft sound of the approaching tires. Arriving with its headlights off, it was there with us before we had a chance to be startled, so we were naked, philosophical, and caught.

"Kipper?" asked a voice, and it was Brad. The old Dodge had entered the roadside park in darkness, its occupants looking for a spot to make out, and they had recognized my mottled white Chevy—the one I made grocery deliveries in, its license plate forever tilted.

"Chase?" came the soft whisper of a girl's awed voice.

The faces of Brad, Tim, Sylvie and Joanna peered at us and we heard our names repeated in sudden amusement. Looking back, though, it was Chase who made the difference. He stood as indifferent as a marble statue, beautiful and muscular, his penis still swollen, arms crossed, and only later did Joanna and Sylvie admit to what desire, jealousy, and yearning they suddenly felt. I wanted to cover myself, but Tib and Dana stood their ground, so there I was: trapped in the naked tableau, seeing the gesture through, taking my unspoken instructions to stay cool. In any case, Sylvie decided that we wouldn't outdo her. She slid out of the car, raised her arms, and pushed her fingers into her dark red hair. For a moment she struck a dancer's pose, legs slightly apart in an arrogant stance. Then she somehow reached back and drew her cotton dress straight up over her head. She wasn't wearing a bra and she came out of her panties in a neat, liquid movement. No one said anything.

■

Twenty years ago, all this.

Our town was small then and now, with a population of less than two thousand, and our families lived in the snug values of times maybe thirty years before that time, in years that hardly seemed touched by assassinations, Vietnam, or any part of the sexual revolution. Middle America: we grew up on church suppers, sports, fair play and honest labor. Each house around the square stood up white and pious, part of a stubborn theology of a time that had long ago passed away.

What set the eight of us apart in those strange days? We experimented with a little booze, sure, but found it ineffective and stupid compared to the inebriations of the flesh. None of us were radicals. We liked each other because we were all psychologically straight without annoying tics or dark corners. Tibby, later, in one of her more psychological moments, offered that it was just all the movies we went to see. Into our consciousness came Michael Corleone, Sally Bowles, James Bond, the shark from *Jaws,* Woody Allen, Peter Sellers, and a hundred couples who talked dirty and did it onscreen. Locked in the middle of the continent, we were hooked on movies, and our parents often relented and let us drive over to Nevada—and, later, places like Fort Scott or Joplin that they didn't know about—to see movies. We became free, Tibby suggested, because life was out there to be seen. Maybe so: made wild and sophisticated by the celluloid stories that flickered through our heads.

"You want to drive all the way to Fort Scott for what? For an Australian movie? I didn't know they made Australian movies," said my father one evening. "And I can't believe the parents of all those girls put up with your late hours, either."

"We just go to movies, get burgers, and talk, that's all we ever do," I argued. "Nobody drinks. We drive slow. All the other parents trust us."

That won my mother to my side again. "We trust you, too," she insisted. "But do try to get home a little earlier."

After the ball game with Jericho Springs—I played shortstop, got a hit, and Chase whacked a homer—we drove to the hillside at the far end of Brad's farm. We could see for miles from that little hillside, so could easily spot the headlights of an approaching car. This was soon after our first meeting, but already our inhibitions had vanished in a barrage of dirty language and sexual acrobatics. We watched each other and had contests. We even gave each other anatomy lessons, huddling together as a group once or twice to pay elaborate attention to demonstrations. We howled with laughter or groaned in unison. Blankets and pillows appeared. Hygiene and the use of the Pill became topics and it became a frenzied class, weekend-night class, we called it, and there were no rules for those who participated or watched.

One night we played hide and seek, but that proved uncomfortable—the young corn stalks raking our thighs and butts. Tim, who was loudest among us, soon settled down, and after the sex we soon started settling into one car, crowding together, to talk. The subjects ranged from life on other planets to the dreary lives of our parents. Dracula. Mick Jagger. Religion. Bums who took drugs.

I was the astronomy freak and out there beneath the stars where the heavens opened up to us we talked about the speed of light, the formation of the galaxies, and the nature of infinity—the concept beyond concepts. It was all teenage excitement and speculation: only a few random facts, but intense.

"Black holes suck," Tim offered wistfully, like a line of melancholy wisdom, and we broke out in laughter.

"Men are just these tiny lost sperm, swimming along in the cosmos," Tibby later offered.

"That's for sure," Joanna agreed.

In the midst of these celestial discussions, Brad wanted to know if any of us could get another erection by just thinking about sex. This was after we had all exhausted ourselves. We sat in two naked clusters, front and back in the Chevy, trying to talk our way back into the rational life that would move us back toward our separate houses before dawn.

"No visual aids," Brad said. "Without looking at the girls. Just close your eyes, concentrate, and get it up."

"I can only do that in study hall," Chase muttered, and we howled again with laughter.

"I've been laid four times tonight, but I think I can do it," Tim asserted.

"None of you can do it," Sylvie added, challenging us.

Standing with our backs to the parallel cars, shutting our eyes tight, the girls acting as judges, we tried to get our lewdest thoughts collected. It was a short contest that we all lost. After that the girls sat in the Dodge discussing Warren Beatty and the guys slumped in the Chevy talking sports.

At the end of the school year we decided who would take whom to the prom. I asked for Tibby because I figured she'd keep up the conversation all evening. Other classmates invited various ones of us to get drunk, to drag race, to go skinny dipping and to meet at the mill in Bolivar for breakfast, but we all knew where we'd spend the night when the official fun ended: back in the cornfield, folding silken dresses and rented tuxedoes into the trunks of the cars, going at each other again.

On prom night we had the first of our several fantasy sessions. In time, we played nurses and interns, bosses and secretaries, and models and photographers.

That summer all the boys and two of the girls worked at part-time jobs while Chase and I played summer-league baseball, yet we all managed to keep up the rendezvous in the cornfield. With summer came the first few small complications, too. Two yeast infections. Then Sylvie was grounded for yelling at her mother, though her parents forgave her in six days. The carburetor in the Dodge went out and Tim's parents promised to fix it, but didn't. All of us found a rebuilt one and struggled to install it.

One day Tibby, who worked mornings at our dinky little town library, brought me a book on astronomy. Telescope photos, mostly, and a few artist's conceptions that are now long outdated. The birth of the stars, all that. I was loading up cardboard boxes for my noon delivery when she stopped off with the book. We stood beside the meat locker as Chase, sweeping the floor, gave us a knowing glance, raising an eyebrow as if to say, hey, no flirting.

Tibby asked if I wanted her to make deliveries with me.

"What for?" I asked, being dumb.

"Just to do it, okay?"

"Sure, I guess so," I answered, and I looked over to see if Chase was watching us.

"Then I'll wait in the Chevy," she said lightly, and she went off toward the front of the store with a nice sway, waving at my father before she went out the door. She would circle back to the car in the alley, I knew, and the deception gave me a charge.

"You two got something up?" Chase asked, coming over with his broom. He wasn't smiling.

"Nah, everything's cool," I told him, and I showed him the book and explained why she stopped by, lying to my best friend, yet it was a lie in the future tense, a lie of possibilities and uncertainties.

Tibby and I made three deliveries in town, then took the back road out toward the Grandy farm, a gravel road that still winds along the curves of the Osage River. Tibby pulled up her knees and hugged them as we drove. She talked about how in two years she'd be at the University of Missouri, then how in two years after that she'd take a junior year abroad, traveling around Europe, and how she planned to be a journalism major, then a writer different from a journalist, not that she knew exactly what sort. As I drove I glanced over at her long legs, the most perfect long legs. She was like a movie librarian, one of those who suddenly takes off her glasses and lets down her hair to reveal that she's really the most beautiful girl in the movie, not just some dog librarian. Seriously good looking, Tim once said about her, but also seriously and unfortunately smart.

Driving along as she talked, I thought how I watched her that first night at the roadside park. In a corner of my thoughts, she was Chase's girl because they started it all. So why did she ask to come with me today? And what was I feeling?

The summer grew suddenly more complicated.

She helped me carry the two boxes of groceries onto the porch of the farmhouse where Mrs. Grandy met us. We were led inside where the old man sat drooling in his wheelchair in a room filled with bric-a-brac, doilies, musty rugs, and creaky furniture. We accepted a sugar cookie warm from the oven. Small talk. Tibby asked all the right questions about the old man's condition and said all the appropriate things. Meanwhile, I felt my chest tighten so I couldn't breathe.

We waved goodbye and drove away. Near the river we found a bower of trees. A curtain of lush July foliage blocked the view from the road, hiding us, and the strong midsummer fragrance of the river filled the car.

"Let's do oral," Tibby said, grinning wickedly. As I turned off the engine, I could only look ahead at the river and nod. It was something the eight of us had never done and I wasn't sure, for my part, how to go about it.

She kissed me, later, with my own taste in her mouth, a kiss like nothing I had ever known, possessive and softly fierce. She was breathing hard and laughing, saying, "Oh god, that's a first, oh my," and I felt unusually successful in my performance, joining her in her laughter.

Afterward, she started talking again. I suggested that we should maybe put our clothes on and I had the overpowering desire to get out of there, but she went on about writing and traveling the world.

"I mean it," I urged her. "Some fishermen might come along. It's the middle of the day."

She might become a novelist, she told me, or a foreign correspondent.

While I buttoned up my shirt, she fixed those dark eyes in mine. "But you'll always be my first love," she told me. "Always."

"Who me? How could I be? You did it with Chase first."

This reply, I realized later, was wildly inappropriate.

"Chase?"

"Sure, at the roadside park that first night."

"What are you talking about?"

"Well, isn't he, technically, your first love?"

"Only my first lay," she corrected me. "Besides, Chase will always have three or four girls wherever he goes. And, believe me, he won't go far. But you will. You're different."

"How's that?" I asked, and I really wanted to know.

"Because you're sensitive. The most sensitive boy I've ever known."

"Sensitive?" It was a word I wasn't sure of, but certainly more in fashion in those days than now.

"Kipper, you're on a completely different wavelength from all the rest of us, don't you know that?"

I didn't know it, yet I quickly wanted to believe it. I only knew that my name was Kipper Jones, and that until this moment I had been a shortstop, a pal, a good son, a sex machine, a movie addict, and a part-time delivery boy for my father's store.

"You're capable of real love, Kipper, don't you even know that?

And I need love, as it turns out. A true heart. I mean, god, we have another whole year of high school before we can get out of this town. And if we don't take love where we find it, god, well, I think I'd just break in half."

Mesmerized by Tibby's husky voice and the strangeness of her words, I just looked at her. Clearly, she was the most beautiful naked object in the world. How could I want more? Yet I wanted to speak about the eight of us, the rules, the magic of the last three months.

Then she addressed all that.

"The eight of us won't last the summer," she predicted.

I made some slight gesture with my hand as if I knew that, too, but I didn't.

"There are lots of little signs, Kipper. I mean, Brad smells a lot like manure these days, and not all of us are happy with him. And Dana, well, she's fragile. She might go goofy on us. And Chase is already looking around. I think he wants to bang every female in school, including Miss Reinhardt in gym class."

Who among us, I wanted to say, doesn't?

"Don't get dressed," she said, sighing. "Come here." She pulled me close and opened herself to me again. "Besides, I don't want to share you with anybody. And now we can do it all the time. Twice a day all summer. Think about it. Three times, if that's what you want, then every day during next school year."

She made a strong argument for love.

"Also, we can talk. I mean you really listen to me, but you also have lots to say, that's why you're special. And maybe we can sleep together. God, I'd love to sleep with you all night. Let me think about it, I'll plan something. Wait, that hurts. Hold it. There, now that's better."

As she talked on, I once again managed to turn myself into molten lava.

We drove back from the Osage River as a couple.

When I saw Chase back at the store, I worried he suspected. That night in the game against Carthage I made my first two errors of the season, booting one easy grounder that I took on the chin. Distractions. The whole team became sullen after the loss and I felt guilty. Still, Chase didn't say anything.

To my amazement we went back to the cornfield that next Friday night, having told our parents that we were driving to Fort Scott to see a Jack Nicholson movie. That whole evening I kept watching Tibby for a signal, expecting her to make an announcement, but she seemed equally wild for all of us. Then, afterward, we all talked music: Tower of Power, Lynyrd Skynyrd, ZZ Top, Stevie Wonder, Aerosmith, Cat Stevens, and all the others. Everybody had a different favorite, so minor arguments broke out, then at last I was alone with Tibby in the front seat of the Dodge while Tim and Dana rutted away in the backseat with their usual noisiness.

"What's going on?" I asked Tib. "What were we talking about there at the river? You said you didn't want to share me."

"Ssh, not now," she replied. "Let's just do it."

While we made out, the title of an album kept buzzing in my head, a Doobie Brothers title: *What Once Were Vices Are Now Habits.* Was there a song by that title, too? Half a moon rose up over the horizon, giving us its lunatic light. Later on I stretched out on top of the Chevy, confused, and nobody even bothered to say anything to me. The music deep inside me was definitely funk.

In the days that followed I suspected Tibby might be giving all the guys special treatment on the side. A clever girl and not an impossible thought. I also decided that Tibby, not my friend Chase, had caused all this to happen, and that what occurred that first night in the roadside park she had orchestrated. She was the one who drove Chase crazy, the one who took off her clothes first, and maybe now, I decided, she manipulated all of us.

Then she phoned to explain.

"Joanna's parents are making her go with them to the Grand Canyon for a whole month. A big summer camping trip. Can you believe it? So that'll break up the group, but also Chase is going to be on the all-star team which means he'll go away for that. What do you call it?"

"The All-State Tour," I answered sadly, wishing that I was better than a .256 hitter with a good glove.

"So why should we take the blame for breaking things up? It's happening anyway. That's what I needed to tell you, but couldn't."

"It seemed to me you were just jacking my emotions around," I complained.

"I meant what I said about this summer. Three times a day if you want me, Kip. We can go back to our spot by the river. There's also a little room in the library I want to show you. And I can get the key to my folks' cabin. By the time everybody gets back at the end of the summer, we'll be together. Just the two of us. It'll be natural. Just one of the things that happened."

"You seemed to enjoy yourself the other night," I accused her.

"I tried to be a good sport," she countered. "Don't be jealous. Oh, god, Kip, I can't wait to get you alone, I really can't."

When I finally got off the phone I passed my mother in the hallway. She might have been listening in, and asked me who I was talking to.

"Tibby," I said with a sigh. "I guess we're in love."

Tibby's predictions came true. Chase was voted onto the All Star squad that finally played a big game in Kansas City. Joanna, crying and begging to be let off, went with her parents. "The goddamned Grand Canyon," she wailed. "Isn't there a movie about it? Can't they just go to a movie and see it?"

We had a last Saturday night together. It was the night I sort of fell for Sylvie. In the backseat of the Dodge she held me close, breathing in my ear, and said quietly, "Kipper, you're the best. Not like anybody else. Gentle and—" Sensitive, I almost said to help her out. She began to cry.

"It's out there, so huge," she whimpered, growing small in my arms. "Life. It's going to gobble us up, isn't it?"

Sylvie was pure feeling. Years later she would be a dancer, dazzling, and that night I kissed her slender neck, watching the tears edge down her cheeks in graceful rivulets. She was soft in a way, I knew, that Tibby would never be.

That night a sadness befell us, a sexual melancholy—although none of us were capable of naming it. We spread out blankets and piled on, all eight of us, our bodies moving over one another in a slow adagio of touching. Only Tibby and I knew it was goodbye, that idyll, that last long kiss of summer, and we didn't tell what we knew, just as none of us would ever tell others in that little town or the strangers who couldn't understand out there in that huge world of which Sylvie spoke.

As I grew older and read some of the books that awaited me, I learned of naked children in the far islands who embraced their sexual lives far sooner than we did—short, happy interludes of abandon before the little girls became pregnant and the brief cycles of romance ended. It was true in many places—along the frozen tundra of the Arctic circle and in the deepest thickets of Africa—children thrusting themselves into nature where lust, unchecked, becomes curiously innocent. If the eight of us were out of step with the normalcies of a small town in the midcontinent, the larger questions remain: what is right, what is natural, what is true, and who speaks with authority about any of it?

Anyway, the ironies overtook us. I became the writer, not Tibby. She became a lawyer in Chicago, married with three children. Brad and Dana were once engaged, then married others. Everyone finally married, except for Chase who kicked around the minor leagues for a few years, then joined the Marines and was killed in the skirmish we now call Desert Storm. Friendly fire brought him down.

A dozen years after we left high school I took Sylvie out to dinner in San Francisco. She was the lead dancer in a West Coast ballet troupe, and I was on a political assignment for my magazine, when I saw her photo in a newspaper and managed to get her phone number at the theater.

We sat in an open restaurant on the wharf, the one that serves such good abalone, and we talked about everybody. She asked about Chase.

"You didn't hear?"

She read my face and tears pooled in her eyes. I told her the few facts I knew. "Oh Kipper," she said softly, and she looked out over the bay. No one had called me that for years.

We sat there holding hands after the meal. I was newly married and she was engaged, and we ached for each other.

"Was it terrible what we did?" she asked me.

"No, I believe it was good for us all," I answered truthfully, though perhaps she didn't quite believe this.

"We were so young," she said, managing a smile. "Sometimes I think nobody was ever that young."

Still holding hands we strolled the wharf while the gulls circled and cried above us. It occurred to me once more that I might have missed Sylvie, missed the great love of my life, but sex, after all, is a mystery; we can possibly be honest about everything except sex, we can know ourselves and not understand it, we can be completely worldly, yet innocent in its wake and impulse.

Sylvie was beautiful and elegant as we walked in silence and I was proud to be at her side. I brought her fingers to my lips and kissed them. In our thoughts, I know, we were in a long-ago time, in that strange American twilight before so many of the brutal vulgarities, hidden in the cornstalks, moving from the old Dodge to the old Chevy, back and forth in a burning game that somehow never burned us out, eight of us, four couples, our sixteen-year-old bodies aglow, far away.

Maryann

Marc Levy

Martin saw the ad in a magazine, plucked from one of several tin boxes chained, "handcuffed," he had said to himself, to a traffic light on 7th Ave. He was in the habit of reading them, and kept a stack of fresh one dollar bills in a desk drawer. *Insert your response in an envelope. Do not seal it. Put the box number you are responding to on the front of the envelope. Put a stamp on the envelope. Now place the envelope and two dollars into a second envelope. Seal the second envelope. Address it to Sity Singles, PO Box 4041, Ansonia Station, New York, NY 10025. Make sure you have placed sufficient postage on the second envelope. For multiple responses, repeat the above.*

Martin was forty-four years old and straight, but he read them all. Women Seeking Men, Men Seeking Men, Women Seeking Women, Couples, Anything Goes. Afterward, he would return to the straight section. On a good day he would think to himself, well, you never know. Bad days he was less positive about himself. He scanned.

"SWF, 40s, attractive, well traveled, successful, outgoing, literate, enjoys Bach to Bon Jovi, museums, art, theater, culture, seeks honest, caring, successful man for committed relationship. Note, photo, phone."

Too much for me to handle, he thought, and continued to finger down the line. The uncommon epithets, those with wit or clever wordplays sometimes made him laugh. Most often it was the odd or eccentric that attracted him. His favorite was, "Yeah, yeah, I know the drill. I am woman, I am strong. Lonely SJF, 46, seeks nice guy to fill a bowl of chicken soup for. Be sane and interesting. Got a job? Great! Let's meet!"

He thought of writing her, but the ad had disappeared the following month. Martin felt he had missed the opportunity of a lifetime.

"So far so bad," he said to the lead painted walls. In five months he had moved six times since returning from a year's travel in Asia and Europe. Depressed and fragmented in the cramped and stuffy $300-a-month YMCA room, he realized it was the same as '92, when he had traveled in Central America for several months. It had taken him a year to readjust. How was it that he could leave and travel, occasionally find himself in good company for extended periods of time, then come back and *crash and burn*? Where had he heard the phrase? From a chopper pilot. After the war.

Good news, Aquarius. Your moon is in transit with Mercury. This is a good time to invest in stocks and bonds. Or buy that new 4X4 Rover you've had your eye on. Your special powers of imagination are now working for you, Aquarius. This is a great time to communicate your innovative ideas to those special persons around you.

Martin settled back onto the dismal foam bed and laughed through the haze of his anxiety. "Who you kidding, man?" he said to the four plaster walls and brown wooden floor. The words echoed off the rusted footlocker two feet from his head. Outside, in the firetrap hallway, someone shouted street directions into the pay phone.

"Left, bitch. Two blocks south, then hang a damn right. You got that? Bitch! Ho! You got it?" It was Larry the Crackhead speaking with his girlfriend.

The phone slammed down hard. A moment later, coins dropped into the machine; a deep voice spoke softly, perhaps to a wife. There were fifteen transient men on the floor. After six weeks Martin had grown used to the human parade.

He turned the page and continued down the list of Women Seeking Men, reading just the first line of each ad.

"Let me be the chocolate icing on your thick fudge cake!"

"SWF vegan sex goddess seeks thick hunk of dark meat."

"SWCFNS seeks Clint Eastwood lookalike with Richard Nixon values for LTR."

He smirked. They were hilarious, they flowed like poems, and took his mind off himself.

"The chocolate icing on your thick fudge cake," he mouthed, tasting the word play.

Outside, Martin recognized the shuffle step of Jeremy the ex-marine, intent on his evening toilette. Sixty pounds overweight, a chain-smoker, the USMC bulldog tattoo still visible on his bloated arm, Jeremy collected welfare, visited his parole officer twice weekly.

Once, Martin had heard Jeremy talk to himself in front of the cracked mirrors over the communal sinks.

"Good-looking corpse . . . gonna make a good looking corpse . . ." he repeated over and over. He had fought in Korea. He drank.

Martin wanted to speak to him, another vet. Jeremy kept to himself.

Fucking Marines, Martin thought. The Cav saved your ass beaucoup times.

■

"Sexy senior seeks gentleman for the company of his pleasure."

"People say I have a lot to give but I give too much of myself."

Martin read on. About women in search of white knights and mensches, about candlelit dinners and all life has to offer, about ballet, sailing, opera, hot times, about requirements like "must like cats" and "unslim"; he ran his finger once more over the black-and-white column of babble.

". . . the company of his pleasure. You will not be disappointed."

He put the paper down, closed his eyes, recalled past encounters. Judy had written back immediately, eager to meet him as soon as she was out of prison.

"The police pulled me over because of a broken taillight. When they opened the hood they found ten kilos. But it wasn't mine. Honest. Anyway, I'll be getting out soon and would really like to meet you, Martin. You sound SO interesting." He'd thrown the scented letter and soft-porn photo into the garbage.

Bonnie promised high heels and negligees. But when they spoke by phone she rattled off a list of unquaint conditions, including $200 each time they had sex. "Well, no thanks," said Martin. "That's your choice," she had countered. "Have a pleasant day," he rejoined, then hung up.

Ann from Canada sent a computer-generated letter, the dot matrix crotch shot poised over, "I *really* want to meet you, Martin Berry, 1482 River Street, Tarrytown, New York 10591, USA. But first I'd like you to see my *very* personal video, only $19.95 plus $4.95 for shipping and handling." He called the postal inspectors in both countries.

Once, three weeks before leaving the country for Central America, he wrote to a woman advertising in a literary magazine. "While the mouse is away the cat will play. Forties SWF has nine months alone while husband is on sabbatical. Seeking good lover." Martin expressed his desire to make love slowly; foreplay was most important. He had a fondness for standing in front of full-length mirrors and undressing women while he stood behind. "I'll raise your skirt up and enter you, your breasts cupped in my hands. Would you like that? I'll kiss you everywhere. Where do you like to be kissed? Afterward, when we're spent, I'll kiss you to sleep." He sent off the note and forgot about it.

Her reply came ten days after the plane tickets for Guatemala arrived.

Dear Martin,

Of the forty-one responses I received, yours was the only one that was straightforward and to the point. I too enjoy lovemaking standing up, but seated as well, and standing face to face, and in the bath. Martin, I would love to see you. Please call me soon to arrange our first meeting.

He wondered what to do. Stay, and lose the chance to travel? She seemed sincere. He wrote her the truth and departed a week later.

■

Martin carefully circled the oblong box. "Sexy Senior." She can't be *that* old, he reassured himself.

Maryann called a week later. Her voice reminded him of cake sales and hand-knitted sweaters. They made small talk, chatted about the weather, music, their likes and dislikes, her garden, his travels.

"And what kind of work do you do, dear? To go to all those places?"

"Well, I get a pension from the Veterans Administration."

"A government pension? Goodness! Were you wounded badly?"

"Yes," he lied.

"But you can, well, you know . . ."

"Make love?" Martin said to the older woman.

"Not that I . . ."

"Yes," he said, "I can do that."

There was a momentary pause.

"You're certainly welcome to drop by," she said flawlessly.

"I'd like to," said Martin, as calmly as possible.

"Three o'clock on the 20th?" she asked.

"You can take a cab from the train station in Crestwood. I'll pay for it, dear."

"Sure," he said. "I'll see you then." He gently hung up the phone. Well, what have I got to lose? he thought. She can't be *that* old.

Martin worked out extra hard for a week. Stretching and calisthenics. His body was trim. He weighed one hundred and fifty-five pounds. Afterward, he would look at the war photo of himself that he had taped to the wall. He could see no difference between then and now. It was a good shot, taken on patrol somewhere off Tay Ninh. In it, he stood bent slightly forward, head tilted up, straining under the weight of his helmet and pack. The M16 hung sideways, a stiff metal flag draped across his chest over three bandoliers of ammo, his aid bag, the .45, his canteens of water, the fragmentation grenades. He hadn't smiled, but looked directly into the camera, the angular features shock-set and weary.

"Say cheese," Larry Roy, the point man had said.

But he hadn't, and they were ambushed soon after. And Bill Williams was dead. When Martin looked at the photo he sobbed.

■

Pools of sweat glistened on the wooden floor. Even the window had fogged up. He stepped out to shower, face flushed, sweat streaming off his body from exercise in the cubicle room.

"What you been up to, man?" Larry whined.

Martin looked directly at the pitiful human being; the endorphins always burnt a pleasant hole through his private agony.

"Fucking," he said, dead serious. "I be fucking."

The communal shower was empty. The cold water felt good on his head and body.

"You's a sick motherfucker, old man," the young addict shouted. "Sick, sick, sick." The shrill words echoed and drowned in the chip-tiled chamber. Martin grinned. The words rolled playfully off his tongue:

"The chocolate icing on your thick fudge cake."

■

He stepped out of the shower, toweled down, brushed his teeth. Why was he doing this, he asked himself, though he secretly knew. Depressed and anxious, Martin saw himself incapable of all but the simplest of casual encounters. Besides, since the war it had always been this way. Only now the government gave him money for post-traumatic stress disorder. He recalled the exam as he looked in the fractured mirror.

"All I know, I went back to Vietnam last year and something snapped."

The psychiatrist had nodded curtly, raised his eyebrows with muted concern. Martin burst into tears for the rest of the hour.

Well, he thought, at least it's a start. As far as he could tell, she lived a few towns over, had money, and they were both discreetly horny.

■

He took the train from Grand Central, got off at Crestwood, walked down to the stationery store, bought a scratch-off lottery ticket, won three dollars, and hailed a cab.

"32 Lincoln Lane," he told the driver, his voice uplifted. "Where you from, man?"

"Haiti," the cabbie said. The whites of his eyes flashed in the rearview mirror, the afternoon sun absorbed into dark-brown skin.

"Haiti," Martin repeated. "You come over here before or after Papa Doc?"

"Ahhh. I left in the time of Baby Doc, my friend. It was hard. Very bad. I am here now many years. I have a house, my wife, children; the taxi, she's mine. For me that is enough. And you? From Crestwood? I haven't seen you before."

"Tarrytown," Martin said. "Just visiting a friend."

"She's nice in Tarrytown, yes?"

"Can't complain. And Crestwood?"

"Oh, Crestwood she's very nice, indeed. What number did you say?" Martin looked out the window at the manicured lawns, the unfenced yards, the well-kept Tudor and neocolonial homes, felt the wealthy sway of the road.

"Thirty-two," he said.

"Yes, my friend. Twenty-eight, thirty . . . thirty-two she is." The driver glided to the curb of a large house with a red-painted door.

"Here," Martin said, stepping out before the man could give him change. "Have a good afternoon," he said, and snapped the door smartly shut.

"Yessss, a good afternoon," the driver said. He eyed the three-dollar tip, then sped off.

■

Maryann looked remarkably like the mother of a friend from college, which, he calculated, would make her roughly sixty-four. She *was* old. They sat at her living-room table.

"Not too long," Martin said, in answer to how long the trip had taken.

He noted her bronze-tinted hair, the over-rouged cheeks, liver-spotted hands, the deep, wrinkled lines of her face. Yet beneath the blue silk blouse, her intriguing breasts. She was not very pretty, he thought, but at least . . .

Martin had not slept with a woman in nearly two years. He imagined how he would unbutton her, take the delicate cups into his hands and mouth. He would close his eyes, suckle long and hard, recall other women, unfasten his pants, penetrate her like he had not done in so long. He suddenly recalled the Colombian prostitute in Amsterdam, where he first crashed and burned on the way home from his travels in Southeast Asia. They spoke in simple Spanish. About the price, what he wanted, and didn't: SIDA. He spoke to her easily, without shame. "I want sex first. Afterward, will you let me hold you? Will you hold me? That's all I want." She undressed, set her clothes on the back of a wooden chair, filled a plastic bowl with warm water, and placed a yellow towel nearby. After the powerful orgasm, she let him fall asleep in her arms. His head spun less for hours.

Maryann said, "Let me show you . . ." She gestured to the rest of her home.

"The bedroom?" Martin said, surprising himself.

"Why, I hadn't really thought of that, dear, but, oh, why not?" she feigned. She offered her hand; he led her upstairs to the second floor of the spacious house.

"It's the second door on the left, dear."

They undressed quickly.

"But why not?" Maryann said, looking from his limpness to her parted legs. "Why won't you do it? Honestly, dear. I thought . . . Don't you like doing that?"

Martin looked at her splayed naked on the double bed. She was spindle-legged, her belly a cummerbund of fat; it was one thing to sit in the company of this older woman, quite another to . . . still, she had well-proportioned, near Venus de Milo breasts. And it had been so fuckin' long.

Maryann rose up, touched him, drew him near. For several minutes he lay with her, not moving. She stroked the back of his neck. How did she know? That's all I want for now, old woman. Just keep doing that. I'll pay you. How much? Thirty guilders? Alright, alright, we'll do it, for God's sake. I'll probably explode. Let me hold you. Hold me. Hold me. That's all I want.

She grew restless, trailed her fingertips up and down the length of his cock.

"Oh dear, oh dear," Maryann said, fondling his splendid erection. "Martin, please."

Martin paused to collect his thoughts, to dilute the anguish of his reply. She really *is* old, he thought, and looked at the white-and-gray-spangled stubble brooding between her legs. In college, the girls had called him "Mr. Hips" in awe of his churning loins. It was something he had learned on R&R.

"Can you, well, help me out a little?" he said to the pretty young prostitute at the Five Star Hotel in Yokohama, Japan.

"I've just come out of combat. I'm not sure I can, you know . . . do it." She smiled, unzipped the black cocktail dress, removed the long-haired wig, counted his 30,000 yen, rapidly circled her hips clockwise, then counterclockwise, ground his virginity to pulp.

"Me good fuck, GI," she yawned.

He took a photo of her while she slept. The college girls went wild whenever he duplicated her technical sex.

Martin looked at Maryann. Not in a million years, baby. Not in a million fuckin' years. Still . . . her breasts were beautiful. Oh, Christ. He lay down next to her. It had been too long.

"Please, Martin, dear. Goodness, look how big you are. Don't you want to make love to me?"

"Like this?" Martin said.

With startling ease he entered her, closed his eyes, performed.

■

They awoke two hours later. He thought of the time it would take to return to Tarrytown. Cab. Train. Walk up the hill. Go to the Chinese takeout next to the VFW hall. He would give them money.

"Buddhist Delight," he would say. They would give him food.

"Goodness, it's late," Maryann said. "Are you hungry, dear? I can fix you something to eat." She began to dress.

"Not yet," Martin said. He pulled her down beside him, nestled his head between her breasts, suckled ravenously, then softly kissed the perfect nipples, the aromatic cleavage.

"Oh, Martin, dear, it's 10 o'clock. I have work tomorrow. And I have to take my pills, you know. Can we make it another time? Shall we?" She slipped forty dollars on the night table. The sight of it made him uneasy.

"I'll call a cab," Martin said, letting her go. In the lamplight he imagined she was good-looking in her youth.

"You'll call me next week, dear?"

"Yes," Martin said. He put on his coat. Maryann hugged him before he walked out the door.

"Goodness, wherever did you learn to do it like that?"

He felt her frailness push up against him. Was she reliving her youth? She was old enough to be . . . he would not admit it. He had fucked her, and fallen asleep in her arms.

"The cab's here," he said. Eyes closed, he kissed her on the cheek.

"Get home safe, dear. Have a safe trip."

■

"Four dollah," the Chinese girl said, handing him the order.

"Chopstick?" he said. She always forgot.

"Soy sauce?"

"Just one, please."

She tossed in three, plus a thimble of hot and spicy mustard and two of the sticky-goo duck sauce. It was their nightly ritual.

"Good night," Martin said.

"Goo' night, mistah," she always replied.

He went immediately to his room, wolfed the food down, slurped water from a cold-water faucet in the bathroom, brushed his teeth, lay down on the foam bed, clicked the overhead light switch off, and drifted to uneasy sleep.

Marc Levy

The Queen of Exit 17

Ernie Conrick

The nicest man I've ever seen
Was the Queen of Exit 17.

If you are driving south on Route 95 past the Mass Pike and the radio towers of Needham Heights (often called the "antenna farm" during morning traffic reports), you will see a blue sign for a rest stop, or "Service Area," near Exit 17 in Westwood. At first glance, there is not much going on at Exit 17. There are no gas stations or restaurants or public facilities there, just a half acre of asphalt and three telephone booths. To a certain type of man, however, the Exit 17 rest stop offers something very desirable—a dark corner. The dark corner is down at the far end of the parking area, toward the access ramp. It is overhung by high, thick trees, and the land there slopes downward into an even gloomier alcove that, in the dark of night, has blackness enough to cover up the most clandestine of acts.

Exit 17 is directly across the highway from the Massachusetts Correctional Facility, which the Commonwealth had the vision to build on the median strip of an interstate highway. This utilizes unused land, avoids the not-in-my-backyard mentality of nearby residents, and provides an additional barrier to escaping prisoners, who would not only have to scale the walls but also avoid the careening vehicles of maniacal Boston drivers. The floodlights that blaze incessantly from the prison reveal a ziggurat-like structure that, like some ancient Sodom, rises in slabs of concrete and barbwire atop chain-link fences. I know about Exit 17 because I seek out dark corners. I have visited enough of them, in fact, to be a connoisseur. I could write a guidebook of dark corners, with ratings for forlornness and isolation. Exit 17 is my unequalled favorite because it is wholly stark and neglected. Nobody would stop at Exit 17 for very long unless they were exhausted, drunk, or loved dark corners like me.

As you may have guessed, I go there for sex. I am a type of sexual being that has no accurate name. You can call me gay, queer, a sex addict, or any number of other names, and you still have not hit the nail on the head. I'm not quite gay, although, as you have also probably guessed, all sex at places like Exit 17 is between men. I love my wife with all my heart. I make love to her often and enthusiastically, and I'm not faking it.

The closest you can come is to say that I have an obsession with anonymous intimacy. I find a strange inebriation in showing an utter stranger the most private side of myself. There is something pure and real in a random encounter between strangers. Perhaps it is because I think that talking ruins sex. In my opinion, the less talking the better. There should be only a naked singularity of genitals, come, groans, grasping and subtle signals. To be an animal for a few moments in a dark corner, unobserved by the world—*that* is what I live for.

Can you understand? Imagine pulling off the highway in the middle of the night. Even the blinking of your turn signal may serve as a signal to others like you. Turn slowly off the highway and drive through the parking lot. Maybe there is a car or two already in the dark corner with taillights that glint in the glare of your headlights like the eyes of a raccoon. Kill the lights and glide dark and silent into the gloom. There is a car next to you and a silhouette in its front seat. Shadows dance as cars pass by on the road. The silhouette shifts so that you are now two silhouettes face to face. You both freeze and wait, shuffling nervously and scanning your eyes in all directions.

Maybe you are ready, but you must wait because now there is another car pulling off of the highway. It parks between you with its lights on, radio blaring. A drunken man stumbles out, oblivious to what he is interrupting, and stumbles forward into the edges of the wood. As the tinkle of his piss fills the still void between cars, you steal a nervous glance at the silhouette. You smile and he smiles back. You can't see him do it, nor he you, but you know it happens because even here, in the dark corner of Exit 17, there is xenophobia, hatred of the foreigner.

The man relieves himself, weaves back to his front seat, fishes in his jeans for his keys for what seems like an eternity, searches for the ignition for another eon, adjusts the radio for a millennium, and then, like a glacier in summer, his car recedes and pulls back onto the highway where he belongs. Now you and the silhouette begin to stir again.

Two strangers in two cars in the dark corner of Exit 17. One stranger leaves his car and stretches as if exhausted, the last of his acting. Now he steps into the woods, pushes his pelvis forward. Pissing or stroking? His shadow shifts; he is looking over his shoulder. With one last check in the rearview mirror for the square headlights of the highway patrol, you are out of your car and into the shadows.

That is what it is like for me to visit Exit 17 late at night. Make what judgement you like, this isn't a confession. It all began as a drunken lark after Thanksgiving dinner one year. Soon I visited regularly and with enthusiasm.

Now, as you can imagine, everybody looks pretty much the same in the pitch black. Even if I had seen them walking down the street, I could not recognize anybody with whom I had tangled at Exit 17. Honestly, I am not entirely sure if I am having sex with many different partners or just a small group over and over again. Cars, however, are easier to recognize under such circumstances, and I began to notice that I was often finding myself parked next to an Oldsmobile Achieva. There were several other things that I began to recognize about this particular visitor to Exit 17. For one thing, he always wore some sort of vanilla cologne that I liked instantly. For another, he was young, probably early twenties, and thin to the point of bony. Other than that I could not tell much about him. He was always quiet and quick, but not nervous. I always felt that I had hit the jackpot if I found the Olds in that dark corner; I hit the jackpot often.

Neither of us was there in that dark corner to make friends, and we both tried to avoid recognizing each other. However, by the fourth or fifth encounter, I felt that introductions were inevitable.

I was leaning against a tree with my back to the highway waiting for him. The young man, knowing that I was waiting, lingered in his car, playing with the radio and dragging hurriedly on a Camel. Over my shoulder I could see the green glow of the dashboard and the pale orange glow of the cigarette illuminating the jawline of his angular face. I leaned my head back and inhaled sharply while rolling my head back and forth over grooves in the tree bark.

At last I heard the door of his car close softly and the dry crackle of leaves and pine needles beneath his feet. I felt his hand on my biceps and covered it with my own. He slid his lithe body up against me and stroked my chest with long elegant fingers, head resting on my shoulder. As the tips of his fingers circled slowly around my nipples, I ran my hands along his side and followed the tight denim of his jeans from his lower back to his upper thigh. Now his hands fell lower and, with a touch so light as to be undetectable at first, he stroked me through my own jeans, finding the spot directly behind the ridge of the head. With a finger as light as an angel's tongue he tickled me so that my back arched and my shoulders ground against the trunk of the tree.

I tried to help him unfasten my belt buckle, but he pushed my hand away, clasping my palm between his thin fingers. He undid it himself. Now I was in the grasp of his cold hand as delicate as icicles. I grabbed at him roughly and placed his weight against me. He stepped away, however, and considered me with a gaze that I could not see but imagined held patience, smugness, and, perhaps, a touch of cruelty. Then I watched as his shadow sank slowly and his icicle fingers guided me gingerly into his hot throat. With both hands resting on my thighs, his head rocked back and forth; my arms, too polite to hold him firmly to the ground, curled backward around the tree trunk as if I were a Salem warlock tied to the post.

As we parted, I asked, "What's your name?"

I could hear him exhale quickly in what might have been a laugh.

He leaned in close and looked up at me. "I," he declared, "am the Queen of Exit 17."

He walked away, glancing backward. His face might have held any expression.

Cruising season usually ends by mid-October, when all the lonely men are driven inside by the cold. Until spring, they are trapped inside with their wives who, month by month, loom larger and larger. By February, their wives are monstrous, so large, in fact, that their heads must bend so as not to go through the ceiling. These poor men can have no secrets until the spring, when the windows open and they escape, gasping, onto the front lawn.

This year I could not bear the reality of the coming winter. I refused to wear sweaters, I didn't change from a summer-weight suit after Labor Day, and I drove home from work without my headlights on. I also kept visiting Exit 17. It didn't help; the days grew shorter and colder, the leaves turned melancholy orange and yellow, pumpkins fell from heaven and landed on every doorstep, and front doors sprouted ears of Indian corn.

The slanting light of autumn somehow makes every object look large, adding deep, cold shadows to them.

The weather didn't stop the Queen of Exit 17 from his appointed rounds either. As October drew near its end, the Queen and I, and possibly a grizzled truck driver or two, were the only shadows left in the dark corner of Exit 17. Encounters, after my brief introduction, again lapsed into silence and became more awkward as the two of us, fingers numb from the chill air, fumbled with down coats, three layers of shirts, and long underwear. Across the highway, the trees, which had lost all but a few random tufts of leaves, fully revealed the prison house. The floodlights blared in electric-blue intensity, catching violet auras in the empty air. These lights, now shining unhindered from behind the bare trees, revealed the rows of barbwire coiled on the tops of the chain-link fences, the spikes catching the light on dull points of metal and giving the illusion of jagged Christmas tinsel discarded by giants.

By early November, there were only a couple of leaves on the trees. Some changing weather pattern, a scrambling of Ls and Hs on the meteorologist's map, had given New England Arctic air. I was drinking hard at the Irish Embassy. A forgotten acquaintance appeared and bought me a shot of Goldschlager. German liqueurs are dangerous. They taste like cough medicine but they hide a powerful spirit, a Teutonic spirit, a berserk Viking spirit, a cold and blond beast. You always get a little crazy after a shot of Goldschlager, and that night I had four. My acquaintance went on about other acquaintances more forgotten than himself and alluded to riotous drunks that he wrongly assumed I had been present at. I could not follow him and became sullen; he eventually turned in his chair and introduced himself to a sweet girl named Bridget. Then a chubby little blonde walked in and smiled at me. The corners of my mouth twitched in involuntary response, my eyes following her to the nearby bar stool where she parked herself. Through the gloom, she smiled again and played with her hair that was intermittently illuminated by passing headlights in the wet, chill night.

This is how it starts: with a sidelong glance from an overfed girl. If I tried, I knew I could have her. With the right lines, the right lies, the right parts played, I could calm myself between her legs. Yes, I could, but the price is too high. I took another shot and turned away. I knew where I would end up that night.

I arrived about one o'clock—drunk. The prison floodlights reflected off the full, heavy clouds, grumbling with thunder. The lot was empty—except for the Queen. By now, I could recognize his car in the pitch black. Gliding up next to him, I turned on the interior light and pretended to play with my hair in the rearview mirror. The Queen turned on his lights and did the same. It was all a good joke. Simultaneously, we stepped from our cars, into the dark and grabbed each other awkwardly. I felt him shiver through his jacket.

"Freezing out," he said.

Even drunk, I sensed that the cold had ruined the mood for him.

"Sure is." I agreed.

The Queen leaned back against a tree and with a tilt of his head glanced at the sky. "Not many leaves on the trees."

He was right again.

The dark corner was not so dark that night. The lights of the highway and the prison were reflecting off of the storm clouds and down through the trees, bare but for a pair of wet oak leaves. In the gloom, his face was striking. His nose was sharp, as was his chin; his hair, hanging down in front of his eyes in greasy spikes, accentuated the angularity of his features.

"You're beautiful." I said, pushing myself against him.

"You're drunk." He laughed, then smiled.

"A bit," I agreed.

The sky rumbled and the wind suddenly shifted from chilling to warm and wet. It felt like rain.

"Do you have a place?" he asked.

"No." Pause. "Do you?"

He shook his head.

It would've, could've, should've stopped right there, but the Goldschlager surged in my blood and spoke for me. "Let's get a hotel room. I'll pay."

He nodded in silent agreement. Then I noticed that he checked his watch.

Hotels are very impersonal places for very personal encounters. Some women swear by sex in cheap hotels. I never understood this until that night. It's hard to say exactly what it is about the sanitized, deodorized interior of a Super 8 room that can make a sexual encounter so special. For one thing, it makes you feel like a seedy, sleazy mook on a lonely stretch of Nowhere Street, streets lined with Kmarts and countless Exxon filling stations. For another, there is supreme solitude. When you are safely locked in room 242 and registered under a name that you stole from the boy who sat next to you in fourth grade, you cannot be found. You are as alone as the guru on the Himalayan mountaintop. There is nothing but you and your lover in a sanitized nowhere.

The few moments in that room as the young man and I quietly disrobed and wrestled with the thermostat was the only time I ever saw him in the light. I have difficulty connecting the shadow that I would see at Exit 17 with the person who stood before me in the cold glow of the bathroom lights. I must say that imagination had been kind to the Queen of Exit 17. My mind had extrapolated on the unknown features of the Queen, making him taller and thinner than he really was. His face, unblemished in the shadows and imagined as tan and smooth, was in actuality pale and scarred. The look of innocence I had seen in the dark was, in the light, an expression of jaded resignation. Eyes that had caught the hard glare of the prison, turning it into soft blue spark, in the light were dull and glossed. It may have been the same for him to now see me. Both of us wordlessly agreed to quickly shut off the lights before completely undressing.

With the lights out the illusion revived. Always restricted in movement in an outside cruising spot, I enjoyed the free range of motion that we now had. We could lie flat, kneel, get on all fours, and stick our feet in the air. Most enjoyable was the sensation of complete nudity. Whatever he looked like, the Queen had beautiful feet.

The sex started and stopped in fits and waves. After the initial rapture we both expected to dress and leave. He sat on the edge of the bed, his hand sweeping the sheets for his shirt, but I encompassed him from behind and ran my hands over his smooth chest— and we were at it again. We traded tongues over his bare shoulder, his thin hand stroking my cheek. I kissed his neck and his nape, all the while caressing his chest. He touched himself between his legs, running his palm over his thick, uncut cock. Suddenly standing, with his hands on his hips as if to scold, he presented his cock to me. Sitting on the edge of the bed, I swallowed him slowly and sucked the viscous, salty drop that hung on the tip. I swirled my tongue around the head, then plunged his entire cock deep into my throat, my lips touching the downy hair beneath his stomach.

During the next pause I felt a strong and feverish sense of failure to my wife. "I've made a mistake . . ." I began, but he quieted me with a *shhhh* as gentle as water from a stream; I lay down again, his mouth on mine.

I awoke with a start the next morning. The Queen was already dressed, fumbling on the floor for his wristwatch. He looked at me but I turned my eyes toward the far wall and locked them there.

"Bye," he said, still looking at me. But I will never know the expression. I smiled at the wall and he turned to go, quietly shutting the door.

The stillness in the room was unbearable, so, despite my pounding head, I dressed. Looking about the room, I saw that we had left no mark that the chambermaid would not wash away. That thought haunted me; for a few minutes, I wandered around the room, sat on the corner of the bed and lifted the burlap curtain.

It was snowing outside. The whole world was covered in white except for the tire tracks of the street, which were wet and black. A chill seeped through the window of the Super 8, and I sniffled. In the drawer next to the come-stained bed was Gideons Bible. There in Gideons was chapter XXI of Samuel I, where Jonathan kisses David in the field; just a few pages away, in the first pages of Samuel II, David cries for Jonathan. It is a speech that inflames many clerics who, on cold winter days, sit inside, quietly reading their Bibles.

Ten Seconds to Love

or, How Motley Crue Popped My Cherry

(A Fantasy of Utter Fiction)

Michelle Tea

There were reasons why my mother didn't want me hanging around with Lola Blanchetta. My father said my mom was judging Lola on the size of her boobs and that wasn't right, and I chimed in in Lola's defense but secretly I knew my mother was right. I was out of my league hanging out with Lola. Her enormous tits, snug and round beneath her tight Playboy-logo t-shirt, was only the most obvious warning sign. Lola was wild.

We were both in the same grade, but only because Lola had been held back so many times. She had better things than school to think about. Lola had boyfriends, lots of them and never for long, all of them older boys with dangerous nicknames and jacked-up cars, greasy hair. Lola had felt Playboy logos ironed on to the sleeves of her shirts; she had a patch of perfect chemical-white bleached into the bottom of her long feathered hair.

She had those gigantic swinging tits, and she had an older brother who filtered his cool toughness down to her, showing by example how to hold your cigarette (cupped backwards into your palm, quick, squinty drags), how to talk (lots of "fucks" and "you wishes") and what bands were awesome (Van Halen, AC/DC, Judas Priest). When the Motley Crue tickets came, it was Lola's brother who got them. I had to lie. I had to tell my mom I was going somewhere else, with a friend she approved of. Lola was ok to sit on the front stairs with, in full parental view, but I couldn't actually go anywhere with her, and especially not with her tough brother who was trouble in his car that he drove screeching down our street, pissing my mother off with heavy metal blaring out the windows. And I could not go to a Motley Crue concert. My mother had curiously lifted the ominous dark cover of *Shout at the Devil,* matte black with its embossed satanic pentagram, slid the lyric sheet out, read the words in quiet horror, and then hid the vinyl under the couch. I Don't Want You Playing That she had said to me in a disgusted voice. That Is Just Awful. How Can You Listen To That. I stole the record back and looked over the lyrics with my mother's eyes. *"Bring your girlfriend, or maybe bring two / got my camera, make a star outta you."*

I was a little ashamed. I had had this dream where I was up in the top bunk of the bunk beds I shared with my sister, and the drummer, Tommy Lee, was crawling up from the foot of my bed, slowly, his long skinny body moving up over mine, his long black hair hanging in his face, and I was frozen beneath him and I knew he was going to do something horrible to me and there was nothing I could do to stop him. I woke up with the soft space between my legs swollen tight and throbbing a steady, hot throb.

I knew I would have to sneak to the concert and I did. Lola did my hair, she did my makeup, she gave me clothes to wear—leopard things—she sprayed my hair up high like hers and ordered me not to blink as she ran thick black eyeliner over my lids. You Look Excellent, she declared, happy with her work. Come On, her brother was hollering from out in the driveway, impatient. He reached up and whacked his fist against Lola's bedroom window. Keep It In Ya Pants! Lola hollered back, and I thought I would have to remember that one so I could use it later on my own siblings.

I don't want to talk about the drive up, drinking cans of Budweiser and flicking Marlboros out the speeding-car window, feeling really free because what I was doing was so bad that if I got caught I would get in unimaginable trouble, and I had done it and it was too late and I couldn't turn back. I don't even want to talk about the concert itself, and how me and Lola hopped empty seats until we were right up front and there was Motley Crue like they'd stepped right out of the posters on my wall, because even that's boring compared to Lola sucking off the roadie. He had picked her out of all the girls clustered at the backstage door, all desperately flirting and pleading for access and Lola just standing there smoking her Marlboro in her tough way, tossing her head so her feathered hair swung. The roadie guy looked at her and said, Do You Want To Meet The Crue, and Lola said, Fuck Yeah and he said Come On and grabbed her arm and she ditched her cigarette and grabbed my arm and we were yanked through the yelling desperate girls into a hallway, the door slamming shut behind us. He leaned up against it, this big, tall Hell's Angels kind of guy with tattoos on his hands and a dirty denim vest covered with patches of skulls and stuff, he put his hands over the front of his jeans and sort of rubbed himself and said You Want To Meet Them Real Bad, Baby? and Lola said Yeah and he pulled his cock from his pants and Lola kneeled in front of him and she slid her mouth around it.

It all happened so fast it practically seemed choreographed, and I leaned into the wall and watched, feeling the beers I drank in the car buzzing in my ears. Between my legs started quivering like that dream I had about Tommy Lee as I watched Lola's face, her eyes closed and her lips, big and dark with lipstick moving up and down the roadie's prick as he thrust his hips into her mouth and moaned, grabbing her long hair with his tattooed knuckles. You Suck Real Good, You Suck My Cock Real Good. His eyes were closed too and I wondered if they even remembered I was there. I moved over to Lola and put my hand on the back of her neck and she put one of her hands on my shiny spandexed leg and squeezed. She was sucking faster, bobbing her head on his thick cock and his hips bucked faster as he fucked her mouth and then he really gasped and slammed into her and Lola gurgled a little and then pulled her lips off his cock and swallowed. The guy leaned there with a little smile on his face, wiped his dick gently with his hand, tucked it back in his pants and *zip,* it was all done. Lola stood and swung her head around and the guy touched her face and said The Boys Are Gonna Like You A Lot.

He looked me up and down and winked. Come On.

OK, so there's this room and Motley Crue are sitting in it, arranged on big couches like magnificent dreams come true, hair like enormous shaggy headdresses, all wrapped up in their costumes of leather straps studded with metal and dangling with chains. They were still sweaty from the show, dabbing at their faces with fluffy towels, trying not to mess up their makeup. It was a pretty unbelievable sight, Vince Neil, his hair yellower in real life than the perfect platinum of my posters, kind of the same color as Lola's little bleached patch. He was passing a bottle of something amber to Tommy, the sweatiest one, his hair soaked and streaming down his back. Nikki had his head bowed to the table, moving his nose over the thin lines of powder that were arranged there. Got Somethin For Ya the roadie guy bellowed, grabbing the band's attention. We stood on either side of him, Lola and I, our spandexed asses sitting firmly in each of his meaty, tattooed roadie hands. There was a collective murmur from the Crue, and Vince leaned forward, squinting at us through his mascara. Well, he said slowly, the word slinking through the air. He licked his shimmery pink lips. Who Are These Two? he said.

I'm Veronica, Lola said coolly with a swish of her hair, and looked at me expectantly.

Uh . . . Kimberly, I said, wondering why Lola did that. This was too confusing already without having to remember fake names. Immediately I forgot hers. She pulled a Marlboro out of her box and lit up, the Crue watching expectantly like she was performing some kind of magic trick. Lola was just so cool. Calm and completely unfazed, she was either really empty-headed and incapable of deep thought or emotion, or things, lots of things, were going on in there, on a level too deep for me to begin to grasp. How Old Are You Girls? asked Tommy Lee with suspiciously raised eyebrows and a hungry smile, and Lola snapped Old Enough, like she was talking to her brother's delinquent friends and not, you know, Motley Crue.

Jail-BAIT! hooted Nikki and swiped the bottle from Tommy's hand.

You Break 'Em In For Us, Rocco? Tommy was talking to the roadie but his eyes were locked on mine and his stare was awful and burning and I couldn't look away. My pussy flared. A Little, chuckled Rocco The Roadie. I Know How You Guys Are About Sloppy Seconds, and he took his hands and lightly shoved us toward the band. Bon Appetit, he called over his shoulder as he left, and I thought about stories I'd read where young, virginal girls are delivered to the king, and I thought how me and Lola were those girls and now we were really in for it.

That Was A Cool Show, Lola said, blowing out smoke. She walked over to an empty love seat and sat down and I followed close behind. I plopped down beside Lola and Nikki handed me the bottle they'd been sharing. It was whiskey, and I took a huge gulp the way I'd watched them do it, and it hit my body like a mallet, shooting right down to my cunt and sending awful choking shivers through the rest of me. Nikki laughed and shook his head, grabbed the bottle away from me. Jail-bait, he repeated, shaking his head. Ten'll Get Us Twenty.

You Liked The Show? Vince asked, peering at Lola from beneath his bleached bangs. We both nodded. You Got A Show For Us? he asked, and I felt my gut swell with dread and my pussy swell with something else. Maybe, Lola said mysteriously, and put her hand on my leg. I thought about the porn mags we stole from her brother, blond-haired girls with their tongues a half-inch from each other's pussies. Eeeeew, I had said, like I thought I was supposed to, but Lola just shrugged and said, It's No Big Deal.

Those Are My Clothes She's Wearing, Lola said, rubbing the shimmery black material. Kimberly, Give Me Back My Clothes.

What? I asked. I was shaking, and the band was all laughing. Shit, one of them said in a kind of impressed voice. Give Me Back My Clothes, Lola repeated, this time smiling, but it was clear she wasn't kidding.

You Know, Nikki said, wiping whiskey from his mouth, You Should Really Give Her Back Her Clothes. Yeah, chimed in Tommy, and Vince just smirked.

Lift Your Arms, said Lola, and she grabbed the clingy shirt I was wearing and slowly peeled it off me. The Shoes, she said, and I kicked the spike heels onto the carpet. Stand Up, she said. The band was hooting, rolling on the couch like a bunch of teenagers at a party. My own black bra covered my tits, and Lola's spandex protected the rest of me. She moved in close and unbuttoned the metal button, unzipped the fly. Lola, I whispered, and she whispered back, Veronica, and covered my mouth with her own, slid her tongue through my lips. Yeah! one of the guys yelled, and Lola slid her hand beneath the tight pants. I had no underwear on—Lola had told me not to wear any, said the panty lines would ruin my ass and inhibit the camel-toe effect. Her fingers pushed through my pubic hair and down toward my pounding pussy, a place only I had ever touched before. She found my swollen clit easily and pushed it like a button and I groaned.

TITS! Motley Crue was hollering, Show Us Some TITS!, and Lola removed her hand from my crotch to whip off her shirt, and there were her tremendous tits, all pushed together by her tight leopard bra. Her hands snaked behind my back and unhooked my bra, and I followed her lead and unhooked hers. The bras fell to the floor and Nikki grabbed for them, for the collection, no doubt. I watched Lola's tremendous tits and found my own fingers playing with her nipples, rubbing and squeezing them, making them get all hard and puckered looking. Lola was tugging down my spandex. It was a tough job; the material clung to me, and I wondered how Lola, with her rounder hips, ever got in them. Will One Of You Help Me? she asked, and Nikki hopped up and came at me from behind. He hooked his fingers into the waistband, and with one strong pull the fabric slid over my ass. Yeah, he murmured, cupping my cheeks with his hands, and Lola pulled them down until I was just naked, standing before the most lecherous band ever. I had read about the Polaroids they took of groupies doing everything, sticking bottles up their cunts, the works, and how the band hung them on their tour-bus wall. Nikki fell into the love seat and pulled me down on top of him, my naked skin instantly sticking to all his leather. Lola climbed on top of me, steadying herself on my hip bone, and she started frenching me again, her tongue moving all around my mouth while Nikki brought his hands up over my tits and squeezed. The hard bump moving up against my ass had to be his cock. I moved my ass over it and he groaned, said into my ear You're Getting Me Hard, Little Girl, and squeezed my nipples harder. Lola pulled herself off me, just when I was really starting to like her there.

She Won't Even Know What To Do With It, she giggled. Kimberly's A Virgin. Lola! I hissed, and Nikki groaned Aww, Shit, and pushed his cock up against my ass. She Ain't Gonna Be A Virgin For Long. I thought about how me and Lola talked about fucking and how I said I wanted to lose it to either Billy Idol or Motley Crue or maybe David Lee Roth, but probably not, with that receding hairline, and now Vince and Tommy were coming at me just like in my dream, rubbing their crotches, and I wasn't sure at all that I had meant it.

Lola moved to make room for them, and I felt my legs instinctively close. Uh-Uh, Tommy said, grabbing my thigh. Open Those Back Up, Come On, Open Your Legs. I tried to twist free and Tommy told Nikki to grab me, hold me tight. I was whimpering, but it turned to moans as Tommy brought his hand down to my cunt. She's Ready To Go, he said, sliding his fingers around my wet lips, and he looked toward Vince, who was busy with his face in Lola's tits. Don't Be Scared, Tommy said with a smile. Aren't We Your Favorite Band? These guys smelled like alcohol and cigarettes and who knew how many drugs they were on. My head swam with it all. You Ready To Get Your Cherry Popped? Tommy teased me, and I said I Don't Know.

Better Get Ready, Then, he said. He was anchored firmly between my spread legs, and my arms were held back by Nikki, who kept thrusting up against me through his leather pants. Tommy's cock was out, he rubbed it with one hand while the other probed my pussy, separating my lips and fingering my hole. My little cunt felt huge, all swollen and wet, and he brought the tip of his cock down to it and started nudging. You Want Me To Fuck You, he said slowly. Dontcha. Tell Me You Do. He was rocking his hips, his cock pushing insistently at my little hole. Tell Me, he said, and I said I Want You To, and he said, Want Me To What? and I whimpered and Nikki laughed beneath me, and I said I Want You To Fuck Me, and they both groaned and Tommy drove his cock right up me and I cried out. Oh, Oh, Oh, Tommy was fucking me, in, out, right on top of me, thrusting back and forth. Nikki let go of my arms, slid his fingers down to my clit and started rubbing on it like I do late at night before I go to sleep. Make Her Come Nikki, Tommy grunted as he plowed into me again and again. You Get Her Next. I pushed my hips up to meet Nikki's fingers. Sweat dripped from Tommy's long hair onto my belly and I felt the small explosion building in my cunt. Come On Little Girl, Nikki breathed into my ear as I strained against his hand, and I yelled as I felt it happen, the big crash in my cunt that made my whole body go thrashing crazy.

Good Girl, Nikki cooed. His voice was so nasty. Tommy was still fucking me, then one deep shove and his body shook too and I felt a quivering deep in my pussy. On the couch across the room, Lola was impaled on Vince's cock, riding it up and down while he tugged at her tits. Let's Trade, said Nikki to Tommy.

Lola got pregnancy tests later. I had to pee on a little strip of paper and then wait. Lola did it too; we both sat in her room with the door locked, chain-smoking Marlboros we stole from her brother. Lola got in trouble for taking off at the concert, making her brother search high and low for us, and eventually he just left and we actually hitchhiked all the way back home in our slutty outfits and no bras. A nice lady picked us up and drove us straight to the door, she was so concerned. Lola's mother screamed at her, but that was it. Lola never really got punished. Nothing happened to me because my parents thought I was someplace safe the whole time and not getting gang-fucked by my favorite band. It was weird to act like everything was normal when I came home the next day. I fucked Motley Crue. Lola thought it would be cool if we were pregnant with their kids; then we'd get to see them again and maybe they'd marry us and we'd get to go around with them and wear cool clothes and maybe be on MTV, but if I were pregnant with Motley Crue's baby I would get in more trouble than I ever ever ever could ever imagine. The strips came out negative, and I was so relieved and Lola said Shit, and tossed them in the trash. Then Lola said Pretend I'm Vince, and pulled me down onto her bed. I laid there with my legs spread as she lowered herself onto my body.

Ideal Assex

Eva Morris

I'm on a long boat on a dark night when a tall man puts a cool hand on my neck. It feels instantly right, as so few things do, so I stay my ground and wait for his next move, one which doesn't come. So the deep, dark sea slips below our feet and under the boat in a mesmerizing pattern, gradually easing me into a sloe-eyed state. Then there's champagne in my hand, and it tastes like good cocaine—as champagne on an empty stomach tends to do. Later, through dinner, he is seated across and down from me, and I relax because I see he interacts well with everyone. He flirts with all the women—more with those who naturally get less, and just enough with those that want more—and when he converses with the men his gaze slips to mine and holds a glimmer. I want him even more now, to have his cultivated attentions, and he, knowing women, has managed to not leave me feeling alone even once. I feel that he thinks I am the hottest, the sexiest, the one. How many men were playing hooky the day that lesson was taught!

■

After dinner, we find each other's hands, and while mine pulses interest, his leads me, gently, a nudge really, up and out of the digesting room. I haven't eaten much, but I hope that he has! If there is a Goddess up in the sky, this windy night will please me in a way I've been aching to be pleased, and by that Goddess, this man will need the energy.

Now I can smell the leather of his boots, the scent of five-hours-past cologne, the cigar and cognac remnants. His beard stubble scratches me; it scratches me purposefully as he kisses my lips directly, wetly, carefully, deeply, with no interruption at all. I float. This man obviously knows the five heights of women—the five stages a woman traverses on her way to ecstasy. He kisses me through the first, second, and to the third, where my back is arched, my nostrils enlarged, and my breath hot, rising from deep depths. By no means are my legs crossed. I lick my lips any chance I get.

He says nothing to me because he's driving. He's driving—I feel like a fine automobile. Yeah, he's driving, he's driving me toward a steep ravine, knowingly, and soon, it's over the edge for me. Soon is coming soon enough! I pull my shoulders back to offer my breasts to him. He politely refrains from pawing them. So, of course, I try harder. I elevate, center, and fire them away in his direction—direct hit! His hands cup them from underneath in the way that only other women have held my breasts . . . as if to support their weight gently, and then his big hand slides up sideways, so slowly that I'm feeling their masculine strength and pleasant roughness right through my silks. He pinches my nipple between his thumb and first finger, holding it, steady and sure, and now I'm aching, but steady and sure he holds it and ouuuuuch, but I won't wrestle out of this slightly painful grip if there's even a tit's chance I might have to live without it. He knows the secret of pleasurable pain.

At this point I really want him. Jesus—he could be covered with trash and rotting on the beach, I'd blow him; floating dead in the water, bloated and rigid—I'd still hook him out and sit on his rigor mortis–hard cock. I'd deep kiss him now even if he were my father. That's the interesting thing about women that dark men on long boats know: that we start up on our own time schedules, but can't turn it off. You cannot stop a woman once ignited, not the way I have been turned on now.

I am hardly sitting on my seat. I do a slow hip twist going from here to there and back in order to rouse his attention. Yet he takes his time and repeatedly says nothing, although he is acutely aware of every move I make.

Please, please, I think, don't . . . don't prove to have a small cock. Or attempt to say something stupid. Or suddenly leave for any reason, but instead, whisper "I'm getting up to lock that door." So—I'm in or I'm out, is it?

Well darling, this minx is *in,* in deep now, as deep as I'll be sucking you in soon enough . . . then he's back and he grabs both of my hands, tucks them into his lap, cradles my face in his hand, and uses the other to squeeze my cheeks together so that I open my mouth wider. Hey, I'm not talking about my face.

Slow, slow he goes; it seems to me like I never had any clothes on at all. I'm naked, wanting, wet down to my knees, heaving my chest with every breath, and thank every damn type of God there is that he doesn't go by the old routine and try to put one yearning mouth to another, now. There will be enough time for tongue-in-sex later, for my fourth and fifth moan and a shudder; now I want a rock-hard, as it is, cock literally shoved into my hungry cat of a mouth. It's wide open and growling now, no, *supplicating,* wanting, wanting, drooling wet with want, and too fucking slowly his right hand lifts his give-stick out of his pants, leads it to the water, in both senses, and a combination of a tiger being fed meat and an Aztec throwing himself to the volcano happens.

He gets it into me in five thrusts—a complement to my tight pussy, his great size, and the rocking of the boat. It's a home run! A jackpot! He won! I won! Bells are ringing as he begins to pull it out partways and do that old Japanese trick of timing his strokes to the timing of a traditional Japanese folksong. *Sakura, Sakura;* long notes are long strokes, short notes a quick thrust; I don't know what's coming, I struggle to keep up, he endures, and I suck each note out of his *Shakuhachi.*

He is on top of me. He has one of my legs over and behind his head, the other trapped down between his legs, elongating, widening, and tightening me, and then he reaches a surprise-slickened bunch of fingers down and behind to slide a choice one right up my ass. Firmly then, he says, "Mine," and Whoa! There I go! A quick shot orgasm #1, going on to the beat of his cock's strokes.

He takes his finger out of my backside before that happens, so I'm not feeling it, just the repercussions of it. But he knows I'm a player now, and I know that he's someone I can let explore hidden secrets. By the virtue of his wealth of experience, he has gained entrance to the gates.

Not knowing my body—and here a miscalculation could ruin all the fun—he smoothly exits, turns me over and sets to nuzzling my neck and massaging the tension out through my back. Although the warm-up he provides could in fact loosen up a *gerbil* enough to . . . His hands continue to knead at any tight muscle in sight, a means of loosening up my whole body—every muscle—as his cock waits, patiently, a certain troll at the drawbridge, right up against my asshole.

Now it's my turn to tantalize. I know how.

■

I wiggle. I squirm. Have I done this before? Am I nervous or a real virgin? Will he succeed, or have to pass GO without collecting $200? Mmmm, he's not sure, and I'm running with the opportunity, twisting slowly to the right, coyly to the left, moaning—but then somehow he's onto me, he's figured out that, rare or cooked, it's his now, and slowly slips the head of his cock into my ass.

Boy oh boy! An Academy Award should be mine for the show that I give—moaning and pleading in half words—as he continues his slow trek home. With every tight centimeter he gains, I near closer to absolutely crying. And with that thought he takes another centimeter.

As he feels me tighten up, for whatever reason, he stops, and if I am still too tight, he withdraws himself an inch so that I relax an inch, then he whispers, "Ummm, baby, baby," in my ear as he continues again. You know, it's not the end but the means, and getting there *is* all the fun. A pro can do it with only a lot of spit as lubricant—but, kids, don't try that at home!

When finally *he* hits home, he doesn't move because for all intents and purposes I'd best not come now. When I come I'll close up like a clam, which is good, but not if he's buried deep in my sweet round ass, up to the hilt.

So he takes a minute and so do I, adjusting to a huge fat presence in my ass. There is simply nothing like it in the world, and I know this world, and I know a hard cock up my young ass, and I'll take that long drive home any day.

He brings it almost out, to 3/4 of the head, licks my ear in a semi-circle, fingers my pussy in a counterclockwise circle for just 30 seconds, and then I'm having an orgasm like I've never, ever had before.

A woman gets it in many ways, touches even can set us a-spinnin', but the orgasm itself always happens with our vaginal muscles. They pulse, and at the same rate a man's penis pulses when he comes, but it lasts longer for us. And it is stronger! (Ah! Equality!) So, to set that absolute myth of size not mattering to the coffin, a thick cock distending us is about the best thing we know. Hence, we use things like cucumbers, in a fix, not toothpicks. But, when we come, squeezing, pulsing, and biting frequently, like a shark eating elusive food, the more space we have to thrash in, the better. So, tongue-induced orgasms, with a finger just one inch in, are the most intense—except for anal sex orgasms, where that cock comes right up behind us to knock us crazy. Our teased pussies grasp at air, spurred on by all the nerves being molested in our ass. The asshole has more erotic nerve endings to offer us stimulation than even our cunts do; oh, but that's not news to me, not now. He goes at it once more. My orgasms give him virgin territory again. But we both know it isn't. I'm not crying now, just moaning, uncuntrollably. And his voice isn't soothing now, it's matter-of-fucking-fact. "Ah, your ass," he tells me, "So tight. So hot. So right. It's mine, you know." He's workin' it now, "popping," that old gay trick where he sinks all the way in, then slides it all the way out, moving like a slide trombonist, his head popping out a second before it's back inside. Like a gopher in a rainstorm. Now it's going in slowly, but this final thrust is deep, and his back arches up as he yells out my name. There he holds it tight, there at the finish line, pumping that last inch of him against the deepest fathomable part of me, again and again, and now I'm feeling him swell to what feels like double his original girth. He's gonna blow! If his feet aren't dug in as deeply as an anchor has to be in a storm, he could literally propel himself out of me. He's nesting the tip in tight, somewhere only a Goddess knows where, when I set to moving my hips in a real slow, big circle. He comes a quart, oiling every groove of my ass, so deep I might not be seeing his come again for days. Those powerful throbs of his have set me off, and then I am there too, holding his hand in mine, my eyes rolled back and the long-lashed lids almost closed, my mouth open, head thrown back.

Soft and half-size now, his come and mine make the difference between my pussy and my ass indistinguishable to both him and me. It's into my strong round ass, then my soft hot trap, then back again, switching partners to a gentle firm beat as he's growing progressively harder. Who wouldn't? Both of my legs are up over his shoulders and my hips are elevated off the sea-rolling bed. His ceaseless insertions hardly rock me at all. It's the best possible feeling. In. Out. In. Out. Everything I have is his. He has conquered me, and now I lay open, wanting more, more, more. He stops, leans back on his heels, pulls my head up and forward and I, in one smooth movement, sink my mouth onto and around the all of him. His cock tastes like real sex. Him. Me. Sperm. Pussy. Ass. Sweat. Time-fermented. It tastes like a mixture of old-fashioned licorice with a touch of soy sauce. It's all down my throat, yum-yum, now it's my turn to be pleasing him. I lick all he's got. Base to tip. It's so stiff and rock-hard that I have to maneuver it down and away from his abdomen. I suck it into my mouth, slide it down my throat, tickling its length with my tongue while I hold it there, the final inch of it lodged beyond where I gag, and I edge it back and forth, that final inch, because when I gag with it that deep, my throat squeezes on his bursting head.

Like a bitch fucked by a dog with a twisted dick, he can't get out because he's hooked deep inside me.

I let him go at some point, poor guy, and that's the time, yes, it's time for him to get on down and lick my clit. I like a steady, rhythmic pressure. Something sure I can relax right into. He's sucking my little accelerator button to the beat, his tongue is running in little tiny circles around it within his mouth. My asshole may be on overtime at this point, but he's got first one, then two, then FOUR fingers three knuckles deep in my love tunnel, and he's slowly moving them around—looking for gold, maybe. But what takes me from the plateau of waving fields to the ragged mountaintop is when he talks dirty, saying, as he comes up for air, "Yes, pretty, yes, you're there. Right there. I've got it. Relax right into it. Come on, here ya go," and there I go.

■

Aftersex is laying on the totally wet sheet, nose up to his tits, sucking slowly on them, as if it's a hot southern summer day and I'm an absent-minded fool. But the night is dark, it would be five in the morning if we gave a damn, the boat is slithering through the deep water, where all the world's fish eat, sleep, and fuck. He kisses so as to make me know that tonight was the best he's ever had, a deep, slow kiss with an incredible attention to detail, then he brings one hand under my sore ass, cupping it, and inserts his middle-fuck-finger into my pussy as he rolls onto his back, Mission Accomplished. Were I to need more, he is still, and probably will always be, in a ready position to give it, with just a tell-tale sign from me. But I'm too had to do that (though 1/10th of me might). I run my feline tongue up his neck a few times, purr into his ear. He sounds contented as I sink my nose into his armpit so as to catch his pheromones, and our breaths count 1-2-3.

Morning comes and I'm on him like a duck on a June bug. We fuck after a deep and tight sleep, rise and proceed to eat four times our combined weight.

From The Leather Daddy and the Femme

Carol Queen

I was looking pretty boyish that evening. Maybe that's why he looked twice at the stoplight when my car pulled up next to his motorcycle. Usually guys like that are moving; you just see a gleaming blur of black and silver. But here at the light was a real done-up daddy, sitting stock-still—except for his head, which turned in response to my eyes fixed on him and found what he saw noticeable enough to make him turn again. When boy energy gets into me I look like an effete young Cambridge faggot looking to go bad: round spectacles framing inquisitive eyes and a shock of hair falling down over one. Not classically daddy's boy, something a little different. Maybe tonight this daddy was looking for a new kind of ride.

A real done-up daddy, yeah. His leathers were immaculate and carried that dull gleam that well-kept black leather picks up under streetlights. Black leather cap, high boots, everything on him black and silver except the well-worn blue denim at his crotch, bulging invitingly out of a pair of chaps. I eyed that denimed expanse quite deliberately; he noticed. He had steely-blue daddy eyes and a well-trimmed beard. I couldn't see his hands under the riding gloves, but they looked big, and from the looks of him I bet they were manicured. I love these impeccable daddies. They appeal to the femme in me.

And his bike! A huge, shiny animal, a Harley, of course—nothing but classic for this daddy. The chrome gleamed as if he did the fine polish with his tongue—or rather, used the tongue of some lucky boy. I'm more for polishing leather, myself, but if this stone-hot daddy told me to do his bike, of course I'd get right to it.

Ooh, he was looking right into my eyes, taking in my angelic Vienna-choirboy face and my leather jacket, much rattier than his with all its ACT UP and Queer Nation stickers. Did he think I was cute enough for a walk on the wild side? I could hear him dishing me to all the other daddies: "Yeah, this hot little schoolboy, looked real innocent but he cruised me like he knew what I had and wanted it, so I let him follow me home."

On the cross street the light turned yellow. I did want what he had. This was it. I leaned out the window and said, just loud enough to be heard, careful to keep my voice low pitched, "Daddy, can I come too?"

The daddy grinned. When the light turned green he gunned the Harley, took the space in front of my car, and signaled for me to follow.

A South of Market apartment—oh, this was perfect. At three A.M. on any given night he could probably open his bedroom window and find a willing mouth down here to piss in—I'd heard about this alley. The entryway was dark. Good. I parked my car and caught up with him there. I fell to my knees as he pulled his keys from his belt. By the time he had his door unlocked I was chewing on his balls through the denim. He let me go on that way for a minute, and then he collared me and hauled me into the dark foyer. I barely had time to grab my rucksack, which I'd let fall beside me so I could get both hands on his hard, leather-clad thighs.

Inside, I pulled off my glasses and tucked them away safely in my jacket. In the future, I guess I'd remember to wear my contacts. Daddy pushed me back onto my knees, and I scrambled to open the buttons of his Levi's. I wanted his cock, wanted it big, wanted it down my throat with his hands fisting the hair at the nape of my neck, giving it to me hard and rhythmically. I wanted to suck both his balls into my mouth while he slapped his dick against my cheeks. Cock worship in the dark. Use me. Daddy, no, don't come yet—I have a surprise for you.

I don't know how long I went on. I get lost in cocksucking sometimes; it's like a ritual that disconnects me from my head, all the more so when it's anonymous. I hadn't even seen this cock I was sucking, and that made me feel I could be anyone, even an adventurous gay boy in a South of Market alley, sucking Daddy's big, hard dick. Any second now he could realize that I was no ordinary boy, and that gave me a great rush of adrenaline, a lust to have it down my throat. Until he discovered me I could believe this illusion myself, and with most men this was all I could expect to be, a cocksucker until they turned the lights on.

Daddy was moaning; guess as a cocksucker I got a passing grade. I felt the seam of my Levi's, wet where they pressed into my cunt. Jesus, I wanted it, I wanted it from him, I wanted him not to care. The scents of leather and sweat filled my head. Finally I pulled my mouth away from his dick—no problem speaking in a low voice now; shit, I was hoarse from his pounding. "Daddy, please, I want you to fuck me."

He pulled me up at once, kissed me, hard. That was a surprise. I was swooning, not feeling like a boy now, whatever a boy feels like, but all womanly, my brain in my cunt. And I was about to be discovered. His hand was sliding into my jacket; any second now it would fall upon the swell of my breast. This was when most guys freaked out and sent me home to beat off. That was okay, usually, but God, it would kill me to break this kiss.

But the kiss went on even when his fingers grazed first one breast, then the other . . . when his other hand followed the first under my jacket, then under my shirt, as if for corroboration, and he felt my nipples go hard under his touch. He squeezed them, eliciting a very unboyish moan, thrusting his tongue deep down where his cock had been, so that even when he twisted my nipples into the shape of morning glories, furled around themselves. I couldn't cry out.

The kiss went on even when one hand slid down my belly and

started undoing the buttons of my jeans until there was room for him to slip a finger down between my pussy lips, root its way, almost roughly, all the way into my cunt, pull the slick finger out again and thrust it into my mouth, where our tongues sucked it clean. The kiss lasted while he slid his fingers back in and fucked me, so slowly, so juicy and excruciating, until I finally broke away to beg, "Oh, Jesus, please, make me come!" He stroked in faster, then; I came like a fountain into his hand. He rubbed the juice all over my face, licked some of it off, kissing me again, then pulled me down the hall into a lit room. I felt weak-kneed and wildly disheveled; he was immaculate yet, but his cock was out and it was still hard. For me.

Those steel-blue eyes were lit with more than amusement, and when he spoke, in a soft, low, almost-drawl, I realized it was the first time I'd heard his voice.

"Well, little boy, I must say you had me tricked." He laughed; I guess I looked a little proud. "Do you make a habit of fooling guys like me?"

"Not very often," I managed. "And most men don't want what they get."

"No, I would imagine not. A little too much pussy under that boy drag. A man wouldn't want to get himself . . . confused. Hey, where'd you learn to suck cock? A bathhouse?"

"My brother taught me. He's gay."

"Shit, bring him with you the next time you visit," said the daddy. "I'll die and go to heaven." He pushed me back on the bed then and knelt above me. His big cock dangled above my face and at first he held me down, teasing me with it, but I begged and he lowered it to my lips, letting me have just enough to suck on like a baby dreams over a tit. "Good girl," he said, smiling a little, running his fingertips over my skin in a most enticing way. The boy energy was gone, but I didn't want to stay a little girl with a man this hot. Anyway, he wasn't acting like a leather daddy any more.

I don't know what gets into me. When I cruise gay men as a boy, I know full well that I have to stay a boy the whole time. Unless they send me out at the first touch of curves, the first smell of pussy, they'll play with me only if I can keep up the fantasy. I lick Daddy's boots and suck his cock and get on my face for him, raise my ass up at the first brush of his cock on my cheeks. I beg Daddy to fuck my ass and promise I'll be his good boy, always. But deep inside, even as he's slam-fucking my ass and I'm screaming from the deep-pounding pleasure of it, even though I love being a faggot for him, I secretly wish he'd slip and bury his meat all the way deep in my cunt. I love being a boy, but I don't like having to be two separate people to get what I want. I really want the men I fuck to turn me over and see the whole me: the woman in the boy, the boy in the woman. This daddy, this leatherman whose name I didn't even know, was the first one with whom that seemed possible—and I wanted to make sure. I wanted to know if he would really play with me.

So again I let his cock slip from my lips. "Daddy, will you let me up for a minute? I want to play a new game, and I really want you to like it." He released me, looking at me quizzically as I reached for my bag and pulled the last of my clothes off. There. A femme hates having pants bagging around her ankles.

Feeling sleeker already, I took the bag into the bathroom, promising I'd be right back. Everything was there—shoes, clothes, makeup. It was time to grow up.

The dress was red and tight and hugged my small breasts into cleavage. Its backline plunged down almost to the swell of my ass. Black stockings and garters (the dress was too tight to wear a belt under, only a black G-string would fit), and red leather pumps with high, high heels. The kind of shoes drag queens named so aptly "Come-Fuck-Me Pumps." You're not supposed to walk in them—you're supposed to offer the toe to a worshipful tongue or lock them around a neck while you get pounded. Which is what I hoped would be happening to me shortly.

With some gel and a brush my hair went from boyish to chic. Powder on my face, then blush. I darkened my eyebrows and lashes, lined and shaded my eyes with green and violet, and brushed deep crimson onto my lips. An amazingly changed face, all angles and shadows and eyes and cheekbones, looked back at me from the mirror. One last glance: I was sufficiently stunning. In fact, the sight, combined with the knowledge that I was about to emerge from the little room into the leather daddy's view, had me soaked, my heart pounding, my clit buzzing. I get so very narcissistic when I'm femmed out. I want to reach for my image in the mirror, take her apart and fuck her. No doubt I'd be riding this energy into the girl bars tomorrow night, looking for my image stepped through the looking glass, out looking for me.

One last flourish, a long, sheer, black scarf, sheer as my stockings, flung around my shoulders, hiding nothing. I stepped back into the leather daddy's room.

He'd taken his jeans off from beneath the chaps. His jacket was off, too, hung carefully over a chair. His dick was in his hand. He'd been stroking it, staying hard. Bands of leather drew my gaze to the hard curves of his biceps. Silver rings gleamed in his nipples. I felt like a *Vogue* model who'd stumbled into a Tom of Finland painting. He was gorgeous. He was every bit the spectacle I was, body modified and presented to evoke heat, to attract sex.

He looked at me hard, taking in the transformation. I saw his cock jump; good.

"So, Daddy, do you still want to play?" I said "Daddy" in a different voice this time, let it be lush with irony, like a '40s burlesque queen. A well-educated faggot ought to pick up on that.

There was a touch of wonder in his voice. "God damn. I don't believe I've ever picked up anything quite like you." Then suspicion. "So what's your trip? Trying to turn the heathens into hets? No wonder all those other guys threw you out."

A new rush of adrenaline hit. Go ahead, I thought, be uncomfortable, baby, but don't stop wanting it. I took a couple of steps, coming near enough the bed that I could put one foot up on it. I moved into his territory, gave him a view of the tops of my stockings and the wet, pussy-redolent G-string. I narrowed my eyes. "Did I suck your cock like a het? You think I can't take it now that I have a dress on?"

He persisted. "Why waste this on gay men? Straight boys must fall over for you."

"Straight boys don't know how to give me what I want." I ran my eyes down his body. "Besides, your cock says I'm not wasting this on you."

He made no move to try to hide the hard-on. His voice was more curious than accusatory when he said, "You get a perverse charge out of this, don't you?"

"Yeah, I do. But I really want *you* to get a perverse charge out of it." I moved to him, knelt over him so that only the insides of my knees touched the smooth leather of his chaps. He was close enough to touch; I had to stop from reaching. This was it, the last obstacle. His hard cock almost touched me. "I'm no ordinary boy, Daddy, and I'm no ordinary woman. Do you want it? Just take it."

There is so much power in being open and accessible and ready. So much power in wanting it. That's what so many other women don't understand. You'll never get what you want if you make it too hard for someone to give it to you. He proved it: he lifted his hands to me, ran them once over my body, bringing the nipples up hard through the clinging dress, pinned my arms at my sides and brought me down into a kiss that seared and melted, a kiss I felt like a tongue in my cunt. I felt myself sliding along his body till his cockhead rested against the soaked silk of my G-string, hard and hot, and he stroked against my clit over and over and over. When he released my arms, one big hand held my ass, keeping me pushed against him. The other hand was fisted in my hair. He held me fast, and once again my cries of orgasm were muffled on his tongue.

When his mouth left mine it went to my ear, talking low.

"Pretty girl, I want your cunt so hot you go crazy. You got all dressed up for me, didn't you? Pretty bitch, you want it rough, you like it like that?"

"Yes!" I gasped, still riding the last waves of come, wanting more.

"Then tell me. Ask for it. Beg me!"

He pulled the scarf from around my neck, threw me easily onto my back. He pinned my arms over my head and bound my wrists with the scarf, talking in his low daddy voice, playing my game:

"You want it, pretty bitch? You're going to get it, Miss Special. So you think your cunt is good enough for my meat? Can't get what you need from straight boys? You're gonna need it bad before you get an inch of me, baby . . . Spread 'em, that's right, spread for me, show it to me, let me have a good look. I haven't seen one of these in a real long time . . . You know what I usually do with this cock, don't you? Is that what you want, is that what straight boys don't give you? Want it in your ass, make you be Daddy's boy again, hmm? . . . No, you want it in your pussy, baby, I can feel it. Just shove it all inside you, you want to feel it open you up. Can you take it?"

Now he was reddening my ass with slaps, the dress was pulled up to my waist, and from nowhere he clicked open a knife. I gasped and whimpered, but he just used it to cut the G-string off and it disappeared again. He slapped my pussy with his cock, scattering drops of my wetness, stopping short before I came, whispering, "Want it, pretty bitch? Want it all?" And I writhed against him and begged him:

"Jesus, please, give it to me, Daddy! Please . . . please!"

He was a consummate tease, this daddy; I wondered dimly if his boys tried to wiggle their assholes onto his just-out-of-reach cock the way I was trying to capture it with my hungry cunt. Not so much difference between one hunger and another, after all.

He reached for a rubber, worked it over his cockhead and rolled it down the shaft. The encasement made his big cock strain harder. As he knelt between my spread-wide legs, I murmured, "Give it to me, give it to me, give . . ."—and in a long plunge, he did.

It felt so good to be filled so full, and to smell the hot leather and cock and pussy and feel the chaps against my legs. The second thrust came harder than the first, and a look of sexy concentration played across my leather daddy's face as he settled in for a long, hard, pounding ride.

It was my turn to talk to him as I met his strokes with thrusts of my own, letting my pinned-down body fill with delicious tension that would build up to even more intense peaks.

". . . Oh, yeah, just like that, give me your cock, baby, fill up my pussy, yeah . . . Give it to me, give it to me, you know I can take it, hard, yeah, come on . . . Fuck my cunt like you fuck your boys' asses, make me take it from you, yeah, don't stop, don't ever stop, just try to out-last me, Daddy—you can fuck me all night, fill that rubber with a big hot load and I'll come just thinking about you, just give it to me . . . Just give it to me, make me, make me . . . come . . ."

And it was all lost in cries and sobs and breath taking over. Somehow he'd untied my hands, and I held him and came and came and came, and the wild ride was over with half a dozen bucking thrusts. I heard his yells mingle with mine, and I reached down to pull cock and rubber free from my cunt and feel the heft of jism in my hand as we lay together in a tangle of sweaty limbs, not man and woman, just animals, two sated animals.

I drifted off to sleep and woke again as he was working the tight, sweaty dress over my head and off. My red leather shoes glowed against the white sheets.

"Hellion," he said as my eyes opened, "faggot in a woman's body, bitch-goddess, do you intend to sleep in your exquisite red shoes?"

I held them up for him to take off, one and then the other, and he placed respectful kisses on each toe before he set them on the bed.

"No," I said, "that's too femmy, even for me."

"And what does a man need to do with you around," he continued, pulling off my stockings, "to get fucked? Call your brother?"

He hadn't seen all the contents of my trick bag. I reached for it and spilled it onto the floor: three dildos, a harness, and a pair of long rubber gloves fell out. I promised that in the morning he could take his pick. I was dying to show Daddy what else a femme can do.

Thief of
Cocks

Susannah Indigo

They say I'm here because I'm a kleptomaniac. The shrink said, in his most serious doctor voice, "Margo, I think this is a deep-seated problem, and I will have to see you daily while you're here in order to help you." I looked him up and down when he said that and smiled. I know what he wants.

I look at the bare white walls in this little room and marvel at the irony of it all. I've never really stolen anything in my life. Nothing criminal at least—no shoplifting, no embezzling, no grand larceny. And no man on earth is ever going to file charges against me.

I'm only here because of my friend Jennifer. I made the mistake of bringing her in my darkroom to let her watch me develop the film from her wedding. I completely forgot that she'd never seen the shelves that house the Collection. I know she was shocked—she's a nice girl, after all. What happened afterward . . . she was only trying to help, I'm sure.

The cute, stocky nurse named Jon is here to take care of me. I swear I am going to try and behave, at least for today.

"Mornin', Margo," he says in that too-familiar voice that nurses everywhere own. "How are we feeling today?"

I laugh. "I am, as always, feeling hot, dear Jon." What luck of mine to get a nurse with a great mustache. "The real question is—how are you doing after last night?" Forget what I just said about behaving.

He blushes. This is the first moment of power. When you can make a man blush using mild sexual innuendoes, it's all downhill from there. Owning his cock is almost too easy.

Jon sits on the side of my narrow bed and begins to brush my long black hair, as though I'm a little girl and can't do it for myself. Truth is, I love it. I let his fingers travel down and brush my nipples beneath my flimsy, tangerine nightgown.

"You have perfect breasts, Margo," he says matter-of-factly. All the men tell me that. There's no logic for this—I'm a regular 36B kind of girl, the kind they invented Wonderbras for. I'd never wear one, though. It's just not necessary.

He brings the stiff hairbrush down over my hard nipple, and holds it there to see how I like the feeling. Suddenly I know this man has potential.

"My turn to check," he says. He reaches down casually between my legs while I moan. There's a short pause as he finds out that my pussy is completely devoid of hair. I shave it perfectly, and it drives men wild. He slides a finger into me with his eyes locked on mine. Bringing his very wet finger to my mouth to taste, he says only, "I win, today."

I never get a word in before he rises and leaves, throwing me a kiss on the way out. Turnabout's fair play, of course, and I did the same thing to him last night after he said he knew my game. He said there was no way I could even make him hard.

I can, though—faster and with no hands.

■

My business partner Gabriel arrives promptly at two to visit me. Thank god they let me wear my own clothes in here, though I did notice that they took away all of my sharp jewelry. I wear a calf-length black crinkle skirt and a white cotton shirt tied at the waist for him. Gabriel knows I never wear anything underneath. I go barefoot on the lawn to meet him, dancing through the dandelions. I'm supposed to be crazy, so I might as well act like it.

"Margo! You look all right!" He kisses me with that magical tongue deep in my mouth. There's a definite reason why all the girls call him the "Angel of Fuck." Gabriel owns the Whacked Porpoise Tavern in the Denver Lodo district, which is a whole 'nother story. He's also a partner with me in my art gallery down the street, "The Phallic Z."

"Gabriel, darling," I murmur, sliding his tongue out of me and catching my breath. "Did you bring what I asked?" Boy, if there was ever a man I seriously thought about learning the art of monogamy with, Gabriel was it.

"Of course, Margo. Paintings for your bare walls, two books, and the top three from the Collection." He laughs and looks over his shoulder. "All we have to do is figure out how to sneak it past the security here."

I tell him it's not a problem, that I already have a friend on the inside. We kick our feet up on the deck railing and begin to talk about how I'm going to get out of here.

■

A couple of years ago I was stretched out flat on my belly on Gabriel's big brass bed, wrists and ankles tied to the bedposts the way only the Angel of Fuck can do just right. He was straddling my bare waist and giving me a deep massage after fucking me silly for days.

He had just pointed out my strange ability to live up to the Stones' words about "making a dead man come."

"Ha," I replied, "I can do better than that."

"You can?"

"Yep. I can pull any grown man away from a tied game in the Super Bowl and make him forget football even exists."

He laughed. "That," he said, suddenly seriously, "is a marketable skill, sweetheart. You should do something with it."

So I did. He designed the flyer for me and it went up right in the gallery lobby. It looked like a work of art, and nobody but those interested ever questioned it. "LEARN TO BE A THIEF OF COCKS," it said, ". . . a special seminar in cultivating fuckability." Gabriel designed a couple of upright cocks in the corners, and most people thought it was about the gallery name. "IT'S ALL ABOUT POWER," the flyer ended.

Every seminar filled instantly. I charge a fortune, but I give those eager women power in return. Power is priceless. And power is what got me in so much trouble.

■

I kick my feet up on the shrink's desk, still barefoot. I'm getting to like this crazy routine. "Dr. Russ," he says to call him, as though I'd call anyone who says I'm a kleptomaniac and a nymphomaniac "doctor." I saw it in writing; that's what the man said.

"I think," he declares, twisting his pipe in his mouth in bad imitation of every movie shrink I've ever seen, "that these desires you have are rooted in a deep childhood trauma. I think we need to explore your relationship with your father. It might be a Daddy thing."

A Daddy thing? This doesn't sound like shrink talk to me, it sounds like his own kink. I spread my legs a little and hike my skirt above my knees. I've tried this Sharon Stone move many times, but it's a Hollywood specialty that usually requires a low camera angle for any worthwhile effect.

"I think, Shrink, that you want to fuck me."

It slows him down. He even blinks and forgets to answer me with a question.

"Perhaps you think that about all men, Margo, while you search for your Daddy's love."

I laugh. "Perhaps, Shrink, it's a fact that every man I meet wants to fuck me." I can walk on this guy. Figuratively. Or physically. It's one of the reasons I like to stay slim—I teach the girls in my seminars this skill, with the maxim, "Don't diet just to capture a man: diet so you can walk all over him."

He just watches in that faux-wise way. I watch him too. I can't help but notice that's he's fairly handsome, in an older, proper, kind of way. Just the kind of man who needs me.

"This obsession with cocks, Margo. What do you think it's all about?"

It's so simple. "There's nothing deep to it. Cocks are like snowflakes. No two are exactly alike."

He laughs. I've already got the shrink laughing. Oh man, I can't resist an idea once it's in my head. "Would you like me to walk on you? What is your first name?"

"It's Jerry," he replies with a slight smile. "Now, why would you want to walk on me?"

That's the end of the words. I get up and flip on the CD player on the credenza behind him. I would have bet my life that classical music would begin, but he surprises me with the soundtrack to *Exotica*. This guy can't be all bad.

I dance around his office, twirling my black skirt, stopping by the door to lock it. He doesn't stop me or call for an orderly. He just watches as I hop on his big oak desk and dance for him.

"Because, Jerry," I say, leaning down close to his mouth and removing his pipe, "you look stressed out, and I know how to take care of you."

He looks at me as though he's taking notes for my file, but I know what he wants.

I hop off the desk and dim the lights. "Lie down on the carpet here, Dr. Jerry, and let me show you just what I have in mind."

I dance over him, his hands holding my ankles tight, my skirt flying. I turn him over and walk on his back, just exactly right, the way I learned it from a kinky Japanese film. I hear him moaning with pleasure, and all the questions are gone. Finally I lower my lips to my point of obsession with every man, starving for the treat of his cock deep in my throat. I take him all in and drink down all of his juice. I have to admit that I was trying to imagine how I'd get away with adding him to my collection even as I was taking that last bit of tension from his body.

■

"So, Margo," says Jon the nurse when he brings me my evening pills. "I hear you fucked Dr. Russ this afternoon."

Oh yes, this man is my type. "Don't be silly, Jon. If I had really fucked him it would have taken a lot longer than that. I just made him shut up for a while."

I put my pills in with the rest of my stash to give to Gabriel on his next visit. There's no way I'm taking these drugs—I'm neither depressed, nor manic, nor oversexed. But god knows I have plenty of friends who can use them. Nobody's going to tinker with my sexuality unless they're doing it with a hard cock and a lot of passion.

Jon doesn't seem to care if I take my pills, though I'm sure he's supposed to watch me take them. He's too busy watching my ass as I change into my nightgown right in front of him. Well, no, I have some modesty, because I turned my back to him.

"Tell me about yourself, Margo."

"You don't have enough time for my story."

Jon locks the door to my room. "I do. I'm covered. Tell me." He starts that infernal gentle brushing of my hair again, with the strokes that make me almost cry.

"I don't know, Jon. I've always had this pull for men—since I was twelve years old it's been happening. Maybe my mother was this way—maybe it's hereditary. But I've turned it into both a fine art and an obsession."

He strokes the brush down over my skin to my bottom and spanks me lightly. "Why?"

"Why what?"

"Why turn it into an art and an obsession?"

"I don't know," I say, turning so he can reach me better. "It's what I know best. It's what I do. I'm a profitable gallery owner, a good artist, and a great fuck."

He smiles and lifts my short white gown, tying it up by my waist. "You are a great fuck, Margo. I don't even have to fuck you to know that. I can tell by the way your body responds to my touch."

He runs the stiff hairbrush down over my bare pussy, and I almost wish I had hair there so that he would never stop.

"Do you ever wonder what your purpose in life is, Jon?"

He smiles at me gently like I'm a child. "I know my purpose,

Margo. I'm clear on who I am. My purpose is to share the gift of strong nurturing that I've been given with my patients. Other than that, my sole purpose is to live in the present moment."

Oh my, hot and sexy *and* deep.

"Well, I know mine too. My purpose in life is to make men hard."

■

An hour later I've somehow finished my tale. I told Jon of my obsession with cocks while his fingers were buried deep in my pussy. I told him of my seminars and about cultivating fuckability while he did things with his fingers that even the Angel of Fuck doesn't know.

After he'd brought me to orgasm several times with only those strong fingers, he finally started to respond to my words.

"The secrets of fuckability? That's great, Margo. They shouldn't lock you up for that, they should give you an award. I feel like I should be taking notes here for all my women friends. What are the first three steps you mentioned?"

I know he's teasing me, but I give them out slowly. STOP, LOOK, SUCK.

"First, STOP—stop spending all that money on clothes and perfume and makeup and hairstyles. It doesn't make a damn difference."

He pretends to write this down.

"Second, LOOK—stand in front of a full-length mirror every night for a half hour and practice getting your eyes and your body to say 'Fuck me,' without ever whispering a word. Study French-women; they've got this down pat. Do it until you can turn yourself on just by looking. If you can't make yourself wet, how can you turn anyone else on?

"Third, SUCK—a man who knows you're obsessed with his cock is yours. Look at a man's cock immediately after you meet his eyes. Then worship it—in words, with your body, with your mouth."

I look directly at Jon's cock after I finish. My hands travel to meet his hardness.

"There's a lot more, Jon, but it works. It gives them the sexual power they all want, without spending an extra dime."

I stroke his cock through his white jeans and we both consider where to go from here.

"So, Margo, what happened to get you in here?"

I don't know if he's ready for this. I don't know if anyone ever is. En masse, it's just too much to know and see, except for people like me and my partner Gabriel. But Jon's eyes are so sincere and his hard cock under my palm is starting to obsess me.

"I have this Collection in my loft, Jon, and it's gotten me in trouble. It started innocently, with an artist friend. Then, it all grew out of control. Just like my sex life started only with stolen moments, and then moved on to stolen hearts. The next thing I knew my sights had lowered and I was into stolen cocks."

"Are you saying you have a collection of cocks, Margo?"

I nod.

"This I have to see. Let's go."

I didn't think he could do it, but he dressed me up and snuck me out of that crazy place, and we were off in the cool night air to the Lodo to view my personal Collection.

■

We climb the stairs to my loft and I feel like a thief sneaking into my own home. I light all the candles so he can get a feel for the place before I shock him. I tell him part of the story, how my friend Jennifer saw the Collection and called up some other strait-laced friends to discuss their worries about my sanity. I try to explain about her psychologist friend who told her to set up an intervention for me. They were all going to surprise me here in my loft, supposedly with love and caring, and make me admit my sex-addiction problems and seek professional help.

"But wasn't it your choice, Margo, whether to seek help or not?"

I laugh at the memory. "Yeah, it was supposed to be. Jennifer meant well. But I missed the intervention meeting because it was the night of the Mass-Seduction Test for my September Cock Seminar with the girls. They did so well that the night ran very long."

Jon holds me tight in the candlelight. "You're not crazy. Margo.

You're just one of a kind. You should write a book about this."

I look at him, and he's serious.

"The shrink who was in charge of the intervention was pissed off, who knows why. Maybe he just hadn't been laid right in years. So he set me up. It was kind of like a sting operation."

Jon is almost on the floor, and I can finally see it all differently, with humor.

"A cock sting, Margo?"

"Yeah, exactly. He came on to me one night the next week and I brought him home, and I even laid him quite right. The next thing I know, I'm doing my cock operation, and it turns out he's videotaping it all through some damn little camera in his briefcase."

Jon stops laughing. "What happened?"

"Oh, he tried to charge me with something. But what it would be is the problem—Involuntary Theft of Hardness? Cock Larceny? So instead, he got me committed, and the cops dropped the effort and are, I hope, entertained by it to this day."

"That's crazy."

"Indeed."

■

I carry one candle into the darkroom. "This is the Collection, Jon."

He stands before my shelves and I can see the look in his eyes as he stares. This man who sees crazy people all the time in his work is wondering if I'm truly whacked and if I might be dangerous.

"How do you do this, Margo?" is all he asks.

I'm afraid to answer.

He walks me closer and we stand in front of the glass-encased shelves. Each cock is painted to perfection, and each one has a little bronze name tag attached to it. Each one is different—some have seams, some have veins, some are curved, and the sizes vary widely.

I try to laugh off the look in his eyes. "Hey, you know, some women collect Precious Moments, I collect Precious Cocks."

"How?"

"It's an art. Each one is a plaster mold. But they're strong enough to use as dildos after they're painted and dried. I do the painting from the photo I snap. I can't make the cast while they're asleep, unfortunately, because they have to be hard." I peek to see if he's still with me. "This is what I tell the girls in my seminar: you're going to be able to make a man so hard that he'd stay that way long enough for you to make a plaster cast of his hard cock if you wanted to. They always think I'm joking."

Jon begins to laugh uncontrollably, but still has me captured tightly in his arms in front of him. "Do they ever crumble in the process?"

"Of course. I had this guy Keith who would say I almost turned him on, and then I'd get him hard as a rock and he'd get too interested in the details of my plaster technique. He was a great fuck, but his member is not of my collection."

"There must be over a hundred cocks here."

"Not everybody cooperates—shyness or something. Did you know you can make a man hard while he's almost passed out drunk? That's what happened to the shrink who turned me in. He claimed it wasn't consensual."

"No, baby, but I can't imagine needing to drink with you around. You make me high just by contact."

I can tell he can't stand it any longer. He lifts my skirt and bends me over the work table and tells me he understands my obsession. He thinks my problem is that I just never get fucked and penetrated right. He tells me he can think of a use for every single cock in the case, and I believe him. He's trying to take my power away from me. I almost want him to.

He lets me have his own cock in my pussy and everyplace else before he moves on to the plaster cocks. I don't think he quite used them all, but it feels that way when I wake up to find us spread across my own soft bed. I feel deliciously fucked, perfectly fucked, powerfully fucked, and I turn to watch him sleeping. Maybe this is the man who can slow me down. He's wiser than any shrink, and he knows what I need. I think I'll wake him up and tell him this. Maybe I can go straight with his help.

But, first, I'll get the plaster mix ready, just in case. This cock just might be the pride of my Collection.

The Agent

Jess Wells

There isn't a New Yorker alive who would fault me for it, and San Franciscans might cut me some slack as well, but I have actually fucked for real estate.

I couldn't help it.

It wasn't just desperation in the face of a small down payment, high expectations, a town with water on at least three sides and a no-growth urban policy. It was that the process was so sexual.

Why do real estate agents have cars with interiors of better leather than my sex toys? I was being transported in a high-class dildo bag—*I Dream of Jeannie*'s bottle, if Jeannie were a dominatrix. She kept saying I would have to open myself to the possibility of love, and I tried to remember that she was talking about loving a house. "Imagine yourself there," she said, handing me coffee, turning on my music, pampering me like I imagine Hollywood babes get treated. She drove me around town, then led me into the houses. "Can you see your bed here?" she'd say, sweeping a long muscular arm around a sunny room, and there was something clandestine about it right away. These were other people's homes. Their owners were at work. And we were in their bedroom in the middle of the day. Or they were vacant homes with polished floors, and she would pop her little butt up onto the kitchen counter and cross her long legs, shake her foot, and describe dinner parties I might have. "A quarter million," she'd say, "and I can get you financing, easy."

Well, I'm sorry, but all that money is so sexy. Makes you feel powerful, legitimate. Capable. It goes into your pants, it does. Besides, nothing about my financing is easy, so when she said that, it was as if she were giving me a quarter mil, not just a house; she was giving the dinner party, the bedroom; she was my wife providing the sunny Sunday mornings she described as she took me through the houses.

"Are you open?" she kept asking. Open to the possibilities?

She wore perfume, or the smell of leather hung on her, maybe she put weed in the car's air supply or something because I wanted her. Right there in a stranger's kitchen, on some old lady's dining table, in an empty room where this beautiful bed in my suddenly beautiful life would hold her sleek nakedness. I was being led around town, through moist basements and narrow secret hallways, by my nose like an idiot bull, and I fucked her during "agent appointments" on seven butcher blocks and three wood floors, in a "bonus room down" and in one dilapidated shed before I got the fever and really wanted her bad.

I wanted her like I wanted a solid foundation, a quick escrow with buckets of cash back from the seller for nothing. I wanted to wheel and deal her on the end of my tongue.

Then she found the place for me. She fucked me so hard in this darling old house that some biddy had died in, just nailed me so good that I laid there on that old area rug, lookin' at heaven through little French doors. Might not have been the doors, but it was French something, so I signed on the dotted line. Moved in like a mistress being settled somewhere.

She was good to me.

Visited me after broker's opens on Tuesdays.

Then I started to follow her. I thought I would surprise her, play a little cat and mouse during an inspection or something, see if I couldn't lay her out in the gazebo. I saw her pull her motored sex toy in front of a house. A sign in front said SOLD. I missed my parking spot and had to circle the block, but as I passed the house, I saw the door open, saw some woman's hand cup the agent's head and pull her into the house.

Very intimate gesture, this cupping of heads.

My agent was in there for nearly an hour, then dashed for her car, pulling out her cell phone. The woman tripped out of the house all dolled up—pert and pressed—made me want to puke. Got in the sex toy and they toured. I was speechless. I followed her. My agent, a lock box, into a house and then out again with the client all glassy-eyed, reaching for the agent's hand, but my agent dodged a bit when they parted. Then my girl's off to another house where she takes down a SOLD sign. Then some ho comes out, flings her arms around my gal in real estate.

That's all I need to see.

I stopped by the stationery store on the way home. I believe escrow has closed, I whined to myself. Two boxes of Kleenex, big bottle of Visine, and a FOR SALE BY OWNER sign for the front of my house.

Homo-ownership, my ass.

Big Hungry Woman

Bill Noble

She barreled along the beach like a locomotive, the imprints of her feet stretched far back along the edge of the Pacific. Matt couldn't take his eyes off her. *Geez, them quads! And them tits! Awesome!* He pictured fucking a chick like that, tearing off the soaking-wet high-cut that barely covered her magnificence and plugging her.

She was at least his own height—more than six feet—and massive. Her trunk and shoulders were huge, her breasts out-thrust towers of flesh, her belly as corded with muscle as his own. Her pistoning thighs were as thick as his torso. She was brown—Polynesian maybe—with broad hungry lips, sculpted cheekbones, and oiled black hair that hung in a tangle of ringlets. She turned enormous dark eyes toward him as she passed. They flicked down over his long blond hair, his muscled body, the proud lump swung in his red thong. He gave her a sexy, swaggering grin and cocked his hips.

She wheeled back in a wide turn. Close up, she towered over him, took his breath away. She took his hand, smiling, and pulled him back toward an alcove in the cliffs. This wasn't the usual way babes hit on Matt, but he flashed her a foxy grin. Her hands were hot and sure as she leaned him back against the rock. She ran her fingers over his face, then over the knotted dragon newly tattooed on his shoulder. She pinched his nipples and palmed his pecs; his anus clenched suddenly and the sensation bulged through his perineum to tingle the tip of his cock. She ran fingernails down his belly, hooked strong fingers in the sides of his bathing suit and ripped the side seams apart. The tatter of cloth dropped to the sand between their feet.

Her smile spread and spread. He thrust his purpley cockhead toward her crotch and reached for her giant boobs, but she knocked his hands aside. She wrapped one hand around his stiffie and grabbed his balls in the other, leaned her full weight against him, opened her mouth, and kissed him. Matt had frenched babes, fucking them with his tongue till they struggled for air, but no chick had ever done him that way. Her mouth was hot and thickly wet. It smeared itself all over his face, and then her tongue probed him. It ran up under his lips, slid back and wrapped around his molars. It arched against his whole palate, then snaked under his tongue, twisted around it. He felt it reach back and hook his tonsils. She laughed a deep, long laugh right down his throat. Her nipples were twin .45s against his chest.

She pulled back and eyed him up and down.

"You're one hot chick," he wise-assed, trying to keep the sudden unanticipated tremble out of his voice. She broke into a monstrous smile again and licked first one of his still-downy cheeks and then the other with the flat of her tongue. She whipped her bikini top off and pulled his head to her breast.

Her nipple had a faint sugary taste. It filled his mouth, her breast covering his whole face. A hot hand pumped his cock, razoring him right to the edge of coming. He couldn't think straight, sucking one whistling breath after another through his nose, half-suffocated. He pulled away. ". . . I'm Matt," he offered, trying to regain the initiative. "You from around here?" She laughed the same honey laugh again, welling it up from way down inside her, and pulled him onto the other breast.

She squeezed his balls till he squirmed, then slid her hand over his ass to run a long finger into him. He felt a surge of anger, but when her pussy lips slicked the head of his cock, his protest died. He didn't seem to enter her, but her lips slithered along his whole length, enveloping him. She moved like a wave over his body, titanic, irresistible. She pulled his head up and kissed him again, her mouth oven-temperature. He breathed her breath, sweet, flower-scented, heavy with heat. She filled his lungs, then sucked the air back out of him. His cock ratcheted at the brink of detonation.

■

Matt's head whirled with pictures: the long-legged redhead and her mousy girlfriend that he'd done X with last Saturday, humping them against a blur of surf roar all night long; the blue-green pipe he'd run in last winter's big breakers; the kid who'd tried to suck his beery cock in the john of some bar. His hips were moving of their own volition. *Inside her! I gotta be inside this chick!*

The big woman pulled him a few steps back from the rocks, laid him on the warm sand and dropped full onto him. *No . . . on top of her,* he thought, *I gotta fuck this chick,* but it was too late. Hips locked between her steel thighs, his cock disappeared inside her. His head fell back. Her smile was blinding above the looming horizon of her breasts. Her eyes were bottomless. Her laughter churned his cock.

She grabbed his hair and fucked him. Gigantically. All thought of resisting vanished.

She fucked the air out of his lungs. Her come was tectonic, a tsunami of surges and belly laughs that milked him dry and left him screaming. *Guys don't make come noises,* some corner of Matt's mind thought, but she shuddered over him and he cried out again.

When she laughed, his spent cock squeezed out of her with a *pop!* She licked his face again, bit his lip with her white, strong teeth, then slid up until her dripping pudendum scooped over his face. She began to fuck his mouth and nose.

Matt had never eaten pussy—*oral sex is for chicks*—but now he did. Her taste, her smells, were meaty—fertile smells that flooded his brain stem. He licked. He lapped. He gobbled her juices, flailed his face back and forth across her thick lips and straining clit. In the moments his mouth found air he panted and howled. His heels spurred the sand. His cock, loaded again, wet and red, slapped side to side against his thighs.

As she climaxed again and then again over Matt, she ground harder and harder against his face. *Wait, wait!* Her vagina gaped and his face sank to the ears in her. He tried to shout, tried somehow to suck air into his lungs. She thrust again. His head popped inside her. Heat. Wet, massive muscle. Darkness.

Her movements were tidal now, her laughter a huge resonant chord inside her body. Matt's arms flailed wildly in the air, fingers clutching at nothing.

She pushed harder. One shoulder slipped inside. Pushed again, and both arms were pinned to his sides. *Help me!* The heat and meaty slipperiness reached the line of his nipples, then his hips. His crimson-headed cock was jacked straight down between his legs, peeping between his vibrating thighs as her lips enveloped his ass. His feet kicked in frenzy as she enveloped his thighs. *Help!* She grunted and pushed harder, head thrown back, huge eyes rolling up in ecstasy. Ropy loops of come flung out of his straining cock.

She rose to her knees, holding her breasts to the sun. Tidal surges of pleasure sucked him in to the knees, past the shins. Finally, only the crinkled, pleading soles of his feet and his frantically wriggling toes showed. She rumbled in deep satisfaction *Help* as his toes fumbled her heavy, hooded clit.

She rose to her feet. Arched her back. Stroked her belly. Her immense dark eyes opened again to sea and sky. Satisfied. Hungry. The last ten, pink, small remnants of Matt winked out of view between her legs *(help)*.

The sun dropped toward the ocean. A surfboard and a twist of red cloth lay on the sand. The woman's figure dwindled down the beach, her elongated shadow rippling and dancing over sand and seaside cliffs. Even from a distance, you could see she was a big woman.

The Fishing Show

Mel Harris

"Oh baby . . . Oh baby! Wheeee, here we goooo. Would you look at the size of that thing! Oh—oh—oh!" Bone Wrinkelman's raspy voice filled the den. For a moment the only sound was a soft wheezing, then: "Oh, noooo! Here we go again." More wheezing. "Come on, baby. Come on. Come to Daddy—oh yeah . . ."

Laybee Wrinkelman reached over, picked up the remote, and snapped off the VCR. She'd had enough of *The Fishing Show with Bone Wrinkelman.* She tossed the remote back on the coffee table.

"Ha! I'd like to see him get half that excited when we make love," she muttered, getting up from the couch and heading for the kitchen.

She glared at the huge muskie, mounted in an upward leap, affixed to the rustic wooden beam above the doorway to the kitchen. "And I *know* you got more foreplay than I've had in the last three months!" she said to it as she walked past.

Laybee opened the refrigerator door, hunting for the pasta salad she'd made yesterday, but all she saw was six-packs of beer, logs of cold cuts, cartons of dip, and six dozen eggs.

Great, she thought. Bone was going on location again, and she wouldn't see him for another two weeks. She wouldn't get near him tonight either: one of Bone's ridiculous superstitions. "Honey, I *gotta* reserve my strength for the big game," he'd say whenever she tried to snuggle up to him before one of his trips.

She shoved a huge jar of mustard to the side and found the salad. Grabbing one of the beers, because it would irritate Bone, she slammed the door shut with her hip, picked up a fork and returned to the den. She flopped down on the couch and turned this week's show back on. Bone liked her to watch it every week before it aired: another one of his superstitions.

"Yeah, yeah, oh *yeah!*" Bone's breathing was quite heavy now, as he skillfully brought a nice largemouth bass close to his boat.

"You're just going to wet yourself, aren't you?" Laybee said, taking a long swig of beer. She watched as Bone leaned over and lifted the hefty bass out of the water and held it up for his viewers to admire.

"There's just *nothing* that compares to the feeling of landing one of these beauties!" Bone gently stroked the glistening side of the wriggling fish.

"That's not what you used to tell me," Laybee mumbled, swallowing another gulp of beer. She remembered the way Bone had been during the first years of their marriage, coming back from his trips all eager and excited, testosterone raging.

They'd jump in the shower and he'd wave his Ugly Stick (Laybee's pet name for it) at her, talking like he did on the show: "Come on, baby, soap up the rudder, baby. Make it nice and clean so it can slip through your wake." He'd made her laugh. And after she'd gotten it squeaky clean, she'd drop to her knees in the shower and ummm, ummm, ummm.

Laybee sighed. Now he just came home exhausted and hung over. She took another swig of beer and sank back into the soft cushions on the couch. She'd just have to resort to "Paddling the Pink Canoe," as Bone called it. She reached down and slid out of her jeans. She was already so wet.

■

Laybee finished her third beer and was on her way to the kitchen for a fourth when she noticed the clock. Oh boy—Bone would be home any minute to pack and he'd want his snack before he laid down for his ritual pretrip nap.

Rifling through the cupboards, she took out some crackers and peanut butter, then retrieved an apple from the refrigerator. "Damn superstitions," she muttered as she cut the apple into wedges. Bone claimed protein built up his endurance and the crackers settled his stomach for the flight. Laybee added the apple so he wouldn't die from scurvy.

She'd just finished spreading the last cracker when Bone walked through the door, hefting several large bags onto the counter. "Hi, hon," he said, walking over to the refrigerator to find room for the six pounds of bacon he'd bought. Laybee busied herself cleaning up from the snack, trying not to move too quickly, as the beer had made her a little woozy.

"Hon?" Bone said, his head in the refrigerator. "What have you done to my supplies?"

She looked up to see him dangling the half-consumed six-pack by one of the plastic rings.

"You *know* I have to have all this stuff accounted for. It's all on the expense records."

"Relax, Bone," she said, not hiding her irritation. "It's just a couple beers. It's not like I sold all your tackle in a garage sale."

"*Lay!* Don't even *think* that!" The veins on his neck bulged.

"Sit down and have your snack before you have a stroke," Laybee said, pushing the plate of crackers toward him. She picked up the bags on the counter. "I'll take this stuff up to the bedroom."

Bone threw her a hurt look but said nothing as he took the snack to the den and flipped on the VCR to watch his show.

Laybee heard him mumble, "Mmmm—yeah. Oh, that was great!" through mouthfuls of cracker as she climbed the stairs to the bedroom.

The master bedroom was the second-biggest room in the house, after the den, which had been specially built so Bone could view the many trophies, awards, and mounted game he'd gotten over the years. The large four-poster water bed occupied the center of the room. At the end of the bed sat a huge aquarium filled with Bone's favorite species of freshwater fish.

Laybee threw the bag on the bed and flopped down. She'd always found the fish gliding back and forth through the water soothing and sensual. The lighted tank threw a romantic glow on the bed. They'd spent many a night with the fish watching them make some waves in the water bed. She reached down and slid her hand inside her panties, still wet from her episode on the couch.

Since turning forty, two years ago, she'd found herself thinking about, and wanting, lovemaking nearly every day. It was worse than being a teenager. She'd been letting "her fingers do the walking" quite a bit more lately, but Bone's fingers were the ones she wanted, and his tongue, and his lips . . .

She sighed again. If only he didn't have this damn trip tonight. The shoot wouldn't even start for another three days, but Bone liked to get there early and check everything out. And, as if he didn't get enough on the shoots, he did some fishing just for pleasure.

Maybe she could talk him out of leaving tonight. He could catch the first flight out in the morning and still arrive in plenty of time for the shoot. Laybee rolled over on her side and propped herself up on her elbow to stare at the fish. Nope, Bone would never go for that. His location shoots were like religious rituals. She looked around the room at the dozen or so boxes of tackle, fishing line and artificial bait that would be soon packed for the trip. She reached over and picked up a bag of glitter-infused, fluorescent-yellow night crawlers. They felt cool and enticing through the package.

Suddenly, Laybee dropped the bag back into the box and started searching through the rest of the boxes. Leaders, lures, floats, weights. She sat back down on the bed, a wide grin on her face.

■

Laybee heard the muffled thumps of Bone's slow, steady footsteps on the carpeted stairs as he headed for their bedroom. She hurried to finish brushing her hair and straightened her robe. She hoped she had returned everything to its proper box so as not to arouse suspicion.

"I'm going to go downstairs and read so you can have some peace and quiet for your nap," she said to him as he entered the bedroom.

"Thanks, hon," he said, his hair tousled, eyelids heavy. "I really am tired. Will you be sure to wake me in an hour so I'll have plenty of time to pack?"

"Sure," she replied, looking at her watch. "One hour. Sweet dreams."

"Thanks, Lay," he said, pulling off his flannel shirt and hanging it over the back of the stuffed bobcat poised next to the bed. Clad only in his underwear and socks, he settled comfortably into the bed.

She flipped off the light and went downstairs to the den to put the finishing touches on her plan.

■

Laybee moved quietly through the darkened bedroom and stood next to the bed watching Bone sleep, sprawled out on his back. She shivered. She'd spent the past twenty minutes pacing the carpet in the den, finalizing her plans and waiting to make sure Bone was fast asleep. He slept like a rock, but still she moved cautiously. She had to have everything in place before he awoke, or it was never going to work.

Spying the large box she was looking for next to the bed, she reached over and gently removed four hinged rod holders, a manufacturer's gift given to Bone to promote on the show. She unfastened the hinges, trying to control her breathing. Her hands trembled as she opened each of the cuff-shaped rod holders. The holders were lined with a soft polyurethane foam, designed to prevent scratching and nicking of expensive fishing rods.

Laybee snapped two hundred-pound test leaders to the ring on the outside of each rod holder, then looped the leaders around each of the four bedposts and fastened them on the ring. Very cautiously, she slid one of the holders around Bone's wrist; fastening it securely to form a cuff, she quickly repeated the process on his other wrist and then on each of his ankles.

Opening another box, she found a large round cork float and set it on the edge of the bed. She also found one of the red bandannas Bone wore around his neck, a trademark of his show.

As she was double-checking the rod holders to make sure they were fastened securely, Bone began to stir. He opened his mouth in a wide yawn, obviously not yet aware of his predicament. Laybee stood back to admire her work and to see if the contraption would hold.

Suddenly Bone's eyes grew huge.

"Ah," she said with obvious satisfaction. "I see you're awake now."

"Laybee?" he said, still not fully comprehending. "What's goin' on?"

He tried to sit up, but when he realized he couldn't, he looked over at his wrists, and then his feet. The look of surprise quickly turned to panic.

"Don't get yourself all worked up, Bone." Her voice was oddly calm.

Bone's panic did not subside, however, and he began pulling his arms and legs, frantically trying to free himself. He only succeeded in pulling the rod holders more tightly around his wrists and ankles, the edges cutting into his flesh. Finally he gave up and lay panting on the bed.

He raised his head and looked at her in puzzlement. His eyes narrowed. "You've been watchin' them talk shows again, haven't you?"

Laybee said nothing.

Bone finally dropped his head back down on the bed.

"C'mon Laybee, you've had your fun. Now, I've *got* to get ready—"

"I don't think so," she interrupted, walking around to the end of the bed. "I watched your show today, Bone. It was real good. Just like it always is with all your hootin' and hollerin' and all those sweet words for the damn fish. You get so excited, I bet you come over the edge of the boat after the camera stops rolling."

"No, Laybee, that's *not* what happens—well okay, maybe once. But just that time in Minnesota when I landed that big muskie. Uh—and that time on Lake Michigan when the drag was set just right and—"

"Shut up, Bone!" she snapped. Laybee was pacing now.

Bone lay back silent for a moment, nervously flexing his hands. He looked at her again.

"Laybee, honey, *please*. I'm *so* sorry you feel ignored, but I have to go on this trip." His voice was pleading, feigning sweetness. "Is it PMS, hon? Is it . . . *that time?"*

She'd heard enough. Moving quickly now, Laybee dropped the float in Bone's open mouth and tied it in place with the bandanna.

"Munggrahhh?" Bone mumbled behind the cork.

"Ah, ah, ah!" Laybee said, shaking her finger at him, as she straddled his chest. "You're going to gag yourself."

"Aaragganth, bblanth, aahh garratsh . . ." He was waving his hands and jerking his head toward the boxes and suitcases next to the bed. "Mmrrrunggah!!" he growled again and started to cough.

"Oh, you're not going anywhere, Bone Wrinkelman," she said with a satisfied smile. "I've been waiting for a moment like this for a long time." Her nostrils flared. "I've spent the last two years waiting for you to stay home long enough to remind you what being with a woman is like. I've barely gotten enough time to watch you milk your monkey."

Bone grew strangely quiet. In Laybee's heated discussion, her arm flailing had caused her robe to fall open, revealing the tight leather teddy she'd slipped into earlier. She stopped for a moment, watching Bone stare at her heaving breasts. He looked nervous. She knew he could feel her wet heat spreading across his chest. A smile returned to her tempting lips.

Laybee slid off him, stood next to the bed and removed her robe, letting it fall to the floor. Bone made some sort of gurgling sound deep in his throat. His eyes were glued to her.

"Ah, you like my new outfit?" She turned around, allowing him full visual advantage. "I got it last year while you were on location in Canada.

"And look at these neat little accessories," she said, peeling off the cups of the bra, revealing her full nipples. Another groan arose from Bone.

Laybee returned to the edge of the bed. Bone's boxer shorts were beginning to crease at an odd angle. She reached over, lifted the elastic waist band and took a peek. "Mmm, it's true. Graphite rods *do* have the best action," she said, slipping her hand inside. The boxers turned and tugged like a squirrel had gotten loose in them.

She removed her hand from Bone's shorts, letting the elastic band snap. Bone whimpered softly, his eyes pleading. Laybee turned again to search in one of the boxes. She came across a small, zippered case. Smiling, she opened it.

Bone could see she held something in her hand as she turned to face him again, but it wasn't until she sat the camcorder on the corner of the aquarium and was carefully focusing it on him, that he realized what she was doing.

"We're going to make our own little show, Bone Wrinkelman." Laybee pushed the RECORD button.

Still searching, she reached into a nearby box, pulling out a multi-purpose pocket tool. She fiddled with it and found it had a pliers, screwdriver, corkscrew, and several knife blades, all in one. "Hmmm. 'The Leatherman.' This is *very* interesting," she said. Bone's eyes widened.

"This should do it," she said, and pulling out the longest of the knife blades, she ran it lightly up the inside of Bone's thigh, lifting at the leg of his boxers.

He squirmed and whimpered, trying to get away from the cool, sharp, blade.

"Relax, Bone," she said. "I'm horny, not stupid."

She grasped the shorts in one hand and cut through the material with several deft strokes, the tattered remains falling back on the bed. Bone inhaled sharply. Before he could recover enough to take another breath, she repeated the process on his T-shirt, exposing his heaving chest and splendid erection.

Bone looked at his erection, then at Laybee, then back at his erection. His eyes begged.

Just then, the phone beside the bed rang. Laybee jumped and Bone whimpered. She picked up the phone. "Hello?" She put on her best housewife voice.

"Hey, Laybee. This is Rog Sparks. We're waiting for Bone down here so we can load up the plane. Is he there?"

"Hi, Rog." Her voice was sweeter than Berkely's Liquid Fish

Attractant. "I'm so sorry, but Bone can't come to the phone. He's all tied up right now—some special research or something."

Bone was waving his hands and making strained grunting noises. Laybee leaned over and pressed the exposed blade of the Leatherman firmly into his flesh, just below his navel. It immediately silenced him.

"Well, is he going to make the flight, Laybee? He knows we leave in half an hour."

"Mmm, well. I wouldn't count on it, Rog. I think he said something about catching up with you guys tomorrow on location."

The silence hung for a long moment.

"Well, I, ah, guess we'd better go on ahead . . ."

"Yes, Rog, I think that's wise."

"Okay then. Bye."

Laybee hung up the phone. Bone's breathing had slowed, his erection flagging.

"Now, back to business." She leaned over. He felt her heated breath. "We'll fix Mr. Wiggley," she murmured, taking all of him into her mouth.

Slowly, keeping a firm suction with her mouth, she pulled back. Bone's breathing quickened as she withdrew, his hips bucking forward in an attempt to thrust himself further into her mouth. Laybee took his wrinkled pouch in her hand and gently but firmly drew his swollen jewels toward his thighs. Letting him slide out of her mouth, she admired him for a moment, glistening and pulsating in the light of the aquarium.

The muscles of his abdomen tightened, and Laybee noticed the escalating bucking and pitching of his shaft. Bone's eyes rolled back in his head and he let out a deep gurgling moan. She reached over and frantically rummaged through the boxes. She recognized that motion; Bone Wrinkelman was about to spill.

"Oh, no you don't," she said, taking one of the glittery neon jelly worms and tightening it firmly around the base of his penis.

The artificial bait did the trick—his erection finally stopped its lurching and stood tall and proud. Bone was now making slow, steady grunting noises.

Laybee returned to pacing beside the bed. Then, snapping her fingers, she rifled through the boxes again. Bone's erection rose and fell, following Laybee's movements as if watching her.

She found a large aerosol can. "BANG! Fish Attractant," she read. She popped the cap off and sprayed a little of the contents into the lid and sniffed it.

"Whew," she said, coughing and waving her hand. "That smells like Rog. No wonder he never has a date." She tossed the can back into the pile.

Holding up a package, she discovered a long carolina leader: a weight and two glowing red beads threaded onto a length of wire and finished on the ends with two snap swivels. She took it out of the package and fastened it around his neck, linking the swivels together.

"There," she said, arranging it. "Now you're dressed for the occasion."

She held up several more packages and read their contents out loud: "Pearl White Lizards, six-inch size. Shaky Tail Worm, in June-bug and watermelon-seed colors. Four-inch Meatheads, and the ten-inch *Old Monster?*"

She looked at him, "Jeez, Bone, what do you guys *do* with this stuff?"

Bone shrugged.

"I might have to keep some of these for myself." She picked out the six-inch Pearl White Lizards and the ten-inch Old Monster in watermelon-seed color and walked over to her dresser, depositing them in her underwear drawer.

Returning to the bed, she opened a couple of packages and pulled out their contents. The smooth, rubbery jelly baits wiggled and danced in her hands. They felt sensual, almost alive. Too good to put on a hook, she thought. Selecting a couple of glimmer-blue Split Tail Trailers, she draped them over her nipples and turned to Bone.

"Do I attract you now, Bone?" She shook her shoulders briefly, the shivers causing the Split Tail Trailers to dance erotically. Then she picked up a bait that looked like a giant red-and-black rubber caterpillar.

"Ooh—a Bush Hogg," she started to moan. "I know *just* where I want you." She slipped aside the leg of her teddy and rubbed the trembling lure along the inner edge of her recent trim. Her head fell back and she savored the prickly texture, beginning a steady rocking motion as she maneuvered the jelly bait. The Split Tail Trailers flipped onto Bone's chest.

He stared at them. He had forgotten to breathe, and he was turning a deep cinnamon red. Suddenly, he took a huge breath.

Laybee looked at him. "We can't have you passing out for lack of air now, can we?" she said, putting down the now-wet lure and opening a big box. She took out a bait aerator, an apparatus that looked like a small aquarium pump, attached a long plastic tube to it, and then plugged it into the wall. It made a quiet hum.

Setting the pump down next to the bed, she inserted the end of the tube under the bandanna tied around Bone's mouth, alongside the cork float. A more normal color soon returned to Bone's face.

"There we go," she said, slapping him gently on the cheek. "Now you'll have plenty of air."

Bone gave her a look that said he knew she had completely and utterly lost her mind. But then he gave another pleading look, nodding toward his penis.

Laybee pressed a finger to the top of his penis and watched it twitch. "Don't worry, Bone. I have big plans for the Ugly Stick." She slid her finger around the edge of his purple helmet.

Picking up the Bush Hogg again, she resumed her exploration, only now she propped one leg on the edge of the bed and faced Bone as she worked. Laybee was thoroughly enjoying herself, finding the texture and sensation of the soft bait exquisite. But she was also keeping a close eye on Bone. His nostrils flared with each breath, his eyes transfixed by the action of the lure.

"Now don't you wish you were Mr. Bush Hogg here, Bone?" she cooed as she slipped the tail of the bait further inside.

Bone had resumed his quiet steady grunting, fascinated with the steady motions Laybee was making with her hands and the lure.

Laybee had to be careful. This lure was very effective, and she felt herself teetering on the edge of an unstoppable freefall. She slipped out the Bush Hogg and climbed on the bed. Kneeling next to Bone's hips, she began rubbing the wet, tensile bait along the length of his shaft.

"Aaaggrrrl," Bone growled, his toes curling up.

She leaned over and followed the motion of the lure with her tongue, causing his erection to make short jerking strokes in her mouth.

"Mmm," she murmured, without stopping.

Bone began thrusting his hips forward again, increasing the motion of her mouth.

Laybee sat up for a moment, but Bone continued his thrusting, moaning in protest.

"Hold on, boy," she said breathlessly. "We're gonna take care of that for you right now."

Laybee carefully straddled his hips. She gripped his erection in both hands and, poised above him, she began her descent. Bone, urgent and shaking, saw her hover briefly above him before plunging downward. It was only at the last moment he saw the split in her teddy that allowed an unencumbered splashdown.

Bone's crescendo was drowned out by Laybee's own ululating. She'd found the Bush Hogg again and was rubbing it on the front side of his shaft, both of them sharing in the pleasure. Laybee rose and fell on Bone like the waves of the sea.

Finally, she could wait no longer, and she reached around and tugged at the jelly worm still tied around Bone's erection, releasing him. Laybee leaned forward and gripped Bone's shoulders, increasing her rocking as together they rode the wild wave.

■

"C'mon, baby . . . that's it. C'mon home to me now. That's it!" Bone's grunting filled the den. Laybee giggled.

They snuggled together on the couch, watching his latest show.

She looked at him and he grinned as he patted her gently on the thigh. It had been a wonderful week since he'd been home from the shoot. Bone hadn't left the house since he'd been back, except for beer and food.

She watched him pull up a gorgeous walleye on the video. "Wow! Did you come after that one?" she teased.

"Naw," he blushed. "I saved my bait just for you, baby."

Laybee giggled again.

Bone traced the outline of her left breast with his finger. "I think I found a new pre-trip ritual, too." He grinned again.

"Mmm, and I have the video to prove it," Laybee said, snuggling into his shoulder.

"Watch this," Bone said, picking up the remote to turn up the volume.

The last few minutes of the show were coming up.

The camera zoomed in on a very relaxed, slightly sunburned Bone standing on the edge of a dock next to a boat. He was wearing the leader "necklace."

"Remember, folks, the key to a successful fishing trip is being prepared." He propped one foot on the edge of the boat. "The right bait, the right lures, and the right equipment for the right moment." Grinning, Bone patted the rod holders, now mounted on the boat.

"But most of all, remember that everything in life is better when you share it with the one you love. Bye now, and cast your line with a friend!" On the video, Bone waved and the credits began to roll.

The Blowfish

Amelia G

I lied to the police about how Jimmy died because I wanted the Fugu for myself. With the price tags on those babies, there was no other way I would ever get one.

"Please, tell me again, Mr. Renaldi, how you found your roommate," the pretty red-haired lieutenant asked me.

"You've already heard my story, and I'm sticking to it." I laughed so she would know I was feebly attempting to make a joke. The chances were slim, as I was possibly on the verge of becoming a murder suspect, but I wanted her to find me charming. Because I wanted to fuck her. Not badly or anything, but it would have been nice. Nothing like hormones to keep me polite.

"I don't think there is any chance you are failing to tell the truth," she purred. "I just need you to repeat what you told me so I can get a taped transcript. Regulations, you know."

"I thought you were recording the first time."

"The tape deck malfunctioned. Joys of technology, you know. It all saves lots of time. Except when it doesn't."

This was one tough lady. The stench of the room in the July heat was making me feel completely ill, but she seemed totally unfazed. I looked over at the white plastic bag on the bed. "Let's go in the kitchen," I said. Not that I was in any condition to eat, but the living room doubled as my bedroom and we were in Jimmy's room, which had the distinct disadvantage of having Jimmy in it.

Even though it was my apartment, the officer led the way. I watched her ass tilt briskly back and forth as she walked. She had the most perfect heart-shaped butt. My dick twitched futilely in my tight blue jeans. But I thought it was more the tantalizing future prospect of the Fugu than the concrete presence of the redhead. I sat down in a folding chair at the gray-and-white marbled Formica table. She remained standing. I pushed aside a coffee tin that had been left out on the table and scratched idly at a blob of periwinkle oil paint that had crystallized on the tabletop.

She clicked the microrecorder on. "How did you know James Woodbern?"

"I met him at *d.c. space.* Some of my paintings were on display there that month and his band was playing one night when I dropped by to see how people were reacting to my stuff."

"That's over by Seventh and E, right?" There was an edge in her voice now. I imagined that she had read some of the press my exhibition had been getting and now there was no chance of her fucking me. I've sold stuff to men's magazines from time to time, but I never got much artistic recognition—or cash—until Women Against Pornography tried to get my paintings removed from *d.c. space.*

"Yes, that is where *space* is." We lived over a tacky clothing boutique on Ninth NW, so she could practically see Seventh and E from the kitchen window.

She nodded and wrote something down. "So, how long have you known Mr. Woodbern?"

"About a year and a half." It sounded odd hearing her call him Mr. Woodbern, because most people we knew didn't even know that was the guitarist's real name. Until about six months ago, I was always answering the door for nubile young things who giggled and said, "Is Jimmy Burn there? Is Jimmy Burn there? You know, the one from Chip-In Passion?" I never told any of them the real reason why Jimmy stopped wanting them. And, hell, Jimmy had always been fickle. He went through cute female mini-starfuckers the way I went through paintbrushes. He claimed he got inspiration from them. (The teenyboppers, not my paintbrushes.) Mostly, I think he got blow jobs.

Personally, I particularly wanted this extra-tenacious babe called Spike. She claimed she got the nickname because she wore a spiked collar to school when she was, like, thirteen. She had long brown hair, except on the right-hand side, where it was shaved down to the scalp. Her mom's a politician and her dad's a lawyer, so she's got this big rebel thing going on. But aside from that, she looked soft, big tits and no bra, only eighteen, but with real womanly curves, not like a Spike at all. Painters just don't get laid like musicians do.

"How long," the cop asked, "did you share an apartment with Mr. Woodbern?"

"Almost exactly one year. Our lease runs out in three weeks." I chipped away at a bit of crimson paint, trying to make the table properly off-white with the bitten-down stub of my fingernail.

She paced over to our decrepit stove. Neither Jimmy nor I ever really cooked. The stove had broken four months ago, and neither of us had felt the urge to really press the landlord. We mostly ate take-out when we had money and boiled Ramen noodles in the hot pot when we didn't.

"Mr. Renaldi," she said, "don't you find it odd that your room-mate is dead? Doesn't it concern you that a man may have been murdered in your home?"

I couldn't quite get up the energy to rip on her for her tone of voice. I just wanted them all to go away and leave me alone. The Fugu was waiting. "Look," I said, "Jimmy was my best friend. I'm upset that he is dead, but carrying on and displaying my emotions in front of you is not going to bring him back. Sure, I suspect foul play. I'm assuming he was poisoned, given that he was twisted all weird when I found him. I paint the human body, so I'm pretty in touch with the fact that human bodies don't contort into a position like that without something being horribly horribly *horribly* wrong. And I don't think I'm assuming too much when I say that was probably his puke all over his damn bedroom. My home is a wreck and my roommate is deceased so, yes, I suppose you could say I'm concerned." Mostly, though, I was just upset because I noticed she was checking out the painting I had hanging on the kitchen wall. It was a really dark night painting of Washington, D.C., lit up with the moon as a beautiful woman's ass. I'm good with detail, and *The Moon* was a work I was too personally attached to to sell or even show. And I could just tell she disapproved of the erotic content in my artwork.

I guess maybe that makes me either a shallow egotistical prick or a deep tortured artist. Or maybe some combo of the two. But, without my painting, I'm just another guy with a slightly unusual haircut and no money who would kind of like to get laid. I decided it would be best if I did not show the lieutenant my current work in progress. I was doing a painting of two friends of ours—well, I guess two friends of mine now that Jimmy is dead. The two of them were fucking doggie style in front of the big main window of the Office of Thrift Supervision. So far, the people looked good, and the building was passable, but the huge elegant potted plants just didn't look as moneyed as the originals.

"Mr. Renaldi, I am not trying to give you a hard time." Lieutenant Whatever-Her-Name-Was was getting that tone of voice my high school teachers always used to get immediately before giving me a hard time.

If I had thought about it, I would probably have tried to get on the cop's good side. If she had been a man, I probably would have tried to get in good. I knew she was a cop, but my brain just kept processing *hotchickhotchickhotchick*—hot chick who thinks she is too good for you. So I responded like a total dickhead, the way I would if some good-looking girl I met in a bar really frosted me.

I picked up the copy of this week's *City Paper* I had lying on the table. I opened it up and pretended I couldn't hear the cop talking. The cover story was about the horrible epidemic proportions the AIDS IV virus had reached in the Washington, D.C., area. Ironically, I noticed a smaller story about the legal battles over the Fugu. I flipped to the AIDS IV story because I knew there was no way I could read about the Fugu with a straight face. Given the circumstances.

Jimmy had written a funny song about what *AIDS IV* really stood for. The song was a super-sappy love song based on the fact that, unlike its predecessors, AIDS IV can survive outside the human body for quite some time, but it doesn't want to. Lots of lines about how I could live without you for a while, but eventually it would kill me, etc. Jimmy almost never did his band's lyric writing, but he wrote the funniest series of songs about STDs right before the band broke up. Chip-In Passion probably would never have made it past the local fame it had achieved, anyway. But it was a shame Jimmy never got to perform the AIDS IV song live.

I realized the cop had not stopped talking. "Hey," I finally addressed her, "there is a good band playing at the 9:30 tonight. The Numlocks have a really hot set this tour, complete with random MIDI, three-D imaging through the audience, and just shuttle-loads full of fog juice."

"Mr. Renaldi," the redhead began icily. I love icy. I like the challenge of warming it up. "I realize that you may be in shock over what has happened here today, so I am going to give you a little bit of slack." With that, she turned on her heel and took her perfect heart-shaped butt elsewhere.

The two male cops carried what was left of Jimmy out on a stretcher. I just sat in the kitchen, shifting uncomfortably in my folding chair. I think one of them made some snide comment about coming back to take me out the same way. At this point, however, I really was starting to go into shock.

I'd left the *City Paper* open to the article on AIDS IV, but I was pretty sure I did not want to read about that. I flipped to the Fugu story, thinking of it as foreplay. That bitchy redhead had looked right at the coffee tin on the kitchen table. She'd never suspected a thing. She would have, I guess, if she'd looked in the sink. I laughed to myself. I had poured the entire can of coffee grounds into the drain before I discovered that our garbage disposal had broken.

The Fugu story was mostly about the legal battles over its distribution in the United States. It included a short interview with Niles Takamoto. The man talked a lot about the delicacy of the product. "In Japan, only the finest chef can prepare the Fugu, the Japanese blowfish, for eating. It is a very special meal. The meal is made more poignant by the knowledge that the diner could die from eating it. Even the finest chef sometimes makes an error. Then the blowfish, although tasty, is fatally poisonous. It is the last supper then."

I stopped reading at this point because my dick was so hard, my tight faded jeans were starting to make it hurt. I unzipped and let the little monster breathe. The air felt good on my hard-on, and it jumped when I touched it, but I had no intention of jerking myself off. Not today.

I opened the coffee can and pulled out the latex figure with the trailing wires. It looked like a rubber fish with a tail of colorful wire streamers. First, I attached the red electrodes to each hip. Then I pressed the dermal patches for the blue electrodes against my butt cheeks. I pressed the big purple wire onto my chest. I gently placed the derm for one of the yellow electrodes against my right testicle. A shudder ripped through me at my own touch. I was so worked up to try this thing, I was afraid I might come before I even got it on. Or so soon after, that I might as well just have been stroking myself. I attached the other yellow wire and carefully lowered the latex fish part over my fat empurpled dickhead. Slowly, my whole rod disappeared inside of the fish mouth. Finally, even my balls were inside the Fugu.

Well, really it just felt like latex. Not all that special. I guess maybe it is just the anticipation and the danger that really gets users off. I lay down on the cool kitchen floor and flipped the switch to ON/FULL AUTO. Immediately, I felt slippery warmth begin to slide around my cock. Wet as the most willing partner. A slight tingling began just beneath my purple helmet. Just a tickle and wetness everywhere. The tickle grew to a gentle stroke, like the stiff tip of a beautiful woman's tongue. I imagined the auburn-haired police lieutenant. I imagined Jimmy's ex-girlfriend, pale young Spike. Finally, I stopped imagining and just lost myself in the sensation. This was better than anything I had ever experienced before. Fantasizing about something else was unnecessary, irrelevant, cheapening somehow.

"Oh yeah, oh yeah, oh yeah!" I heard moans and cries and eventually recognized my own voice.

The tongue sensation expanded. Something warm and wet nuzzled at the tip of my swollen member. Another invitingly slippery tendril of sensations twirled around the base. And I began to feel two long strokes along each side.

And the Fugu gave off this scent. Musky. Musky, like someone was fucking up a storm and a half on my kitchen floor. The sweet fragrance of a woman in heat going neck and neck with my own feverish excitement.

The Fugu suddenly gripped me tightly. I jumped, terrified, waiting for the prick of the death needle in the left side of my dick. But the pinprick never came. Instead, the thing's innards began rotating in such a way that I felt like I was plunging into the deepest, most perfect, just-tight-enough, but not too-tight vagina. Holding me, urging me deeper, caressing, and I plummeted farther and farther in. I actually tried to hold back for a moment, but then the thing reversed its motion and I felt like I was pulling out, being pulled out, being cast out of Eden, like there were only a few moments left in which I could come. Even as I rocketed backward, the part around my balls began to massage them slowly. My balls were so full of jism, it felt like they were pressing up against the inside of the head of my dick.

Just as I was about to shoot my load, like it knew I was on the verge (I guess with those electrodes, the Fugu *did* know I was on the verge), the Fugu clamped around the top of my balls and the base of my dick, forcing my orgasm back, holding it screamingly at bay. If the Fugu were a woman, at that moment I would have promised it anything if only it would make me come, let me come, let me come, let me come, come, come come come comecomecome.

I cried out as my body tried to raise my arousal level to the point where I could overcome the Fugu's clamps. Then it unclamped abruptly and began treating me to the sensation of the perfect blow job. Then, just as I was about to climax, it clamped down again. "Please, please let me come," I begged aloud. But the machine was implacable. It kept urging me on, stroking me, warming me, lubricating my blue-steel erection with what felt like a beautiful woman's spit, love juice, love. And then my balls would rise to fire out my chisel-stiff cock—and the clamps would clasp me and stop me from reaching what I was sure was the only destiny that mattered.

And then, when I had despaired of ever getting to have an orgasm, whatever internal mechanism felt like a blow job started again. And my tormented testicles rose and expanded and the world exploded. My cockhead was squeezed slightly and my hot come flew through it with the most intense sensation. My come was a spray of solder, the molten steel of my erection, hot, powerful, intense, heaven, an opening at the Corcoran, at the Guggenheim, at the Museum of Modern Art, love, romance, being with someone else, being someone else, *coming*.

When it was over, I lay back on the cool kitchen floor, an idiot smile on my face. The world felt like a just place. I fell asleep to the sensation of the Fugu licking me clean.

While I slept, I dreamt that Jimmy's babe Spike was trying to get me to have sex with her. "Come on," my dream girl whispered seductively.

"I don't think I can do it again just yet," I told her.

"Come on," she purred, reaching between my thighs. To my surprise and delight, I began to stiffen, responding to her touch.

"COME ON!" I woke up to the sound of loud knocking on the front door. Embarrassed, I turned the Fugu's switch to the OFF position and quickly disconnected the wires. I pulled my jeans up from around my ankles. While I stuffed the Fugu back in the coffee can, I shouted that I'd be right there.

"Hi, Spike."

"Hey, Ren. Jimmy go through with it?"

"What are you talking about?"

Spike swept past me even though I sure hadn't asked her in. "I talked to Jimmy last night, and he sounded bad. Worse than when he first found out. Said he'd like to die of pleasure."

Feeling like a traitor, but needing to talk, I said, "He had a Fugu, you know."

"Yeah." When she shrugged, I couldn't help noticing the way her breasts jiggled.

"I don't know where he got it, but I guess he had a real problem with it for the last six months or so."

"I bought it for him, and I don't think he had a problem," Spike said. "You know what a womanizer he always was. The guy had appetites, but he had the decency to satisfy them at home when he found out he was a foregone conclusion."

I hadn't quite gotten it yet, but there was a growing premonition of doom. "What do you mean? Weren't you jealous? I mean, you didn't sleep with anyone else after Jimmy stopped sleeping with you."

"That's because I wanted to sleep with you, but I didn't think I should do it while Jimmy was alive. It would have been cruel." She gave me a smile so inviting, I could have fallen into it.

Suddenly it clicked. "Jimmy was foregone?"

"Yeah," she said, "I thought you knew."

"No."

"Maybe he didn't want you to know, Ren. 'Cause you lived in the same apartment. Maybe he was afraid you'd get the scare. Not like you could catch AIDS IV from your apartment mate, unless you were trading off blow jobs or sharing a vibrator. But you know how some people are." She put a creamy hand on my shoulder.

"I wish he'd trusted me."

"I'm sorry," she said solemnly. Then more brightly, "I bet I can make you feel better."

I'm only seven years older than that sweet, soft eighteen-year-old is, but somewhere along the way, I misplaced that enthusiasm. I reached out and cupped one of her large, soft breasts in one hand.

"That feels nice." Spike smiled and rubbed against me.

"I wish Jimmy'd trusted me," I repeated.

"Because you wouldn't have held it against him?" she offered.

I let go of Spike's breast and stood back from her. "No, because I wouldn't have used his Fugu."

"Oh," she said. "Thanks for telling me." There was a long, awkward silence. Finally, she added, "Seriously, thanks for telling me. A lot of guys would have just fucked me and oh well for my welfare."

"I couldn't do that to you," I said.

We stood there awkwardly for a minute, not saying anything. I wanted to ask her if she'd bought Jimmy the Fugu because she loved him and wanted him to have what he wanted or because she hated him for not loving her back and wanted to kill him. After the second minute of silence and shuffling feet, I realized that I was not going to get up the nerve to ask her about where she'd purchased the Fugu, much less why. So I told her I had some painting I had to get done and which I needed to be alone for. Which was true as far as it goes.

"Thanks," she said again as she headed out of my apartment. I locked the door behind her and checked it twice to be sure it was locked.

I opened the coffee can and took out the Fugu. It leered up at me knowingly—if fish can leer. I wondered if there was something special I should clean it out with, but I figured I had used it already, so I just kind of dumped some antibacterial Dial soap into the receptacle and rinsed it out. I began to make the connections.

Probably just as well Spike didn't know quite where my surprising honesty came from. Before I tried the Fugu, I might not have thought too seriously about any danger to her health. Of course, there might not have been one then . . . but now I knew that there was something I could enjoy more than fucking Spike, or any other woman, for that matter. Something I could enjoy whenever I wanted. Entirely without pressure, without rejection, without guilt.

I figured I'd get some painting done later. I thought about the punk-rock girl getting it from behind in front of the glass doors to the ironically ornate lobby of the Office of Thrift Supervision. I thought it might be the best thing I'd ever painted, even better than my *Moon* painting.

I closed my eyes and shivered with excitement.

Casting Couch

Serena Moloch

The Job Applicant (Trixie)

I'm so nervous about this interview. I really want this job.

Let me go over it all again. Why I want the job: I'm interested in getting into film and video production and I'd like to learn from the ground up; producer's assistant would be perfect. Why they should hire me: I'm organized, responsible, learn fast, and . . . what was the fourth? Oh, right, *responsive,* I'm responsible *and* responsive to my employer. Previous experience, two years as personal assistant to an executive director. Why I left that job: tricky, but stick to the standard answer, no more room for growth. I just hope Gillian wrote me a good reference, like she promised. Typing speed, 80 words per minute . . . I certainly did Gillian enough favors—a good letter is the least she could do for me in return. Oh, I'm tapping again, I have to stop that. Should I go fix my hair? No, better stay here. Do I have copies of my résumé? What time is it? Early still. Ten more minutes to go.

The Boss (Jane)

As soon as I saw her file, I knew she'd be perfect. With its royal-blue letters leaping off a mauve page, her résumé was eye-catching in a vulgar way that suggested initiative coupled with inexperience. She was underqualified for the position I'd advertised, and I'd be sure to let her know that, so she'd be even more grateful to be hired and even more eager to please. Furthermore, some suggestive phrases in her former employer's reference interested me. Trixie was "a model assistant who never hesitated to provide any service asked, even if that meant helping in ways that some might construe as more personal than professional." She was also "devoted and solicitous."

Trixie must have worked pretty hard, I thought. I leaned back and imagined using that wonderfully ridiculous name in a variety of situations. Trixie, come in here, I'd say over the intercom. Trixie, sit down and take a letter. This is my assistant, Trixie, I'd tell people. Trixie, get me a drink. Trixie, lie down . . . Trixie, take off your clothes . . . now mine . . . very good, Trixie.

I sighed and let the chair come forward again. Too many years of reading scripts had fostered a bad habit of associating names to types and spinning off into little fantasies. Sure, I saw Trixie as a ripe peach, with big round eyes and nipples to match, traipsing her luscious ass around the office in a tight skirt, eager to please. But Trixie would probably be more concerned with her paycheck than with me. Or she'd be all too interested in her effect on me, if the past week's interviews were any indication.

The applicants had been very good looking, and perfectly competent for the job, but they were all actresses eager to break into the business, and it was obvious they had only their interests in mind and not mine. I had certainly been offered a variety of services.

I didn't enjoy remembering what had frankly been a tiring and unpleasant series of encounters. Jill had stared at me oddly until she finally got up the courage to make her move, opening her blouse and fondling her very beautiful breasts while maintaining intense eye contact. "Do you like my titties?" she asked, and I said, "Yes, I like them, Jill, but I don't like you. Thanks for coming in today."

Then there was Pamela, a redhead in spandex. She was quicker than Jill. After two questions about her secretarial skills she walked around my desk to stand directly in front of me, then lifted up her skirt and started to play with herself through some very transparent underwear. "I could really show you a good time," she whispered as she probed her pussy through the silk. "Not now, Pamela," I'd said, "and not ever."

Lenore had a more sophisticated appearance but an even less subtle approach; as soon as the door was closed she came up to me, got down on her knees, and started tugging at my pants zipper. "Tell me what you like," she said, and though I enjoyed imagining what her tongue might do to me, I wasn't interested; I quoted *All About Eve* to let her know why: "I'll tell you what I like, Lenore. I like to go after what I want. I don't want it coming after me."

Maybe Trixie would be better behaved.

The Interview (Trixie)

Oh, no, the receptionist is telling me to go in, and I just slipped my shoe off, okay, got it, here I go, now she's calling me back, oh, great, I left my bag on the chair, good work, Trixie, all right, review the four points, learn fast, organized, responsive, and responsible. No, responsible and responsive.

"Oh, what a nice office," I hear myself saying. Stupid, stupid, not a good way to begin.

"Yes, I like it very much," she says. "Have a seat. No, no, on the chair, not the couch. I save that for more informal occasions. Well, Ms. Davis—or can I call you Trixie? Yes? Good. Trixie. Why don't you tell me what you like about the office. Why do you find it nice?"

This is a funny way to start an interview, but she's the boss. "Well, it's very comfortable." She's staring at me. Maybe she's checking out my analytical skills. "The colors are warm and there's a mix of office furniture, like your desk and all those filing cabinets, and then furniture that's more, um, cozy, like the couch and the bar and the mirrors."

She's smiling, that's good. What's she asking now? Oh, okay, normal questions, typing speed, my qualifications, why I want the job, why I left my last job. I think we're getting along well. She's very attractive—forties, sharp suit, pants, very short hair.

"You know you're not really qualified for this position, don't you, Trixie?"

I blush, but remember to hold my ground. "I may not be right now, but I'll work hard and—"

"But I'm going to hire you anyway," she interrupts. "Because I can tell that you'll be amenable to training, and that you have the makings of a truly gifted assistant. You had a very special relationship with your previous employer, didn't you? Gillian Jackson?"

Now I'm blushing even more, because the way she mentions Gillian makes me nervous. "We got along very well and I really enjoyed working with her."

"And she enjoyed you. She speaks highly of you and mentions qualities that I've been seeking as well: your ability to help her relax, to devote yourself personally to her needs, never to fuss at unusual requests. If you can provide me with the same attention and if you don't object to some supplementary training now and then, you'll have no problem with this position."

Why do I feel that she's saying more than she's saying?

"Can you start tomorrow morning? Good. Ten o'clock: we're not early birds in this line of business. Any questions?"

"I was just wondering what your specialty is here. The notice just said Top Productions, film and video."

"That's a very good question, Trixie, and in fact we do have a specialized focus, but why don't you and I discuss that in the morning. And, Trixie, please call me Jane."

The Job (Jane)

Trixie's first day turned out to be a busy one: in the morning, a casting call, and in the afternoon, a wrap. With any luck, the day would reveal some significant gaps in Trixie's knowledge and skills that would require the kind of extra training session to which she had so readily assented during the interview. Ah, but I was letting myself get carried away again. I can't help but experience the world in cinematic terms, and from my first view of her, her voluptuous body straining as she frantically tried to put her shoe on, Trixie struck me as a complete ingenue in whom sweet awkwardness and powerful sensuality existed side by side. In another era, she'd have been the script girl in glasses who saves the show by shedding her spectacles and becoming a beauty just in time to replace the ailing star. Perhaps she could replace one of my stars today.

Dreams, idle dreams.

She arrived promptly, wearing a red wool suit.

"Trixie," I said sharply. "You mustn't wear red to the office. It's very becoming on you, and I'm sure someone has told you it's a power color, but it's too loud and doesn't give the right impression."

"I'm sorry." She looked hurt and anxious. I tingled.

"Try black or gray or brown. Not blue, though—too corporate. Now, look. You should keep track of these things on a list. You have paper? Write down, 'I will not wear red to the office.' That's right. And that goes for your nail polish, too. Stick to clear. Now, I know we were going to spend the morning getting an interview, but the day is packed and you're going to have to jump right in. This morning we have a casting call. You'll sort the files and run through the audition scene with the actresses. Okay? Tryouts start in fifteen minutes, so go through those folders. The scene is in that binder over there."

I watched Trixie bustle, gathering her materials, somewhat ill at ease because I'd criticized her outfit. I sat behind my desk and scanned budget sheets, looking up occasionally to enjoy her growing discomfiture as she began to understand just what it was we were doing. She looked so sweet when flustered. Perhaps she *was* the assistant of my dreams.

The Job (Trixie)

I was glad to be involved right away in the details of a casting call, but nervous about running through scenes. Oh, well, I thought, the actresses will probably be more nervous than I am. I opened up the first file, Rochelle King, and looked at her head shot—stern, unsmiling. I flipped to the next shot and nearly yelped, because there was Rochelle in a black leather corset and thigh-high boots and nothing else except for studded bracelets all over her arms and a whip in her hand. Her breasts spilled over her corset and her legs were planted wide apart. Was she trying to show off her body to get the job? I wondered if I should warn Jane. I looked up, but she seemed busy.

I went through Rochelle's résumé next. She'd done a lot of movies, but according to her résumé they were all "pornographic feature films, with female casts with an emphasis on bondage and discipline." I wasn't sure that *Taming Lola, Slut Punishment* and *Put It All in My Pussy, Now!* were the proper qualifications for this role. Maybe some of the other actresses had more appropriate experience. I opened the next file, and the next, and the next, and they were all the same—scary women in leather wearing all kinds of whips and chains. Some of them even had their noses pierced. Three of them stood out, though: Rochelle King, Vampi Calda, and a woman called Mike.

Maybe the scene is some kind of comic sidebar, I thought, with a bit part for a dominatrix. I turned to the scene to check it out before the run-through. But when I started to read it, I couldn't believe it. This was no sidebar, and we weren't casting a bit part. And there was no way, no way I was going to be able to run through this scene.

"Trixie? I'm ready to call in the first actress."

The Run-Through (Jane)

"Trixie," I repeated, "let's get the show on the road. What's the matter?"

"Um, Jane," she stumbled, "could I talk to you before we begin?"

"Sorry, we really don't have time. Later. What's in the files? Who looks good to you?"

"I'm not sure, but I pulled these three."

I looked at the files. For an innocent, she had quite an eye for experience. "Very good, Trixie. Two of these actresses are my top choices for the part, and in fact we're beginning with Mike. If she reads well, we'll just hire her."

Trixie looked even more troubled. "Is that okay? What about the other auditions we have scheduled?"

"Trixie," I said sternly, "we don't have time for questions like that. I've been in this business for ages. If I say we can do something, we can do it. Where's that list of yours? Go get it. Write down, 'I will not waste time contradicting Jane.' Great. Terrific. Now tell Mike to come in."

The Run-Through (Trixie)

How was I going to run through this scene?

I trudged to the waiting room and got Mike, who looked tall in a leather trench coat and high boots.

"Mike, hello," said Jane, shaking her hand. "How've you been? Working hard or hardly working?"

"Working hard, Jane, working hard."

"What do you think of our script?"

"It's nice," Mike said. "I like it."

Nice, I thought, about as nice as being caught in a shark tank. I bustled around while they chatted and ignored me.

"Are you ready to run through the scene with Trixie, Mike?"

"Sure," she said, and took off her coat. I'd expected her to be wearing leather, but she had on a white t-shirt and black jeans. Metal chains dangled from her pockets.

"Trixie," Jane said. Something in her voice reduced my resistance. So I'll look like a fool, I thought. At least the pay's good.

I sat down opposite Mike.

"Okay," said Jane. "Let's review the plot up to this point. Mike's character, Big Red, works as a jail warden in a female prison. We've seen her on the job, restraining and disciplining various prisoners, helping the doctor administer exams, humiliating her favorites by making them do their exercises naked and pee in public. In the scene right before this, we watched her break up a gang bang. The problem is, she got all turned on by the woman she was saving and couldn't do anything about it. So now she's getting a drink at her local bar, which moves into a fantasy sequence about the prisoner she rescued. Okay, let's start reading. Trixie, you're the prisoner, obviously, and Mike's the warden. I'll read the bartender's lines."

I crossed my legs and opened my script. My lines were highlighted in yellow.

"Hey, Big Red, what can I get you tonight?" read Jane.

"Double bourbon on the rocks."

"Coming right up."

"Okay," Jane said, "so now we do some business to indicate fantasy mode, and when the fog clears, Big Red sees the luscious piece who only hours ago was being viciously humped by five bad girls. She walks over to her."

"Hey," Mike said, looking straight at me, "I thought I told you to stay in your cell."

"I didn't feel like it," I said, using my finger to hold my place in the script. "I wanted some air."

"Who cares what you feel like?" Mike's voice was as sculpted as her arms. "You do what you're told. You especially do what you're told when I tell it to you."

"What if I don't want to? It's a free country, even in jail."

"Hah! You've been spending too much time in the library. You're in my jail, and you'll do what I say. Or I'll let everyone else do what they want with you, and believe me, it won't be pleasant. You didn't like those women putting their hands all over you, did you?"

"It wasn't so bad," I read stiffly. The directions said I should be pouting, but the way I saw it, they were lucky I was doing this at all. "At least they're prisoners like me, not some nasty pig guard."

Whack! Jane made a smacking noise by clapping her hands together, hard. "Okay, so in the scene, Big Red slaps the prisoner, and then we move into the action. Why don't you two play it out in front of the mirror so I can see more of the angles?"

I stayed glued to my chair. "I thought this was a reading."

Jane smiled. "It's a run-through. I have to see how actresses use their bodies. Don't worry, Trixie. Mike knows what she's doing, and you just have to stand there. After all, she's the one who's auditioning, not you. Unless you'd like a part!"

"No!" I said. "Um, Jane, could I talk to you for a minute?"

"I don't like to break the flow of a scene," she said.

"Only a second?" I wheedled.

"Okay," she sighed. "What is it?"

I looked at Mike. She was smiling pleasantly. I wanted to ask her to leave the room, but didn't feel I could. "Is there any way, do you think, that I could just read the lines sitting down?"

"Trixie," Jane snapped, "where's that list we were keeping?"

"On your desk," I said nervously.

"Get it."

I did.

"What does it say?"

"I will not wear red—"

"No, not that. The next thing."

"I will not waste time contradicting Jane."

"Right. Now underline that. Twice. Now write down, 'I will not make Jane repeat herself.' Okay. Now get up and do the scene, for God's sake."

I felt totally humiliated. Mike held her cool smile. I heard Jane say, behind me, in a kinder tone, "I know you haven't done this before, and that it may be embarrassing. But it's just a scene, and we're all professionals here. Okay?"

"Okay," I said.

So we continued the run-through. There actually wasn't much for me to do; I guess this movie was a star vehicle, and Mike was the star. After she supposedly slapped me, she pulled my arms behind my back and pushed me up against a wall, telling my character what an ungrateful cunt she was. "I think you'd better show me some gratitude," she said. "I don't think I'm going to give you a choice about it." Then Mike got to show off how quickly she could get me gagged and bound in a bunch of devices. Still holding my arms behind me, she snapped cuffs around my wrists, tied my arms together near the elbow with some ropes, gagged me with a scarf, and put a chain around my waist that she connected to the cuffs at my wrists.

I kept telling myself we were all professionals while Mike read her lines and ran through simulated sex movements. At least I still had clothes on.

"Who's the pig now?" she asked, while she stood a couple of

inches in front of me and pretended to grind her hips into me. She looked really convincing, her body strong, her movements lustful, her voice charged and powerful. I even felt myself getting caught up in the scene, wondering how I looked.

"Are you my little heifer?" she grunted, and kept up her air-grinding. "Are you my little sow?" She whirled me around and pushed my hands onto the sofa. Now I could see myself in the mirror. I looked like a cross between a prisoner and a trussed-up farm animal. A twinge between my legs took me by surprise, but before I could focus on it, a stronger sensation took over. Mike had taken some kind of whip out of her bag and was whacking the seat of my pants. It stung like hell.

Luckily, Jane intervened. "Whoa, Mike, hey, it's just a rehearsal." Mike stopped. Thank God.

"Sorry, Jane," she said. "Got a little too into the scene."

Sorry, *Jane*? I thought. I'm the one getting my ass whacked.

"Why don't we just skip ahead to page forty-five," said Jane.

"Where I take the gag off and force her to go down on me?" Mike asked.

"Right," said Jane.

If you'd asked me twenty minutes before whether I'd even read that scene, never mind act it out, I would have said no. But I'd crossed a line. Maybe it happened when I saw myself in the mirror; I was excited now.

"Have you learned your lesson, you little bitch?" Mike barked. "You ready to show a little gratitude?"

"Yes," I read. "Let me show you. I'll do whatever you say."

According to the script, Mike was supposed to bring me to my knees, force me to open her pants with my mouth, lick her clit, and then, as the script put it, "etc." But Mike was doing something different. She was pushing up her t-shirt on one side, exposing a breast, and pushing my mouth toward her nipple. "Go ahead," she said, "show me what you can do. Suck on that."

Something about the authority of her voice and the authority of that brown, pointed nipple made me forget myself. I leaned down and took it into my mouth. I'd barely closed my lips around it when Mike yelled "Hey!" and shoved me halfway across the room.

"What's the deal, Jane?" she yelled, pulling her shirt down. I was confused.

The Run-Through (Jane)

"I'm sorry," I laughed. "Trixie's new. She just got a little carried away. She didn't know that it's impolite to touch an actress during a run-through. Did you, Trixie?"

Trixie looked mortified and stared at the ground.

"Say you're sorry, Trixie," I said, more sternly.

"I'm sorry," she mumbled, still looking down.

"Not like that. Like you mean it."

"I'm sorry," she said, only a little more clearly. Mike stood with her arms crossed.

"Trixie, you've offended one of my best actresses. I think you're going to have to show how sorry you are a little better than this."

She looked up, flushed. "What do you want to do? Whip me? Throw me on the floor and teach me a thing or two? Or maybe I should kiss her feet?"

"Those are all fine ideas," I said coolly. "You pick."

She was mad now. "Or maybe I should read my little list while Mike holds me down and you spank me, since I've been *such a bad girl.*"

Mike spoke up. "Hey, Jane, I'm out of here. I'll call you later about the contract." Out the door she went. Trixie and I were alone.

The Training (Trixie)

I don't know what made me say all those things, but I meant them. I was quiet with Mike gone, silently daring Jane to make it all a joke now that we were alone.

She sat down behind her desk and said, "Well, Trixie, what will it be?"

I remained silent.

"I think we're both agreed that you're in need of some correction.

You've made several mistakes this morning, and it's best not to defer our discipline and training session too long. Since you don't seem able to decide on what your punishment should be, I will."

I felt nervous, excited, unreal. The boss and I were about to go over.

"Take your list, Trixie, and put it on the desk."

I did.

"Now pull up your skirt and hold it up."

I did. My body blushed, my pussy contracted, and the blood rushed to my clit.

"Look down at the list and read it out loud, over and over again. Don't stop, and don't look up."

I did. I read, "I will not wear red to the office. I will not waste time contradicting Jane. I will not make Jane repeat herself." While I read and held my skirt up, I heard Jane rustle around in her drawer. What was she doing?

She got up and came around behind me. Her arm snaked around me and removed the list. "I think you have it memorized by now, Trixie. Keep reciting, but put your hands on the table and your ass in the air."

I tried to do it right, but she had to push on my pelvis and spread my legs apart to get me in the position she wanted. Then she grabbed my pantyhose and ripped them apart from the waist down. They floated free of my legs and settled around my ankles.

"Keep reciting," Jane said. "Your punishment will only get worse if you stop. But if you absolutely can't take it anymore, start saying 'I will not type letters to my friends on the job.' Got that?"

"Yes," I said, and hastily resumed. "I will not waste time contradicting Jane. I will not wear red to the office . . ."

Whack! Her hand landed where my butt cheeks met, and my skin heated up. *Whack!* again! She spanked one cheek, then the other, hard. I almost collapsed onto the table, and I lost track of my place in the list.

"What's the matter, Trixie? Did you forget your orders? Maybe this will help you remember."

A barrage of slaps on my ass, even harder than before, vindictive but controlled. My skin felt crisp and burned. I imagined the marks of her fingers on my butt and my pussy got electric. I felt completely out of control even though I knew I could make her stop. I liked the feeling. She was the boss, and I was a bad, bad girl.

"I'm going to spank you ten more times, Trixie. Keep count now. If you mess up we'll have to start all over again."

Whack! "One," I gasped.

She made me wait, then dealt me another enormous slap. "Two," I said, wondering if I could make it through eight more. But after teasing me by making me wait a long time for a few more vicious wallops, she dealt the rest of my punishment out rapidly, then undid my skirt and pulled it down around my ankles.

"Turn around, Trixie," she said. I did, but I was too embarrassed to look at her. "That's right, Trixie, don't look up. I'm the boss. I'll look at you." She put her hand under my chin and raised my face. I made sure to keep my eyes averted. "I'm going to undo your blouse now, Trixie. I want to see what you're hiding from me." Her hands were warm, her fingers deft, and as she exposed my breasts, I worried about my pussy. It was getting so wet I thought my juices might drip down my thighs and onto the floor.

Her hands cupped my breasts and her fingers teased my nipples. "Nice," she said, "very nice." Her voice had gotten sweeter, but it still commanded. She moved over to the couch and lay down. "Come here. Trixie." I went to her, my movements hampered by the skirt around my ankles. "Get up on the couch, between my legs." I did what she said. "Open my pants." I started to, but was alarmed when I felt something big and hard in her pants. "Take it out," she said, and I did—a long, thick, and very lifelike dildo. She reached under the couch and brought up a condom. "Put it on," she said, "with your mouth." I was clumsy, but I did it. The condom was lubricated, so when she told me to start fucking my tits with her dick, the dildo slid right between them. She groaned as if she could really feel every inch of it. "Suck it," she said. "Get it in your mouth." I moved my chest up and down on it, feeling the friction on my breasts and enjoying it when my fingers occasionally rubbed my nipples. I lowered my mouth onto the head. I sucked and licked it enthusiastically. I moaned and sighed. I felt crazy, and for a second panicked, when I realized that anyone could walk into the office and see me there, naked except for the torn hose and disheveled skirt that held my feet together.

"Oh, that's good," Jane said. "That's it, really put your head into it. Show me how sorry you are that you did your job so badly. Show me what a good slut you can be." She fucked my breasts and mouth some more, then pulled away from me. She got up and rearranged me so that my skirt was completely off and I was kneeling on the couch and looking straight into the mirror. She got behind me.

"I want you to see what you look like when you get fucked," she murmured in my ear. "That way, you'll learn your lesson even better." She explored the entrance to my pussy with her dick. "Spread your legs, you bad thing." I moved them. "That's right," she said, "show me your pussy." She edged the dildo in more. "The boss is going to fuck you now," she warned, and pushed it in hard and deep. My pussy swallowed it up and I started moving against it.

She moved with me, working it in and out, watching my face in the mirror. She grabbed my hair and pulled my head up and back. "Watch yourself get fucked," she hissed. I saw her, still perfectly dressed in her executive clothes, knowing that her dick was lodged inside me. I saw my face, tense with arousal, my flushed neck, and my heavy breasts. I felt something change and realized that Jane had put her fingers between the dildo and her skin and was stroking her clit. "You're going to make me come," she told me. "Do you want to come, too?"

I nodded. In the mirror, I saw her stare at me.

"Please," I said.

"The boss comes," she smiled. "The assistant doesn't."

"Please," I begged. I pushed my pussy onto her dick even harder, but I needed my clit touched.

"Why should I?" she asked, stroking herself more and more.

"I'll be good," I promised, "so good. I'll make you come all the time. I'll fuck you whenever you want, and your clients, too. I'll give you blow jobs at lunch and a hand job with your morning coffee. Just please, please let me come now."

"All right," she said. "Touch yourself."

And I did, digging my fingers into my clit, hard, thrusting myself onto her dick. In seconds, I was coming so much that I didn't even realize until after that she was coming at the same time. I sank into the couch and she collapsed on top of me.

When our breathing and heartbeats got back to normal, I realized how awkward the situation was. She was mostly dressed, but I felt ashamed of my partial nudity and my exposed, reddened ass. If I can't see her, I thought, maybe she can't see me, and so I stayed face-down even when I felt her get up.

"Trixie," I heard. I turned my head. "Trixie! Sit up!"

I sat up. Jane looked perfectly composed. Her pants were closed up.

"Button your blouse. Put on your skirt. What kind of a spectacle are you making of yourself?" She smiled as she spoke.

"I don't know what we're going to do with you." She took her wallet out of her pants. "Here's some money," she said, and as I struggled into my skirt, I saw that she was giving me $200. "Get yourself some new stockings. And keep the change. Consider it a disability payment—I'm assuming you might have some trouble sitting down for the next two days."

I took the money and smiled back. My first day at work was certainly turning out nicely.

"I hope to see you again after lunch," Jane said. "I think we could work very well together."

"I'd like to come back," I said. "And I'm sure you'll do everything you can to see that I do."

Jane looked puzzled at first, then cleared her throat. "Hm, well, yes, certainly, of course. It's clear that we should be paying you far more than the initial salary we settled on. You're so much more qualified than your résumé suggested. I'll have the new contract drawn up and you can sign it when you get back. How does that sound?"

"Beautiful," I said.

And then I took a very, very long lunch.

Scent

Susan St. Aubin

Evelyn lies on the couch with her robe open, smoothing lotion over her breasts and belly, still damp from her bath. The lotion tickles her nose with jasmine as she massages it into her moist skin, moving her fingers in circles around her nipples and navel. She has forty minutes before Hal is due home from work. She estimates how long this will take her, she who likes to take her time. Maybe half an hour? It's now twenty past five, and predictable Hal will walk up the steps at six. Her nipples harden. The daffodils in the vase on the coffee table seem to stir and straighten. Yes. She could do it in half an hour.

She pours more lotion on her stomach, letting it slide down to the sponge of hair between her legs. Her whole body seems to soften as her cunt creates its own cream. She massages both lotions into her pelt, jasmine mingled with her own musk, then breathes deeply. Like a birth in reverse, everything comes into her: the room, the house, the trees, the stars and sky. She inhales the universe with each breath.

Evelyn is aware of the hands of the old wooden clock on the wall, the second hand jerking forward with each tick, and, from the bedroom, she hears the faint click of the alarm clock as it flips through its numbers, although she can't see either clock from where she lies with her legs spread. In her mind, she sees one of the screen savers on Hal's computer, stars moving as though you were flying through them; the universe moving, pulling the clocks with it. Five minutes pass, or ten—she doesn't know. Time binds her, yet she's outside it. Her fingers spread lotion around her clit in a one-second motion, *clit-clock, clit-clock*.

Always the clocks, always the present sliding minute by minute into a future she can't escape. She puts a finger to her mouth and runs it over her tongue and lips, tasting jasmine and savory cunt, then returns it to the heart of her universe, pulsing now in time with each passing second. Her fingers move quickly over her soft lips to the center bud that swells like a seed pod about to burst—but not yet, because every car that passes on the street outside could be his. Too often her body is his, but now it's so much hers that she sees him as an invader coming, like a blip on her mind's radar screen, and she gathers her armor to fight him. Come, come, she calls to the pulsing center, but the cells and atoms of her body don't respond; instead they say, "He's coming, he's coming" in a counter-rhythm that slows the motion of her fingers.

He *is* coming. Her body hangs, timeless, while the clocks jerk past it. She hears a car stop, a door slam, and footsteps. She glares at the front door opposite the couch, then drops her hand to her side. He's climbing the stairs. The stars freeze with her body sealed in them, high in the universe. To break the spell, she sits up, ties her robe, smoothes her hair; she holds the moment inside herself, away from him. When she stands her head seems to float high above her actual height as she glides across the carpet.

She opens the front door, she smiles, she says (even she can't believe the tone of disappointment in her voice), "You're late! It's almost 6:15."

"I gave Joe a ride, and then he wanted me to take a look at his computer—something got spilled in the keyboard." Hal takes off his jacket, kisses her forehead, throws the jacket on the couch. He sniffs the air. "Haven't you started cooking yet? What are we having?

Snails and eggs? What's your latest trick?"

The real world pulls her head down from the ceiling. She doesn't what to think about Chouette, the restaurant where she's working with the chef in his quest for the world's most unique omelet. She's bored with cooking, at home or at work. When Hal kisses her mouth, her lips are numb, her teeth are rocks of ice. She wants to bite him.

He walks to the bathroom, taking off his clothes as he goes. His body seems as remote as a painting. She sniffs her own scent: heavy and sweet like her jasmine lotion, but also like earth after a hard rain, like chopped mushrooms, like eggs fresh out of their broken shells, like raw meat. She's amazed he can't smell her—it's all over, spilling from between her legs, from her skin, from her fingertips.

She pours him a glass of sherry and hands it to him in the bathroom. "Aperitif," she says, telling herself that that'll keep him busy.

"Thank you." He's surprised; she can see him wondering if this means anything. "After dinner?" he asks.

Always food first, before sex. Her head starts to float again at the sight of the steam enveloping his body as he steps inside the shower. When he's safely under the water, she shuts the bathroom door and returns to the couch.

Her hands go like magnets to her moist cunt, where she feels the firm berry, like a grenade of seeds ready to explode. She imagines the glowing clouds of a sunset blown apart to reveal stars stabbing the night. The sound of water falling drowns the ticking and clicking of the clocks. She licks the fingers of her right hand and begins a circling massage that stops time, putting it in her hands.

When he sings under the sound of the water, she finds her fingers moving to his song. This annoys her, so she pictures the water washing over him, filling his ears, his nose, and finally his mouth until he stops singing. He really has stopped singing. She listens closely, hearing his feet suck against the shower tiles as he scrubs himself, then moves her hand again. Now time controls her: How long will he take? How long will she take? How much time is there? She pictures him in the steamy shower, washing his cock now, soaping it with one hand while the other is behind him, massaging the crack of his ass. White soap bubbles spread across his body like fog over the hills, streaming into all the crevices of the earth. Maybe she should wait until after dinner.

But her fingers are moving faster, apart from her, as though she were two people, one stroking, and the other passively taking pleasure with no thought of return. She feels her pulse move from her heart to her clit, which seems to lift and harden, pulling on the skin around it. Hal calls it her third nipple, but she doesn't care for that, because it seems to say more about his desire to feed himself than to please her. To her, it's a berry that bursts and reseeds itself. He can eat it if he wants, but it'll always grow again.

When her cunt cream soaks her fingers, she rubs the excess on her thighs before continuing. Her pulse is steady, solid, synchronized with her firm little bud, all the clocks in the house, and Hal under the steady throb of his shower. Water falls over all of them. Evelyn feels a pulsing beneath her fingers that makes a counterpoint to her own heartbeat. Her berry has a beat of its own now, faster, then faster, opening her cunt, turning her outside of herself. The pulsation moves up her spine, up through her head, quick as lightning. Her hand is limp, but still she throbs.

Hal shuts off the water. He whistles as he rubs himself dry—she hears the flip of cloth against his skin. She sits up, fastens her robe, and stands. Her head is exactly where it should be—five feet, three inches off the ground. She goes into the kitchen and washes her hands, then starts frying hamburger for chili. Gourmet food no longer interests her; she wants cheap meat, tomatoes, hot peppers. She forgets how many kinds of pepper there are in chili powder— just to be sure it's hot enough, she chops a fresh jalapeno, not even seeding it, and throws it in. This will be the hottest ever; it will burn the sky. When Hal comes in wrapped in a white robe, she asks him to chop onions.

Her scent hangs in the air around her, along with the chilies and onions, so strong even she can smell it. Hal sneezes because onions always make him sneeze; they've probably deadened his nose. She goes to him and wraps her arms around his neck, with the spatula in one hand dripping fat down the back of his robe. She still sees him in the shower, disappearing into the mist, slick with soap. She can almost feel him sliding across her body.

"Breathe deep," she whispers in his ear. "Breathe me. I'll wipe out those onions."

He puts his arms around her, rubbing the onion juice on the back of her robe, which she unties and lets slip to the floor. She waltzes him away from the onion smell as he buries his nose in her hair until they come to rest against the kitchen table, where she pushes him until he's leaning backward over it. Then he pushes her until they're upright again, when they slide to the floor.

The hamburger begins to sizzle in the pan, the blood smell of it rising. Evelyn thinks she should get up and stir the meat before it sticks to the bottom, but Hal is on top of her. His nose is at her neck now, beneath her ear, and he breathes deeply as he takes her ear lobe between his soft lips and sucks. His thigh is between her legs, pressing her berry, rolling it around under its skin hood. Evelyn's own dark, sweet odor, which reminds her of the taste of mushrooms, spreads over the room. She wonders if mushrooms would be good in chili—she's never seen a recipe that calls for them, but decides she'll try it anyway, if it's not too late to add them in five or ten minutes. Her head is rising to the ceiling fast.

Hal's cock is a sausage poking her leg, poking between her thighs, then sliding into her nether mouth, the toothless mouth that can't bite. Her clit, squeezed between his pelvis and penis, begins to pulse. As he strokes, she feels all the clocks in the house going *clit-cock, clit-cock*. He goes in and out of her like a metronome.

Hamburger pops and crackles on the stove, fat spitting into the air, its smoky essence blending with her own musk. Yes, mushrooms would taste good in chili. She imagines she feels a mushroom cloud rushing from her cunt, which pulses as her berry explodes. She sees flames with her eyes closed; she doesn't care if the hamburger burns. Hal comes, biting her ear lobe so hard she thinks he's drawn blood. The smell of mushrooms and burning meat swirls around them.

"The hamburger," she whispers in his ear. "I've got to get up."

But they lie on the cold linoleum, breathing into each other's ears, until Hal jumps off her shouting, "You forgot the meat!" as he turns off the burner. He takes up a spatula and scrapes the bottom of the pan.

Evelyn crawls off the floor, finds her robe, and wraps it around her. She takes the spatula from Hal and stirs the hamburger. It's not very much burned, she decides—a little blackened in spots, and the onions and chilies are crisp, which will add a campfire taste to the finished dish. When she begins to chop the mushrooms, releasing their cunt scent, Hal comes up behind her and sniffs. She asks him to cut some tomatoes. He takes another deep breath, and kisses her bruised earlobe.

"I never noticed how mushrooms smell," he says. "They're unique, sort of earthy." He hangs over her, inhaling her, kissing the back of her neck.

"I'm amazed at what you don't notice," she says.

"Where's a knife for the tomatoes?" he asks.

She pulls one off the knife rack on the wall and hands it to him with a smile, then dumps the mushrooms into the chili and turns up the flame. The scent of mushrooms and scorched meat fills the air. Hal slices tomatoes, licking his lips, and dumps them on top of the sizzling meat and mushrooms while Evelyn stirs.

"Tomatoes smell like water," he says. "I thought they'd smell like blood." He slips his arms around her waist.

"They smell like piss when they burn," she warns as she stirs. She opens a couple of cans of tomato sauce and pours them in. Hal is bending over her again, his nose in her neck. She turns the flame down as low as she can get it, and takes his hand. This time she'll lead him to the bedroom, where the only scent will be her own.

Quiet Please

Aimee Bender

It is quiet in the rest of the library.

Inside the back room, the woman has crawled out from underneath the man. Now fuck me like a dog, she tells him. She grips a pillow in her fists, and he breathes behind her, hot air down her back, which is starting to sweat and slip on his stomach. She doesn't want him to see her face, because it is blowing up inside, red and furious, and she's grimacing at the pale white wall, which is cool when she puts her hand on it to help her push back into him, get his dick to fill up her body until there's nothing left of her inside: just dick.

The woman is a librarian, and today her father has died. She got a phone call from her weeping mother in the morning, threw up and then dressed for work. Sitting at her desk with her back very straight, she politely asks the young man, the one who always comes into the library to check out best-sellers, when it was he last got laid. He lets out a weird sound, and she says, *shhh,* this is a library. She has her hair up and the glasses on, but everyone has a librarian fantasy, and she is truly a babe beneath.

I have a fantasy, he says, of a librarian.

She smiles at him but asks her original question again. She doesn't want someone brand-new to the business, but neither is she looking for a goddamn gigolo. This is an important fuck for her. He tells her it's been a few months and looks sheepish but honest and then hopeful. She says great and tells him there's a back room with a couch for people who get dizzy or sick in the library (which happens surprisingly often) and could he meet her there in five minutes? He nods; he's already telling his friends about this in a monologue in his head. He has green eyes and no wrinkles yet.

They meet in the back, and she pulls the shade down on the little window. This is the sex that she wishes would split her open and murder her, because she can't deal with a dead father. Is it true? He's really gone? She didn't really want him to die; that is not what she meant when she faced him and imagined knives sticking into his body. This is not what she meant, for him actually to die. She wonders if she invented the phone call, but she remembers the way her mother's voice kept climbing up and up, and it's so real and true that she can't bear it and wants to go fuck someone else. The man is tired now but grinning like he can't believe it. He's figuring when he can be there next, but she's sure she'll never want him again. Her hair is down and glasses off and clothes on the floor, and she's the fucked librarian, and he's looking at her with this look of adoration. She squeezes his wrist and then concentrates on putting herself back together. In ten minutes, she's at the front desk again, telling a youngster about a swell book on aisle ten, and unless you leaned forward to smell her, you'd never know.

There is a mural, on the curved ceiling of the library, of fairies dancing. Their arms are interwoven, hair loose from the wind. Since people look at the ceiling fairly often when they're at the library, it is a well-known mural. The librarian tilts her head back to take a deep breath. One of the fairies is missing a mouth. It has burned off from the glare of the sunlight, and she is staring at her fairy friends with a purple-eyed look of muteness. The librarian does not like to see this and looks down to survey the population of her library instead.

As she glances around, she is amazed to see how many attractive men there are that day. They are everywhere: leaning over the wood tables, straight-backed in the aisles, men flipping pages with nice hands. The librarian, on this day, the day of her father's death, is overwhelmed by an appetite she has never felt before, and she waits for another one of them to approach her desk.

It takes five minutes.

This one is a businessman with a vest. He is asking her about a book on fishing when she propositions him. His face lights up; the young boy comes clean and clear through his eyes—that librarian he knew when he was 7. She had round calves and a low voice.

She has him back in the room; he takes one tentative step forward, and then he's on her like Wall Street rain, his suit in a pile on the floor in a full bucket, her dress unbuttoned, down, down, one by one, until she's naked and the sweat is pooling in her back again. She obliterates herself and then buttons up. This man too wants to see her again—he might want to marry her, he's thinking—but she smiles without teeth and says, Man, this is a one-shot deal. Thanks.

If she wanted to, she could do this forever, charge a lot of money and become rich. She has this wonderful body, with full, heavy breasts and a curve to her back that makes her pliable like a toy. She wraps her legs around man number three, a longhaired artist type, and her hair shakes loose, and he removes her glasses, and she fucks him until he's shuddering and trying to moan, but she just keeps saying *shhh, shhh,* and it makes him so happy she keeps saying it even after he's shut up.

The morning goes by like normal, except she fucks three more men, and it's all in the silence, while people shuffle across the wood floor and trade words on paper for more words on paper.

After lunch the muscleman enters the library.

He is tan and attractive, and his arms are busting out of his shirt like balloons. He is with the traveling circus, where he lifts a desk with a chair with a person with a child with a dog with a bone. He lifts it up and never drops anything, and people cheer.

He also likes to read.

He picks this library because it's the closest to the big top. It's been a tiring week at the circus because the lion tamer had a fit and quit, and so the lions keep roaring. They miss him, and no one else will pet them because they're lions. When the muscleman enters the library, he breathes in the quiet in relief. He notices the librarian right away, the way she is sitting at her desk with this little twist to her lips that only a very careful observer would notice. He approaches her, and she looks at him in surprise. At this point, the librarian assumes everyone in the library knows what is going on, but the fact is, they don't. Most of the library people just think it's stuffier than usual and for some reason they are having a hard time focusing on their books.

The librarian looks at the muscleman and wants him.

Five minutes, she says, tilting her head toward the back room.

The muscleman nods, but he doesn't know what she's talking about. He goes off to look at the classics, but after five minutes he follows his summons, curious.

The back room has a couch and white walls. When he enters the room, he's struck by the thickness of the sex smell; it is so pervasive that he almost falls over. The librarian is sitting on the couch in her dress, which is gray and covers her whole body. Down the center, there is a row of mother-of-pearl buttons, and one of them is unbuttoned by accident.

The thing is, the muscleman is not so sure of his librarian fantasies. He is more sure that he likes to lift whatever he can. So he walks over to her in the waddly way that men with big thighs have to walk and picks her up, couch and all.

Hey, she says, put me down.

The muscleman loves how his shoulders feel, the weight of something important, a life, on his back.

Hey, she says again, this is a library; put me down.

He twirls her gently, for the absent audience, and she ducks her head down so as not to collide with the light fixture.

He opens the door and walks out with the couch. He is thoughtful enough to bring it down when they get to the door frame so she doesn't bump her head. She wants to yell at him, but they're in the library now.

Two of the men she has fucked are still there, in hopes of a second round. They are stunned and very jealous when they see her riding the couch like a float at a parade through the aisles of books. The businessman in the vest stares, and after a minute he removes a book of poetry from the shelf behind him and throws it at her.

Get down! he hisses, and she ducks, almost cries out, then clamps her hand over her mouth. Her father's funeral is in one day. It is important that there is quiet in a library. The book flies past her knees, skidding on the floor, landing on the foot of a regular library man, who is reading a magazine at a table.

He is startled, then stands, defensive. The businessman is already throwing another book, which also slips below the librarian, and now the regular man, confused, throws his magazine in its plastic coverlet, which flaps and thuds unsuccessfully, and then, in a storm, they're all over: books are falling off tables; books are flung into the air; the dust trapped between chapters is slapped up into her mouth. The pages rustle as they fly, and the librarian covers her face, because she can't stand to look down at the floor and see her books splayed open on their bindings as if they've been shot.

The muscleman doesn't seem to notice, even though the books are hitting him on his legs, his waist. He lifts her up, on his tiptoes, to the ceiling of the library.

Stand up, he says to her in a low voice, muffled from underneath the couch. Stand up and I'll still balance you; I can do it even if you are standing.

She doesn't know what else to do, and she can feel him pushing upward from beneath her. She presses down with her feet to stand and puts a finger on the huge mural on the ceiling, the mural of the fairies dancing in summer. She can hear the men below her. Right away she sees the one fairy without the mouth and reaches into her bun to remove the pencil that is always kept there. Hair tumbles down. On her tiptoes, she is able to touch the curve of the ceiling where the fairy's mouth should be.

Hold still, she whispers to the muscleman, who doesn't hear her, who is in his own bliss of strength.

She grips the pencil and, with one hand flat on the ceiling, steadies herself enough to draw a mouth underneath the nose of the fairy. She tries to draw it as a big, wide, dancing smile and darkens the pencil line a few times. From where she stands, it looks nice, from where she is, just inches underneath the painting, which is warmed by the sunlight coming into the library.

She doesn't notice until the next day, when she comes to work to clean up the books an hour before her father is to be put into the ground, her back aching, her thighs sore, that the circle of fairies is altered now. That the laughing ones now pull along one fairy with purple eyes, who is clearly dancing against her will, dragged along with the circle, her mouth wide-open and screaming.

Contributors

Aimee Bender lives in Los Angeles and is the author of *The Girl in the Flammable Skirt,* a collection of short stories. She teaches creative writing at the University of Southern California and is currently at work on her first novel.

Debra Boxer is a writer living in New Jersey. Her poetry and nonfiction have appeared in *Nerve* and *Moxie* magazines. In addition to writing book reviews for the *San Francisco Chronicle* and *Publishers Weekly,* she also writes fiction and is currently working on a novel.

Poppy Z. Brite is the author of four novels—*Lost Souls, Drawing Blood, Exquisite Corpse,* and *The Lazarus Heart*—as well as two short-story collections, *Wormwood* and *Are You Loathsome Tonight?*; and the nonfiction *Courtney Love: The Real Story.* Her work has appeared in numerous books, magazines, and Web zines, including *Spin, The Village Voice, The Mammoth Book of New Erotica,* and *Nerve.* She edited the anthologies *Love in Vein* and *Love in Vein II.* She lives in New Orleans with her husband, Christopher, a chef.

Nell Carberry is a writer living in New York City. Her work has been published in *Bust, Libido, Paramour,* and *Bitch*. She is forever grateful to her late father, who used to swipe her Richard Pryor albums. Dad's motto was: "There is no such thing as a dirty word."

Ernie Conrick is a twenty-eight-year-old writer and scholar living in Brooklyn, New York. He is the author of two unpublished novels and a growing collection of short stories. Widely traveled in South and Central Asia, he was the recipient of several research grants through the University of Hawaii.

Bret Easton Ellis is the author of *Less Than Zero, The Rules of Attraction, The Informers,* and *American Psycho,* all of which are available in Vintage paperback. He lives in New York City.

Amelia G was born in London and raised in Europe, the Middle East, and, finally, the United States. Her fiction has ranged from sci-fi to horror to erotica to literary. Some of her short stories can be found in the anthologies *Dark Angels, Sex Crime,* the *Noirotica* series, and *Eros Ex Machina*. She edits the glossy Gothic magazine *Blue Blood* and does freelance writing, design, and photography with her partner in crime, Forrest Black. She can be contacted c/o *Blue Blood,* 8033 Sunset Boulevard, #43, Hollywood, CA 90046.

Gabrielle Glancy's work has appeared in *The New Yorker, New American Writing, The Paris Review, The American Poetry Review,* and many other journals and anthologies. She has recently completed a novel chronicling the sometimes comic, sometimes kinky exploits of a girl-Casanova in search of her Russian lover, who has mysteriously disappeared. Born and raised in New York City, she currently lives in London.

Mel Harris is a forty-one-year-old mother of two who lives on the Gulf of Mexico in northern Florida. She is currently working on a novel about a woman on a spiritual journey. "The Fishing Show" is her first published short story. She has only recently begun to write erotica and is enjoying it thoroughly. The bumper sticker on her car reads: I TRIED TO CONTAIN MYSELF—BUT I ESCAPED.

William Harrison is the author of eight novels, two collections of short stories, and screenplays including *Rollerball* and *Mountains of the Moon.* A Texan, he has lived in Arkansas for a number of years.

Vicki Hendricks is the author of three noir novels: *Miami Purity, Iguana Love,* and *Voluntary Madness.* Her story "Penile Infraction" appears in the popular collection *Dick for a Day.* She lives in southern Florida and teaches writing at Broward Community College. She is a passionate scuba diver and sailor, and has taken up skydiving, too, which provides the background for *Sky Blues,* her next novel of obsession.

Susannah Indigo is a consultant and writer based in Colorado. Her serialized erotic fiction is published by *Erotasy* (http://www. erotasy.com), which was named Best Erotic Web Site by the *San Francisco Bay Guardian.* Indigo's work is also published in many magazines, including *Libido, Black Sheets,* and *Howlings: Wild Women of the West;* it also appears on the new *Libido* CD and in *Herotica 6.* She has won awards for her writing from both *Libido* and the National Writers Association.

Linda Jaivin is not an alien, though her hair *is* blue (today). She likes sex and rock 'n' roll and is the author of the novels *Eat Me* and *Rock 'n' Roll Babes from Outer Space,* as well as the essay collection *Confessions of an S & M Virgin.*

Bombay-born **Ginu Kamani** is the author of *Junglee Girl,* a collection of stories exploring sexuality, sensuality, and power. Published in various anthologies, journals, and magazines, her essays and talks deal with gender, sexual self-knowledge, and hyphenated American identities. She is a Visiting Writer in Fiction at Mills College in Oakland, California, and is working on a novel.

Marc Levy served with the First Cavalry in Vietnam and Cambodia in 1970. He has traveled extensively in Central America, Southeast Asia, and Indonesia. His work has appeared in *Vagabond Monthly, Peregrine, CleanSheets, Slant, The Higginsville Reader,* and in works from Masquerade Books. He lives in New Jersey.

Adam McCabe's erotic mystery stories have appeared in a number of erotic magazines and anthologies. The thirty-something author lives in Cincinnati with his lover and muse.

Serena Moloch lives in San Francisco and can type 180 words per minute. "Casting Couch" is dedicated to her seventh-grade typing teacher, Ms. June Bogart, and to all secretarial talent awaiting discovery.

Eva Morris is the author of *Bad Girls' Bedtime Stories,* and "Why It Is More Important to Have a CB Radio Than a Basset Hound on a Road Trip," and her own *Sex Kitten* newsletter. She recently completed a cross-country quest as the only woman among 150 other hot-rodders.

Jack Murnighan is a columnist for and senior editor at *Nerve* magazine. He recently received a Ph.D. from Duke University, where he studied medieval and Renaissance literature. "Three Shades of Longing" is his second published story; his first, "Watershed," appeared in *The Best American Erotica 1999.* He lives in Manhattan's Chinatown.

Bill Noble (noblebill@aol.com) is a poet, writer, naturalist, community activist, and mischievous person in Northern California. His erotica has appeared in *Libido* and *Paramour. CleanSheets* was his first online publishing venture. He has a fiction award from the Southwest Writers Conference, and his poetry has appeared in *New Millennium Writings, Grrrrrr!,* and elsewhere.

Carol Queen (http://www.carolqueen.com) has a doctorate in sexuality and is the author of *The Leather Daddy and the Femme, Real*

Live Nude Girl, and *Exhibitionism for the Shy.* She is also the coeditor of *Sex Spoken Here, PoMoSexuals,* and *Switch Hitters.*

Simon Sheppard is the coeditor, with M. Christian, of the new anthology *Rough Stuff: Tales of Gay Men, Sex, and Power.* His work has previously appeared in *The Best American Erotica 1997,* as well as the 1996, 1997, and 1999 editions of *Best Gay Erotica* and dozens of other anthologies. He's lived in San Francisco for quite a while, and dedicates "Midsummer of Love" to the memory of too many men to mention.

Susan St. Aubin's work has appeared most recently in the anthologies *Going Down: Lip Service from Great Writers* and *Herotica 6.* She's a full-time office manager and part-time writer who reads cookbooks in her spare time.

Mark Stuertz is a restaurant critic, wine writer, and reporter for the *Dallas Observer,* an alternative weekly newspaper. His work has appeared in *Paramour* and *The Best American Erotica 1997.* He lives in Dallas with his wife and daughter.

Michelle Tea is the author of the novels *The Passionate Mistakes and Intricate Corruption of One Girl in America* and *Valencia.* She is cofounder of the yearly all-girl performance tour Sister Spit, and she would like to thank her Spit Sister Shar Rednour for encouraging her sickest rock-star fantasies.

Claire Tristram (http://www.tristram.com/claire) wrote her first story in 1994, shortly after a near-death experience on her motorcycle. Her fiction and personal essays have since appeared in *Fiction International, The Alaska Quarterly Review, The Massachusetts Review, The Chiron Review,* and in several anthologies and commercial magazines.

Bob Vickery (http://www.bobvickery.com) has published stories in a wide variety of magazines, and he is a regular contributor to *Men* magazine. He has published two anthologies of his stories, *Skin Deep* and *Cock Tales*, and stories of his have also appeared in numerous other anthologies, including *The Best American Erotica 1997, Best Gay Erotica 1999, Friction, Friction 2,* and *Queer Dharma: Voices of Gay Buddhists.*

Molly Weatherfield is the author of *Carrie's Story* and *Safe Word.* She has written about pornography and pornographers for *Salon,* and maintains an annotated bibliography on porn theory at http://www.mtbs.com. She's currently writing a historical romance set in the forbidden-book trade of prerevolutionary France.

Jess Wells has published ten volumes of work, including the new erotic novel *The Price of Passion* and the anthology of erotica *Lip Service.* Her previous novel, *AfterShocks,* was nominated for the American Library Association Gay and Lesbian Literary Award. The anthology, *Lesbians Raising Sons,* was a finalist for a Lambda Literary Award. Her five collections of short stories include *Loon Lake Duet* (publication forthcoming), *Two Willow Chairs,* and *The Dress/The Sharda Stories.*

Shay Youngblood is the author of a novel, *Soul Kiss,* and a collection of short fiction, *The Big Mama Stories.* Her plays *Shakin' the Mess Out of Misery* and *Talking Bones* have been widely produced. Her other plays include *Black Power Barbie* and *Communism Killed My Dog.*

Reader's Directory

Alfred A. Knopf

Glamorama, by Bret Easton Ellis, was published by Alfred A. Knopf in 1999. Knopf also published Ellis's novel *The Informers* in 1994. Both are available in Vintage paperback, along with his novels *American Psycho, The Rules of Attraction,* and *Less Than Zero.*

Alyson Publications

Alyson Publications Inc. was founded in 1980 and publishes books for, by, and about lesbians and gay men. 6922 Hollywood Boulevard, Suite 1000, Los Angeles, CA 90028, (323) 860-6070; http://www.alyson.com.

Anchor Books/Doubleday

The Girl in the Flammable Skirt, by Aimee Bender, was first published by Doubleday in 1998. The book is now available in trade paperback from Anchor, a division of Doubleday (http://www.randomhouse.com). A general-interest trade publisher, Anchor has also published *Erotique Noire: Black Erotica; The Wild Good: Lesbian*

Photographs and Writing on Love; On a Bed of Rice: An Asian American Erotic Feast; Wild Women Don't Wear No Blues: Black Women Writers on Love, Men, and Sex; and *The Anatomist.*

Arsenal Pulp Press

Arsenal Pulp Press is an independent Canadian publisher with a wide range of titles. In addition to *Hot & Bothered: Short Short Fiction on Lesbian Desire,* Arsenal Pulp Press also publishes *Hot & Bothered 2, Quickies: Short Short Fiction on Gay Male Desire,* and *Quickies 2.* For more information, write to: #103, 1014 Homer Street, Vancouver, BC, Canada V6B 2W9, or see http://www.arsenalpulp.com.

Broadway Books

Rock 'n' Roll Babes from Outer Space, by Linda Jaivin, was first published by Broadway Books in 1998. Broadway also published Jaivin's first novel, *Eat Me,* in 1997, and both books are available in trade paperback. A general-interest trade publisher, Broadway has published *In the Garden of Desire: The Intimate World of Women's Sexual Fantasies; How to Be a Great Lover: Girlfriend-to-Girlfriend Techniques That Will Totally Blow His Mind;* and *Nerve: Literate Smut.*

CleanSheets

CleanSheets is a free online erotica magazine that is updated every Wednesday and showcases intelligent and sexy erotic fiction, poetry, and art, as well as information and commentary on sexuality and society. The editor in chief is Mary Anne Mohanraj, and fiction editors are Kristine Hawes and Jaie Helier. *CleanSheets* may be found on the Web at http://www.cleansheets.com.

Cleis Press

Cleis Press publishes America's most intelligent and provocative sex-positive books for girlfriends of all genders. P.O. Box 14684, San Francisco, CA 94114, (800) 780-2279; cleis@aol.com.

Down There Press

Down There Press is an independent publisher devoted exclusively to publishing sexual self-awareness books and erotica since 1975. The best-selling *Herotica* series originated at Down There Press, 938 Howard Street, #101, San Francisco, CA 94103.

Erotasy

Erotasy is a Web zine devoted to extraordinary erotic literature: compelling short stories and a popular, free weekly serial that celebrate the mystery, suspense, longing, humor, and passion of authentic sexuality. Wide ranging in style and content, *Erotasy*'s stories are created by notable contemporary erotica writers of all sexualities, and the site's free library posts new material regularly. The collectibles section of the Web site sells handsomely formatted stories, at a nominal fee, through a secure server. Find *Erotasy* at http://www.erotasy.com.

Fiction International

Fiction International's twin biases are politics and technical innovation, either integrated in a particular fiction, or apart. The outfit also publishes articles, art, photos, interviews, satire, criticism, reviews, excerpts from novels, and nonfiction. Each annual issue is devoted to a unique theme. Direct editorial correspondence to Harold Jaffe at San Diego State University Press, San Diego State University, San Diego, CA 92182. To subscribe or purchase individual issues, write to the above address.

Libido

The journal of sex and sensibility—*Libido* is an all-embracing, heat-generating quarterly that breaks down the dualities that divide us all: good/bad, gay/straight, and man/woman. *Libido* publishes some of the best-written, most demanding, and provocative erotica in America. Marianna Beck and Jack Hafferkamp are its publishers/editors. Subscriptions: $30 (4 issues); single issue: $9.00. Write to P.O. Box 146721, Chicago, IL 60614, or call (800) 495-1988.

Masquerade Books

Richard Kasak, publisher. 801 Second Avenue, New York, NY 10017.

The Missouri Review

"Two Cars in a Cornfield" by William Harrison was first published in *The Missouri Review*. A triannual literary magazine, *The Missouri Review* publishes the brightest new as well as established voices in fiction, poetry, and creative nonfiction along with interviews, book reviews, cartoons, and historical literary discoveries of interest to the general reader. A one-year subscription is available for $19: contact *The Missouri Review,* 1507 Hillcrest Hall, University of Missouri, Columbia, MO 65211; http://www.missourireview.org.

Men Magazine

Men magazine is the premier publication for gay-male erotica. In addition to photo layouts, the magazine features three pieces of erotic fiction per issue. From the same publishers comes *Freshmen,* the magazine all about young men. Both magazines are monthly; subscriptions are $39.98 for *Men,* at P.O. Box 589, Mount Morris, IL 61054-7845, and $39.99 for *Freshmen,* at P.O. Box 591, Mount Morris, IL 61054-7825, or at (800) 757-7069 (both publications).

Moxie Magazine

Moxie focuses on real women doing real things in the real world. Themed issues on love, the body, sheroes, art, and work include fiction, poetry, photography, illustrations, and reviews by emerging writers and artists. Emily Hancock, publisher/editor. Published quarterly; subscriptions are $12 per year; samples are $5. Write to *Moxie,* 1230 Glen Avenue, Berkeley, CA 94708; http://www.moxiemag.com.

Nerve Publishing

Nerve is an online magazine of exceptional photographs and writing about sex and sexuality, intended for both men and women. *Nerve* publishes Pulitzer Prize–winning authors alongside MOMA photographers, and was likened to a *New Yorker* of sex by *Entertainment Weekly*. Much of the best of the first year of *Nerve* is collected in the book *Nerve: Literate Smut* (New York: Bantam Books, 1998); http://www.nervemag.com.

Paramour

Paramour is a luscious, cream-filled pansexual magazine featuring fiction, poetry, photography, illustrations, and reviews. Amelia Copeland, publisher/editor. *Paramour* is no longer in publication, but fans may write or e-mail for info on back issues: P.O.Box 400949, Cambridge, MA 02140-0008; amelia@paramour.com.

The Permanent Press

The Permanent Press of Sag Harbor, New York, is best known for publishing artfully written fiction, both erotic and otherwise, that has garnered more than fifty literary honors for its authors. Among Permanent's books are the complete literary output of Marco Vassi, perhaps the most accomplished erotic writer of his generation. Contact Martin Shepard at 4120 Noyac Road, Sag Harbor, NY 11963.

St*rphkr

St*rphkr is the best jack-off material to hit the planet! It's filled with satire, dark sex, and out-of-this-world fantasies about our favorite public figures, written by erotica's finest writers. Single issue: $6.00, including postage. Order from 3288 21st Street, #94, San Francisco, CA 94110; http://www.thehailmarys.com/shartopia.html.

Three Rivers Press

Three Rivers Press is a division of Crown Publishers, Inc., and publishes a wide variety of fiction, nonfiction, and African-American interest books. If you enjoyed Shay Youngblood's work, be sure to check out such recent best-sellers and crowd pleasers from Three Rivers as *The Sweet Potato Queens' Book of Love,* by Jill Conner Browne; *Close to the Bone,* by Jake Lamar; *The Vibe History of Hip-Hop,* from the editors of *Vibe* magazine; and *The Essence Total Makeover,* from the editors of *Essence* magazine.

Credits

first appeared in *Herotica 5,* edited by Marcy Sheiner (Down There Press, 1998).

"Maryann," by Marc Levy, © 1998 by Marc Levy, appeared in *CleanSheets,* February 10, 1999, edited by Mary Anne Mohanraj (Clean Sheets 1999), and also in *The Unmade Bed: 20th Century Erotica,* edited by Marti Hohmann (Masquerade Books, 1998).

"The Maltese Dildo," by Adam McCabe, © 1998 by Adam McCabe, first appeared in *Sex Toy Tales,* edited by Anne Semans and Cathy Winks (Down There Press, 1998).

"Ideal Assex," by Eva Morris, © 1999 by Eva Morris, first appeared in the self-published *Bad Girls' Bedtime Stories* (1999).

"3 Shades of Longing," by Jack Murnighan, © 1998 by Jack Murnighan, first appeared in *Nerve,* November 18, 1998, edited by Rufus Griscom and Genevieve Field (Nerve Publishing, LLC, 1998).

"Big Hungry Woman," by Bill Noble, © 1999 by Bill Noble, first appeared in *CleanSheets,* February 24, 1999, edited by Mary Anne Mohanraj (Clean Sheets, 1999).

"After the Light Changed," an excerpt from *The Leather Daddy and the Femme,* by Carol Queen, © 1998 by Carol Queen, first appeared in *The Leather Daddy and the Femme,* written by Carol Queen (Cleis Press, 1998).

"Scent," by Susan St. Aubin, © 1998 by Susan St. Aubin, first appeared in *Libido,* vol. 9, no. 4 (Winter 1998), edited by Marianna Beck and Jack Hafferkamp (Libido, 1998).

"Ten Seconds to Love," by Michelle Tea, © 1998 by Michelle Tea, first appeared in St*rphkr, 1998, edited by Shar Rednour (Shartopia, 1998).

Reader Survey

1. What are your favorite stories in this year's collection?

2. Have you read previous years' editions of *The Best American Erotica*?

3. If yes, do you have any favorite stories from those previous collections?

4. Do you have any recommendations for *The Best American Erotica 2001*? (Nominated stories must have been published in North America, in any form—book, periodical, internet—between March 1999 and March 2000).

_____

_____

_____

_____

_____

5. How did you get this book?
___ independent bookstore
___ mail-order company
___ sex/erotica shop
___ library
___ chain bookstore
___ other type of store
___ borrowed it from a friend

6. How old are you?

7. Male, female, other?

8. Where do you live?
___ West Coast
___ Midwest
___ East Coast
___ South
___ Other

9. What made you interested in *The Best American Erotica 2000*? (check as many as apply)
___ enjoyed other *Best American Erotica* collections
___ editor's reputation
___ authors' reputation
___ enjoy "Best of"–type anthologies
___ enjoy short stories in general
___ word-of-mouth recommendation
___ read book review
___ was attracted to advertisement

10. Any other suggestions? Feedback?

Please return this survey or any other *BAE*-related correspondence to: Susie Bright, BAE Feedback, P.O. Box 8377, Santa Cruz, CA 95061, or e-mail BAEfeedback@susiebright.com.

Thanks so much; your comments are truly appreciated.